BLADE AND BONE

Blade and Bone Book 1

D.K. HOLMBERG

Copyright © 2022 by D.K. Holmberg

Cover art by Felix Ortiz

Cover design by Shawn King

All rights reserved.

No part of this book may be reproduced in any form or by any electronic or mechanical means, including information storage and retrieval systems, without written permission from the author, except for the use of brief quotations in a book review.

Want a **free book** and to be notified when D.K. Holmberg's next novel is released, along with other news and freebies? **Sign up for his mailing list by going here**. Your email address will never be shared and you can unsubscribe at any time.

www.dkholmberg.com

Chapter One

KANAR

The dust of the road coated everything, working its way through the scarf Kanar Reims had pulled up to cover his face. A man learned to deal with almost anything, but that didn't mean he had to like it.

He scanned the horizon for possible dangers. Not that he expected to find any out here. The journey had been uneventful, and barely worthy of his services. Kanar would take the coin, though.

The wagons weren't far from Sanaron now, and the job would be complete. Get them to the docks and unloaded safely, and they'd be done with another assignment. Then Kanar could get himself clean.

"Go check beyond the hillside," he said to Jal.

The tall man glanced up from beneath his wide-brimmed hat and regarded Kanar with his almond-eyed gaze. "There's nothing up there, Kan. Just more of the same dirt we've seen."

"Then it shouldn't take you long."

Jal looked as if he wanted to argue but instead shifted

his bow, touched his quiver—a nervous tic—and then loped off, his quick stride chewing up the ground between the wagon caravan and the slight rise in the distance.

"Think there's anything up there?" Lily asked from where she sat on one of the wagons.

Kanar shook his head, not needing to look over to her. She'd taken to riding early during the assignment, choosing to sit on the wagon while Kanar and Jal walked alongside the slow-moving caravan. She had claimed to Heatharn, the merchant owner of the caravan, that it was because she was so much shorter than them and couldn't keep pace, but the truth was that it gave her a chance to see—and hear—more than she could from the ground. Kanar had thought to teach her that sometimes dangers didn't come from outside, but she already knew that truth.

"Probably not," he said. "Been a quiet trip."

"Too quiet, for what they're paying us," Lily said.

Now Kanar did look over to her. She was perched on the top of one of the container wagons. Her feet dangled over the edge, and her oiled boots kicked at the painted fox symbol of Heatharn's house. She had to lean down to look at Kanar, and her long black hair fell to either side of her face.

"If it helps, I'll keep your cut," he said.

"You've probably thought about it already," Lily said.

"I've always paid my debts." Even when it cost him everything, Kanar didn't add.

Jal jogged back to them. His gait reminded Kanar of a horse at full gallop, though that had something to do with his long legs.

"Nothing there," Jal said, not even breathless from his run. He looked over to Lily, who worked to twist her hair into a braid while surveying the hillside in front of them. "City isn't far, though. It's been a far sight too long since we've been back in Sanaron. I'm ready for a bath and a cool mug of ale."

Kanar grunted. It wasn't the first time Jal had said it, as if talking about a thing brought it to life. A man got used to the dirt and stink on the road. *Women do, too*, he thought, glancing over to where Lily continued to run her fingers through her hair. He'd assumed she was braiding it, but now he saw that she was smoothing the dust out of it.

"You need it. The bath, at least," Lily said to Jal.

"I suppose you think you smell like flowers? Even a pretty girl like you starts to stink."

"Well, I *am* a Lily."

"Only in name," Jal said.

"Would the two of you be quiet?" Kanar snapped.

He glanced behind him. Heatharn sat atop the rearmost wagon, holding the reins to the pair of chestnut mares leading it tightly. The wagon was smaller than the other four in the caravan, little more than a flat bed with a bench seat, along with the black lacquered trunk chained to the wagon.

As if the chains don't give away what he values here.

They had been hired to protect the entire caravan, though from what Kanar had been able to determine, the other wagons carried more commonplace items. He'd seen the silks in the lead wagon and the ceramics in the second one, but hadn't figured out what the other two carried. That wasn't the job, yet it didn't stop him from trying to come up with answers. It was the rearmost wagon that had always caught his attention. Kanar was careful not to show his interest, but he *was* curious. The four armed toughs who were seated on top of the other wagons should be able to protect against most threats. Why hire Kanar's team—unless whatever Heatharn was carting to Sanaron was extremely valuable?

Or dangerous.

That was the other possibility, though Kanar wasn't sure how something small enough to fit into that trunk would be dangerous.

None of that was the job, though.

They were to help escort Heatharn and his wagons from the border town of Jerat to the port in Sanaron. For that, he and his team would make ten silver brals. Not a huge haul, but not terrible for a week of work. And easy work, at that.

"Say, Kan," Jal said, his voice turning serious, "I see something up ahead. Either side of the road. Near the trees."

Kanar frowned. From the ground next to the caravan, he couldn't make out any danger, but he didn't have Jal's sight. Or Lily's, for that matter. Not that he had bad eyesight—it was just that the two of them had better.

"I thought you scouted the road," he said to Jal.

"There wasn't anything up there then. There is now."

Kanar couldn't quite determine what Jal had seen. The peak of the hill would make a perfect spot for an ambush before they had a chance to descend into Sanaron. After that, it was mostly downhill, which meant the wagons would have a chance to outrun any highwaymen who thought to attack.

"Let Heatharn know we might have a touch of trouble," Kanar said to Lily.

She popped to her feet. With how fast she raced atop

the wagon and jumped to the next, it wouldn't take long for her to reach Heatharn to warn him. The question now became whether Heatharn would follow Kanar's instructions. Like other merchants, he'd probably think he knew better than the man he'd hired to protect him and would decide to stop the wagons, but Kanar wanted him to get the wagons moving faster, if anything.

"Check the trees on the left," he said to Jal. "I'll scope out the right."

"What's the plan?" Jal asked.

The unspoken question was a simple one: How much force would they use?

It was something too many teams got wrong. Killing was easy—Kanar had done that under the banner of the king for long enough to have learned that—but knowing when to exercise restraint was harder. That was a lesson he'd tried to instill in his team. Take out the wrong person, even if for the right reason, and you might find yourself hounded and any job you try to take that much harder. Or worse—you may find yourself hunted.

"Use your best judgment," Kanar said.

Jal pulled an arrow out of his quiver and nocked it to the bow, but didn't draw back. He rode off toward the trees.

Kanar checked his own weapons. He had a pair of knives strapped to his side, though he'd prefer not to use them. The short axe he carried offered an intimidation factor that he could take advantage of, but it would be more likely to maim or kill. He had the most control with the sword, but he almost never used it.

The blade had been a gift. A marker of his service. There had been a time when he'd been honored to carry it, but now it was reminder of who he'd been: the Blackheart, with a blackened blade to match. The artisanship of the sword was too skilled for him to abandon it, though.

Kanar slipped away. When he neared the trees, he glanced back to see the wagons lurching faster. Lily stood on Heatharn's bench, eyes surveying everything around the caravan. The four toughs Heatharn had hired for his caravan had dislodged themselves from their seats, and now most of them held crossbows at the ready.

I really should have worked with them more during the journey.

They'd spent the better part of three days escorting this caravan. There had been time, but he doubted it would have made any difference. Men like that only thought of one thing—violence. There had been a time not that long ago when Kanar had been that way.

At least Heatharn had listened and gotten the wagons moving. The hillside wasn't far from here. Once they crested it, the wagons would have an easy time getting down into the city.

Beneath the canopy of the leaves, the air was almost damp. That seemed strange considering how dry and dusty the road was.

Something moved about two dozen paces from him.

Idiots. Had they not seen him head into the trees?

Kanar slipped around one tree, then used another to shield his approach. By the time he came upon the figure, who wore a deep-green wool cloak, they had veered back toward the road.

A quick blow to the back of the man's neck knocked him out.

Kanar rolled him over. He had tanned skin and a thin

beard. Nothing to suggest where he came from. Or who he might serve.

He checked the man for weapons, found a knife and a crossbow, and tossed the knife deeper into the trees. Kanar kept the crossbow.

Another slip of movement caught his attention, and he picked his way carefully toward it. He found another person wearing a similar green cloak—heavily tattered and dirty—pulling an empty cart through the forest.

They weren't after the entire caravan.

What was in that trunk?

Kanar raced forward, the damp soil and pine needles muting his steps. His training as one of the Realmsguard elite soldiers to the king of Reyand had taught him stealth. The figure started to turn, but Kanar was too quick.

He spun his knives. Darkened eyes beneath the cloak started to widen at the sight him. Had they recognized him?

Then he struck with the flat of his blade, and they crumpled.

Kanar glanced at the cart, which was small and meant for moving through the forest. The wheels were a dull gray metal, and the silvery wood looked to be sturdy. Someone with money or resources had made it.

What were a pair of highwaymen in the forest doing with something like that?

There were no other figures around.

He jogged through the trees until he reached the edge once more. The wagons had stopped.

What is Heatharn thinking?

Honaaz, one of the hulking toughs Heatharn had along with him, stood at the rear of the caravan. He held his crossbow up, ready to fire.

As Kanar approached, Honaaz pointed the crossbow at him.

"Fire at me, and my sword will go through your belly," Kanar said.

Honaaz lowered the crossbow only a little, but enough so that it was no longer pointed directly at him.

Kanar searched on his side of the forest. There was no further sign of ambush. That meant it would come from the other side.

"Get the wagons moving again," he said to Heatharn.

Heatharn looked down his long nose at Kanar, his scarred cheeks catching a hint of the midday sun. "I had to check my cargo. Besides, they said they can't protect the wagons while they're moving," Heatharn said.

"But I can. Get them moving," Kanar snapped. "Wait. What cargo were you checking?"

There was a soft scraping coming from one of the wagons.

"It's none of your concern," Heatharn said.

All of this is my concern.

"Just go, then."

We can figure that out later.

Heatharn glanced to Honaaz, but Kanar shoved the man out of the way. Or attempted to. Honaaz might be the largest man Kanar had ever seen. Still, Kanar gave him a hard push, and he moved.

Honaaz didn't need to argue, not when there could be an ambush. If they didn't get the wagons to the docks the way they'd all agreed to, Honaaz wouldn't see one bral either, let alone all ten they'd been promised.

Thankfully, the wagons started to move, albeit more slowly than Kanar preferred.

He jogged ahead. He found Lily still seated. "Two men in the trees. Reasonably well equipped," he said, tossing the crossbow up to her.

Lily examined it. "Not bad quality for simple robbers."

"Think that's what they are?" Kanar asked.

She looked at the crossbow again, then got to her feet and stood with them apart as she squinted toward the trees. "Thought it was quiet."

"It was."

A dark figure near one of the trees up ahead caught Kanar's attention, but before he could react, Jal was already driving his elbow into the back of the man's neck. He crumpled.

As Jal crouched down, Kanar noticed another figure creeping closer to him.

"Think you can hit him from there?" he asked Lily.

"Not me. Jal's the sure shot."

Kanar went running. He didn't need to get all the way to Jal, just close enough that he could use one of his knives. He might not have the same skill with the bow that Jal had, but he was deadly with his blades.

When he reached the trees, he let one of the knives fly. It tumbled end over end until it stuck into the man's shoulder.

That gave Jal enough of a window that he looked up, realized that someone was closing in on him, then swept his leg around to knock the man down. With a brutal blow to his attacker's head, the fight was over.

Kanar retrieved his knife, wiping it on the fallen man's wool cloak. It matched the others they'd come across. Four of them, all dressed the same, and with weapons of reasonable quality. That, and the cart he'd seen.

"It would've been easier if you'd just let me shoot them from the wagons," Jal said.

"Easier for now," Kanar said. "Everything has consequences."

As Jal finished checking for weapons, he pulled a knife from the fallen man and handed it to Kanar. "How many did you have to deal with?"

"Including the one that nearly killed you? Three."

Jal nodded to the man Kanar had struck with his knife.

"See if he has any weapons on him, and let's get moving," Kanar said. "We need to get these wagons to the docks before sunset. I'm ready to be done with them, especially as Heatharn seems to be transporting something else inside one of those wagons."

Jal looked over to them, his gaze narrowing. "Like what?"

Kanar shrugged. "Some sort of creature."

Jal almost hissed in annoyance. "Something doesn't feel right, Kan. Not sure what it is, but we should be ready."

Kanar sighed. "One of *those* feelings?"

Jal had good instincts. Kanar knew to trust the man.

"I don't know."

Kanar headed over to the small hill and looked down at the city in the distance. Fog engulfed Sanaron the way it often did, to the point where he couldn't even see the bay stretching out from the shoreline. Through the fog, he caught a few glimpses of buildings near the shore, but not so much that he could make out the distinct Sanaron architecture and the white buildings that occupied the center—and oldest—part of the city.

Kanar motioned to the wagons, encouraging them to keep moving. Now wasn't the time to stop or slow. Now was the time to expedite this and move toward the city as quickly as possible. If there was one crew thinking to attack them here, it was possible there would be another.

"Find anything else?" Lily asked.

Kanar looked up to her. She had perched on the edge of the wagon again, though now she faced straight ahead rather than dangling her legs. She bit her lip the way she did when she was thinking.

"Nothing more than a few men who decided to make a run at us," he said.

"Another? We haven't had anybody try that on us so far. Like I told you before, it's been—"

"Quiet. I know."

He should've known that quiet only lasted so long. Certainly not long enough to reach the city. Not when there were ten silver brals on the line. He wouldn't have been hired were there not something to the job. Heatharn hadn't said anything about the details, but he hadn't really needed to. Kanar had seen enough to know there was more going on than what he'd been told.

As the wagons rumbled along, he kept pace, keeping his sword unsheathed and his gaze sweeping from side to side. There was no further movement, nothing to suggest that they had another attack coming. But it didn't change anything for Kanar. If Jal felt like things weren't quite right, then they probably weren't.

"Well, the easy part is upon you," Heatharn said. He had scrambled down from his wagon, one of the few times Kanar had seen him climb down. He had left Honaaz to guide the wagon instead. "I thought you were some notorious killer. Why did you leave those rogues alive?"

Kanar ignored the second part and focused on the first.

It was easier to deal with stupidity than the ignorance of someone who could so easily discard another person's life. "What makes you think this is the easy part?"

Heatharn seemed disappointed at the omission. "We are almost to the city. We just have to get through there, get to the docks, and get the wagons loaded. Then you can get paid."

Kanar glanced over to him and frowned. Heatharn wore an overly long jacket that covered a shirt embroidered with brightly colored flowers. He looked like every other merchant that Kanar had escorted in the time since he'd abandoned his service to the Realmsguard. They always made a point of dressing too formally for the road, as if they couldn't stand traveling in clothing that was actually suited for the task ahead. He was unarmed, at least seemingly so. Kanar had observed him slipping a slender jeweled knife beneath his cloak, though the blade would probably be of little use against a sword like the one Kanar carried, and certainly of no use against Jal and his bow. Were he to have to deal with Lily... It was probably for the best that Heatharn had no idea what Lily was capable of doing.

"I'll get you to the docks, as we agreed," Kanar said. "You have to do what I tell you is necessary. That is, if you don't want to die along the way."

Heatharn started to smile, but it faded as he watched Kanar. "Have you seen something?"

"It's not a matter of seeing anything."

"Then what is it a matter of?"

"An instinct." Kanar motioned to the wagon. "You should get back to your bench."

Heatharn opened his mouth as if he wanted to argue, before clamping it closed once again and shifting his jacket.

That was for the best. If he decided to argue, he was going to find that Kanar was in no mood. Heatharn wasn't going to be the one to pay him, anyway. Kanar had already been paid by the person Heatharn had contracted with. He didn't need to appease anyone. He just had to finish the job.

The road curved sharply down the slope toward Sanaron. A straight shot to the city was possible, but not unless the wagons went by road. They would roll too quickly, likely out of control, and end up crashing somewhere before they reached their destination. Were he on horseback—something that was far too rare these days—he could take the direct approach, even if it would be difficult. Kanar was experienced enough to handle such a ride.

"What do you see down there?" Kanar asked.

Jal leaned close, and he shifted so that he could look from the same vantage that Kanar had. "I just see the fog. Why? What do you see?"

"I see the job coming to a close."

"Why do you look like you think this isn't going to end well?"

Kanar shook his head. "Because it *isn't* going to end well."

They fell into silence, hearing nothing more than the creaking of the wagons as they finished the meandering descent. When Kanar motioned for them to head to the northern side of the city, Heatharn looked as if he wanted to argue, but Kanar shot him a hard expression and silenced the merchant. Jal frowned but didn't question. The only one who seemed to understand why Kanar was choosing this path was Lily, but that didn't surprise him. She had a quick mind.

Traveling this way might be longer, but it also had the

advantage of traditionally having less fog than the quicker route that Kanar suspected Heatharn wanted him to take.

"I don't have a good feeling about this," Jal said as they reached the outskirts of the city.

"I figured you would be pleased that we've finally returned."

"I'm pleased that we're back," Jal said, and he turned in place, his gaze darting all around him. His fingers twitched as he reached for his quiver again. He pulled an arrow out, holding it loosely in hand. "But something doesn't feel right."

"That's what I was afraid of."

From anyone else, Kanar might brush aside instincts like that. There were plenty of men who were superstitious, and often for no good reason. When it came to Jal and his instincts, though, Kanar had come to trust them. At least, he had come to trust that something would come of them. He'd worked with Jal often enough over the last year—and exclusively lately—that he trusted his instinct.

Kanar whistled softly at Lily, who scooted closer. "Keep your eyes alert. Something might happen."

She nodded.

Kanar slipped back, darting from one side of the street to the other. The fog made it difficult for him to make out the detail of the buildings, but he could practically imagine the bright colors found even in these outer city sections. It was one of the distinctive features of Sanaron, as if by painting the buildings as brightly as they did, they could stave off some of the dreariness of the fog and create a separation from what was found deeper in the city.

When he reached the rear wagon, he nodded to

Honaaz. "You and the others need to join me on the street."

"I don't work for you," Honaaz said.

"Fine." Kanar turned to Heatharn. "Tell them to get onto the street."

"But we're almost to the docks," Heatharn said. "You made us take the longer road, but the distance we travel doesn't mean you're going to get paid any more."

"I had you take the safer route. And I'm telling you now to have your men get down here."

"Why?"

"Because," Kanar said, "I'm afraid you might have your opportunity to see the killing you wanted to see before."

As if on cue, shouts rang out on either side of them.

Chapter Two

KANAR

THE WAGONS ROLLED TO A STOP. WITHOUT HESITATION, Kanar whistled and slapped one of the horses on the flank, getting the wagons moving again. The fog swirled, as if it were alive and being controlled, though he knew it was little more than the heavy fog typical of Sanaron. Had they reached the city later in the day, most of the fog would've burned off already. Perhaps he should have waited to enter.

He focused on the sounds around him, as sometimes sound told more than sight, before tossing a fistful of alisalts. They could be expensive, but they were one of the few ways of clearing the fog in front of him, even if only temporarily.

The streets had been quiet. That should have been one of his first indications that something was amiss, but he had thought it little more than the muted quiet of the fog.

As they got closer to the shoreline, the cool breeze gusted in the smells of the salt water. The briny odor overpowered the stink of fishmongers and dockworkers. There was a shout, a whistle, and a slight scraping sound from above.

He whistled, and Lily darted across the wagon tops. She crouched down next to him.

"Rooftops," Kanar said. "I hear two to my left, maybe another to the right."

Lily nodded, reaching into the leather satchel she kept with her at all times. She pulled out a rope and her folding grappling hook, then tossed it. The rope wouldn't support someone of his weight, which was one of the advantages of her slight stature. But he wasn't nearly as skilled as she was, either, and he doubted that he would be able to scale the side of the building as quickly and easily as Lily could.

She disappeared into the fog.

Kanar whistled again. Jal immediately appeared, as if he had been waiting for his signal. "Rooftops."

"How aggressive?"

"We're in the city. Fair game," Kanar told him. "She'll understand if we put some heat on the others."

Jal smirked before heading away. Fair game meant that they would not hold back.

Outside of the city, the highwaymen they encountered were often poor farmers or villagers, or those displaced by one of the many recent wars. That was a reason Kanar tended to hold back. They didn't need to slaughter everyone they came across.

In the city, circumstances were different. Especially in Sanaron. This place could be brutal and violent, and it was a place where he fit in well.

He looked over to Heatharn but still swept his gaze around the street, looking for any sign of attack. It was coming. He knew it. Thankfully, Honaaz had gotten down from the wagon and had moved forward to talk to the other three hired men.

"What's the priority?" Kanar asked Heatharn.

The merchant frowned at him. "What? You were hired to protect the wagons. And me, I might add."

"I know what I was hired to protect," Kanar said.

The fog swirled near him, but it was the faint stink of the docks that caught his attention. He pulled one of his knives and whipped it in that direction, then heard a soft grunt as the attacker fell. He didn't need to check that his throw was accurate. Kanar had thrown countless knives in his day, and he scarcely had to aim.

"If it comes down to saving the entire caravan or you, what's the priority?"

"Why, me," Heatharn said. "And this trunk."

Kanar nodded.

"But you were hired to protect all of them."

"I know my job."

Half a dozen figures appeared near an alley through the haze. He needed the fog to burn off or a gust of wind to blow through or something. The obscured surroundings made everything far too difficult to see.

He whistled twice, and Jal appeared next to him. "We stay near the wagons. Near Heatharn."

"If you say so," Jal said. "I dropped two on the rooftops. There might be others."

It was more than Kanar would have been able to make out through the fog. "Lily's up there."

"Then she has it covered."

They would trust Lily to protect them. They didn't need to watch over her. She was deadly competent in ways that very few people Kanar had worked with were.

Now they had these six newcomers to deal with.

He unsheathed his knives. Before he even had a chance to move, Jal had two of them down, arrows protruding from their chests.

Kanar lunged forward toward the remaining four attackers. He couldn't see faces or clothing, but they had a distinctive stench to them. And they had come after the caravan.

They must have been waiting. Kanar had thought that the highwaymen they'd thwarted had been the extent of the threat, but he should have known better than that. There was always something more coming.

He had suspected more danger on the road, and he'd overlooked the threat they might face inside the walls. Had he been the one assigned to capture the caravan and its contents, he wouldn't have attacked out in the open like that. It made the fight far too fair, and it gave Kanar and his team the upper hand. They could watch for any oncoming threats.

But in the streets, in the fog, it would be easy enough to take any advantage to slow the wagons, kill the escort, and make off with the prize. It was how he would've done it.

Then again, he would've been smarter than this.

He stabbed and spun, kicking one of the men in his knee and hearing the crack as it fractured. As Kanar turned, he drove his fist up into a chin, then brought his blades around and cleaved through an arm.

Just like that, the four were down.

Jal worked his way through to the two men he had struck, checking for any valuables.

Kanar hurried back to the wagons. They were still moving along the street, the wheels creaking steadily as they rumbled over the cobblestones. The fog was starting to lift around them.

Lily dropped down from the shadows overhead and landed on the wagon in front of them. "Jal got two on the rooftops, and I took out the other two. I don't know if there are any more, but they would have a hard time seeing anything from the other buildings."

Kanar nodded. He climbed onto the wagon, peering into the lifting fog until he caught sight of one of the buildings. The door stood slightly ajar, and fresh scratches ran along the green paint—likely from someone trying to pry the door open.

He motioned to Heatharn. They stopped in front of the door, the largest of the wagons blocking access to it.

He nodded to Lily. "Keep an eye out."

Kanar found a window along the building and jabbed at it with the hilt of his sword, breaking the glass with a crash. He darted inside.

A flurry of movement came toward him. Five men were all dressed in dark gray jackets and pants, each armed with either short swords, crossbows, or knives. Two of them had markings on the back of their hands that he recognized—a tattoo of a snarling dog, which indicated the crew they ran with.

Kanar didn't have a tattoo. He didn't care to mark himself like that, but it was also partly because he didn't want anyone to think he could be owned. He was his own man, and no one would force him to take a job he didn't want to. He could be hired, but that was the extent of it.

Kanar didn't recognize any of the men, but that didn't matter.

He stabbed the nearest of them in the stomach, ducked

beneath a sword that swung toward his head, and jabbed forward with his knives, catching the next man in the thigh. Kanar jumped, kicking out, and when he landed, he was left with only one more attacker. A sharp strike to the side of the man's neck dropped him as well.

One of them had landed a lucky blow. Pain bloomed in Kanar's arm where he'd been cut. He healed fast enough, but something like that could slow him.

He started to head back outside and stopped when a face appeared in the window. Honaaz.

The man looked past Kanar, and his broad face deepened into a wide frown. "What did you do?"

"Get back to the wagons."

"You did this by yourself?" Honaaz said.

"Yes, by myself. Now get back."

He suspected that Honaaz had never had any formal training in fighting, so seeing what Kanar had been able to do must look almost supernatural. Those were not the rumors he needed spread about himself. There were already rumors about him, and he didn't care for them.

He scrambled out of the window, back onto the street, and whistled. It wasn't long before the wagons began to rumble forward again.

Kanar made his way to the rearmost one again.

"Are we done?" Heatharn asked.

Kanar snorted. "Done with what?"

"The fighting. How many can they send?"

"You've got the Rabid Dog crew after you. So… another hundred, maybe more. I doubt they're going to send everybody they have for something like this. But they've already sent over a dozen, so they must think that whatever you have is valuable."

"Just finish the job," Heatharn snapped.

"I told you I would."

Jal loped over to Kanar and peered around. "They lost some of their muscle," he said.

"How?"

"Other side of the street."

Kanar looked and realized there was another door slightly ajar, another window shattered. He hadn't even seen it. *Why have so much pressure put on this caravan?*

He glanced over to Heatharn, to the trunk, and to the rest of the wagons.

And he let out a heavy sigh. "I need you and Lily to get the other four wagons ahead."

"What?" Jal asked.

"We'll be coming up to Wedel Street. Take that and lead the other wagons. I'm going to keep Honaaz and Heatharn with me."

"We don't split up," Jal said.

"Not usually," Kanar said. "This time, I'm afraid we need to. That's the Rabid Dog crew out there."

Jal clenched his jaw. "Then they really won't stop, will they?"

Kanar didn't have to tell him no. They both knew the truth. This was one of the most aggressive and violent crews in the city. They were headed by a man who went by the moniker of the Prophet—someone Kanar had never seen, though he didn't know anyone who had. The man was ruthless.

"Make sure Lily knows what you're doing," Kanar told Jal.

"I don't like it."

"Your objection is noted."

Jal looked as if he wanted to say something more, but he hurried toward the rest of the wagons and left Kanar near the rear.

Kanar climbed up onto the wagon and held the bench so that he got closer to Heatharn. "The wagons are splitting up," he whispered. "Before you say anything, you, me, and Honaaz are going to take this wagon toward the docks. We're going to meet the others there."

"Why?" Heatharn asked.

"Because we have too many after us. It's safer this way. Split them up. I can handle whatever comes this way, and the rest of my team can handle the others."

"Just you? If this crew is as dangerous as you say, how do you expect to protect me?"

It was about more than just protecting Heatharn, but Kanar wasn't going to debate that with him. "Because I can."

They reached the street, and the other four wagons started to turn. A shout rang out, and then a series of soft twangs came as Jal's bow fired, followed by several grunts.

"Now!" Kanar said.

Heatharn whipped the horses into action. They galloped forward, no longer encumbered by the other wagons that had slowed their progress. This wagon was smaller and lighter, and Kanar had anticipated that they would be able to move more quickly and easily. As soon as the other wagons were off the road, theirs surged ahead.

Kanar looked around, watching for additional attackers. He couldn't tell if anyone else was there, as the fog had settled once again.

Honaaz stayed seated on the bench next to Heatharn. Kanar was tempted to jump back down but was no longer certain that he would be able to keep up with the pace of the wagon. At this point, it might make the most sense for him to stay right where he was.

They weren't that far from the docks.

As soon as they reached their destination, he would make sure they loaded the wagon contents onto the ship, and then he would leave Heatharn and the rest of his hired help to finish the job. Kanar had only been hired to get them onto the docks, partly because the docks themselves were considered a safe zone where the crews generally didn't operate openly.

"The road is going to curve up here, and as soon as it does, you will have a straight shot to the docks," Kanar said. "I don't want you to slow down until I tell you to. Do you get that?"

Heatharn nodded.

"Good. Because I think we have a bit more excitement ahead of us."

A pair of figures stood near an alleyway. The fog made it difficult for Kanar to distinguish much about those figures, but he doubted they were merely out here to keep an eye on the street. More likely than not, they were also part of the Rabid Dog crew, and possibly even keeping a lookout for—

A powerful explosion ripped through a nearby street.

The suddenness of it took his breath away, which was for the best, as he would've ended up coughing too much had he been able to breathe. The smoke billowed around them, competing with the fog to obstruct his view.

Kanar's mind was already going to work, and he thought through the different scenarios. There was another side street, though it was going to be just wide enough for the wagon to make it down.

He reached for the reins and pulled on them as hard as he could, forcing the horses to the left. They fought him. He wasn't gentle, but now wasn't the time for gentle. Now was the time to get the damn horses to do what he needed.

Right now.

They pulled against him, but he forced them to follow his direction. The wagon turned.

"You're going to crash us into the buildings!" Heatharn shouted.

"I'm not going to crash us into anything," Kanar said, teeth clenched.

The smoke and fog lifted for a moment, long enough for him to see the alley. The wagon eased down the tight space. He could reach out and touch the wall—and would probably lose an arm in the process. But they were out of the street, out of the thickest part of the smoke, and they were able to navigate through the alley.

If he was right—and he had a pretty good sense of the streets in Sanaron—then this would lead to Maulod Street, and then he could use that to intersect with the shoreline. If he was wrong, then it was entirely possible that he was leading the wagon away from the docks and they would have to fight their way back.

"What happens if we get stuck?" Heatharn asked. His words were clipped, and despite the growing chill in the air, sweat beaded on his brow.

Likely the man hadn't even considered the possibility that they might actually get attacked. The muscle like Honaaz, as well as the hired guards like Kanar, were more for show.

"We're not getting stuck," Kanar said. "Now, would you let me deal with this?"

He was done talking—and listening.

The wagon rolled through the alley, but the wagon wasn't the issue here. The two horses leading it were turning out to be the greater concern. They didn't seem to care for the narrow confines of the alley and started to slow, forcing Kanar to push them. They weren't war horses and were certainly not trained to follow the same commands that Kanar had once used on his horse, but he figured they should be able to follow basic commands.

"Just keep moving," he whispered, trying to sound as soothing as he could. "Not much further. We get to the next street, the rest of it will be easy. I promise."

"You told me that already," Heatharn said.

"I'm not talking to you. I'm talking to the horses."

Kanar found Honaaz watching him. Honaaz still seemed spooked by the sight of the five men Kanar had taken out.

Lily hadn't found anything to worry about with any of the other people in the caravan, but she might not have checked thoroughly. It really was a short journey, and they hadn't expected this kind of trouble, though Kanar always tried to anticipate the potential. He saw danger even when there wasn't going to be any. That was how he managed to stay ahead of most trouble—and how he'd managed to stay alive as long as he had. What if Honaaz had betrayed them? Kanar couldn't think about that now, but he would have to be ready to watch him when they reached the docks.

"We're about there," Kanar said as fog swept toward them.

Then they were out of the alley, and he turned toward the denser fog rolling in from the sea, using it to help guide him. If there were other people in the street... they would just have to get out of the way.

They hadn't gone very far when another explosion thundered.

This one came from behind them.

"What is that?" Heatharn asked, his voice rising an octave.

"Nothing you want to see," Kanar said.

He was scarcely aware of the intersection they reached, only noticing it by the faint stir of the fog that told him they were reaching a wider street. He jerked on the reins again, turning the horses to follow the shoreline once more.

"Take them," he said, handing the reins back to Heatharn. "I might need to take care of a little business up here."

Kanar stared through the fog but saw no sign of anything more.

There *was* danger, he was certain of it.

Then he felt an arrow strike the wagon behind him.

Kanar turned.

Now was the time when he wished for Jal and Lily. The two of them would take care of any rogue archer, but it was going to have to be up to him.

He scanned the fog and then caught sight of the man who stood atop a nearby building, standing tall as if he had nothing to fear. And he probably thought he didn't.

Kanar grabbed another blade. He took aim and whipped the knife, sending it tumbling end over end. It missed.

An arrow streaked toward him. Kanar ducked, and he

tossed another knife, which struck the archer in the neck. The man clasped his hand over his wound, before falling forward and collapsing to the stone. Shouts rang out.

"Now," Kanar said.

Thankfully, Heatharn seemed to know what he needed to do. The horses galloped forward, and as they neared the rows of docks, the fog shifted, caught in the wind that always seemed so prominent near the shore.

"Which one?" Kanar asked.

"Pier seven," Heatharn said.

Kanar held his hand on the hilt of his sword, ready for another attack, but they reached the dock without any further obstacles. He had them pause, not wanting to go too far onto the dock until he had a chance to surveil everything. He reached for a spare pair of knives, ready to toss them at any Dogs who might come their way, but none did. Yet.

"Here," Kanar said, jerking the reins from Heatharn and getting the wagon to stop near the others. "Make sure you send word that we got you here in one piece. I don't need anybody grumbling about failure to complete assignments."

Heatharn ran his hands up and down his chest and onto his stomach before wiping his brow.

"Now you get to tell me what you have," Kanar said.

The merchant frowned and shook his head.

Kanar stalked toward him, reaching for his sword but not unsheathing it. "I need to know why so many Dogs came at us. What are you carrying?"

"Relics," Heatharn said. "Just some Alainsith relics. I don't know what the Dogs might be after them for, but—"

"Where did you get them?"

"They started their journey near Verendal," Heatharn said, staggering away from Kanar. "I'm merely transporting them. That's it."

Verendal. It was near the edge of Reyand, and close to Alainsith lands. Kanar supposed that he shouldn't be surprised that someone would be interested in those relics. The Alainsith were an ancient race of people who had their own natural magic. That was reason enough for him to want to destroy these relics, but he had agreed to the job.

Most Alainsith relics were buildings, not anything portable, and he had little curiosity about what Heatharn might be carrying. That wasn't what he'd been hired for.

Why would the Dogs be interested in something magical?

"Get moving," Kanar said. "Take your cargo and get out of the city. I'd hate for something to happen to you while you don't have us here to keep an eye on you."

Hate was a bit strong. He would be disappointed to have gone through all this, only to have them end up dead because of stupidity. But his assignment was done.

Heatharn nodded. "Yes. I suppose… Thank you. You did well."

Kanar snorted. He wasn't sure he had done well, but they were still alive. The cargo had reached its destination, and if he had anything to do with it, the ship would leave with what he'd been hired to protect.

All in all, it was a good job.

But where were the others?

Chapter Three

LILY

Lily perched on the top of the wagons as they careened around the corner. The fog made it difficult for her to see anything, but she had an advantage that Kanar didn't. Not that it mattered. Not with this. They might be dealing with some Rabid Dogs, but she wasn't afraid of them. They were Dogs, after all. And she was a cat—quick to prowl, quick to jump, and able to easily escape.

Jal held on to the wagon as he looked over to her. His bow was unslung from one shoulder, and his gaze darted around with a nervous energy that he often had. She smiled at him, and he shook his head, as if he were scared more than excited.

How could he be afraid? They hadn't even gotten in any real trouble yet.

"I don't like him leaving us like that," Jal said above the sound of the wagons rumbling.

They hadn't encountered more Dogs, but she suspected that it was only a matter of time before they did. And when they did, she had her knives and the crossbow Kanar had given her, but she also had other ways of slowing them down.

"I thought you were tougher than this," she said, grinning at him. "I didn't expect the great Jal Olassa to be afraid of a few Dogs."

Lily looked through the fog and whipped a knife, which sunk into a man's chest. Even though Kanar had said that everything was fair game, she wouldn't have held back now anyway. Not in these tough conditions, and not against the Dogs. She did not care for them.

"Am I great?" Jal smiled back at her, and his eyes narrowed slightly before he grabbed his bow, tapped his quiver, and fired an arrow. She looked behind her as a man tumbled from a rooftop.

She'd missed him. They would've passed right by, and she hadn't seen him?

She was getting too complacent. But then, they'd been out of Sanaron for the better part of a week. Even a short time away from the city took away some of her skill, making it so that she was not as competent as she normally would be. She'd trained far too long to acquire her skill.

"That's what you like to tell us," Lily said.

"I really do," he said with another grin.

The wagons continued to rumble, and then they slowed.

Lily cursed under her breath. "Tell them to keep moving," she hissed.

"You tell them."

"How am I supposed to tell them anything? They aren't going to listen to a little girl like me."

Jal arched a brow. "They've seen you helping."

"Just go," she snapped at him.

He chuckled, then shrugged and released the wagon before loping ahead.

When he was gone, Lily reached into her pouch and grabbed one of the small fragments of bone formed into a ring, slipping it onto her finger. When she did, the fog seemed to lift a bit.

She scanned the rooftop and spotted three more.

How many Dogs had they sent out here?

More than she had expected.

More than Kanar had expected.

He was a skilled planner, and if anybody would have anticipated the dangers of this job, it would've been Kanar. The fact that he hadn't counted on this bothered her. She would've expected him to pick up on the signs that the job they were pulling was dangerous, but somehow even Kanar had missed it.

Or there was more taking place than they knew about.

They had been gone from Sanaron for the better part of a week, so that was possible.

The wagons lurched forward again, and Jal took up a position near the foremost wagon. These wagons were wide enough that it made it difficult for them to navigate on any of the side streets. They had taken the main thoroughfares through the city. She had agreed with Kanar that coming out of the forest, heading to the city along this northerly route, and following the shoreline made the most sense—at least at the time. The density of the fog made it difficult for anybody to see much of anything here, but it also was a more indirect path.

It probably gave their attackers some advantage that they wouldn't have had otherwise. They could see their caravan more easily as well.

But not more easily than she could.

Lily whistled, and Jal looked back at her for a moment before nodding.

It was all the signal she needed to give for him to know what she was going to do. She reached for her grappling hook, unfolded it, and then tossed it as they passed a nearby building—a butcher shop, from the sign out front. It smelled like it as well. There was a hint of smoke, and her mouth almost watered at the idea that she could grab some smoked meats, but she would have to do that another time. They had to finish this and get the stupid wagons down to the dock, and then she could bathe and eat and drink and chase down that pretty little florist she'd been flirting with before leaving the city this last time.

The grappling hook held, and she hurriedly scaled the line. When she got under the rooftop, she folded the hook up, looped the rope around her arm, and scanned the roof. The roofs here were all made of smooth slate and were slick with dew. If she stepped wrong, she would go tumbling down to the cobblestones below, ending with a splat. She had traveled these rooftops long enough that navigating wasn't difficult, but with everything they had been through in the last leg of their journey, she needed to be careful. Lily wasn't very tall, so was a target on the ground, but the rooftops were another story.

Lily slipped along the roof until she found one of the men holding a crossbow and lying on his stomach. With a flick of her wrist, her knife sunk into his back. She scrambled toward him before he could recover, grabbed the crossbow from his hands, and gave him a kick. He grunted and rolled off the side.

"Don't you go falling for me," she muttered.

She looked at the other rooftop across the street, where another man had his crossbow aimed at the back of the wagon. She took aim, focused for a moment, and then fired the crossbow. The bolt struck true, and the man fell down and dropped his weapon.

That was two. How many other Dogs were up here?

But would they be Dogs if they were on a rooftop? She didn't know of any dog that could climb up to a roof. Maybe they were something else.

Lily checked for the mark they had on their hands and found that this man had a Dog tattoo, much like the last one had. The Prophet certainly didn't care if he sacrificed his people, not when there was something to be earned in doing so. He was cruel, often callous. Most people who dealt with him ended up on the losing side. Lily was determined not to be one of them.

She scrambled along the tiles, reaching the place where she had jumped up, and found that the wagon had turned and was now heading the wrong direction.

What was Jal doing?

Jal was sweet and was useful in a fight, but she never *really* knew what he would do when he had his "hunches." Worse, he'd slipped away once during this battle—and for what reason?

Lily secured the grappling hook to the rooftop, dropped down to the cobblestones, and then jerked the line free. She ran while looping the rope around her wrist, ready for another jump if it came down to it.

By the time she caught up to the wagons, they had turned another corner.

And then she saw why.

There had to be a dozen men converging on the wagons.

All of these Dogs for this?

Not for this. For whatever Kanar had gone off and protected. She couldn't help but wonder what was in it. Not that they could ask. That wasn't the way jobs worked. Not when Malory was involved.

Before Lily had caught up with Kanar and started working with Malory, she had asked the questions. Now she allowed Kanar to take the lead. It was probably for the best. He was skilled in ways that most men who worked in Sanaron simply weren't, and they took interesting jobs. Besides, when people heard rumors about Kanar, they forgot the rumors about her.

She would've expected some of the Kalenwatch to be out in the city by now. They should have intervened, if only to slow the Dogs. Of course, anyone could be bribed, and given the Prophet's reach—and his money—Lily wouldn't be surprised that he had a way of bribing the watch.

A darkened shape in a nearby alley caught her attention. She darted toward it with a pair of knives already in hand, and she pushed off the ground, driving her blades up into the man's belly. He fell without a sound. She sat on his chest, bearing her weight on him, and waited.

The crowd moved past where she hid in the alley. Not just a dozen. There were probably fifteen, maybe eighteen Dogs. All of that for the wagons.

With her knife, she hurriedly carved off the man's fingers one by one, then stuffed them into a pouch. She'd have to clean them later, but if it came down to it, she wasn't going to end up with the Dogs overrunning her just because she wasn't prepared to use her skills.

Lily wouldn't be able to get back to the wagon on the street, and if she did nothing, the Dogs were going to take over the wagons. Jal would be able to protect them to a certain degree, but there were limits to what he could do, limits to how much he could offer them.

She decided to go to the rooftops again, where she might be able to slow some of them. But by how much?

She had a few different options.

Once on the roof, she raced along, jumping from building to building. The wagons were not far from her, and Jal made a valiant effort of trying to bring down as many of the Dogs as he could. Lily knew that the fog diffusing through the streets made it difficult for him to be able to see much of anything. He was talented, but he needed to be able to see in order to target the shots.

Which meant that she might have to use her other skills.

She reached into her pouch. There was a reason she didn't let Jal handle it. He was foolish enough that he might end up blowing himself up. Kanar probably wouldn't kill himself, but he would ask questions. Questions about her past, how she ended up in Sanaron. Questions she didn't want to answer.

She doubted that Jal would understand. He was like an open book. Kanar, on the other hand, had his own demons. He had come to the city after leaving the Realmsguard, and she'd been searching for information about what had happened to him and why he had left, but she'd found it difficult to get anything on him. There were other soldiers from Reyand here, but none of them would speak to her.

Maybe Kanar had bought their silence. She would get his secrets. She was determined to do so. And when she did, then maybe she would share her own.

The throng of Dogs below moved through the street and headed toward the wagons. They seemed unconcerned as they raced forward, and as far as Lily could tell, all of them were armed with crossbows and swords.

Once she got to a point where she was looking down upon them, she reached into her pouch until she found the specific bone fragment she was looking for. When she pulled it out, she twisted it in her fingers and ran her thumb along it. Then she took out a knife, jabbed it into her thumb, and smeared a layer of blood across the bone. She murmured the necessary words and tossed it down onto the street.

Smoke streamed from it as it dropped. It wasn't going to be a subtle effect, but she didn't need subtlety.

The bone exploded. As soon as it did, the jarring pain that came from that explosion burned through her. She paused on the edge of the rooftop, gritting her teeth and waiting for that pain to pass. When it finally did, the Dogs had already started to scatter.

She had other bones like that, at least similar enough that they would explode if she added what was necessary, but she didn't really want to use them. Not here, and not with the cost it incurred.

Lily scrambled forward and reached the wagons as they rumbled along the street. As soon as she did, she swung down. She jerked the grappling hook from the roof, stuffed it into her pouch, and darted toward Jal.

"What in the name of Isan do you think you're doing?" she said.

Jal looked over. "There you are. I've been waiting for you. Did you find the Dogs?"

He *had* to have heard the explosions. He certainly saw

things well enough, and she figured he could hear things just as well.

"You had an entire throng of them chasing you," Lily said.

He furrowed his brow. "We did? What happened?"

"They must've gotten distracted by the fog." She waved her hand behind her. "But you're going in the wrong direction," she said, pointing off to her right. "That's the seashore."

"That's the seashore all right," he said, "but in order for us to get there, we have to head this way."

"Why?"

He shrugged.

She didn't share Kanar's appreciation of Jal's hunches, but then again, she hadn't been privy to some of the more impressive circumstances with it. Kanar always loved to take Jal with him when he was gambling, as if Jal would somehow afford him winnings that he wouldn't have on his own. And unfortunately, it had worked, more often than not. She hated that it did. More than that, she hated that she hated it.

"So what else is your instinct telling you we need to do?" she asked.

"Well, we need to go a little further this way, and once we reach the next road, we're going to take a hard right, and then we're going to go straight along it until we get to the dock." He grinned, then fired an arrow. It flew back in the direction she had come from and struck a man perched on the rooftop.

Had that man seen what she had done? How many Dogs might she have missed? And would they have known it was her? There weren't too many people who would recognize her use of magic, but there might be some.

"Are you ready?" Jal asked.

"I'm ready," she muttered, shaking her head. "But if you get me killed…"

"If I get you killed, Kanar is going to kill me. And if we don't complete the job, I think Malory is going to kill all of us."

"It's kind of a stupid job."

"For what she's paying?"

"Oh, she could pay more than she did," Lily said. "But I doubt Kanar will push her."

"Why not?"

"He's afraid of her," she said.

Jal watched her, a hint of a grin on his face. His eyes went wide, and then he drew another arrow and fired. Another Dog was down.

All of this for a caravan? Just how many had been sent after them?

This was too much. There was something going on here. Even if Kanar didn't want to dig into it, Lily wasn't about to let it drop.

"I don't think Kanar is afraid of anyone," Jal said. "Certainly not Malory."

Lily bit back any retort she might have. She could imagine Jal falling under Malory's spell all too easily. He was exactly the kind of person she would use her charms on, and one who would never know they had been seduced by her. Kanar, on the other hand, likely knew better than to allow himself to risk that seduction. More than that, Malory probably appreciated that about him, which made her work all the harder at Kanar.

Lily had known women like that, and when she had been training, those women had worked to get her to end up like that. She had resisted, but she knew how that technique worked, especially on somebody like Jal.

"Now," he said, and the wagon driver suddenly turned, veering the wagons off to the right.

She watched the rooftops. There had been attackers all along the last pathway, as well as the gaggle of Dogs that had chased them until she dropped her explosive in the middle of them. So far, there had been no sign of any further stragglers, but she wouldn't put it past the Dogs to keep chasing, especially if they thought it gave them an opportunity to capture these wagons.

There was no sign of them.

The street was nearly empty. There were the usual people out and about—merchants, shoppers, and even some fishmongers coming in from a day out at sea—but no Dogs. It was almost as if turning that street corner had left them all behind.

Lily glanced over to Jal. His hunch, huh? She had never really given much stock to it, but maybe there was something to it. Who was she to question, anyway?

When they reached the dock, they raced forward to pier number seven, and then she finally allowed herself to relax. There weren't going to be any attackers out here. The Dogs weren't stupid enough to attack on the dock. This was a no-contact zone that would draw the attention of the watch, and that was something even the Prophet made a point of avoiding.

The wagons slowed, and she jumped down when she saw Kanar. He was talking to Honaaz and Heatharn. Was that relief that swept over his face when he saw her?

Lily whistled, and Kanar made his way over to them.

"You got here," he said.

"We got here," she replied. "Now what?"

"Time to go. Get paid, get a drink, and let Jal clean up. He stinks."

Chapter Four

KANAR

Kanar never liked his visits with Malory.

She offered jobs, made sure he got paid, and provided a measure of protection in a city where he was something of an outsider, but he still didn't trust her. Not because she was a woman—there were plenty of people in Sanaron who dismissed Malory for that reason, to their own detriment— but because she had a cruel streak that he never cared for.

Kanar struggled to avoid the Kalenwatch as he made his way from the docks. Dozens upon dozens of men swarmed and filled the streets, stopping everyone they came across. They forced him to duck into an alley and loop around the long way before getting to Malory. He didn't like the idea of dealing with questions, nor did he care for the possibility that he might be checked for weapons.

At least the watch had finally decided to get involved. After the Dogs' attack on the caravan, he had expected more of a response. Normally, they kept things better locked down.

One more thing to talk to Malory about.

She had an apartment above the Painted Nails brothel near the Mill district. The location offered easy access to the docks, but it also offered her an air of legitimacy that she wouldn't have otherwise. She could pull from those with no money—dock workers, fishers, street thieves all among them—as well as some of the well-off merchants.

The brothel itself tended to do brisk business, and the women were all attractive, if pushy, which was typical for what he'd seen of similar places in Sanaron. Getting to Malory's apartment meant that he had to go through the brothel with its dim lantern light and plush purple carpet, then past the guards hiding in the smoke-filled shadows, and up a narrow staircase in the back. Anyone else would be stopped before they even reached the stairs.

Kanar took them two at a time. At the top of the stairs, he knocked on the door.

A small slat in the door opened, revealing a round face. The frown on the full lips quickly faded. "Good to see you again, Kanar."

"And you, Bec. She in?"

It was always best to get to business here. The workers tried to seduce everyone out of the last coin they could, even when they knew they'd fail, as they would with Kanar.

"She's not in a good mood, but she's here."

"What happened?" Kanar asked.

"You don't want to know."

He didn't, but dealing with Malory meant that he was at a natural disadvantage. If she was in a foul mood, having any insight about what had happened would put him on better footing.

"Sure I do. Maybe I can do something about it."

"Don't go making promises you can't keep," Bec purred.

She pulled the door open, revealing a darkened hall that led to another door at the far end. The brothel rooms were in a different section, but Malory made a point of keeping up appearances so that if the Painted Nails was ever raided, they could make it look like Malory was nothing more than another of their girls.

Bec leaned on the door and watched him with a curl to her lips, the sheer white gown she wore clinging to her curves. "Sounds like she missed out on a job she'd been angling for. You know how she gets."

Unfortunately, he did. That was how he knew Malory could be cruel.

Whoever had pulled a job out from under her would suffer the consequences. He only hoped that he wouldn't be asked to be a part of it.

"Do you want to let her know I'm here?" Kanar said.

"She knows," a hard voice replied from the end of the hall.

Kanar pulled his gaze away from Bec and tipped his head politely to Malory. She expected polite. Despite—or perhaps because of—the fact that she was a brothel mistress, Malory carried herself with a measure of authority. She also dressed in a far more distinguished way than anybody else in this part of the city ever dared. It was more chaste, as well. Today she wore a flowing high-necked dress with a single gold band hanging from her neck.

"Job is done," he said.

Malory's eyes narrowed and she flicked her gaze past him to Bec, who stepped onto the staircase and closed the door behind her. Kanar couldn't help but feel trapped, though he wasn't.

Unlike most people who came to the Nails, he wasn't searched for weapons and didn't have to check in with anyone at the entrance. He was a known entity. Trusted. That didn't mean he would ever make the mistake of crossing Malory. He might get out alive, but he wouldn't stay that way long.

"Why do you sound like you had to kill a cat?" Malory said.

He sniffed. "Dog. Rabid ones. Probably a dozen of those bastards, maybe more."

She watched him for a long moment before waving for him to follow.

Kanar made his way down the hall. Malory was selective with how often she invited him back, and when she did, it usually meant a business discussion. Kanar wasn't sure he was ready for another discussion at this point. He had just finished the last job, and considering how poorly it had gone, he wasn't terribly eager to jump into another right away.

He'd only ever seen the outer room of her apartment, which was elegantly appointed. A pair of high-backed chairs were angled toward a hearth that always crackled with a warm flame. Two oil lanterns glowed with soft orange light, and a sheer maroon veil draped over them made the light shift, giving it a hint of red. The air hung with a lilac fragrance that was mixed with rose and even a bit of mint, though it took him a few moments to pick up on that. She motioned for him to take a seat, which he did, however reluctantly. It meant that he would be staying for a while. All he wanted was to get paid and then get to the others. They were waiting for him to celebrate.

Malory stopped at a shelf on the far side of the room, and he heard the soft clinking of coins. When she turned back, she set a small purse on the table between the two chairs. She rested her hands on the back of the empty chair, though she didn't take a seat. "Tell me."

He liked to think that he was all business when he came to the Nails, but Malory was always business first.

"The job was easy," he said, "at least until we got close to the city. A few highwaymen jumped us, but they were easy enough to dispatch."

She frowned, shifting her navy-blue dress. "I wouldn't expect you to have trouble with any simple highwaymen. Unless…" She frowned, tipping her head to the side, and Kanar could practically see the gears in her mind starting to work. She was smart. One of the smartest people he had ever been around. "I see. They sent word back to the city. That's where the real trouble was."

"Right," Kanar said. "We got pinched in the warehouse district."

"Why did you take that way?"

"Better to mask our approach."

She nodded.

"They had men on roofs, a few more in one of the buildings, and there were a couple explosions." He looked up at her carefully then. He hadn't told Lily or Jal about the explosions, though he suspected they had heard them. Of everything he had dealt with, that was what he was most concerned about.

"The Dogs don't deal with magic," Malory said.

"Are you sure about that? Besides, can't say that they were all magic."

Her brow furrowed, and her lips pressed into a tighter line. "Not as sure as I would like to be." She took a deep breath and straightened her spine, patting the back of the chair with one hand. "You got away. You got the cargo to the ship. Except for one small item Heatharn had procured. An exotic marmoset, from what I understand."

Damn you, Jal.

He'd probably snuck the creature away during the fight. *Which meant he'd left Lily unprotected.*

"You already knew," Kanar said.

"Of course I knew. The moment you reached the dock, a runner sent word."

He shook his head. Kanar never had a chance to keep anything from her, not that he actually would. He wouldn't dare conceal anything from Malory. The consequences would be too dire.

"What else was he transporting?" he asked.

"That's not part of the job, Kanar."

"Not usually. But I also don't usually have a dozen Dogs chasing me down when I'm trying to escort a caravan to the city."

"You were hired for protection," Malory said. "You provided it. That was the job."

"You hired me to protect Alainsith relics. Who are you moving them for?"

She said nothing.

"The Prophet is after them," Kanar said. "They nearly killed us to get to those relics."

"There are always people who are after power. And it doesn't matter. Heatharn came looking for protection, and it was easy enough to push him to pay a premium, especially given the kind of cargo he had. He tried to renegotiate after his pet went missing, but I passed."

She had known—and she hadn't said anything to him. It was enough to anger him, if it weren't for the fact that he still needed her and her jobs.

That was about all the admission he was going to get from her about how much Heatharn had paid for Kanar's protection. It would be more than what Kanar was paid. Malory took her cut, and most of the time he didn't care. That was the price of doing business, especially in a place like Sanaron. In this case, though, it wasn't just the Dogs that worried him. It was the use of magic.

An *open* use of magic.

"If someone's using magic in Sanaron—"

"That's none of our concern," Malory said.

"It is. I've been around enough magic in my day."

Her smile turned darker, more dangerous. "Would you like to talk about it?"

"Not with you."

She chuckled and turned away, moving to a table near the hearth. She lifted one of the glasses that rested on a tray and filled it with wine. Without turning, she took a swig. Kanar didn't know her tastes, but he imagined they ran expensive. Sanaron was a port city and was able to draw goods from many parts of the world. The wines that came here would likely be incredibly expensive and exotic—nothing like the piss he often bought.

"I will give you an additional five silver for hazard pay."

"Ten," he said. Her offer told him she was willing to negotiate.

Malory turned back to him. "Fine. Ten. For that ten, I expect silence."

"About Heatharn?"

"About everything."

"Why?" Kanar asked.

This wasn't the kind of thing he normally cared about, but then again, he normally wasn't involved in magical dealings. He tried to steer clear of it. Most people did, but given his own personal experience, he had even more reason to want to stay far away.

"Heatharn was carrying relics," Malory said. "I don't know what they were exactly. I haven't been able to determine that, but there was an urgency to his transport. You did well ensuring that he got to the dock unscathed. From what I could tell, there will be other similar transports." She looked over to him, holding the glass at her lips. The wine had stained them red. "Given what you encountered, I will negotiate better terms for the next one. I doubt we will have any difficulty getting paid."

"I'm not sure I want to go through that again."

"I didn't figure you for somebody who was afraid of a few stray dogs."

Kanar grabbed the purse, stuffed it into his pocket, and got to his feet. "This was an entire pack. What happens if they send more the next time?"

"Then you need to be prepared."

He wanted to argue with her, but he also wanted the coin, so it put him in a difficult spot. He didn't want to lose the job. Lily and Jal would want to keep the job as well. The Rabid Dog crew had been unusually sloppy today despite their numbers—maybe they'd brought in new recruits. He tried to remember if the brand he'd seen looked fresh.

"Let me know when you have the next job. I'll let you know my terms."

"That's not how it works, Kanar."

"Not usually," he said.

That she had so easily paid him an additional ten silver suggested that he could have gotten more. How much had she cleared for this job? How much did she think she could get for another?

When Kanar reached the door, he paused for a moment, hand on the handle. "What job did you miss out on?"

"She told you that?"

"I hear rumors."

"From my girls."

He shook his head. "No. I hear rumors from people in the street."

Malory glanced at the door. "I'm sure you do. In this case, the rumors are unfounded. I have missed out on an opportunity, but it's not uncommon for that to take place. I will have plenty of others. As will you." She took another sip of her wine and set her glass down. "The attack offers an opportunity, and we will take advantage of it. Now go and celebrate. I will get word to you soon enough."

Kanar didn't like the dismissal, but he also didn't care to stay with her any longer than necessary.

Bec sat on a stool outside the door, and she rested a hand on his arm as he approached. "That didn't take you very long. I figured you for the kind who would take your time and enjoy it."

"I'm not sure anyone could enjoy their time with her,"

he said. "Does she have you here to keep an eye on her? Or are you here because she's keeping an eye on you?"

"A little of both. I made the mistake of getting a bit too friendly with one of the Kalenwatch. She didn't much care for that. She thought it would draw attention to the Nails."

The guardians of the city were simple foot soldiers, and about as skilled as the Archers from his home. They were easy enough to avoid, but Malory was probably right to want to keep from attracting their attention. If the Kalenwatch caught wind of her crew, they could disrupt her business. Malory was too skilled of a businesswoman to permit that to happen.

"Maybe you need to find better men," he said.

Bec smiled. "Is that an offer, Kanar?"

"Not this time."

He made his way down the stairs, through the brothel, and out to the street. He took a deep breath. In this district, the air didn't have quite as much salt to it, and he couldn't smell the fishmongers like he could closer to the shoreline. There was a hint of sawdust in the air, a remnant from the mill, but the steady wind that gusted through often pulled that away and left the air smelling fresh—if such a thing were possible.

Kanar walked up the steep hillside toward the Yol district, which was situated halfway up one of the many hills of Sanaron. The street narrowed, as no horses or wagons could make their way up.

He stepped into the Roasted Walnut tavern. As soon as he was inside, he breathed more easily. This was a familiar place that he had found early on in his time in the city. There was a comfort to it, a measure of safety. He didn't have to look over his shoulder, worrying about what Malory might try to pull or whether there would be some other crew attempting to jump him. He could simply enjoy a mug of ale. Never wine, though. He knew better than to trust Porten's taste in wine.

He found the tavern owner leaning on the counter, wiping off his ale glasses. He looked up, the perpetually surly expression on his face not fading one bit when he caught sight of Kanar. He motioned to the back, where Jal and Lily sat at a table with two others.

Breck was a younger man, barely twenty, and had been useful on certain jobs. He was good with the sword, at least as well as anyone who was raised in Sanaron could be considered good with the sword. He had a decent head on his shoulders and never made the mistake of fighting when he could run. It was a trait that Kanar always appreciated.

Olivia was with him. Another local, she had been running through the streets of Sanaron since she was only a few years old. Kanar had always thought it was a wonder she didn't get pulled into Malory's brothel, or any number of similar establishments scattered around the city. That she hadn't suggested that she was clever, or perhaps she had connections. Kanar had always been careful with her because he didn't know her well enough to know which it was.

Kanar pulled a chair over to the table and took a seat.

Jal arched a brow. "Well?"

"We got paid."

"We were always going to get paid," Lily said.

"We got some hazard pay too."

Breck slapped his hand on the table. "Wait. She's paying hazard pay now? I never known her to do that."

"Because the jobs you pull aren't dangerous," Jal said.

He took a long drink of his ale before setting his mug down and wiping his hand across his mouth.

"I can handle dangerous. You just have to include me next time, Kanar."

"If the job is right," Kanar said. He looked up when Porten strolled over to the table and set a mug down in front of him. The man didn't say anything—just slapped his towel over his shoulder and trudged back to the bar. "It takes time to know what I need out of my team."

And even more time for him to convince Malory that he needed to expand it.

"Well, I just want you to know that I can be useful," Breck said. "I can keep a lookout, and can fight, and can—"

"I've seen you fight. You shouldn't be bragging about that," Lily said.

Olivia grinned. "Don't give him such a hard time. He might not be as quick as the two of you, but he's skilled enough."

"High praise, that is," Jal said. "Just what I've always wanted to be told: 'You're skilled enough.'"

Lily snickered. "I doubt you've heard that before—in any circumstance."

Kanar leaned forward toward Breck and Olivia and dropped his voice to a low whisper. "If the two of you want to be part of what we're doing, I need anything you hear about jobs that Malory might have missed out on."

He took a drink of his ale. It was more bitter and warmer than he liked, but it was decent. That was more than could be said about many of the places he had found in this city.

"What happened?" Lily asked.

"She didn't really say, but she's not too thrilled about it," Kanar said. "Between that and what happened with us, I'm starting to question whether there might be more at play here than we know about. And you know how I feel about not knowing."

Lily nodded slowly. "Don't keep anything from him. Can't have Kanar upset."

"Not our fearless leader," Jal said with a smile. He took another swig of his ale, then set it down. "You know what, now you're the one who stinks, Kan. I figured you'd need to get all prettied up before you go and visit Malory. I heard she liked you like that."

Breck covered his mouth, as if trying to hide his reaction.

"You ever kissed a snake?" Kanar asked.

"Kind of a question is that?" Jal said.

Kanar shrugged. "Given how you're from Yelind, I figure I would at least ask."

"No, and I can't even imagine who would."

"Exactly. Who would?"

Kanar took a long drink of ale and realized that maybe Jal wasn't wrong. He did stink. Rather than stopping at one of the bath houses along the way to the Roasted Walnut, he had come straight to the tavern. It might be good to soak, wash off some of the dust of the road.

Then he could start digging into what the Rabid Dogs were after. He wasn't going to let that drop. He didn't know how much time he had before Malory would hire him for another job, but suspected he had a little. Heatharn had his ship to deal with, and if he was her primary contact, he would need some time to finish this shipment, return to the city, and then go after another one.

Kanar stood. "I think I'm going to get a bath. Then I'll be back."

"Oh, maybe he's going back to the Nails," Breck said to the others. He elbowed Olivia before he seemed to realize what he was doing, then sat up straighter.

"Careful," Lily said. "You don't want the great Kanar Reims to come after you."

"Not so much great about me these days," he muttered.

He nodded to Porten as he made his way out of the tavern, then paused in the street. It had gotten dark. The fog had lifted, which it always did at this time of day, though a thin layer still hung along the shoreline. It would build closer to morning, billowing in on the steady breeze, as if some angry god were trying to sweep it in from the sea to erase the city.

Kanar started up another hill. One thing he had always liked in his time in Sanaron was to have a view. Too far down and too close to the shoreline, the fog often made it difficult for him to see much of anything. He preferred to be higher up, perched on one of the hillsides, away from most of the crews that ran the city. His place might be in a merchant section, but it also kept him safer. There weren't many who were willing to spend the coin on an apartment in the area he did.

He made his way forward before taking a side street and angling to the south. The calls of seagulls circling ahead filled the night. Everyone else was quiet. As he stepped out onto another street, he paused. He couldn't shake the sense that somebody was following him. He pressed himself up against one of the nearby buildings. The bakery windows were dark, though he could see shadows moving inside.

Somebody was there working, probably preparing for

the morning rush. Maybe that was all he had felt. He didn't like to think that he would overreact in such a way, but maybe he had.

Kanar took a few steps. He smelled ash, then noticed a feeling of tension along his skin.

When the explosion struck, he was tossed forward, and his head crashed into the cobblestone road. Before he blacked out, he saw a pair of figures approaching.

Chapter Five

LILY

Lily looked across the tavern as Kanar left. Something was not quite right with him, though she wasn't exactly sure what it was. He could be a challenge to read, though that didn't mean she wouldn't try. Jal jabbered on, leaning toward Olivia while smiling broadly at her. He was a fool, and Olivia was far too easy of a target. She wouldn't fall for somebody like him, anyway.

"I think I'm going to get some sleep," Lily said, getting to her feet and frowning at Jal. His long face looked more comical with the froth of his ale smeared across it.

"Why are you looking at me like that?" he asked.

"Just because." She reached over and ruffled his hair. "If you see Kanar again, let him know that I'll catch up with him in the morning."

"He might come back," Jal said.

"This is Kanar we're talking about. He's not coming back tonight. He's done."

They all had their experiences with Kanar leaving abruptly like that.

"You plan to follow him?" Porten asked as Lily made her way past the bar.

She glanced over to the old bartender. He and Kanar had some sort of agreement, though she had no idea the terms of it. She'd noticed Porten was gruffer with everybody else than he was with Kanar. He seemed to have a soft spot for him. Lily wanted to know what it was, as it was one more thing about Kanar that she struggled to uncover. If she was going to work with someone, she wanted to know them.

No surprises.

She shook her head.

"Looks like you might," he said, glancing toward the door. "A man like that doesn't really care to have anybody chasing him."

"Sometimes he needs people to follow him," she said softly.

He regarded her, gaze going to her pouch a moment, and then he grunted. "Might be right at that."

Lily stepped outside and hurriedly scanned her surroundings. There was an emptiness to the street. Situated where this was, up on a hillside and looking down toward the seashore, it could often be lovely here. She could see the ocean on a clear day. It was clear enough now—the fog had mostly lifted, though it never *really* lifted—and it gave her a chance to see the moon reflecting off the water, sending a streak of silver shooting toward the city. It was beautiful.

She reached into her pouch and pulled out a bone. It was a fresh one, cut from the Dog and cleaned. She would have to treat it before she could use it, but she needed time to do so.

That was part of the other reason she wanted to leave the tavern. She needed an opportunity to work through her collection—especially if they were planning to take another job for Malory. Lily wanted to be better prepared the next time. She wasn't going to have any Dogs spring up and surprise her, leaving her questioning whether they'd be able to get away safely.

Today had been a near thing. Far closer than it should have been.

It was unfortunate that Kanar did not like to work with too large of a team. When it came to payment, though, Lily appreciated that. A smaller team meant fewer people to split the coin with, which meant they were better off. Most of the time. Some of that was Malory's preference, though she knew *most* of it came from Kanar.

The lower city was chaotic tonight.

There were times when it was quiet, when the fog itself seemed to be a heavy blanket that weighed down upon Sanaron and muted everything. There were times when the wind that gusted through carried away the voices and sounds of the city, pulling it out to sea or pushing it deeper onto land. There were times when the rains were heavy enough to drown out all noise.

Tonight was not one of those nights. Tonight was a night when the sounds were vibrant and vivacious, and music drifted from someplace along the shoreline. Shouts sprang up from time to time, and every so often she heard the cawing of seagulls and the distant howl of a wolf.

It was comforting.

Lily enjoyed being inside the city and having this sort of commotion around her, where she was not as isolated as she had been when she was younger. The energy filled her, and it gave her an easier time making collections. Especially when it came to ones that would be used on jobs with Kanar.

She didn't see where he'd gone, though Kanar could slip away more easily than almost any man she'd ever met. He obviously had some training. She doubted that his training was similar to hers, though they accomplished the same goals. They could both sneak away, but she tended to go up to rooftops, while he tended to go by ground.

She decided to head toward the shore, as Kanar often scouted there. Sanaron could be safe in the daylight despite the fog, especially with the watch out ensuring the crews didn't operate freely. But night was a different matter. Though she'd admired the moonlight shining off the sea from the hillside, she didn't think she could go and simply *walk* along the shore.

There were other ways she could, though. And she would need to. Before the night was over, Lily thought she had to find different answers than what Malory had given Kanar.

The Dogs bothered her more than she could put a finger on. She needed to understand what had taken place, what she and the others had protected, and why the Prophet had sent so many after that caravan.

Had she been feeling brave about it, she would've found a way to sneak aboard the ship and figure out what was in that trunk. But if she had done that, there was no telling how long she'd be stuck out at sea. She wasn't a swimmer. She could probably find some nearby vessel, claim that she'd gotten thrown overboard, and get brought back to Sanaron, but it would only expose her to different questions she didn't want to answer.

Lily hadn't climbed very far when she heard voices behind her. She scrambled to the rooftop right as a pair of Kalenwatch came strolling up the street. Since the attack earlier, the watch had been almost too thick to maneuver through. These two were armed with crossbows, as most of the watch were, and moving quickly. Lily kept pace.

"Doubt we will find another like that," one of the men said. "They aren't supposed to be active here."

Who were they talking about? The Dogs?

"You know what that is, don't you? Hegen magic. It's dangerous. It's not supposed to be here," the other replied.

"You don't know that's what it is," the first one said. "Besides, I'm not nearly as superstitious about magic as those shits in Reyand."

"If that magic is spreading here, it might mean the war is coming this way too. We don't need any of that."

"The war should be over. At least, it's mostly over."

They moved on, but Lily hung out for another moment. They'd found her collections.

She wasn't concerned about the watch finding anything she had taken. She was more worried about Kanar or Jal learning about it. They weren't questions she was eager to answer.

She found her way down the hillside, moving past brightly colored buildings, and then turned down a narrow, twisting side street. This one led toward an alley that opened up into one of the more distinct streets in the city. The place had once been filled with nefarious people, but it had been gentrified so that the homes were some of the nicest, and most expensive, in the city. Lily always enjoyed walking along it.

Most of the homes had flowerpots outside the windows,

and vibrant flowers bloomed in the bright sunlight that shone here. She always appreciated the fact that the fragrance from the flowers mingled, creating the smell of a garden in the midst of the city. It was a place she always came to on her own so she could think, where she knew it would not be occupied by dangerous people.

She took a seat on a bench in a small plaza right before the alley opened into a wider street. She pulled out her pouch, set it on her lap, and began to work at the bones. Lily rubbed the bones until they were fully cleansed. She would need boiling water and would have to process them fully, but for now this would be enough. If it came down to it, she could even use them, but it would take more out of her to do so.

She worked her finger along the bones as her mind traced back to when she had first learned this technique. She'd been barely eleven years old when she had first begun her journey toward the art and understood her own potential. It was so different than what her parents could do, though her mother had certainly tried to help her find a similar gift to her own. For all of Lily's attempts to be like her mother, she had failed. She simply didn't have that same predilection.

Not like she did when it came to bone.

She remembered the first time she'd been brought to claim her own prize. That was what they were considered, after all—prizes. The man had been hanged for some crime against the kingdom, and once she and the others had climbed up the white stone, her instructor had waved her hand toward Lily and then to the corpse.

"You have to claim it yourself," Ezra had said. "There's more power in it. Once you claim it, then you can clean it, and then you can use it. All part of the stages involved in this."

Lily approached slowly. The others had backed away, especially when Ezra had gotten there. They revered her, not only because of her experience but because of her skill. If Ezra was training a student, as she was with Lily, they gave her the necessary space to do what she needed to do. In this case, Lily was being given an opportunity to claim her own prize so that she could begin to have some mastery.

"It feels wrong," Lily said.

She couldn't take her eyes off the man's face, with his grizzled beard and sallow cheeks. His brown eyes were open and staring at her, as if condemning her for what she was going to do. She shivered and backed up a step, knowing that she should not. Ezra would not allow her to abandon this part of her training.

"What about it feels wrong?" Ezra asked.

Lily looked over to her. Ezra's blonde hair was pulled back into a braid and wrapped with a pale blue silk that shone in the moonlight. Her smile was warm and comforting as she looked at Lily.

"Taking from him," Lily said.

"Does he need his fingers?" Ezra asked. "His toes? Even his ears or his manhood?"

Lily glanced back at the corpse, and for a moment she could practically feel as if the man were watching her, his eyes demanding that she walk away, that she not touch him.

"He's dead," she whispered.

"Then he does not need those things. They are part of his flesh, and now they will be part of something greater. But only if *you* turn them into something greater." Ezra reached forward and grabbed the man's hand. She gripped his thumb, and with large silver scissors she cut through the thumb before holding it up. "It is our responsibility to ensure that those who have gone can still offer something to those who remain behind. Do you feel that you do not have that potential?"

"You said that I do," Lily said.

"And what do *you* think you can do?"

"I don't know."

It wasn't a matter of what she could do, it was a matter of what she was willing to. And in this case, she was going to have to be willing to do what Ezra had just done: claim a prize. Lily had known that was part of her training and had tried to prepare herself for what she would have to do, but now that she was here in front of this man, she found it more difficult than she had imagined.

The wind picked up, stirring a hint of the rot of this place, but it was mixed with the flowers that bloomed all around the stone. Lilies, just like her name.

"What did he do?" Lily asked.

"Will it make it easier for you?"

"I don't know."

Ezra glanced to the city in the distance. It was hidden behind a wall, obscured from her view, though Lily had wandered the streets of that city. She had learned to sneak through them, skulking like the others who had been training with Ezra.

"He took advantage of several women," Ezra said. "That was his crime. Crimes." She smiled tightly as she corrected herself. "The mistakes he made in his life can be redeemed in the afterlife. The mistakes he made can be paid for with the offering that he makes."

"He's not choosing to make this offering, though."

"By agreeing to his sentencing, he agreed to the offering."

Ezra looked over to those around them. Lily was one of the very few who did not grow up among the people of this holding. She had been sent here to train, to learn. In that, she felt like an outsider, but never more so than she did now. Now that she was here with Ezra and the others, instructed on what she needed to do next, she could not help but feel as if she did not belong.

"He didn't agree to his sentencing," Lily said.

"He made the walk. You saw it."

Lily nodded. She had seen. The man had walked out to the stone, climbed the stairs and the small ladder, and placed his neck inside the rope. Maybe he had agreed to his sentencing. Not that the man had any choice in the matter, but perhaps at the end he had known what was coming and hadn't objected. Maybe he knew what would become of his body, the way the people would claim their prizes. None of that was a secret in this part of the world.

Ezra watched her. Lily reached out and took hold of the man's pinky finger. She would start small. That had been the lesson she'd been given. Not just because claiming the prize was easier when she started small, but because the art she would create would be easier to make that way.

The wind whispered along her face and tugged at her hair. She looked over to the others, all of them standing in the shadows as if waiting on her to make her decision—and to claim her prize.

Ezra nodded in encouragement. Lily placed her small silver scissors up to the base of the pinky, and with trembling hands, she snipped. The finger came off cleanly. She held it out, unsure what she was supposed to do next. Ezra had told her before, but she hadn't given enough thought to it. In her mind, this had never been something she would have done.

The pinky felt surprisingly small and cold. Lily hadn't known what it would feel like, but other than the sticky blood, it was just cold. She would have to clean the flesh before she could use the bone in the art, but it seemed to her that the hardest part had been done.

"Very well. Now that you've claimed your prize, you get to decide how you'll use it," Ezra said.

Lily nodded. "Just this one?" Her hands still shook, but she'd cut one finger off now. What would be another?

"We'll start with this. When you feel comfortable with it, you can begin to try another. Does that sound fair?"

Lily looked at the dead man again, meeting his blank eyes. *Was* it fair?

Was anything?

She didn't know how she felt.

She nodded and stepped away from the hanging body, letting others move in to take their prizes. She'd been so focused on what she'd been doing that she hadn't paid much attention to them as they waited on her and Ezra. Now they were there, quiet as they worked, the steady *snip* of the scissors cutting through flesh and bone the only sound.

Lily blinked away the memory, turning the bone in her hand as she looked around the small courtyard. That seemed like a lifetime ago, though it wasn't that long. It was easier on her conscience now. Claiming prizes was a matter of practicality. When someone was gone, why *shouldn't* she use their remains?

But it was harder to actually do because getting to the bodies wasn't easy unless she was the one who killed them. Then it didn't feel so much like she claimed a prize as it felt like her taking something that wasn't hers.

Sitting here wasn't going to help her prepare any better, but there was something relaxing about it. Ezra would understand. She'd taught Lily so much, but it was only one aspect of the training Lily had received. The other parts of her training had been harder earned but no less important. They were the parts that had kept her alive all this time.

Lily stuffed the bones back into her pouch and sealed it shut.

Kanar wouldn't understand. She had to keep him from learning about her prizes and about the reason she claimed them. Though he was from Reyand, most there didn't care for the kind of subtle art she used.

Not so subtle these days.

Not with what she'd done with the Dogs.

Then again, there hadn't been the chance for subtlety. She'd needed quick action, or else Jal and the wagons would have been captured. She wasn't about to let that happen just because she'd been trained to try to keep her arts hidden.

The Dogs…

That was what she needed to learn more about.

When she did, then she could let Kanar know what kind of a threat they really posed. He probably expected her to get involved anyway, though he would never tell her that. Kanar could be difficult to read. Stubborn. He was the kind of man that she would have relished the opportunity to go after had she been given the job, though. She would have taken a careful approach, perhaps even something of a delicate touch to ensure that he didn't know she was coming.

And then...

Lily smiled at the thought. What kind of art could she create with a prize claimed from Kanar? That thought wasn't just hers. It came from the lessons Ezra had given her. Lessons that her other mentors in the citadel had trained into her mind.

A bark sounded in the distance, and she got to her feet.

It seemed as if even the strays wanted her to get moving. And it was time.

The Dogs weren't waiting on them, so she wouldn't wait on the Dogs.

Chapter Six

KANAR

When he came awake, Kanar half expected to be in one of the Dogs' strongholds. Having survived the attack, he knew there was a danger of them coming after him. It wasn't as if he wasn't a known entity in the city. Quite a few people would recognize him and his sword, along with the members of his team.

But he wasn't in one of the Dogs' strongholds. If he had been, he would smell the seashore, the stench of fish, the salt in the air.

Instead, it smelled like Malory's room. She wouldn't have jumped him, though.

Whoever was responsible for this had used some sort of explosive—or magic, he had to acknowledge—and knocked him out. Malory didn't need to do any of that. If she had wanted talk to him, she would simply have sent for him.

His hands were bound. His legs as well. He was sitting in a chair, but it was too dark to see. It wasn't the first time Kanar had been bound like this, and he immediately began to work on the knots. Most people got sloppy, afraid of cutting off the prisoner's circulation. That was one thing Kanar knew how to do well—make sure the bindings were taut.

He rubbed his wrists together. It was tight, but not completely.

Somewhere nearby, a door opened. He heard the soft thud of boots along the floor. The sounds were muted more than they should be on wood. That meant carpet. Was he in some sort of merchant stronghold?

Maybe Heatharn had decided to betray him. Though he expected that Heatharn was already out to sea, taking his treasures beyond Sanaron to wherever he sailed.

Not Heatharn, then. Not Malory. And not the Dogs.

A lantern came on, and Kanar blinked.

He was in a wood-paneled office, seated in front of a heavily lacquered desk stacked with books and papers. There was a yellow veil over the lantern. He couldn't easily see the figure seated at the desk, though he suspected it was a man.

Kanar continued to work at the bindings around his wrists. They started to loosen, but not nearly as fast as he wanted. He didn't see anyone else in the room with them, though that didn't mean there wasn't anyone here. Somebody was probably hiding behind one of those paneled walls, watching to make sure that he didn't escape—or spring across the table and strike this person.

"Mr. Reims," the voice said. It was slightly accented but sounded as if it belonged to a Sanaron local, not one of the city's many outsiders. Not somebody like himself. "I apologize for the nature of our visit, but given your reputation, I thought it was best to bring you here in a way that would ensure all of our safety."

"All of it? Seems to me you weren't all that concerned about my safety. What did you use on me?"

"Just a little incapacitating measure. Nothing to be too concerned about."

"A magical measure?"

There was a moment of silence. "Yes," the man finally said. "Your reputation is well earned. Not many would pick up on that. You have experience with it, don't you?"

Did the man know about his past serving the Realmsguard? Or *how* he had served them? Or was this person only aware of his recent history—the time he had spent in Sanaron and what he had done since coming to the city?

That he was unsurprised by Kanar's exposure to magic suggested that it was the former. There were not many people here who knew of it. Malory was one, he suspected, but he didn't know with certainty. Jal and Lily, to a certain extent, though neither knew the full truth.

"I get around," Kanar said.

"It's more than just getting around, though, isn't it? That it makes you a bit of a predicament."

"It only depends on what predicament you're getting at, but maybe you can release these bonds and we'll have a mature conversation."

"I'm afraid that can't be done until I have your full attention."

"You have my attention," Kanar growled.

The man leaned forward. The glowing lantern light cast shadows about his unfamiliar lean face. He had hard lines around deep green eyes, and a heavy beard.

Not a merchant, then. Most of the merchants were clean shaven, at least those who traveled beyond Sanaron.

There were too many people who had judgmental opinions about beards. And about tattoos.

Kanar sat forward just enough that he could smell the man's perfume. Definitely not a merchant.

"That's good. Very good. I would hate to need to do something more to get your attention. I believe your colleagues Mr. Olassa and Ms. Lily would not be quite as receptive to conversation as you are."

That left only a few options, and all of them made him feel increasingly troubled.

"Are you threatening them?" Kanar said.

"Do I need to?"

Kanar worked his hands again, finally jerking them free and lunging at the same time. The bearded man flinched and leaned back, but not before Kanar had his hands around the man's neck. He flipped his legs to the side, cracking the chair on the desk so that he was freed of it. His legs might still be bound, but he had his arms, and now he had the man in his grasp.

A soft *click* came from behind him. Either a panel sliding open or, more likely, a crossbow drawn and ready.

"You are everything I heard you might be," the man said.

"Not everything," Kanar said. He squeezed tightly, just enough that he could suffocate the man or break his neck if someone were to fire a bolt at him. "Call them off."

"I'm afraid I can't do that." He wheezed the words out while Kanar squeezed his neck. "Not while you hold me here."

"I'm going to count to three. I don't care if they fire at me. I've been shot by crossbows before." It was a gamble, especially as Kanar wasn't sure that crossbows were the only things being aimed at him. "But I can guarantee that I will snap your neck before they have a chance to kill me. Call them off."

The man licked his lips, and Kanar relaxed his grip slightly, holding one hand on the back of his head. He wasn't kidding about snapping this man's neck if it came down to it.

"Leave us," the man said.

"Are you sure?" a voice replied. "But—"

"I am sure. Now leave us."

Kanar stood, still keeping one arm wrapped around the bearded man's neck. He pulled the veil off the lantern and twisted the dial, burning more oil so that it lit the room more brightly.

He looked around. In addition to the wood paneling on the walls, wooden beams crisscrossed the ceiling. A table stood along the far wall, with a bottle of brown liquor resting on it, the stopper shaped like a wolf head.

He noticed an opening in the corner of the room. Kanar positioned himself so that the bearded man was in front of him, and in front of whoever aimed down from above. He scanned the rest of the room and found another bolt hole in the opposite corner.

Maybe he *wouldn't* have gotten out of here alive.

He released the man and shoved him back, then took a seat on the desk. He unwrapped the ropes from around his ankles before tossing them at his captor.

"Where's my sword?" Kanar said.

"I'm afraid I won't be able to provide that to you until we have finished our conversation."

"Then I'm afraid we won't have a conversation. Where is my sword?"

The man cocked his head to the side, and a wide smile parted his lips. "Not at all what I would expect. You are more concerned about your sword than about what I called you here for?"

"You called me here because you want my services. Otherwise, I'd be dead. So hand me my sword. You don't intend to kill me because if you did, I'd be gone. I don't intend to kill you because if I did, you'd be dead. So, where is my sword?"

The man turned and pressed a section of the paneling, which split apart. Three swords hung on an exposed section of wall, but none of them were Kanar's. His rested on a countertop. The bearded man pulled it out, holding it carefully, and then offered it to Kanar as if he were the one bequeathing him the blade.

"An interesting weapon. As you can see, I'm something of an aficionado myself."

"Have you ever used one?"

The man's eyes narrowed. "Oh, a time or two."

Kanar forced himself to reevaluate the man. His first impression had been that the man was soft. His reaction when Kanar had jumped him had been one of nervousness —or had it? What if he had instead been going for his own sword?

Kanar glanced at the blades. One of them was curved, wider at the end, and tapered as it came toward the hilt. The other two were short swords. All three blades had intricately carved scabbards and jeweled hilts.

He moved to the middle of the room, figuring that gave him the best opportunity to look around and to be prepared if they shot at him. There were the bolt holes in the ceiling, and now that he surveyed the room further, he saw that several of the panels looked as if they could move to the side as well. He didn't think they were open, but he suspected it would not take more than a shout for the room to be filled by this man's soldiers.

"So which one are you?" Kanar asked.

The bearded man frowned. "Which one?"

"Of the royal heirs. Can't say that I have much experience with Sanaron royalty, but you have the look of them."

He thought he had it right. Sanaron had once been part of a larger nation, but over time it had shrunk. Now the only land the Sanaron royalty could claim was that of the city itself. That wealth and control of the port was what kept them positioned in such a way that they maintained their standing. The king ruled, but everybody knew he was sick. Eventually, his daughter would take the throne, though there were rumors that she wasn't terribly interested in it.

The king's brothers, on the other hand, were interested.

The man sitting in front of him was one of them, Kanar believed.

"Clever," the man said. "You really have lived up to your reputation, Kanar Reims." He smiled tightly, and gone was any pretense of softness. Now there was a hard edge to his eyes that reminded Kanar of Malory. "I am Edward Visaran, currently second in line to the Sanaron throne."

On the streets, Kanar had always heard Edward's ruthlessness described in relation to his pining for the throne. Perhaps this had something to do with his desire for it too.

"I imagine you're trying to decide why I have called you here."

"Well," Kanar said, "seeing as how you didn't necessarily *call* me here, I am trying to figure out what you hope to gain from me, more than anything else."

"It was the only way to get you here without raising questions."

"There are other ways."

"None that were satisfactory to me," Edward said.

That was all there was to it. The only thing that mattered to Edward was what he wanted. This was a man who was accustomed to getting his way. Kanar had been around royalty before and had seen how clueless they could be about what life was like for those who weren't royals. Edward seemed to fit that mold as well.

"Get on with it," Kanar said, strapping his sword back onto his belt. He still had to replace the knives he'd lost in the street fight before he ultimately got around to digging into what the Dogs had been up to. For now, it didn't really matter. "You keep mentioning my reputation, so obviously you want me here for a job, as I said earlier. And given that you claim to know all about me, you must know that most of my jobs come through an intermediary."

"Oh, I'm quite aware that you work for a Malory Ohal. The Painted Nails, I believe?"

Kanar tipped his head in a nod.

"Why don't I share with you the details of the opportunity, and then you can decide how much you would like to get your mistress involved."

Kanar bristled at the idea that she was his mistress, though perhaps he shouldn't. He did work for her, after all. And he already knew what he was going to do. There was no way he was taking a job without letting Malory know.

Could this be the job she'd been angry about? Maybe she'd been angling for something with Edward, though if she had been, Kanar doubted she would have shared that with him. That suggested there was something else going on.

"I would offer you to take a seat, but given that you have destroyed yours, I'm afraid you're going to have to stand," Edward said, taking a seat of his own. When he looked up at Kanar, he forced a smile. "Recently, there was a meeting outside the city of Verendal."

Kanar tensed. *Reyand.*

"If you think I intend to betray my kingdom—"

"Is it your kingdom? Given everything that had taken place, I thought perhaps you might have a more open mind."

"I will not betray them," Kanar said, keeping his voice steady.

"Of course not. I would never dream of trying to pit you against your kingdom. As I was saying, there was recently a meeting outside of Verendal. It was a delicate meeting, one your King Porman had tried to keep quiet, as he has done for many years."

Kanar had served in the Realmsguard before taking his assignment in the Order during the war. He had been a part of many different discreet meetings over the years.

"And?" Kanar said.

"And I can tell from your face that you can already see where this is going. Yes. It was a meeting with the Alainsith, brokering further peace with their people. Unfortunately, following that meeting, nearly the entire contingent of Alainsith was intercepted, along with a relic they carried— one of twelve, I believe. They were slaughtered in a brutal fashion, in a ceremony that can only be described as—"

"Witchcraft," Kanar said, breathing out the word.

Alainsith slaughtered, and a relic stolen? What had Kanar *already* gotten into?

Edward nodded, leaning back and pressing the tips of his fingers together. "Now, I don't have the same view as many in your land do about magic. I am a practical man, and I can see the benefit to it."

Kanar shook his head. "We don't fear magic."

He just hated it.

"You do fear witchcraft and Alainsith magic. And you force hegen to the outskirts of your cities."

The hegen were tolerated, mostly because they used what was considered a minor form of magic. They traded favors for their craft, and that magic had long been considered useful to the king. It was benign, or at least it was traditionally considered that way.

For Kanar, it was *still* magic.

Witchcraft was different. It involved pain and suffering in order to call upon power, and those who came to learn witchcraft had to master such pain first. It was the reason that Kanar despised it. He had seen witchcraft used to destroy too much of his kingdom.

Then there were the Alainsith. Unlike the hegen and witches, the Alainsith simply possessed magic as part of their essence. They lived beyond the borders of the kingdom, somewhere past the forest. There had been a time when the kingdom had battled with the Alainsith. Many had died, but King Porman, like many of his predecessors, had made a point of forging peace with them.

"You understand the consequences of Alainsith being used in such a ceremony," Edward said. "From what I've been able to learn, the Alainsith blood was taken, then brought somewhere beyond Reyand where it could be used. I haven't been able to determine where."

Kanar couldn't move.

Edward was playing him, he was certain of it now. And worse, he didn't know if he could ignore it. If this had truly happened, then the danger was significant.

"Why do you want it?" Kanar asked.

"Let's just say that I have an academic interest in it."

"For the throne." That had to be his reason.

Edward shifted in irritation. "My sources tell me that there was a person present at the time of the attack who knows where they intend to take the blood. What I need from you is to rescue that person from Declan prison in Verendal before they are executed. You've got a week at most. That's all."

Getting into *that* prison would be difficult. Verendal had a reputation. If the person had already been sentenced, then they had a limited time.

But getting there—and breaking in—in less than a week?

"So I don't have to go after the Alainsith blood?" Kanar said.

"Would you have?"

"No."

"I thought not," Edward said. "Break them out"—he said that with more force than Kanar would have expected —"and I will make it worthwhile for you. Go after the blood, and I will make it *quite* worthwhile for you."

Which part was Edward most concerned about? The captive—or the blood?

Maybe it is both.

Alainsith blood used in witchcraft meant that magic

would spread, creating more of the kind of violence that he'd spent years trying to stop.

Still, none of that was really his concern.

"You seem to have me confused with someone who cares about all of this," he said.

Edward leaned forward, his eyes hard. "I think you care, Mr. Reims. Or am I supposed to believe your reputation was ill earned?"

"I don't give two shits about what you believe."

Kanar started toward the door, flicking his gaze to the bolt holes, not sure if he'd make it to the door or not. If Edward really wanted to stop him, it wouldn't be difficult for him to do. A shot through one of those openings would slow him all too easily.

Then what?

Would they kill him simply for refusing?

He had to think such a thing was possible. Edward was royalty, and Kanar had enough experience with royalty to understand what kinds of things they were capable of pulling. They didn't give two shits either.

"The job will pay well," Edward said.

Kanar paused.

"I believe your *team*"—somehow Edward made the word sound despicable—"doesn't have the same luxury you do. Your past has put you in a position where you don't necessarily have to take every job you're offered. A courier arrives in the city the first of each month and deposits a pension into the Reyand bank."

Kanar stiffened. Banks prided themselves on their privacy. The Reyand bank did so especially, and Kanar wasn't the only retiree in the city on an allowance.

Kanar turned toward him. "I'm sure Porman would not

look favorably on you pilfering the pension from one of his men."

"And I'm sure he would be most curious to know *which* man is receiving that pension while living here in Sanaron." Edward smiled tightly. "I'm sure he would have questions about how you received the pensioner's mark, and I suspect that he would very much appreciate learning where the great Kanar Reims disappeared to after the war."

The witchcraft war had pitted Reyand against a coordinated magical attack that sought to conquer all of the kingdom. Because Kanar had served in the Order, tasked with removing the dangerous threat of witchcraft before it could spread throughout Reyand, he'd learned far more about magic than he had wanted.

But the Order—and those who allied themselves with the Order, including the citadel itself—had defended Reyand. They had stopped witchcraft. The war had ended.

The pensioner's mark had not been fully earned, though Kanar had not felt any remorse for having it. Given what he'd done and what he'd been through, he thought of the mark as his reward for service. He could take it to any Reyand bank in the world and receive his monthly pension. The amount wasn't much, but he didn't have to worry about coin for as long as he lived.

Not like his team did.

And not like *he* would have to if Edward revealed his presence.

That was a different threat. The real one.

As much as it irritated him, Kanar couldn't help but feel impressed that the man had played him so well—first, with the threat of magic, and when that didn't work, the financial card.

Kanar wasn't about to tell him which worked best on him.

"You haven't told me anything about this person I'm supposed to go after," he said.

Edward watched him, an expression that looked quite predatory. "The Priest of Fell. I believe you know her as Morgan Raparal."

Everything within Kanar went cold. Of course, that had been the intent.

From the way Edward looked at him, he knew he had Kanar's attention.

"How much?" Kanar said.

Edward leaned forward. His hands were clenched in his lap. "You're interested?"

"Seems like you aren't going to give me much of a choice. At least you had better make it worthwhile. Something like this is dangerous, especially if what you claim is true. Not many people are capable of the job."

"There are not."

"Which is why you need me. So, how much?"

Edward straightened. "You do this, and I will be in the principal position to assume the Sanaron throne. At that point, the—"

Kanar shook his head. "No. Not at that point. How much are you offering now?"

He had a hard time thinking that *this* job would help anyone get the throne, regardless of what Edward claimed. It might make a difference—but *might* wasn't the same as money in hand.

"I am prepared to offer you one thousand gold vans."

Kanar fought to keep his face neutral. A prize like that would be impossible to ignore, and Edward knew it. Why throw out the other pieces first? Did he think that tempting Kanar with the possibility of stopping magic or threatening his pension would work better than just paying him what a job like this was worth?

"Triple it," Kanar said.

"I'm afraid—"

"You're not afraid, but you should be," Kanar snapped. He noticed movement near one of the bolt holes and attempted to ignore it. "If what you say happened the way you say it did, I can tell you how the blood will be used. I've seen it myself. How many men have experience stopping it?" He waited, letting his words sink in. "I can probably count them on one hand, and I can start ticking off those who are still alive." He held his hand up, then began to bend fingers inward as part of his show. "You want this done, you'll pay triple. Then when you assume the throne, I'll take another two thousand."

"*Five* thousand gold vans?" Edward sputtered.

"That's my price. You see, it's not just about this job. It's about what's involved in the job, as well as what I'm going to have to do"—and where he'd have to go, as he wouldn't be able to stay in Sanaron—"when it's done. Is it worth that for you?"

Edward leaned back, the corners of his eyes twitching slightly. "I will agree to your terms and have the papers drawn up. I assume that will be acceptable?"

"You can assume whatever you want," Kanar said as he headed to the door.

"You don't have much time, Mr. Reims."

"Then you'd better get your contract together."

Chapter Seven

LILY

Darkness swallowed the blacksmith shop.

She'd had to question five Dogs before she'd gotten the information she wanted, but eventually one of them revealed what she needed to know. She hadn't killed any of them—Lily didn't need Kanar to know that she'd gone off on her own—but she'd made sure they wouldn't follow her or alert anyone that she was looking.

In the morning, the sound of hammering would radiate from inside. The man crafted decent knives at a fair price. Lily had visited this shop before and knew her way around it.

Well, in the daylight. Not quite so much now.

The only light that streamed down—at least here along the shore—was that of the moon, the occasional star that peeked out from the haze, and the distant glimmer of lanterns. There were no streetlights, as this was a place meant for thieving. It was a place meant for danger.

The blacksmith shop was the key.

The stupid Dogs didn't even try to conceal the fact that

this was one of their hideouts. They had others, and though she had uncovered a handful, she knew this to be a more important one. The Dogs were too numerous to be able to fit into a single building. She could imagine an entire pack attempting to bed down in a warehouse somewhere. How did the Prophet meet with all of his people? He might be able to command them all from afar, but doing so wouldn't be easy. It was a wonder that he managed to keep them under as tight a degree of control as he did.

Her gaze drifted to the sky for a moment before she slipped around the shop and then the buildings on either side of it. If she were the one to protect it, she would've stayed on the rooftop, making sure that no one could approach from the street. The Dogs were arrogant, though, and they didn't have the roofs covered. Of course, they probably didn't think there was a danger of anyone coming.

A quick flick of her wrist, and the grappling hook caught on the roof. She tested it, then scaled up the side of the building. Once she was settled on the top, she let her gaze work its way along the contours, searching for any dimple in the shadows that was out of place.

"You need to be careful how you use the art," Ezra had said to her.

Lily had never learned whether Ezra knew what happened to her, though given what she knew of Ezra, it wouldn't be surprising.

She crept forward. From here she found another rooftop, jumped over to it, and then looked at the blacksmith shop. A high window angled up the side of the building, allowing access to the shop. She could scale down the chimney, but there was no telling how much soot and smoke was inside of that thing, nor how recently the forge had burned. No. It was far safer and smarter for her to go through the window.

She sent her hook across again, adjusted the length of rope, and swung over, causing her to hang up against the building. Even in the darkness, she would probably be visible to anybody in the street, but she had not seen patrols of either the watch or the Dogs.

If Kanar learned that she was doing this…

He isn't going to learn.

The only thing Kanar would find out about was that she had information he could use. He would appreciate that; she knew he would. She wasn't about to give him any opportunity to object to her taking action that would protect them all, but her primarily.

Lily felt for the window, then reached for her knife and slipped it along the edge. The window popped open with a soft *click*. She hung there for a moment, waiting.

She could hear her own breathing, though it was steady and controlled, not erratic the way it had been the first time she'd tried a job like this. Distantly, she could still hear the music from the hillside, along with an occasional shout that carried now and again. But there was nothing suggesting that the Dogs were anywhere nearby.

She might be wrong about this. She didn't think she was, but there was the possibility that they no longer used these hideouts. After the attack from earlier, though, she couldn't help but think that they would return and take advantage of their hideout. She knew she needed to learn as much as possible about what they had hoped to accomplish.

Lily pulled open the window on the upper level, then

slipped inside. She jostled her hook, but it didn't come free. It dangled, the line hanging along the side of the building. She would have to claim it later.

The grappling hook was one of her prized possessions. Not *a* prize—she could acquire those anywhere, with the right preparation and the right willingness to kill. Like she had earlier today. No, the hook was an expensive piece of equipment. It had been built by a master blacksmith, crafted in such a way that it would be easy to fold, and with such impossibly light metal that she still had a hard time believing it held her weight. She suspected it would even hold Kanar or Jal, though she'd never tested it on either of them. She didn't want to take the risk of bending the prongs.

She had received the hook after proving herself at the citadel. It was to have been a simple climbing exercise. The rocky coastline could be difficult, and she'd used a few pieces of art to make the climb easier. When she'd succeeded where others had failed, her mentor had pulled her aside.

"What happens when you have none of your supplies available?" Tayol had asked.

"I gather more."

"And if they're not available?"

She'd shrugged. She had wanted to prove herself—and had. The citadel was the place where she had learned how to take the art she'd learned from her people and turn it into something more subtle, something far more dangerous.

"Then I try not to fall."

Tayol had sniffed, then handed her the hook. "There are ways we *want* you to use your art. And ways we want you to use your skill. Take this. Use it well. Sometimes simple is safest."

Simple.

Not this time.

She had to do this right. If she made a mistake here, she was going to lose the hook.

Lily turned her attention to the inside of the shop. The air was heavy. She was in a loft with dusty floorboards, though she wasn't sure if it was dirt or soot.

Before her was a faint outline of the door. That was what she had come for.

She hesitated long enough to get her bearings. The walls angled up toward the pitched roof, but there wasn't anything else here. It was a wonder that there was a window at all. What purpose would there be in having it? Ventilation, she supposed.

Lily cursed herself for trying to solve a problem that had no purpose. Now wasn't the time. If the Dogs discovered that she'd been here, Malory and her entire operation would be targeted. Lily wasn't willing to risk that.

Stepping carefully, she slid her feet along the floorboards, listening for any creaking that might come. There was nothing.

She appreciated the silence and continued sliding her feet forward. She knew how to move as quietly as possible, to shift her feet in a specific pattern. All she had to do was glide one forward, then the next, and then…

She stepped on something.

It was sharp, but not just that—the floorboard creaked.

Lily tensed. She stared into the darkness, at the door ahead of her, waiting for it to open. If it did, she would have to make a decision. Hide in the darkness, banking on the light from the other room to provide poor night vision. Or she might have to jump through the window.

There was no sound.

Letting out a relieved breath, Lily continued to slip forward. She had no idea what she'd stepped on. She moved forward again, and she heard a faint creaking once more, but now she was closer to the door.

A low wall blocked her. If she had the details of the blacksmith shop correct in her mind, there should be a room on the other side. Somewhere, she suspected, there would be a staircase leading down into the shop itself. There was no sign of a staircase, so it must be through that room.

The Dogs would be on the other side of the door.

Using one of her knives, Lily poked it. It wasn't very thick, and she hadn't expected that it would be. As she jabbed at it, some of the light began to spill into the space.

Then she heard voices. That was what she had hoped for. She crouched down, putting her eye above the small hole she'd made.

The room on the other side was small, with the stairs leading down. A large, heavyset man stood near the stairway, one hand on the smooth wooden rail. His other hand was on his belly, and he had a long sword buckled at his waist. She smiled to herself. A man that size probably wouldn't be able to use the blade quickly in a small space.

There were five others in the room. Four of them were sitting at a table playing cards, and the fifth stood with his back to her, staring at the source of light—the crackling hearth.

The men at the table groused over the hands one of them had been dealt, the way men often argued when playing cards. Most of the time, they felt they were skilled and believed that chance didn't have anything to do with it, though Lily had met very few men who could actually play a hand with any real skill.

"You have to be pocketing one of them," the man at the left end of the table said. "You don't get tens that often."

"I do, Lem."

The other two laughed, sounding like barking dogs. Or more like whining dogs, she decided. They dealt out another round of cards, but she tore her attention away from them and focused on the man standing near the hearth and the one by the staircase.

They were waiting on someone.

If she were lucky, they might be waiting on the Prophet, though she doubted she'd be *that* lucky. The Prophet wouldn't make himself known so easily, and she had a hard time thinking that he would come to a place like this. Of course, Lily didn't know if this was important to him in any way. Maybe this blacksmith shop was somehow meaningful to him.

"I don't want to hear any of you grumbling," the man near the fire said. He had a quiet voice, one that sounded too much like Kanar for her comfort. "When *he* gets here, we need to have our shit together. Got it?"

"We know what we're supposed to do," Lem said. He sat up, set his cards face down on the table, and looked at the man near the hearth.

Lily studied Lem. He had the look of a man who thought *he* should be the one in charge. She'd seen that from people before. Gods, she'd had that look before. It was hard to follow somebody you thought incompetent. Not that she had that problem now.

"Then let me think while we're waiting on him to arrive," the man by the fire said. "Can you do that much for me?"

Lem looked as if he wanted to argue, but the big man near the staircase turned to him and shook his head briefly.

Who *really* had the power here? Not Lem, though he wanted it. The others playing cards with him didn't strike her as having authority either. That left the man by the fire or the one by the stairs.

The big man made his way over to the hearth. He was a good hand shorter than the other, but twice as wide. He pitched his voice low, but Lily had ways around that. She opened her pouch and flipped through several prizes before taking out a small bone wrapped in a band of seaweed. She'd made this one herself when she'd first come to Sanaron, but she'd never really had the need to use it.

There were different ways of creating the art. Typically, raw bone had power stored within it. You could use that raw power and then harness it, depending on what shape you carved it into. Plenty of people used dried flesh, hair, nails, or even blood. For Lily, it was always bone. She knew what it would take, which gave a predictability to the art.

As she traced her finger along the seaweed, the big man's voice came up through the bone and became clearer.

"You sure this is the right play, Devin? You know what's going to happen if he finds out you're making deals behind his back."

"I'm doing nothing behind his back," Devin said softly. He tipped his head to the side as if listening for something.

There was a danger in using this particular creation. The right person might realize their voice was echoing.

She wrapped her hand around the bone for a moment until she saw Devin relax.

"—think that it's a problem, but I wanted to—"

"I know what you're trying to say," Devin said, "and I'm telling you not to worry. Watch for them to come."

The large man shrugged and headed away.

Devin remained near the hearth, staring at the fire as if he would find answers within the flames.

Lily leaned on her heels and shifted her head so that she could get a better look. She'd come hoping to get a little gossip from the Dogs about what they had been doing, but she'd fallen into something more. She hadn't expected that they would use it for anything important.

Maybe it wasn't exactly important, though. Whatever was going on here was intriguing.

She settled in to wait.

Lily could wait. Kanar was already done for the evening, having gone off to bathe and sleep, so why shouldn't she take advantage of her own freedom? It might've been smarter for her to have at least warned Jal that she was coming here, but she did plenty of things that weren't necessarily smart, especially when it came to finding information.

When she'd still been working for the citadel, Lily had needed to take plenty of jobs like this—jobs that involved sitting, scouting, and ultimately using her subtle art to accomplish a specific goal. Since she'd left the citadel—more like since she'd been forced away from it—her jobs had been different. Kanar had given her another chance.

She listened to the men play cards for a while. Their grumbling about pocketing cards picked up again, or about how a man named Nate happened to win a series of hands in a row, which was a surprising coincidence according to Lem. What would they think if they played her? Lily smiled at the thought. She rarely gambled. She played dominoes, as there was certainly an element of chance there, though skill was involved as well. But cards…

She'd watched them for less than twenty minutes, and she already knew that Nate telegraphed his aces by gripping too tightly, and Lem's voice got softer when he had a bad hand. Perhaps she should have simply walked through the front door tonight. She'd seen children's books that were harder to read.

Finally, she heard a creak on the stairs.

She shifted closer, poking her head up against the hole in the wall so that she could look through it more easily. The steady creaking sound came slowly, but she caught sight of a flash of dark blue.

The man who now appeared was dressed in a jacket and pants, all in navy fabric. But he had a gleaming silver scabbard strapped to his waist, the bronze hilt equally shiny.

What if this was the Prophet? No one outside of the Dogs had ever seen him before. Anyone who betrayed him ended up dead, little more than a stray who was strangled and left to rot. She had come across several dead Dogs during her time in Sanaron and had dutifully claimed her prizes, especially as she didn't have to do any work in killing them.

Having been targeted, she'd been tempted to suggest that they question a few of them, but she wasn't exactly sure how Kanar would feel about it. She'd been working with him for the better part of a year, but he was unpredictable. For a man who had been a soldier, and a deadly one at that, he could be surprisingly touchy about killing.

Not Lily. As Ezra had told her, death was a part of life. Sometimes she had to complete that cycle a bit sooner.

The navy-clad man glanced at the hearth and at Devin before he made his way over to the table. The men had quickly put their cards away, and Lem had gotten to his feet, clasping his hands behind his back as if he were a soldier coming to attention. Now that he was standing, Lily saw the crossbow resting against the chair. It was of decent quality, though when it came to it, even a poorly constructed crossbow would generally do the job.

The newcomer looked at the wall, in the direction where she was sitting with her eye up to the hole she'd formed, but his gaze drifted past her.

"He will be here in a few moments," he said.

"Good. Figured we been waiting long enough," Lem said.

Devin looked over to him, and there was murder in his eyes. Lem might not know it yet, but he was already dead. Obviously, this newcomer was somebody of importance, and Lem had misspoken. Lily could already play out what was going to happen, could imagine Lem returning to his home, thinking nothing was wrong, only to walk inside and have a knife suddenly protruding from his back.

No, not a knife. A bolt, probably from his own crossbow. That would be a fitting end for somebody like him.

She'd never run with a crew like that, but her training was similar enough. Learning the art, and then learning the subtle art, had been akin to working with a crew. You learned to always be careful with what you said and who you said it to, knowing that any misspoken word could result in you being on the wrong end of an explosion of uncontrolled power.

That was part of the reason she was here.

"You wait as long as necessary for someone like him," the man said. "You should be lucky that he's coming to you and not the other way around."

"We understand," Devin said. "The boys are just getting a little restless."

"You'll get your opportunity to hunt soon enough," the man said. "And if you do this, and do it well, you might even be able to have your own pack."

The voice sounded familiar, though Lily didn't know why. Maybe one of the Dogs she'd dealt with before?

She caught a glimpse of Devin's face, and the firelight reflecting off his features revealed the slight curl to his lips. That was what this was about. He wanted to split off from the Prophet? What kind of fool was he?

Better yet, who had he gone to that wouldn't fear the Prophet?

The newcomer's gaze swept around the room again. This time, she was certain that he paused as he looked directly at her.

Now she knew why she recognized that voice.

Tayol Borgis.

He'd trained her. Helped her learn to throw knives. To climb. To become a true citadel operative.

Then he'd pushed her to use her art in ways she increasingly felt uncomfortable with, all in service of stopping witchcraft. Lily had wanted to do that, but hadn't shared his enthusiasm. While she'd lost her family, he'd lost his wife and child to witchcraft. They'd both suffered, but he'd taken it to a place she could not.

Would not.

And he was the reason she had left.

She hurried away from the wall, unmindful of the noise she made now. There was nothing she could do other than to start running. They might know that someone had been listening, but they didn't have to learn who she was and who she worked with.

The floor creaked again as she stepped on a loose board.

The door behind her came open. Light spilled out.

"What is it?" she heard someone inside ask—probably Lem.

"You've got yourself a little mouse," Tayol said.

Lily reached the window.

Something struck her from behind.

The blow was hard and unexpected. No one should have been able to reach her that quickly.

That's not true. There are some who can.

She tried not to think about that as she jumped.

Lily twisted as she exploded out the window and grabbed for the rope, thankful that she hadn't been able to free her grappling hook from the roof before coming inside. She swung out and away, before smacking against the building. Pain bloomed in her shoulder.

She started to climb the rope, but something grabbed her. She kicked at it but was held.

The only thing she could do was use one free hand, so she reached into her pouch and grabbed one of her prizes. She had to pick it carefully.

She chose one of the Dogs' fingers.

It didn't take much for her to activate it. It wasn't going to be as powerful as some of her prizes would be, but that didn't matter at this point. She just needed to get away.

Lily tossed the finger at whoever held her. A burst of air sent her sweeping back out away from the window, and she hurriedly climbed the rope now that she was freed. Once she reached the rooftop, she grabbed the grappling hook and scurried along the roof. When she made it to the far end of the building, she glanced back. There was a flash of dark fabric.

But they weren't chasing.

Now her heart was hammering. Now her breathing wasn't controlled.

She had no idea who this was, but there was no doubt they were skilled.

If the Dogs were working with someone like that, they needed to be far more careful than they had been.

How was she going to explain this to Kanar?

Chapter Eight

KANAR

Ever since he'd ended up in Sanaron, Kanar had found the shore to be relaxing. There was something about the energy of the waves crashing against the rocks that was so drastically different than what he had grown up around.

The evening was still early, judging from the hubbub at the alehouse he'd just passed. Kanar must not have been unconscious for long. When he'd finally gotten out, he'd been tempted to go to the Roasted Walnut, but he'd changed his mind and wandered down to the shore. He needed to decide how much he was willing to do for Edward.

The job itself was not going to be straightforward. They would have to break into a nearly impenetrable prison, get back out with a person who would be heavily guarded because of the kind of power she possessed, and then find what she and the others like her had done with the Alainsith blood.

Kanar wasn't sure it was possible. But he wasn't sure he

could say no, especially not if there were now Alainsith relics involved. That suggested a dangerous power at play.

And here I thought the war was mostly over.

Which was exactly the reason why Edward had come to him. Kanar couldn't leave the Alainsith blood for others to use, which meant that once he rescued Morgan, he and his team would go after the blood—if they were willing to join him.

Five thousand gold vans if it all worked out.

He kept coming back to that.

He didn't think his team of three would be enough to pull the job, though a thousand split to each of them upon completion was a good motivator. Kanar wasn't the kind to keep the majority of the cut, though he certainly could on a job like this since he was the one responsible for getting it in the first place.

But three of them wouldn't be enough. Not for what they would have to face.

That said nothing about the issue of Malory. He would have to let her in on it, but he wasn't prepared to split the profits with her the way he suspected she would want.

That left deceiving her, though he didn't care for that either. If Malory learned that he had kept something from her, he had little doubt how she would react. She would not take kindly to him pulling a job without informing her, especially not this particular one. It would likely turn him from ally to enemy.

That meant he had to come up with a different strategy.

He paused near the docks and looked out along the piers. The air stunk of fish, of the ships, but it carried the promise of a certain kind of freedom. The salt in the air, the fog that shrouded everything, all seemed like an offering. Pull this job and he wouldn't need to stay in Sanaron any longer, wondering what might be. He wouldn't have to hope that Porman never learned of him while he collected his pension, here in one of the farthest places where he could still draw his pension without notice. Across the sea, he could take his gold and start anew.

All of that was predicated on succeeding.

All of that was dependent on him and his team managing to find a way to break into a place that was nearly impossible to reach, while surrounded by the kind of power he had learned to destroy. And coming out alive.

It might be too much.

Greed only got them so far.

Kanar had learned that he didn't need that much money to survive. In Sanaron, he could continue helping Jal and Lily and wait on Malory to find them jobs—or go after their own. He could start trading on his reputation. Plenty of jobs would open up to him. Maybe they would be more dangerous, like the job he had just done for Heatharn, but they had managed that well enough.

It wasn't as if Kanar was averse to money. He needed funds as much as anyone did. With a significant haul, he might be able to finally invest in a real search for his sister, not a cursory one as he did now, hoping to hear rumors of where she might've ended up. With enough money, Kanar could truly look.

He wasn't foolish. He had fought in the war, had killed in it. He knew that someone caught up in witchcraft would have likely perished.

All Kanar wanted was some word of it.

He took a deep breath, letting it out in a long, heavy sigh.

It was time to go to his team.

Fog had started to roll in again. It coated the seashore in a blanket of thick moisture, and within it was the shroud of silence. He picked his way from the shore and hadn't gone far when he saw shadows looming.

People were heading toward him.

Quite a few of them, at that.

Having had the encounter with the Rabid Dogs earlier, Kanar suspected that was who came at him now.

He unsheathed his sword and paused, giving them an opportunity to come closer to him. He would bring them in, and then he would do what was necessary.

Two men approached. Both were part of the watch, and neither of them should pose much of a danger. Kanar darted toward an alley to keep from drawing attention, and the sound of more footsteps came storming in his direction.

Ever since the Dogs had attacked, the city had been on high alert, and Kanar had suffered for it. He hadn't been able to move as openly as he was accustomed to. Though the fog might be denser than it usually was, he had not expected the watch to spring on him.

He had to make a choice—stay and fight or sneak away.

Targeting the watch would raise a different kind of suspicion. If Malory found out, jobs would become more difficult.

He looked up the road to where it started to slope upward. When another figure came toward him, Kanar drifted into the alley, thinking to hide until the threat moved past.

The figure followed. Kanar reached forward and

grabbed their wrist, then spun before slamming them against the building.

Not one of the watch.

Not one of the Dogs either.

The man jerked away, and as soon as he did, the air started to thicken. Kanar found it difficult to breathe, and though he sucked in sharply, it felt as if he were underwater. His chest was heavy.

This was magic. It had to be.

Was it coming from this man, or was there someone else?

Kanar didn't dare linger here and wait to find out. He jabbed forward, driving his blade toward his attacker before darting back.

He felt his way along the buildings until he found another alleyway. From there, he backed into the darkness and then raced off. The alleys near the shore could be of varying widths, some of them easier to navigate than others. As he ran, he could feel the presence of magic beginning to fade. The weight that had layered upon him started to ease, and he found it easier to breathe. He sucked in another sharp breath and continued running.

When he reached an intersecting street, he took a roundabout path where he headed to the eastern edge of Sanaron before veering back and making his way up. From there, he followed the hillside and the contours of the city, until he found himself just a few streets away from the Roasted Walnut. If the others were still there, they had to discuss the job.

He wasn't sure the others would agree to it. While he thought Jal would, since he liked money more than anybody else he'd ever met, Kanar wasn't entirely certain that Lily would say yes. She was comfortable here. She only took jobs she thought were appropriate for her skill set, and though she had willingly worked with him over the last year, there was always the possibility that she would decide otherwise.

He searched the street for any further movement, and when he was satisfied there was nothing else, Kanar made his way toward the tavern. He'd been jumped not too far from here, so it wasn't just whoever was down near the shore that put him in danger. It was also Edward and the people working with him.

Kanar hesitated with his hand on the door, then stepped inside.

Porten looked up from the bar, pausing with a rag resting on the surface. Kanar tipped his head to him. Porten frowned but dropped the rag and headed to the two occupied tables, saying something quietly to the patrons. It didn't take long for them to head out, leaving the two tables empty and the rest of the Roasted Walnut for Kanar. Jal still sat in the booth near the back, though he was alone. It didn't surprise Kanar that Breck and Olivia were gone, but he had expected that Lily would still be here.

Porten returned to the bar. He wiped his towel across the faded surface, then pulled a mug from beneath the bar and set it on top. "Care to tell me what this is about?"

"Trouble," Kanar said.

Porten grunted. "Seems to follow you."

"Unfortunately, it does." Kanar grabbed the mug of ale. He wasn't really in the mood for a drink, but seeing as how Porten had emptied out his tavern on his behalf, he owed him that at least. He paid for it, along with the drinks of the men who had just evacuated—an agreement he had made with Porten when he'd first come upon the Walnut.

He carried the mug of ale over to the table and took a seat across from Jal.

Jal looked up, frowning. His almond eyes were slightly red, and there was a loopy smile on his face. "I didn't expect to see you back so soon." He sniffed, then leaned forward. "You didn't even bathe."

"Got offered a job."

Jal straightened, then rubbed a knuckle in one of his eyes, blinking the other for a moment as if trying to work out some blur from them. "Malory?"

"Not her. A new employer."

"She's not going to care for that, you know."

"I didn't say I took it," Kanar said.

"You came here, though." Jal looked past him, seeming to take in the empty tavern, and he breathed out a soft whistle. "She's not going to like it at all."

"I'm not sure that *I* like it at all."

"What's the job?" Jal asked.

"Where's Lily?"

"She took off, not long after you left. Said she wanted to clean up, take care of some supplies. You know the kinds of things she does. She never lets me look into that pouch of hers."

"Probably thinks you'd break something in there," Kanar said. For that matter, Lily never let him look in her pouch. It was one of her most prized possessions, though the faded leather didn't look all that impressive. Still, she felt about her pouch the same way he felt about his sword. He never wanted anybody else to handle the blade, much like Lily never wanted anybody else to handle the pouch. He had been around people who had stranger obsessions, and he figured it was none of his business. So long as she did the jobs he asked of her, and did them well, what did he care what idiosyncrasies she had?

It wasn't as if Jal didn't have his own quirks. He enjoyed his drink, and he tried to keep quiet about his background.

"I'm not going to break anything in her pouch," Jal said. "Not if it's important to her."

"Probably as important to her as your bow is to you."

The bow was slung over Jal's chair. Kanar had often wondered if he slept with it.

Jal ran his fingers along the quiver. "It's all I have left."

"You can make another. Or buy one. The jobs have earned us plenty."

At the thought of coin, Kanar immediately reached into his pocket, having not even considered whether Edward had stripped the pouch Malory had given him. To his surprise, it was still there, as was his pensioner's mark.

"Just like you could buy another sword?" Jal said.

"Well, my sword is a different deal."

Jal took a long drink and then sat up. He rubbed knuckles over both eyes this time so that when he was done, his eyes were watering but no longer looked as red. "What's the job?"

"We wait for Lily," Kanar said.

"And if she doesn't come back?"

"Then we go look for her." He told Jal about how he had gotten jumped along the shore. Jal frowned, though Kanar hadn't even added his concern about magic. He wasn't even sure if he had detected what he believed he had. What if there had been no magic and it was merely his overreaction? "If the Dogs are going to hunt us, we need to make sure they know we aren't going to be easy prey."

"We might need to stay clear of the docks for a while. Let things settle down."

"We don't have to worry about that," Kanar said.

"That kind of a job?"

"That kind of a job."

The door opened, and Kanar glanced toward it. Lily strode in, rubbing her shoulder before shifting the leather pouch strapped around her and taking a seat at the table. She nodded to Porten, who simply grabbed a mug and filled it with ale.

"Thought you were getting yourself all prettied up," she said. She leaned back in the chair, tipping it on two legs, and crossed her arms over her chest.

"Something happened to you," Kanar said.

Lily was tense. If there was one thing he knew about her, it was how to identify her moods. She was small, feisty, and could easily be described as powerful, but she also had a certain temperamental nature to her. With all the time they spent working together, he had needed to come to know her moods so that he didn't end up on the wrong end of one of them.

"Just a couple of Dogs," she muttered, rubbing her shoulder again and adjusting her pouch. "I took care of it."

"How?" Kanar asked.

"I got away. That's all that matters. I don't know what they're after. Probably some snack."

"I'm starting to wonder if it might have been something else."

"Why?" she said.

"Because now they've jumped both of us," Kanar said, and he looked over to Jal. "You need to be careful when you leave."

"Maybe I just stay here." Jal grinned widely. "Hey there, Porten. I don't suppose you have a place I can sleep? I'm fine just curling up on the floor in the back here. Just make sure to refill my mug from time to time and—"

"I'm not hosting anyone overnight," Porten said. His voice was gruff, and it sounded almost as if it pained him to speak.

"It's a wonder he lets us come here in the first place," Lily said.

Jal shook his head. "Not a wonder. He lets us in because Kanar has a hold over him."

"I have no hold over him," Kanar said.

"Is that right? Then he just lets anybody come in and kick out his paying customers?"

"We have an agreement. That's all."

Jal leaned forward. "An agreement. Probably sort of like the agreement Lily has with the young man she meets over in the Wen district." He winked, and Lily looked as if she wanted to stab him with one of her knives. "You don't have to be ashamed of it. I've seen him. He's pretty enough, though I doubt you have trouble getting men to look. Maybe a little too tall for you."

"Says the lumbering buffoon," she said.

Jal sat back and frowned. "Buffoon? Why, I'm not sure I appreciate that kind of comment. Lumbering, I'll take. I do lumber."

"We need to talk about the job we were offered," Kanar snapped. If he let them, they would go on like this for most of the night. He needed their focus, but more than that, he needed to make a plan. Edward hadn't given him much time. The job itself wouldn't allow for it either. They had to act quickly. Otherwise, they would run out of the time needed to get the job done. "Neither of you needs to take the job. It's not going to be easy, but it will pay well."

"Now you're speaking my language," Jal said.

"As if he's never paid us," Lily muttered. Definitely on edge than usual.

"I've always paid," Kanar said. "But I've never suggested a job I wasn't sure we could complete. This one is different. I'm not going to agree to the job unless we all do."

Well, that wasn't entirely true, but they didn't need to know that he would probably have to pull the job regardless. Given the terms, Kanar couldn't imagine not agreeing to take this assignment. It wasn't the money, though. There was far too much at stake.

"It's going to take us out of Sanaron. Far from here," he explained. "And if we do this, there's a real possibility that not all of us are going to make it back."

Jal frowned, and Lily leaned forward in her chair again, resting all four legs back on the ground. She bit her lip.

"But if we do this, the payout is unlike anything we've had before. We'll get three thousand gold vans upon completion, and then another two thousand at a later date."

Jal looked as if he'd stopped breathing.

"What's the job?" Lily asked.

"Oh, something fairly straightforward," Kanar said.

Lily didn't smile, but Jal did, however briefly.

"We have to keep magic from overwhelming the world."

Chapter Nine

KANAR

Silence filled the tavern, and it seemed to linger longer than it should. Kanar had no intention of breaking it. He needed both Jal and Lily to come up with their own decision about this job.

"Magic?" Jal said. He grinned and glanced over to Lily. "What do I care if magic spreads?"

"You know who I was," Kanar said.

Jal shrugged. "Only that you used to serve in the Realmsguard, got tired of the fighting, came out here. Now you get to regale us with old stories of warfare and make sure we complete jobs that are seemingly impossible."

Kanar fidgeted for a moment. He reached for the hilt of his sword before catching himself. "It was more than that. I had a very specific purpose."

Jal looked at Lily. "So, what do you think? Just because his king got a bug up his ass and decided to take on one of their religions—"

"It wasn't a bug up his ass," Lily said, her voice soft. "And it wasn't a religion."

Kanar glanced over to her. She knew.

He had known Jal and Lily about as well as he knew anybody since he'd left the Realmsguard, but there was still a measure of distance between them. It was necessary, especially given the kind of work they did. He needed people who were competent, and when he had come across Lily in Sanaron, scaling rooftops and slipping past a series of guards while breaking into one of the shoreline warehouses, he'd found one part of his crew.

He suspected that she'd trained in the citadel, though he had never pressed her on that. Kanar didn't have any issue with the citadel, though they tended to operate independently of any of the neighboring nations. And while they had been an ally during the witchcraft war, that didn't mean they would always be one.

Malory had put him in contact with Jal, claiming that Kanar could use the young boy. When Kanar had come to meet Jal, he hadn't anticipated a fully grown man. Kanar still wasn't sure why she had referred to Jal as a boy. It was one of Malory's quirks.

"It wasn't a religion," Kanar said. "The witchcraft war was just that. A war. It was different than any war I'd been a part of when serving the Realmsguard. It started with the priests—the priests of Fell had been acquiring wealth—but that was not the concern."

"I'm sure not," Jal said. "Most priests acquire wealth." He sat up straight, held his hands in front of him, and tipped his head slightly. His voice took on a serious intonation. "You must tithe a quarter of your earnings to the church for you to find peace in the After." He grinned. "Of course, it's not peace in the After they care about, is it? They want comfort in the *now*."

Kanar shook his head. "The king didn't care about wealth. He was more concerned about power."

Jal shrugged. "Does it matter to your king if priests gain power? How many churches do you have in Reyand?"

"Too many," Lily said.

Kanar looked over to her. He hadn't known that she felt that way. "There are different churches that serve different gods. During the war, Fell became more prominent, until we discovered that some of its priests were serving witchcraft and using the money they drew to fund additional training." Kanar squeezed his eyes shut. "I was a member of what was called the Order, which was part of the Realmsguard, but not. We led the fight against witchcraft users."

If Lily was from the citadel, then she would know some of that. She watched him silently, with no expression.

"Why are you telling us this?" Jal asked.

"Because the job we were offered involves witchcraft," Kanar said. "I'm not sure the extent of it, but if what I have been told is even partially accurate, it's dangerous." He took a sip of his ale, his mind working over the problem. There was no way around the solution that had come to him, regardless of whether he wanted to take that action. "A caravan of Alainsith was intercepted during a treaty talk with King Porman. They were slaughtered and their blood was preserved, intended to be used in another ceremony. I think that's where the relic that Heatharn had us escort to the city came from."

Jal froze. "How could anybody kill Alainsith?"

"I don't know. I don't have much experience with them. Even though I served in the Realmsguard, I never faced an Alainsith, but I've heard stories. They have magic and are powerful, and it was a wonder that Reyand managed to push them back when we fought them before."

"So, we were offered money to go after the one responsible?" Jal said.

"Not exactly. We were offered money to break out someone who might have been present when the Alainsith were slaughtered. That can't be all *I* do."

They were involved now. After helping with the relic, they had no choice but to be.

"But they're not the one responsible?" Lily asked.

Jal had fallen silent, probably because he had no interest in leaving Sanaron. It was difficult enough to get him to head out on some of the missions outside the city in the first place. Only when Kanar promised that they would return did he relax.

"Probably not," Kanar said.

"Probably?" she said. "Didn't you used to take care of this kind of thing?"

"Not like this."

"And what kind of power do you think this is?" Lily asked softly.

"The kind that can change the use of magic in the world. The Alainsith are powerful, but they don't use their magic the same way the priests did. Gods, for that matter, they don't use it the way that even the hegen use their little prizes. If whoever is after the Alainsith blood manages to accomplish what they intend, it will destroy more than you could even know."

"Is this all about your kingdom?" Lily snorted. "Even the hegen in Reyand are peaceful, regardless of whatever rumors you may have heard."

"It's still magic," Kanar said.

She frowned at him. "And what about you? I've heard the rumors, Kanar. A disgraced Realmsguard, hunted by those he once worked for."

"Disgraced is right," he said, his voice dropping to a whisper. "But not hunted. They don't care that I've left."

"Why are you pushing him?" Jal asked. "We know Kanar."

"We know what he wants us to know," Lily said. "All we know is that he is Kanar Reims. He didn't even want to tell us about his role in the war, though we've suspected." She watched him. "But now he is telling us this because there's something that won't permit him to hide his past from us anymore."

Kanar met their gaze, before turning his attention down to his ale and taking a long, slow drink. He set the mug back down. "She's not wrong. The issue here is that the person I need to go after is somebody I have a bit of a past with."

"What kind of a past?" Lily asked.

Kanar looked up. "The only kind that matters. When I learned who she was—what she was—I couldn't do it anymore. I took a few more missions for the Realmsguard, and then the war was mostly over. My last assignment was to kill her. I couldn't, so I came to Sanaron." His voice had gone almost silent at the end.

That was when he had fallen in with Malory and gotten different assignments. Ones that he actually could pull off.

"Where is she?" Lily said.

"I didn't know she'd been imprisoned, not until Edward informed me. I have a familiarity with the city, enough that we should be able to pull the job off. It's going to be challenging, though. We get her out, then the real work begins."

"We get to start with a prison break? I kind of love it," Jal said, slapping his hand onto the table.

"Where is this prison?" Lily asked.

"That's the problem," Kanar said. "It's not terribly far from here, but far enough." The proximity was part of the reason he thought his plan might actually have a chance of working, but it was also just on the edge of where he thought they could reach in time. "If you're willing, then we will take the job, make a run for the prison, break out the person we're hired to get, and stop this plan."

He sat back and took a long drink of his ale. Now it was their turn to decide what they were willing to do. He suspected he knew how they would decide. At least, he had a strong suspicion of what Jal would do. Lily was being surprisingly quiet.

"You want us to do this with just the three of us?" Lily asked.

"No," Kanar said. "We might need something… extra. I have somebody in mind."

Assuming Kanar was right about him. He had his suspicions, but nothing concrete enough to know if it were true.

"I don't care for that," she said.

"No, I figured you wouldn't, but I'm not exactly sure we have much choice. I need to talk to Malory as well."

"You're going to give her a cut," Jal said. "I wasn't sure if you might keep this one from her."

"She'd get her cut one way or another. But I'm going to need her resources." Kanar had given that some thought. He needed her access, but more than that, he was going to need her supplies. "The two of you are going to have to make your own preparations."

"How soon do you intend to leave?"

"As soon as possible. We have to get her out before they kill her."

Morning came too early, and the heavy fog rolled through the city. Somewhere distantly a bell tolled, though Kanar couldn't tell the direction it was coming from. There were nearly a dozen bells in Sanaron, and they rang for different reasons than they did in Reyand. Those rang on behalf of the gods, as reminders of service asked of the people.

Kanar made his way toward the Painted Nails. He had the conversation phrased in his mind, but conversations with Malory often took a turn, making it difficult for him to feel as if he said what he really wanted.

He and the others had stayed up until late in the evening making plans. At least, that had been his intention. Instead, Jal had peppered him with questions about the Order and the Realmsguard. There were aspects of that he had no interest in discussing. He had shared all he could about the Order and what he knew about witchcraft, while Lily had sat quietly. She was keeping something from him.

That didn't surprise him. He knew that she had her own secrets. They all did. And when it came to Lily, her utility outweighed any secret she might keep from him. That was what he had told himself the entire time they had worked together. As far as he believed, it was true.

Or had been.

With a job like the one they were going to take, he needed everyone to be on the same page. If they weren't, then there was a real possibility that something could happen that would put them all in danger. He didn't want anything to happen to any of them, but especially not if it was because they hadn't shared some secrets of their past.

It was something he'd have to press Lily on before they left.

He stepped inside the Nails. Most brothels were quiet at this time of morning, given that the briskest business came in the overnight hours. Kanar nodded politely to Ima, who sat at a desk near the entrance. He didn't see the morning guards, but he suspected that if Ima made any sort of motion, they'd be on him in a moment.

When Kanar reached the stairs in the back, he heard Malory's voice.

"I'm here."

He turned to see Malory striding down a long hallway from the back of the brothel. There were rooms in that direction, along with a bar, some tables, and a gathering hall. He hadn't spent much time there.

"Didn't expect to see you so soon, Kanar," Malory said. "Did you miss me? Or would you like to have some time with one of my girls?" She swept her hands around her, while a wide smile curled her lips. There was nothing friendly about it.

"Business, Malory. Always business."

"Of course." She glanced to the doorway before turning her attention back to him. It wasn't like her to be down in the brothel like this. She was waiting on something. "What sort of business?"

"A job I've been offered."

Her brow furrowed, and he noted the surge of irritation that swept across her face. "I wasn't aware that you've begun working for someone else."

"That's why I'm here," Kanar said. Already his speech

had been disrupted. He hadn't expected to see Malory down here, and certainly hadn't anticipated having this conversation now rather than getting more of an opportunity to come up with a plan. But Malory often made things difficult for him. "Are we going to have this conversation now?"

"I don't know," she said, smiling at him. "Are we?"

"I just needed to tell you about the job, and to get your help."

Her smile turned into a frown, and her hand went to the pink pearl necklace she was wearing today. She drummed her fingers along the pearls, then motioned for him to follow her to a booth in the back of the main room. Kanar was all too aware of the purple carpet he walked across, of how soft it felt and how strange it seemed for him to talk with her here of all places. Most of the time, he met with Malory in her apartment. Sometimes, he did so through the brothel, though there were other times when he would meet with her through the back entrance to her apartment. That was often the easiest and safest for him to do.

She took a seat along the wall, looked toward the door, and waited for Kanar to sit across from her. He did so, even though it left his back exposed—something he despised. He wondered if she knew that.

"What's the job?" she asked.

"I was asked to acquire an item of some danger."

"And?"

"And it will take me out of the city." Kanar wasn't sure how much information to offer, but he suspected that he needed to share some piece of it. He didn't want to tell her about the magic, nor did he want to tell her about his role in removing magic from the kingdom. "In order for me to be successful, I need to travel quickly."

She locked eyes with him for a brief moment. "And you want access to my resources for this?"

"I was thinking that it might be helpful," he said.

"What will I get out of it?"

"I will pay you a fixed amount of the job."

She crossed her arms. "That's not how our arrangement works, Kanar."

"Normally, I would agree with you," he said, shifting in the seat. It felt firmer than he would've expected, especially given the plush carpet that covered the floor inside her establishment. Maybe it was meant to be uncomfortable. Maybe they didn't want people sitting here for long periods of time. In fact, he suspected that was the case. They'd rather have men going elsewhere with the girls to spend money. "In this case, I can offer you something more than just money."

"I'm a businesswoman," she said, spreading her hands out. "So whatever you feel you can offer, it had best be of significant value."

"What if I told you that the person who hired me for the job was Edward Visaran?"

Now she turned her attention fully on him, and her eyes narrowed. "I would say that you are lying, but I've never known you to lie."

"I'm not lying."

"What would Edward need from you?" She frowned, studying him. When Lily looked at him like that, he could tell that her mind was working through a puzzle, but when Malory did, it was more than that. It was almost as if she were trying to read his mind. The feeling was unsettling, but at least it was short lived. "He needs access to Reyand," she said, her nose wrinkling. "Not exactly Reyand, though. He needs access to the Realmsguard."

"Something like that," he said.

Malory sat back and pressed her hands together, and her gaze once again turned to the door. "How much did he offer you?"

"He made it worth my while."

She smiled but didn't look at him. "I'm not going to take any coin from you. Not if it comes from Edward. I just want to know how much he offered you."

If he lied, she might find out. If he told her the truth, she might want more than just a cut. When it came to Malory, it was always a challenge for him to know what to do.

"He offered me three thousand gold vans."

She blinked and turned her attention back to him. "Too much," she said.

"Too much for what?" Kanar asked.

"Too much for everything I've heard that's taking place around the city. I told you about the job I didn't get."

"Actually, you told me nothing about it. You only told me that you intended for us to be hired for other jobs."

"Others by Heatharn," Malory said. "Perhaps more like him. They've been moving relics. Ancient artifacts. I don't know anything more than that, but I wanted to have a role in it. I anticipate that it will be quite profitable for me, and for you. But what Edward is offering you is too much for that, so it's not about relics, is it? And if he is involved, it means that he thinks that whatever he has access to will position him to sit on the throne."

"It seems to me that it's about the relics, at least a little bit," Kanar said. "Edward mentioned an Alainsith relic that was stolen outside Verendal, and with what you're telling me about Heatharn and moving relics, something is taking place."

Something involving magic.

As much as he wanted to take the job only for Morgan, Kanar didn't think that could be the only reason. Not if there was something more—something dangerous—taking place.

He might have left the Realmsguard and the Order, but he still didn't want magic to spread.

"Whatever is going on involves Edward trying to elevate himself," Malory said.

Kanar shrugged. "I'm not sure that it matters."

"That's because you're not from Sanaron. If you were, you would care. You would care very much."

"What does it matter if one royal or another sits upon the throne?"

"What do you know about Edward Visaran?" Malory said.

"Only his name and his position."

"If you work for him, you should find your answers. Your own answers."

"Why?" Kanar asked the question carefully, then glanced behind him when she suddenly stiffened.

He didn't see anything, though there had been a shadow moving in front of the door. What was going on with Malory? Something was happening, and whatever she was dealing with left him with questions. But if he took this job, which he anticipated doing, then he wasn't going to be in Sanaron. He wouldn't have to worry himself with what was taking place here.

She got to her feet and nodded toward the door. "You will have whatever assistance you need."

"Fast horses. I need to get to Verendal."

She frowned. "That's where he sent you? It will be a week's ride."

"I can't take a week. I need to get there in a few days."

She sniffed, then smiled tightly. "It's going to be uncomfortable. Unpleasant, even. But I can provide you with a change of horses and can see that you are given all the help I can. For a fee, of course."

"I thought you said you didn't want Edward's money."

"Oh, my fee isn't going to come from your cut. Though, if he does give you what he said he would…" It was clear from the way she said it that she doubted that he would. For that matter, Kanar was starting to question whether Edward would actually pay that, either. "You won't have any problem paying me a small cut, will you?"

"What do you want?" he said.

"What I always want, Kanar. Information."

"Because you intend to make sure that he doesn't sit on the throne?"

"Because," Malory said, "I want to know what he thinks he can acquire that will enable him to do so."

"I can tell you whatever you need. I don't have any loyalty to him. It's a job. Nothing more."

"Good. Now, here is what you will need if you are going to Verendal." She took a seat again and began to write down directions on a slip of paper she pulled out from beneath her dress. When she was done, she tapped on the series of towns she'd listed. "You stop here and here and here. That should get you to Verendal in three days. Perhaps faster if you can tolerate it. This," she went on, handing him another slip of paper, "will provide you with my resources. Go and finish this. And remember who made it possible for you to succeed."

Kanar took the documents she gave him, knowing that there would be no way for him to ever forget what role she had in any of his success.

The fog was starting to lift by the time he was back outside, though not so much that it made it easy for him to see. Still, it was bright enough that he thought he could navigate the city streets more easily, and it was much less likely for him to get jumped.

He reached the docks after an uneventful journey, and he made his way down until he found pier seven. He wasn't exactly sure that he would find the answers he wanted here, but he only had to ask one fishmonger before he was pointed in the direction of a small tavern on the far side of the street across from the dock. It had a view of the shore and the fog that rolled through. He had never been to this place before, though having spent some time in Sanaron, he had wandered along the shoreline and taken note of many of the docks here.

When he pulled the tavern door open, he scanned the inside until he found the person he was looking for. It was hard to miss him.

Kanar took a seat at the rough wooden table and rested his arms on it, then looked across to the massive bald man picking at a plate. A stack of dominoes lay next to him, and several copper coins rested near them.

"Interested in taking a job?" Kanar asked.

Honaaz, big as he was, he didn't have to look up much even while seated. He held Kanar's gaze with boredom.

"Figured I wouldn't see you again after Heatharn got done."

"Is that a no?"

"What kind of a job?"

"The kind that will pay you well," Kanar said. "One hundred gold vans." He might split the coin with the other two, but not Honaaz. He didn't know him well enough, and he wasn't sure he could trust him. But for a job like this, there was bound to be a time when he needed muscle. To break into the prison, he was going to need someone with a certain build, as well as a certain look. Honaaz fit the bill. Kanar had seen him fight, so he knew the man wasn't helpless. He figured that Honaaz was unaffiliated with others in Sanaron, as Kanar had traveled with him and not seen any tattoos. It left him thinking that Honaaz was just a man looking for work. A man who could be hired for a dangerous job.

For the right price.

Honaaz looked around the tavern before scooping the dominoes off the table, stuffing them into his pocket, and getting to his feet. "I'm in."

"I didn't tell you the job."

"You said one hundred gold?"

Kanar nodded.

Honaaz shrugged. "Then you said enough."

Chapter Ten

LILY

Lily didn't care much for the horse she'd been assigned. Kanar could have offered to let her choose but had given her a stubborn dappled mare named Nanal. Truthfully, Lily might have grumbled about any option she had. None of them suited her the way her old horse Rank once had, though it had been long enough since she'd ridden her short stallion that she started to question how much of her memory of him was accurate.

Tayol being in Sanaron suggested that the citadel was active. She hadn't found any further sign of him before departing, though she'd been careful. She didn't want to draw his attention. It was better to keep him from learning that she was in the city, which was even more reason for her to take this job. If Tayol learned of her presence…

She didn't know what he might do. His actions had chased her from the citadel, but that didn't mean they wouldn't act against her if they learned she was using what they'd taught her.

Their small group reached the hillside overlooking

Sanaron, and Kanar paused to look behind him. He was seated atop a gray stallion, back straight, his dark gaze sweeping over the city like some general surveying the battlefield. Lines of worry worked along the corners of his pale blue eyes.

"What do you see?" Jal asked.

"Nothing," Kanar said with a grunt. "Just the damn fog. Can't tell if we have anyone tailing us." He looked over to the other man now traveling with them, a note of suspicion lingering on his face.

Honaaz dwarfed his poor mare as he gripped the reins in a meaty fist. Lily still didn't know why Kanar thought they needed someone like Honaaz, but this was his plan, so she knew better than to question him. He'd tell them all the details when he thought they needed them, though it was just as likely that he didn't fully know why he'd wanted Honaaz. For a military man, Kanar often went by what felt right, which was part of the reason he liked having Jal around. That way he had someone else who would tell him he was doing the right thing.

"The Dogs might send someone," Lily said. "I saw something, Kanar. Before we left the city. I didn't think it mattered, and it might not." She squeezed her eyes shut. "There was a man from the citadel. He was recruiting some of the Dogs."

She looked over to Kanar, and his face was impassive.

"You knew about the citadel," she said.

Kanar shrugged. "I suspected. You have the kind of skill that can only be taught in a few different places."

And that wasn't even her only skill, though she wasn't going to tell Kanar that.

"You aren't disappointed?" Lily asked.

"Does it matter? Besides, I don't know that I get to be the one to pass judgment on keeping things secret. We need to have a measure of understanding among our team, but you have your skill, I have mine, Jal has his…" He turned back to her. "It doesn't matter. I'm curious why you left the citadel. Were you part of the war?"

"I finished my training after it was mostly over," she said. She had missed out on her opportunity to get revenge for what had happened to her family.

"Did you come to Sanaron on a mission?" Kanar asked.

"Not exactly," Lily said.

She expected him to press, but he didn't.

"When I was in the Realmsguard, we had a natural distrust for citadel operatives," he told her. "The king permitted them safe passage throughout Reyand, but that didn't mean we didn't keep an eye on them. We knew they had their own agenda. But once we got into the war… Well, let's just say that I came to understand that they were useful. I do wonder if they might have had something to do with the Alainsith blood."

Lily shook her head more vigorously than she intended. "They want understanding. That's what I was taught, and that's about all we tried to do: understand. Not use magic, which is what you are suggesting."

At least, not for the most part. Again, she had been pressed to use her art.

"But I want to get back to the Dogs. I don't feel like they would've sent so many after us if they didn't think they could've gotten something out of it. What if they're after the same thing? Or gods, Kanar, what if they're using magic now?"

Kanar stared, then nodded slowly.

Lily imagined that he was still trying to work through what to make of Devin and the strangely dressed man that she'd seen. Had they stayed in Sanaron, they would have been able to look into him, the Dogs, and Devin. Malory would have helped, Lily was certain, though she got tired of Malory having her fingers in everything they did. Too often, the woman forced them into taking jobs Lily didn't really want to do. Kanar didn't push back hard enough, which surprised her.

"The Dogs don't have resources outside the city," Kanar said.

"They've got money," Jal said, walking over to them. "If you've got enough money, you can buy what you want anywhere you go." He grinned. "Sort of like I plan to do when the job is over."

Jal flicked his gaze to Honaaz. Neither Lily nor Jal knew what Kanar had agreed to with Honaaz, but she doubted that he'd offered a full split.

There were times when having muscle was useful. She'd wished for it when they'd been tasked with intercepting cargo after it had been unloaded from a ship out of Men'lar. It was an easy job, but anything to do with shipping and cargo ran the risk of attracting the attention of the watch, so they had worked carefully to make sure none of them—or Malory—could be implicated. Lily still didn't know what that shipping box had contained, but she hadn't been willing to sneak into Malory's little place to find out. If she'd been caught…

The thought of it made her shiver. She didn't think that Malory could force her to work there, but she didn't know, and certainly didn't want to take the risk. Kanar might have saved her when he'd first come to Sanaron, but there might be limits to how far he would go to cover for her own stupidity.

"Let's get moving," Kanar finally said, tearing his gaze away from the city, as if it were painful for him to do. "We need to reach Howenal tonight."

"You're going to kill the horses if that's your pace," Honaaz said.

Kanar shook his head. "I've got a plan for what we have to do. I just need everyone to do their part. Let's ride."

He started off, pushing the horse at a hard gallop, with Honaaz following him. Lily shared a look with Jal, who seemed more amused than anything. Having seen Jal run, she couldn't help but wonder if he might even be able to keep pace with the horses. He always claimed that he'd grown up on a farm and worked outside every day, but there was something about that answer that didn't sit well with her.

"What kind of plan do you think he has?" Jal asked as they both started to ride.

"The kind that might get us killed," she said.

"Not with the great Kanar Reims leading us, it won't." Jal grinned at her, but the expression faded as he saw that she didn't share his smile. "What's the problem?"

"It's nothing."

"Does it bother you that much that he never told us about his past with the Realmsguard? That's not him anymore, Lily."

"We don't know what's him or not."

She kicked the horse to move faster. Nanal might not have been her first choice, but there was no doubt that the mare moved quickly. All of the horses did. Malory hadn't held back when it came to providing them with mounts, though Lily wondered how much of the job Kanar had shared with her. Probably enough to convince her that they needed her access, but was it enough for them to lose some of the coin they'd earn?

One thousand gold vans.

That was a hard thought to shake.

That kind of money could certainly change her fortunes. She wouldn't have to stay in Sanaron, where she ran the risk of her people learning how to find her—and worse, sending someone after her. From the port in Sanaron, she could sail to dozens of different places. Men'lar intrigued her, but even beyond there, she could visit Oostrang or Xianal or anyplace in the Isles that she couldn't reach without the funds to cross the sea.

One thousand gold was enough to make the crossing.

It was enough to fully disappear.

Maybe that was what Kanar wanted too.

He leaned forward on the horse with his back hunched and his entire body tight, the hilt of that fantastic sword of his sheathed on his left hip. Ever since seeing the blade for the first time, she'd wanted the opportunity to just hold it. But touching a man's sword was like touching his wife. She'd have to wait until Kanar was dead.

At least she could better understand why he seemed so competent.

During her training, she had encountered others of the Realmsguard. Traveling as she did and doing the jobs she had done, she'd been confronted by skilled soldiers from all over. That wasn't an issue for her most of the time. Men like that—and they were always men—were trained to fight with the sword, sometimes hand-to-hand, but they had limitations that she didn't have. The subtle art helped her move past any barriers like that. But Kanar had been more skilled than most she'd encountered. Skilled enough that she couldn't help but wonder how she would fare if she were sent after him.

Not as well as she had on other jobs.

But the prize…

It wasn't only the sword that intrigued her, it was what she could do with a prize like Kanar. Ezra had taught her the art and how to draw power out of life and death, skills that Lily still found useful. But what Ezra had not shared was that it mattered *which* life she drew power from. Some people simply had *more*. That, she had learned later.

Not that she would ever try to act on that, but she could think about it. Were something to happen to Kanar, she wouldn't hesitate to collect from him. She couldn't.

Of course, if he learned about her past, he might not hesitate either.

Knowing what she did of him, she worried that he would find out sooner or later. When he did, what might he do to her?

Lily wouldn't linger to find out.

The road carried them through the forest, farther and farther from the coastline. An occasional daring seagull ventured this far, though it seemed out of place amid the other birds, crows mostly, that circled overhead.

Lily glanced over to Jal and found him smiling slightly. It was disarming, and to anyone other than Lily, it might be flirtatious. She couldn't see him flirting with her, though. Jal was too loyal to Kanar to risk the team. Though he *was* pretty enough. More reason for her to be careful.

"What are you going to do with your cut?" Jal asked as they rode.

The trees had started to block the gusting wind so that it wasn't nearly as difficult to talk, despite the steady pace.

"Probably find another grappling hook," she said.

Jal gave her a quizzical look. "That's all you're going to do with it? You could buy… I don't know, a hundred with your cut?"

"Not the kind I have my eye on."

Jal sighed. "I was thinking that I might try to buy a farm. Maybe not one quite as far away as where I grew up, but find a place where the soil is good, settle down with a nice woman, raise a family…" He grinned. "I hear there are places not far from Sanaron where grapes grow well. Maybe I could start a winery."

"That sounds… boring."

"Only because you prefer a different kind of excitement," he said.

Lily shrugged. "What can I say? I like adventure."

"That's why you want a grappling hook?"

"That's only *part* of what I'll buy. I'd have to get the rope too."

Jal shook his head and leaned down closer to the horse, patting the stallion's side. He looked too tall for the horse he'd been given, though he also seemed more comfortable than the rest of them, as if this were *his* horse. Then again, Jal seemed comfortable wherever he went.

"Have you ever been to this place?" he asked.

She shook her head. Now Jal's nerves were starting to show. She wasn't surprised. Given that they were heading into Reyand, it was reasonable for them to be concerned. Reyand had known too much war lately, and that wasn't the kind of thing you ventured into without a little caution.

"Not there. Places like it, though," Lily said. It didn't

matter if Jal knew whether she'd been to Verendal or not. Many of the cities in Reyand were similar. The king liked to make it seem as if he prized law and order, but she'd seen the effects of his laws. She'd seen his order. While it might make for good collection, it didn't make it a safe place to live, and certainly didn't make it a place where people could explore the arts.

"I've heard of Verendal," Jal said. "Supposed to be dangerous."

"That's what people say about every place, but once you get into the city and get a handle on the people, you'll find that nothing is quite as dangerous as you once believed." She flashed him a smile. "Think of Sanaron."

"I am. It's dangerous."

"But you know your way around it. It might be dangerous, but after a while, you learn which places to avoid if you don't want to get jumped. You learn where you need to go if you want safe food, passage, or shopping. Even where to go if you want to find yourself a nice friend."

He winked at her. "Like you did?"

She shrugged. "What do you think he intends to do with Honaaz?"

There was enough distance between them and the other two that Lily didn't think that the much larger man would overhear, but he seemed to straighten slightly.

"I don't know," Jal said. "Kanar probably wants him to carry whatever it is we're after."

That wasn't it, though she didn't know with any certainty what Kanar might have wanted someone like Honaaz for, other than as muscle. They weren't going after anything that would be too heavy to carry. Not if what Kanar had told them was real. And if it *was*, she had to worry that she might be more intrigued by it than she let on.

Whatever had happened with the Alainsith would be terrible, but that didn't mean the prize shouldn't be collected, and it certainly didn't mean that it couldn't be used in a way that would benefit them. She just had to try to get to it before Kanar did.

That was, if she could. And if the prize was real.

But then what?

The entire reason they were taking this job was for the money, not for the prize and the art she could do with it. Though if it was what Kanar claimed, something greater than money might come with it.

He would never understand.

Not Kanar Reims.

The horses ahead of them slowed. Lily tried to peer over the others to see what might have triggered the stop, but she didn't spot anything obvious. Knowing Kanar, he was being careful, though in this part of the world it was equally likely that there were highwaymen.

The last attackers hadn't been highwaymen.

Stupid, filthy Dogs. Now she didn't even know if that attack had been the Prophet's doing or if it'd been this Devin that she'd seen. He'd had some agenda of his own. Learning what he was after seemed like it needed to be the next thing she did, though it *was* possible that she wouldn't be able to do that even if she *had* stayed in Sanaron.

"What is it?" she asked as she neared Kanar.

"Village. Probably Dulfarn, but it could be Obadan. I haven't traveled through here enough."

They'd taken plenty of escort jobs in the year that they had all been working together as a team, but the jobs didn't generally force them very far from Sanaron. They'd been riding *hard*, and along one of the narrower roads out of the city that some of the wagons couldn't traverse. Partly that was because it was the direction they needed to go, but partly that was out of a need for speed. The road itself might be narrow, and it might lead up steeper hills—such as what they'd been climbing for the better part of the last hour, so it was a strain on the horses—but if they could take a path like that, they would reach Verendal much faster.

"What are you trying to decide?" Jal asked. "The Dogs wouldn't have followed us out here."

"That's what I'm trying to figure out," Kanar said. "And it's more than just being safe. I don't want word of our passing through to get out."

"Here?" Honaaz said. "There's not a whole lot out here but trees and dust. Not that much dust even, so I guess it's mostly trees."

"There are some weeds, and I've heard a few critters. Maybe even a wenderwolf," Jal said, looking into the trees and smiling. When he turned back to them, the smile faded. "Some flowers and crows and *lots* of flies… but you aren't asking about any of that, are you?"

Kanar shook his head. "I'm not concerned about the people here, but you saw what the Dogs were willing to do for those wagons."

"Thought this was a different job," Honaaz said.

Lily hadn't noticed it before, but Honaaz had almost a thick way of talking, as if his tongue were slightly too big for his mouth. He wiped a hand over his head, and she decided that he probably needed a hat. It would take away from his lumpy, bald scalp.

"It should be a different job," Kanar said, "but the

Dogs were out there and still chasing. Seeing as how I don't know what they're after, I figure we need to be careful. Can't have a few strays following us where we're headed."

"You might be able to chase them away," Honaaz said. "Out here, figure a man like you could take care of a couple Dogs."

Kanar looked like he wanted to snap at Honaaz, which Lily couldn't help but feel a hint of amusement about. Let someone else take the brunt of his irritation. It didn't always have to be her and Jal. Mostly Jal. Kanar seemed to recognize that he didn't want—or need—to get after her. Though if he did, she wasn't exactly sure how she would react. Probably not well. She never did well when someone snapped at her.

"That's the point," Kanar said. "I'd rather not have to kill them. That's going to draw attention to where we're going."

"I could go make a false trail," Jal offered.

Kanar scratched his chin. It was strange seeing this side of him. Lily would almost call it cautious, but that wasn't quite what this was. Nor was it nervous. Suspicious? That suited Kanar.

"You'll have to double back to do it," Kanar finally said. "I don't want to risk you and the horses getting too tired."

Jal shrugged. "Won't be that hard. Why don't I make a false trail when we get to the village, then I'll clear our passing. I can head through the trees and meet you. I've got a hunch that it shouldn't take that long, and I should be able to catch up to the rest of you in… where are we stopping tonight?"

"Awahn," Kanar replied. "Not a large town, but should

be large enough to trade horses. Malory's marker should get us what we need there."

Lily smiled at the thought of someone like Malory having reach all the way out here, though with the right marker, they didn't need to know you. They just had to know that what you offered was good for something.

"You can do that?" Honaaz asked, looking at Jal with a different expression. "Why didn't you do that with Heatharn?"

"Because there wasn't the need," Jal said. "We were just a merchant wagon."

"We're going to loop around the village," Kanar said. "We'll take to the trees and keep clear, then you make your pass. We don't want them to know what we look like. Villages as small as this will remember us, and I don't want anyone remembering us."

"Then why make it seem like we went through there at all?" Honaaz asked.

"Because I'll make it seem like we went north—away from the village, not through it," Jal replied. "That way when they're asked, they won't know, but they'll have *heard* something of our passing. It should be enough to draw them away."

Lily was tempted to go with Jal. She was curious as to what was involved in creating a false trail, but she also didn't want to leave Kanar alone with Honaaz.

Kanar nodded. "Let's get moving." He guided his horse into the trees without saying anything more.

Honaaz looked back, watching Jal for a few long moments.

"Don't worry about him," Lily said, tilting her head in Kanar's direction and pushing the horse forward. "He cares. He just does that sometimes." She glanced at Jal, who smiled tightly, saying nothing. Jal knew his role, much like she knew hers.

What neither of them knew was what role Honaaz would play.

"I'll meet you after I get this done," Jal said, handing his reins to Lily.

When Jal had disappeared around a bend, Honaaz shook his head and patted his horse on the flank. "Think he can do what he claims?"

"Which part? Obscuring our tracks? I'm pretty sure Jal can do it," she said. "He's got a way with the forest. Something he learned on the farm, from what he tells us. I'm not sure I buy it, but then Jal likes to attribute everything to his time on the farm. Or are you asking about whether he can actually meet us? He won't lose our track, if that's what you're wondering. I've never known anyone who could follow a trail like him."

Honaaz regarded her with a hint of amusement in his eyes. It was the most she'd spoken to him, even though they had already spent several days together on the road back to Sanaron. "You don't look like you got that much experience."

She flashed her most disarming smile and patted the pouch for a moment before thinking better of it. She knew Kanar and Jal wouldn't go digging around in her possessions, but she didn't know what Honaaz might try to do.

"I might have a little experience. Sort of like Kanar," Lily said.

Honaaz swiveled in the saddle, looking through the shadows that slipped around the trees and toward Kanar's back. "That one's got secrets. I've heard of a man who fights like him."

"It might *be* him, then. Kanar has a reputation."

"Maybe in Sanaron. If he's active there, I'm not surprised. But this reputation came from someplace different. Might not be the same man. Called him *Shavrian*. It means—"

"Death," she said.

Honaaz looked over. "That's right. Not a word most people know."

"I'm not most people."

Lily did touch her pouch then.

Shavrian.

It couldn't be Kanar. Not the same person. But as she looked at him, she started to wonder if maybe those *were* the secrets he kept from them.

And if so, what would happen when he learned of hers?

Chapter Eleven

JAL

JAL RAN OFF INTO THE TREES.

There was a certain comfort in doing so. He could move as quickly as he wanted and didn't have to worry about his horse. Didn't have to worry about anything, really. He enjoyed riding, but only when the horses enjoyed it as well. Too often in Sanaron, along with some of the neighboring lands, the horses weren't treated well. Men thought they needed to use a firm hand, when a soft voice and gentle touch and an occasional treat would be more than enough.

As he'd expected, it was easy work to clear the signs of their passing. The horses had left their imprints, but the road was hard packed, and there hadn't been any recent rains. It was a simple matter for him to go through and erase any evidence of their crossing.

Jal hadn't been paying much attention to where the village was, but as he hurried through the trees, he caught sight of it in a clearing. Most of the small buildings were made out of wood. Woven branches were worked together to form the roofs. They reminded him a little of his home. There wasn't the space, and certainly not the same wildlife that he was accustomed to, but there was a coziness to the village that he could appreciate.

He wasn't entirely sure if this journey would be worth it. Kanar certainly believed it would be, and Jal trusted him. The man had proven himself time and again and had made such a difference in helping him. If Kanar thought this was important, then it was. Jal wasn't going to challenge that assertion.

Still, he wasn't entirely sure the reason behind it. He knew Kanar didn't care for magic. Jal didn't have the same view of it as Kanar did, and probably not the same view as Lily, who liked to hide her collection of magical items in her pouch. She seemed to think that she had kept them from him, but he'd seen her use some of them. He still wasn't sure where she acquired them from.

Jal started to turn away from the village but stopped when he noticed a small pen not far from the road.

Cages.

He hated cages.

There was never anything good kept within them. People kept animals in cages because they didn't have the knowledge to train their charges, which irritated him even more. Any animal could be trained.

These were small cages, though. He couldn't tell what was kept inside, and he knew he probably should leave it alone, but he was curious. He slipped forward, careful to avoid making any tracks in the ground, and reached the outskirts of the village. He leaned over a narrow wooden fence to look through it and at the cages. A man was tending to them, and Jal noticed a dark, furry shape inside the nearest one.

They had rabbits.

Outside his homeland, trappers and hunters would try to catch them, though those critters tended to be larger. Also, they had a bit more fight to them. These rabbits were small—and the cages looked to be meant to fatten them up.

Not like this.

Jal wasn't supposed to draw attention, but he couldn't leave this, either.

No one watched him. He grabbed two of the cages and set off toward the trees.

He hurriedly set them down, then spun back, grabbing two more, making the same trip four more times. By the time he got to the last, a villager had spotted him and started toward him. Jal loped off to the trees, where he released the rabbits all at one time.

As he crouched there, hiding from the villager—who now called to someone else—he caught sight of three men on the road. Even from this distance, Jal could tell they were Dogs. They had on the dark gray jacket and pants that many of the Dogs in Sanaron wore, and one of them had an obvious tattoo on the back of his hand. As Jal studied them, he realized that he recognized one of the men.

They had been followed, which surprised him. Kanar had been pushing hard enough that the Dogs should not have been able to reach them. Unless the Dogs had gone ahead of them? That didn't make sense either.

There was another possibility, but it was one that didn't fit with what he had seen of the Dogs so far. Could they have started to use magic? They'd be even more dangerous if so.

The Dogs would make their way through the village and question the people, and when they discovered that Kanar's crew hadn't passed through here, they would start to look in another direction. They might loop around the village, thinking that the group had tried to conceal their passing, but what Jal needed was to draw them away.

Or he could try something else. Force them to pay attention.

He pulled an arrow from his quiver, brought it to the bow, and then focused. The aim was easy. He'd held a bow for as long as he could remember, and targeting something —or, in this case, someone—wasn't terribly difficult.

One thing that had often surprised him, especially given Kanar's obvious level of significant skill, was that he did not want to kill if he didn't have to. There were so many who thought that killing was the best course of action, and the way they seemed to devalue life had always amazed him. Having grown up where he had, Jal didn't necessarily see things the same way. Sometimes animals needed to be slaughtered for food, but there were times when you didn't take a life. There were times when compassion was the stronger approach.

He aimed, then loosed the arrow. It struck a tree trunk beside the nearest Dog.

Jal grinned at them before spinning and running off.

They gave chase. Dogs were easy to train. At least, most of them were.

When he had first gone to Sanaron, those initial days had been difficult. Most people had a tough time when they arrived in the city, and Jal was no different. He'd been searching for answers for several months, always coming up empty. In the end, he settled in Sanaron, thinking that it would only be a brief time.

He'd slept on the street, along the shoreline. Fog had been his blanket at first, though when that lifted it left him lying in the open.

And then they found him. There had been three Dogs that day, much like today. They usually traveled in packs, and there was always an alpha Dog.

That day, it was Rayl. He was strong and confident, with a cruel streak Jal could smell from a distance. Even though he'd known that about Rayl, Jal had also recognized that he didn't want to lose out on the possibility of protection. He'd been sitting on the street, watching the passersby, struggling to decide what he might need to do, and then Rayl had shown up. He'd been terrible even then.

"Look at you," Rayl had said. "You look like a little street mouse. Well, maybe not so little. A big street mouse." The two Dogs behind him snickered.

Jal had been in the city long enough to recognize the Dogs. He got to his feet and looked around. The street had abruptly emptied.

He turned his attention back to Rayl. "I was just resting," Jal said.

"Really? A good place to sleep. Pretty easy to get run down by wagons, or worse." The other Dogs snickered again. "You know, we could help you."

Jal was ignorant. He thought he could work with anyone. Where he had grown up, with the life he had known, he believed he could train any creature, even the Dogs in Sanaron.

"What kind of help?" Jal asked.

"Depends on what you're willing to do. Someone your size?" Rayl backed away, looking him up and down as if trying to decide how he was going to use him—which, in hindsight, was exactly what he'd done. "You'd have a few different options. Maybe we should see how strong you are."

"He don't look too strong, Rayl," one of the Dogs from behind him said. Dreg was part of Rayl's pack and rarely left his side. Not that Rayl needed the help, but it was more that Dreg preferred to spend time around Rayl. "He's got a bow."

Rayl looked past Jal, noticing the bow and quiver resting on the street. Jal had forgotten about it when he'd gotten to his feet. He never went anywhere without his bow. His grandfather had made it for him, and he'd been known as one of the most skilled craftsmen of such things. It was the same bow Jal had learned on.

"Maybe I should hold on to that," Rayl said, smiling at him.

Jal stepped forward. When he blocked Rayl from reaching for his bow, the look of irritation on Rayl's face flared brightly. It was in that moment that Jal started to think that maybe he'd underestimated them.

But it was not just the Dogs.

"That's mine," Jal said, and he grinned. Most people were disarmed by his smile. Since leaving his homeland, he had taken to smiling as much as possible. He knew that it drew attention away from his height, and from his bow. "I don't want to lose it."

"If you want to join us, you're going to have to make a few sacrifices. For the good of the pack." Rayl sounded as though Jal was the one who was being unreasonable.

Jal took a step back, using his heel to kick up the bow. He grabbed it and squeezed it. Catching the quiver was a little more difficult, but he hooked that as well and then held it behind him.

"You don't look like you have your own team," Rayl said. "Might be best for you to come with us. For your own safety."

Jal grinned again. His fingers slipped closer to the quiver.

In Sanaron, it didn't take a person too long to learn of the Dogs' reputation. He had discovered that quite early on, and had come to know that they were a threat to someone like him. Someone who was unaffiliated.

He felt drawn to the city, though. That was the reason he had stayed and kept looking for what had compelled him to come. He hadn't found it at first, but he'd felt something deep within him that told him he would.

That was the reason why he couldn't keep moving from place to place.

But the Dogs didn't give him that option.

Rayl made a motion with his hand. Jal was used to interpreting tells from animals, and these Dogs weren't so subtle.

Before Dreg and the other Dog could move toward Jal, he whipped his bow around. He caught Dreg on the wrist, brought the other end of the bow up, and smacked the other Dog on the cheek. Then he started off before they had a chance to react. They chased him, but if there was one thing Jal was good at, it was running. He was gone before they ever had a chance of getting close to him.

But from that point on, he'd been forced to avoid the Dogs.

A tall man with a bow would draw attention anywhere, and one who had attacked two Dogs, regardless of which pack they were a part of, would continue to draw attention. He knew that, and he knew there wasn't a whole lot he'd be able to do other than stay away from them, which was exactly what he intended to do.

Jal shook those memories away as he glanced behind him.

Dreg. He hadn't thought of him in a while, but Jal was always good with faces and recognized him even now. Rayl had trained Dreg, so he was about as obedient as any Dog could be. Jal didn't know the other two Dogs but doubted they would pose much of a threat. None of them really did.

He reached the woods. He didn't go far before ducking behind one of the trees, holding an arrow at the ready. Jal was prepared to attack, but also wasn't sure whether he wanted to. How many more were out here? Could Rayl be one of them?

He had a certain cruel streak to him, and Jal had kept his eyes open to watch for any sign of Rayl in the time he'd been in Sanaron, but he hadn't ever come across him again. He'd heard rumors, though. He'd learned that Rayl was moving up the ranks, gaining more power, expanding his own pack. The Prophet valued those like him, those who took a certain initiative and were willing to do what they viewed was necessary.

In order for Jal to be certain that they could avoid the Dogs, he knew he might need to draw them in, find out how many others were with them. He hesitated a moment and pulled an arrow out, then aimed and fired.

It flew true, striking the Dog in the thigh. He dropped and cried out.

"Did you think I wouldn't remember you?" a voice called out to Jal.

That was Dreg. He was certain of it.

"A tall bastard like you gets stories spread about him. Now, where's Reims? It don't look like he's around here to watch over you now."

Jal ducked his head around and felt the air whistle. He jerked his head back and glanced to the tree behind him, a crossbow bolt now jutting out of it.

Dreg laughed. "Think you can still stay ahead of us? How many do you think are here?"

Jal had hoped there was just the three of them, but he seemed to be wrong. He didn't want to take that risk if others were there. He hesitated for a moment, then began to move deeper into the woods.

He slipped around one tree trunk and saw one person move in the distance. Then another, and then another. Six Dogs.

One of them was injured, but there might be even more.

He didn't have enough arrows for that, and he didn't think he could outrun that many, especially if they surrounded him.

Dreg cackled again in the distance. "We see you. We're going to get you, and then you're going to tell us how to find Reims."

What did they want Kanar for? Revenge?

That might be all it was. Kanar had escorted the wagon past the Dogs and their attempt to claim its contents, but Jal had never known the Dogs to push so hard over losing a prize like that. There had to be more of a reason for the Dogs to be out here, and an explanation that would fit why they seemed to be moving as quickly as they had.

Jal scanned the forest. He had claimed to Kanar that he would be able to slip through the forest and keep ahead of them, but perhaps he was wrong. One thing he knew from his life back home was that there were times when animals surprised you. Sometimes they acted according to their nature, but occasionally he misunderstood it.

In this case, that might be what had happened. The Dogs were serving the Prophet, but what else were they serving?

He had to get past them, but he wasn't exactly sure how he would be able to do it.

Jal slipped forward and looked to the trees.

There.

One of the oaks was larger than the others. He could climb the tree, but when he did, he would have to decide how he would approach this. He could fire down on the Dogs from above, but he would run out of arrows. Then he'd be stuck.

The Dogs converged.

They *were* somehow working in unison.

That surprised him. Most of the time, the Dogs played at working together but needed someone to direct them. That was how the Prophet had managed to maneuver himself into his position as the alpha Dog. In the time that Jal had been in Sanaron, he'd hoped to learn more about the Prophet, mostly so he could discover who he was, but he wasn't the only one hoping to learn more about the man. Plenty of people were looking to discover his secret.

Jal got to the tree and started up it. Climbing trees was easy. It required knowing which branch would lead to another, and before any of the Dogs had gotten close to him, he'd already scaled fifty feet.

"Might as well climb back down," Dreg said. "Once we get up there to you, you're going to wish that you'd cooperated with us."

Someone laughed, and Jal felt the whiz of a crossbow bolt streak past him. He grabbed for it, snatching the bolt out of the air. He might not be able to fire the bolt, but he was sure that he could use it if he was stuck here for too long.

He didn't worry that the Dogs would reach him anytime soon. They couldn't climb as well as he could, and he doubted they'd continue wasting bolts unless they thought they could get to him. His real concern was about how long he'd be able to stay in the tree.

Kanar was waiting on him. If he or the others came looking for him, the Dogs might jump them, and Jal didn't want to be the reason for that.

Another bolt flew past him.

Jal tried not to let that bother him. Instead, he looked down. Dreg was directing the others, though he didn't appear to be the one holding the crossbow. From this vantage, Jal could make out nearly ten Dogs.

Too many.

He'd thought there were too many who attacked the caravan, though.

What had the Dogs gotten involved in? Something that was enough to risk leaving the comfort of Sanaron. Enough to make coming out here worthwhile for them, though Jal had a hard time thinking the Dogs had anything here that would matter for them.

"You're going to have to come down sooner or later," Dreg called.

A branch rustled below. Jal waited until he saw an arm gripping a branch before he fired. The arrow struck the man in the forearm, and he dropped with a pained cry.

Jal knew he didn't have an endless supply of arrows. He could keep them from climbing up to him—at least deter them, even if he didn't stop them altogether—but eventually he'd run out of arrows. Then they would only have to wait on him.

Dreg wasn't wrong. He would have to come down. Eventually, Jal would probably fall asleep and tumble down.

He could either save the arrows—which might be the smart play—or just get it over with by firing as many as he had now and figure out how to take out the remaining Dogs that might be left when he was done.

A familiar low howl sounded in the distance—one that he'd come to know well in his homeland. Most thought the wenderwolves dangerous, and they could be, especially when they hunted as a family.

This was a different animal entirely—and far more dangerous.

The howl was meant as a warning from the berahn, creatures that shouldn't be found in this region. He'd have to think about *why* they were here another time.

Jal tipped his head, cupped one hand to his mouth, and offered an answering cry.

Now all he had to do was wait for the slaughter.

Chapter Twelve

HONAAZ

Honaaz was getting tired of the saddle. He'd done his share of riding over the years, but that didn't mean he liked it. Much better to have a ship beneath his feet, feeling the swaying that came from swells on the sea, than the jostling of the damn horse each time he hit a rut in the road. Given where Reims had them traveling, they hit a rut every couple of steps. It was enough to make anyone angry.

Not that Honaaz would show it—and certainly not to Reims.

Let the man think he was going to come along for whatever they wanted. Pull some job in a place the gods didn't intend his kind to be. Then get back out. All for a hundred gold.

More than that, he reminded himself.

"Can we get the damn horses back to the road?" he muttered.

Reims looked back at him. His gaze always looked like he was trying to work through how best to gut a man, and this time was no different. It had been like that from the very first moment Honaaz had met him on the job for Heatharn that *should* have taken him away from Sanaron. Then there had been the attack, and the fucking merchant didn't think he could trust anyone he'd hired in that city.

Honaaz wasn't the reason they'd been jumped, and he hadn't had a chance to go through and interrogate the others Heatharn had hired to find out if they were the culprit. Two of them were dead, though. They probably weren't responsible. The last had been Ferith, and Honaaz had vouched for him. Bastard better not have been the reason Honaaz didn't get his transport away.

In hindsight, the whole debacle might have been a gift. Had he gone with Heatharn, he wouldn't have had his chance to learn about Reims. Even if it meant riding on this fucking horse, he was going to do it.

"You're too slow," Lily said.

Her horse weaved around the trees, and he made a point of moving off to the side, not wanting to get too close to her. He wasn't exactly sure what she could do, but he had growing suspicions that she had a form of sorcery found in his homeland. Regardless of how tiny she might be, she was powerful. And the others seemed oblivious.

"I'm just trying to keep this damn horse moving the way he's supposed to," Honaaz said. "Neither of you seem that concerned that we still haven't gotten back to the road."

"Because it doesn't matter," Reims said. "Jal will let us know when it's safe to get back there."

Honaaz said nothing. Jal. Another man he wasn't quite sure about.

The entire team had him digging for clues but coming up short. That wasn't his usual experience. Most of the time, he could get a handle on a person within a few minutes and would know weaknesses. With Reims and his strange team, they were each dangerous, but for varying reasons.

Lily's horse brushed up against his, and he stiffened. Maybe they weren't equally dangerous. There was no way he would challenge someone like her.

"I thought you said we were looking for speed," Honaaz said to Reims. "Can't have much speed heading through the trees like this."

Not that he *really* wanted to get back onto the road. That meant setting the horses at a gallop. That meant his backside—and back—aching like he'd just brawled with half the crew on his uncle's ship, and everyone knew Castor had the roughest crew on the Salin Sea.

"And we can't have the Dogs chasing us all the way to Verendal," Reims replied. "Just be patient."

Honaaz didn't say anything.

Patient.

He could be patient.

After getting stranded in a place like Sanaron, Honaaz knew how to be patient for far longer than most men. And now it seemed like he might finally have a chance for his patience to pay off. He just had to bide his time a little longer.

Lily flashed a smile at him, then laughed softly when he turned away from her. She was probably already thinking of ways to use those knives she had on her. Or maybe reaching for something in her pouch. That was where the danger lay with someone like her.

Not only there.

He'd been around a few others like her and knew they

had other ways of causing trouble. Not just the pouch where they hid all sorts of horrors. A woman like her might be quick with the knives, but she was also quick with other skills.

They wove through the trees, silent as they could be. There weren't many sounds in the forest other than his occasional grunt as the fucking horse bounced him off tree trunks and forced him to duck. It was almost like the horse knew that Honaaz didn't want to be on him.

The other two didn't seem to have the same struggle. Reims especially seemed comfortable, but someone like him *would* be comfortable.

"It's getting dark," he mumbled later in the day when they'd finally stopped to let the horses drink.

"He's not wrong, Kan," Lily said. "We shouldn't stay here too much longer. Get back to the road and to Jal. I told you I've heard a few wenderwolves, and if they're here, you know what can follow."

Honaaz looked over to her. "What the fuck are wenderwolves?" As soon as he'd uttered the swear, he wished he could pull it back. Someone like Lily wouldn't take well to that kind of language, but that was just how the crew always talked when he was learning the ropes. She'd probably drive her knives into his gut just for daring to speak to her like that. The others didn't seem concerned about her, which left Honaaz thinking they had to be fools. Only, Reims didn't strike him as a fool.

She smiled, and he fought against flinching. "Massive wolves. Or something like them. They don't hunt in packs but in families. If one gets your scent, it's pretty hard to shake them. You don't want to be run down by a wenderwolf. They'll devour a person in little more than an hour."

She laughed, as if that were some kind of entertainment for her.

Maybe for someone like her, it was. Having come by sea, he had no idea what animals were in these lands. "Sounds fucking horrible," he muttered.

"Yeah. They really are."

"Quiet," Reims said. "We shouldn't be too far from town."

Honaaz had heard Reims tell them to be quiet more times than he could count. It was something he wouldn't tolerate from most men, and he wasn't thrilled that he had to listen to Reims tell him to shut up, but this was his job, so he'd do what the captain said. Besides, he'd seen how Reims had handled those Dogs in that building. Honaaz could have done the same, but it would have been a harder job. Reims had been *fluid*. Like waves crashing.

Darkness started to settle through the trees.

It was one thing to be standing on the deck of a ship underneath the stars, with moonlight rippling off the water around you. It was something else altogether to be under the canopy of the forest, with strange shadows that seemed to stretch and draw out around you.

He knew that they had to be getting close to town, but how much longer would Reims force them to ride? Better yet, how much longer would it be until the tall bastard returned?

"I see lights," Lily said.

Honaaz looked over to her. He couldn't figure out why the others didn't share his concern about her. How fucking clueless could they be?

"We aren't far from it now," Reims said. "Told you we didn't have to worry."

Honaaz had to worry, but maybe they didn't. Of course, neither of them probably cared all that much either.

Reims guided them onto a wide road heading into the town. It was much wider than the path they had taken away from Sanaron, where Reims had forced them to ride at a full gallop. At least within the forest, they hadn't been pushing the horses nearly as fast, but Honaaz also suspected they had taken far longer than Reims had wanted. He had wanted to get them to Verendal as quickly as possible, and the delay through the forest had cost them time.

"Have you ever been here before?" Honaaz asked.

Reims looked over with that hard, murderous expression. It was almost enough for Honaaz to grab for his own daggers, but he resisted. He probably wouldn't have an opportunity to do anything against someone like Reims, and certainly not with Lily here to help him.

"No," Reims said. "But I know towns like this. They're all much the same. Once we find the stables, we can use Malory's marker, and then we can make the swap in the morning. We can be on our way, and a day closer to Verendal."

Honaaz twisted in the saddle to look behind him and found Lily watching him. She had that slight lilting smile on her lips that told him she was thinking of a way to slit his throat or drive a knife into his belly. He was sure of that.

At least, he was mostly sure of that.

"What's so special about Verendal, anyway?" he asked.

"Not much," Reims said. "It's a city on the edge of Reyand. Close to Yelind. And it's surrounded by an Alainsith forest."

"Am I supposed to know anything about Alainsith forests?"

"Only if you want to live," Lily said, and laughed softly.

"That's not funny," Honaaz snapped.

"She's not wrong," Reims said. "The Alainsith are people who live beyond the border of Reyand. They once warred with Reyand." Reims regarded him, and there was something in his eyes that suggested that he knew something about him.

Honaaz asking about the Alainsith might be a mistake. Maybe he should be cautious with his questions.

"They aren't bad people," Lily said.

Reims glanced at her, and Honaaz couldn't tell what he was thinking. He looked at her with a little less darkness in his eyes than he did with others, though Honaaz didn't know if that was his imagination or not. It might be. If so, it meant that Reims knew just how dangerous someone like Lily would be. It meant that he would be careful with her. Or maybe they were just fucking. Lily was certainly pretty enough, if you didn't mind the possibility of a blade in your side.

"Not all are," Reims said. "But I've had enough experience with them to know just how dangerous some can be. There aren't many people who can make the same claim."

Honaaz looked over and realized that Lily was keeping quiet, but she had a dangerous expression in her eyes that left him wondering how much experience she might have with these Alainsith people.

Reims continued riding forward, leaving the two of them behind.

"Why are they dangerous?" Honaaz said.

"Just focus on your task," Lily said.

He clenched his jaw. He should've known better than to think that he could befriend someone like her. It wasn't even about befriending her, though. It was more about trying to be kind to her so that he didn't end up with a pair of her knives stuck into his back. He shrugged, dismissing her as much as he could, but he knew that he couldn't dismiss her entirely.

They kept riding forward. They weren't far from the outermost buildings of the town, which looked to be small farms. Most of them had light that glowed within windows. The sight was almost comforting. Farther into the town, the buildings stretched taller. At least the trees had spread apart. A man like Honaaz was accustomed to the open skies.

When they reached the outskirts of the city, he looked over to Reims. "At least tell me more about Verendal before we get there."

"There isn't much to be said about it. I told you that it's on the edge of Reyand."

"Did it get affected by the war?"

Honaaz didn't know all that much about the war itself. He had been traveling the sea during that time and had been kept distant from it for the most part. And had he been in port, he probably wouldn't have heard much about it anyway, other than watching for those that needed escorting away from Reyand.

People like that tended to pay a pretty penny. His uncle had been more than happy to take coin to escort Sanaron people across the sea, to where they believed they'd find a new life. Rarely did anyone ever stop to think about what they might find on the other side of the sea, and whether the new life would be any better than the old one.

"Every place got affected by the war." Reims frowned as he looked at one of the storefronts. Honaaz followed the direction of his gaze and saw an instrument shop. His hands were too big for anything musical, not that he'd be daring enough to try. "This job will be hard. Not the part about getting into the city. The king keeps the city open. He doesn't restrict activity. Not sure that he could, anyway. It's an old city, and the protections there are old as well. It makes it unique. Easy enough for people to get in, a little harder to get out, if that makes any sort of sense."

"You can get in anywhere," Honaaz said.

"Me, or you?"

"I don't know about what you can do."

Reims climbed down from the saddle, grabbed the reins of his horse, and started leading them. Honaaz followed, with Lily not far behind.

She was short, only up to his shoulder, something that was easy to forget when she was seated on her horse. When she was on the ground, barely up to his shoulder blades, Honaaz could almost imagine throwing her if she were to attack.

"The job is to break into a nearly impossible prison," Reims explained, "and break out the person who knows details about what happened during the Alainsith attack. I need my team to focus on this task. And we need one more. Otherwise, I don't know that we can do the job completely."

"And once you get this person?"

"Then we have to get back out," Reims said. "And we have to hope that they can tell us where we need to go next."

Honaaz stiffened. This wasn't what he had agreed to. He had believed that Reims knew what he was doing and knew where he was going. He didn't expect the man to lead them into Reyand, only for them to be stranded there without a plan.

"How much time did you say we had?"

Reims shrugged. "Not enough."

They kept moving forward, and Lily flashed a wide smile. It almost looked friendly on her from this angle. "Don't mind him. He can be a bit of a sourpuss. What he's not telling you is that Reyand has a bit of a reputation," she said. "As does the one who runs the prison."

"It's not just the wardens you have to worry about. Especially in Verendal. You'll see," Reims said.

Lily guided her horse past him, patting the animal on the side.

Honaaz pulled on the reins of his horse, and it seemed like the stubborn creature pulled back, forcing him to yank even harder. It seemed as if Reims had given him the largest horse he'd been able to find. He probably had felt like he needed to so that Honaaz could ride safely, but Honaaz wished that he would've had some choice in the matter. He might have preferred a gentle pack mule rather than the tall, powerful stallion.

"Would you just come on?" Honaaz grunted.

"You have to talk nice to them," a voice said out of the darkness.

Honaaz spun and reached for one of his daggers, when he recognized the tall bastard striding toward them while leading his horse.

"Sometimes, you have to tell them how good they are, even when they aren't." Jal scratched his horse on the nose. "Some people like to say that horses don't understand you, but I've never felt that way. I always feel like they know things, even if they don't understand it in the same way we do. Most animals are like that. They have instincts that have been honed over thousands of years."

"I have my own instincts," Honaaz said.

Jal shrugged. He glanced over to Honaaz's stallion and patted it on the side. The horse turned to him, almost as if comfortable with that gesture.

"We tend to be too dumb to recognize our own instincts," Jal said. "You have to learn which ones to listen to, and which ones not to listen to. That's what separates us from the animals."

"Where did you say you farmed?" Honaaz asked.

"Oh, my farm was far from here," Jal said, his voice taking on a sorrowful tone. "I've been away for too long."

Honaaz regarded him for a moment, taking in the deeply tanned skin, the curly black hair, and his chocolate-colored eyes. "Wustan. That's where you're from." They'd hit a few ports not far from there, which would fit the accent he heard to Jal's words too.

Jal shook his head. "Close, but not quite. I've been through there, though."

They continued onward. A pair of lanterns cast the street in a warm orange glow. A pair of people moved in the opposite direction, away from them. From somewhere in the distance, Honaaz caught the strains of a song, a warbly voice, and a steady drumming sound that accompanied it. The music had to be from some minstrel in a tavern, or perhaps even a street performer.

That was something he missed in Sanaron. There weren't many street performers. The fog didn't really allow that kind of thing. Plenty of shoreline merchants set up their carts to sell different wares, and people shouted for customers, but there were none of the entertainers that he always associated with some of the larger cities. No acrobats, no singers or minstrels, and no poets. Honaaz always liked the poets. He couldn't imagine putting words together like that, something that was almost a song, but that carried a story behind it. They had always impressed him.

"How is Kanar?" Jal asked as they neared another intersecting street.

"About the same as he was during the last job," Honaaz muttered.

"Oh, he gets in different moods. You just have to learn them, and then you can learn how to deal with them. But I don't think he likes going to Reyand," Jal said. "It's too close to who he was."

"And you know who he was?"

"Not as much as I'd like to," Jal said carefully. "But Verendal shouldn't be all bad. Did you know it's where the king keeps his jewels?"

"Then why isn't *that* the job?"

"I don't think anybody can get into the palace," Jal said. "During my travels, I heard a story about a thieving crew that thought to break into the palace. They were surprised by the king and his soldiers, and all of them were slaughtered." He shook his head. "Supposedly, they stuck the leader's head on a pike, showing the rest of the city what would happen if they attempted it."

"That kind of message would work," Honaaz said.

"You agree with it?"

Honaaz shrugged. "Sometimes you have to show others what you are willing to do if they cross you."

Jal watched him, his expression dark, and a question burned in his eyes: what would Honaaz do if someone betrayed him?

Instead, his gaze drifted to Reims, who stalked forward along the road and made his way steadily deeper into the town.

What would he do?

He would do what he was doing now, taking a journey that was possibly dangerous for himself. He would risk everything, especially for answers about *why* his people had stranded him in Sanaron. Especially if it meant that he might finally have a measure of closure.

And Reims would be the one to give it to him.

Chapter Thirteen

KANAR

THE QUIET TAVERN DIDN'T HAVE ANYTHING ON THE Roasted Walnut, but it was cozy enough. In front of Kanar was a tray of roasted squash, venison, and a sweet-smelling roll that he had only picked at so far. Across from him, Jal was lounging back, having already finished his food.

"Relax, Kan. We need to rest and eat to keep our strength. We've got time before the new horses arrive."

Kanar looked around, twisting his hands in his lap. He didn't like sitting and waiting—not when so much was on the line. And this place felt wrong. Too relaxed.

For one thing, it wasn't very busy. Most of the people here looked to be locals. Many of them sat together, playing cards or dominoes, while a couple had sidled up to the bar and were talking to the barkeep. There were only a few stragglers like him and Jal. That would draw attention to them, but at this point, Kanar didn't think it mattered. If Jal had been as effective as he had claimed, then there was no point in worrying about the Dogs chasing them.

"What's eating at you?" Jal asked.

Kanar glanced to the back of the tavern. That was where he would have rather sat. Not near the kitchen where the door brushed his elbow every time it opened. "Nothing. I'm just making plans."

"For the rest of the ride, or for—"

"For Verendal. I need to know that we're going to be ready for what we'll face."

And he wasn't. Not yet. There had been no further sign of the Dogs, though Jal had dealt with them in some way. Kanar wouldn't push. If Jal had to shoot a few Dogs to keep them from following, that was his business, and nothing that Kanar would intervene on. As long as they didn't follow, he was happy.

Jal seemed fine as well. That wasn't always the case. There were times when Jal could be a little uneasy, especially when it came to some of the things they had been forced to do together. Malory had often found them complicated jobs to pull, but those complicated jobs had brought them closer together, turning them into a real team. First him and Jal, and then later Lily had come along.

"Do you want to talk about it?" Jal asked.

"I thought I was."

"You're mentioning it, but I'm offering—"

"I know what you're offering," Kanar said. "You don't need to worry about me. I'll make sure we are in a good space when it comes down to it."

"That wasn't exactly what I was concerned about," Jal said.

Kanar watched him for a moment. "Are you going to talk about what happened?"

Jal shrugged. "Didn't think I needed to."

"You were gone longer than I expected."

"Sometimes you have to take a little time to make sure everything falls the way you want. You know how that can be."

When somebody entered the tavern, Kanar looked up, watching for any danger. He didn't expect any real danger here. They were too far removed from any place of note, but there was the possibility that a Dog might come strolling in. If that happened, he wanted to be ready.

Honaaz and Lily were off scouting the town to make sure they didn't encounter any difficulty. That left him and Jal to sit and eat.

"I've never seen you like this before," Jal said. "Not nervous, but on edge. That's how I would describe it. Gods, I couldn't describe the great Kanar Reims as nervous. But you certainly have an edge to you."

Kanar turned back to him. He snorted, then reached toward his sword without meaning to. Every time he thought of Verendal and everything else he was going to have to do, he began to get increasingly uptight. Maybe it was just the idea of heading back into that world. He'd left Reyand behind and had thought he was done with it. And he had been. For so long, he had been done with it. Kanar hadn't necessarily wanted—or needed—to return to Reyand.

"I'm just uncomfortable," he said. "Not on edge."

Jal grinned. "Seems to me they're the same thing. First about the job, and then you go and get Honaaz involved." He shrugged. "I don't disagree with pulling in someone else. Honaaz is big enough to be useful, but are you sure you want to trust somebody who hasn't done a job with us before?"

"Honaaz has done a job with us before. Just not under my command."

"A job that went well, then. That escort didn't work out quite the way we hoped it would."

No. It certainly hadn't. It had been easy from the beginning, and then it had become a disaster. That disaster had been fully preventable, and somehow he had not managed to do so. That thought irritated him.

"He's going to be useful," Kanar said.

"What do you think we're going to face when we get to Verendal?"

Kanar picked at his food. "What makes you think it's Verendal that I'm worried about?"

"Gods, Kan. Do you even know what we're going to deal with?"

That was part of the problem. Kanar wasn't sure how he could know. If everything worked out the way it was supposed to, he hoped that they would get in, grab Morgan, and then get back out.

If he were honest with himself, the hardest part would be seeing Morgan again. He had left. When he had learned what she was, Kanar hadn't been able to stomach it. He had felt betrayed—again.

"We need to get Morgan so that we can learn where to find the blood," Kanar picked his words carefully.

He had explained as much as he thought was safe to do with Jal and Lily, but even less with Honaaz. He trusted the man as much as he could bring himself to, but he also needed to keep a measure of separation with him. Honaaz didn't need to know what the others were going to make on the job, and given that Kanar trusted that Lily and Jal wouldn't say anything, he figured that he was safe. But Honaaz would play a role. Kanar would see to it. And it was the role that he would play that Kanar needed to ensure worked as planned.

"We have to save her before her execution, which can be difficult," he continued. "Executioners in Reyand are a different breed. They're skilled and powerful, and the rumors out of Verendal are that the executioner there is among their greatest."

"So we get in. We get this Morgan, who's someone you have a past with," Jal said. There was a slight twinkle in his eyes, as if Kanar's past involved some woman he had scorned rather than chasing someone with the kind of power that had nearly unsettled the kingdom. "And we use her. That about sum it up?"

"About."

"And this is all about you and magic."

"It's complicated," Kanar said.

"We have those who practice what you call magic around my farm. Or had," Jal corrected himself. "Nobody really seemed to mind. Most people went to them for poultice if they were hurt, sometimes for healing balms, and I remember one of my neighbors had gone looking for a love spell, though he stayed single. He did, however, find a nice cat, so maybe it worked." Jal grinned. "My people never really got that excited about what you call magic."

"We had that in Reyand," Kanar said, his words soft. "Witches, but of a different kind. They don't use witchcraft, but they have their own kind of magic."

"And what kind is that?"

"It might not be the same, but it's no better."

"Why?" Jal asked.

Kanar sat up, hands resting on either side of his tray as

he met Jal's gaze. Jal started to look away, before seeming to steel himself and holding Kanar's eyes. It was almost enough to make Kanar smile, though he was not in the mood. Not with this.

"Have you ever been to an execution?" Kanar said.

Jal's smile slipped. "What kind of question is that? Not if I could help it. Gods, why would you even think of such a thing?"

"They become something of a festival in Reyand," Kanar explained. "Entire cities turn out for them. The people feel like it's their right to get vengeance on the bastard who wronged them. Most of the time, the person involved did something horrible. Hurting women. Killing. Crimes against the kingdom." During the war, there had been quite a few crimes against the kingdom—more than before. Enough that it had kept Kanar busy. Enough that he had attended far more executions than he had ever imagined he would. "After a man is sent to the gods, through hanging, beheading, or whatever sentence he might've been given, he's left out by the gallows. And that's when it gets bad. That's when *they* come in. They take fingers, toes, ears, and worse."

"You're talking about the hegen," Jal said.

Kanar nodded. "So you know of them?"

"My people have them as well. That's who helps. Those who die aren't going to need their fingers or toes, and apparently there is power stored in the body that can be gifted back to the world. Why shouldn't it be returned?"

Kanar didn't really have a good answer. Not for Jal. He had his own answers, but even in his kingdom, he'd been an outlier with how he felt.

"That's what you were responsible for taking care of?

People like that?" Jal asked.

"Not like that. But it's not all that dissimilar," Kanar said. He breathed out, squeezing his eyes shut. "Witchcraft is bound by pain and suffering. That's where the power comes from. I've seen pain and suffering. I've experienced it." He swallowed, jaw clenched. "I learned how to hunt it so that it could be expelled from Reyand. And we succeeded as well as we could."

"Then you shouldn't be upset."

"I shouldn't be, should I?" Kanar said, opening his eyes.

Jal regarded him for a long moment. "You know, I once had a pup I was training. Cute little thing. Had a long snout, and these deep brown eyes that would look at you as if he could know what you're thinking."

Kanar looked down at his tray. Jal often went back to his farm experiences when it came conveying a point. Kanar had long ago given up trying to argue with him. He would let Jal say his piece, and after that, they could move on.

"He was about two, I suppose. You know how dogs go through their phases. We always said that they were little turds for about three years, good dogs for about three years, and old dogs for about three years." Jal smirked. "Even when they were turds, I still loved working with them. You know me and animals."

"Probably not as well as I should," Kanar said.

"Well, this little guy—Inaran, we called him—might've been cute, but he was stubborn. I've had plenty of experience with animals that didn't want to take their training, but he might've been one of the worst of them." Jal smiled at the memory. "One day, I was trying to work with him on a new command. We had to train them to keep track of the herd, you know. He wasn't ready to be unleashed on it, but I had a soft spot for him. Maybe I shouldn't have, but there are some things in your life that you get a soft spot for that aren't the best for you." Jal looked up, as if somehow knowing Kanar's own weaknesses. "Anyway, this good boy got a little irritated when I was trying to correct him. Lashed out at me." Jal pulled up his sleeve and revealed a massive scar along his arm. "Got me right here. Nearly took a chunk out of my forearm. I'd been bitten before, but this might've been the worst of it. He was snarling, snapping, and trying to tear me apart. Figure had he succeeded, gotten a taste for me, he might've finished me off."

"What's the point of the story?"

"Oh, maybe there's no point. I had to pry his jaw open and needed to go to one of the hegen you don't care much about. They patched me up, got it to stop bleeding, and healed me so that it didn't get infected."

Kanar frowned as he moved over to grab the sweet roll off his tray and took a bite. "So you wanted me to know that the hegen have helped you."

"No, but they did help. Can't spend any time out on a farm and not suffer an accident. Things happen. People get hurt. Animals act like… well, like animals. Not much you can do about it. Just have to keep moving."

"And what happened with your pup?"

"Oh. I think that was my point," Jal said. "After that, I kept working with him. I didn't give up on him. He might've done something bad, but he wasn't all bad. And when the herd wandered a bit, you know who was the first one to sound the alarm?"

"Let me guess. Inaran."

Jal grinned. "Gods no. He didn't sound the alarm, but

he stayed near them, and kept back an entire attack all by himself once. That wildness paid off." He sat back and crossed his arms, as if he'd made some wonderful point. Kanar didn't see it, but that was the norm when it came to Jal's stories.

"I'm going to check on Lily," Jal said. "I didn't like the way Honaaz was looking at her."

"Do you really think you need to worry about her?" Kanar said.

"Probably not. But somebody needs to keep the peace, don't they?"

Kanar nodded. "Somebody does."

Jal flashed a smile, grabbed his bow, and got to his feet, then sauntered out of the tavern.

It was always going to be Jal who kept the peace. That was his gift. That and his intuition. Kanar had learned to trust those who had earned it, and Jal, for all his quirks, had definitely earned his trust. He was an interesting man, the kind of person Kanar never would have anticipated bonding with, and yet here Jal was as one of his most reliable people, and somebody that Kanar couldn't even imagine pulling a job without now.

He breathed out heavily and thought back to their conversation. He had always been taught that the hegen were harmless. Even during the war, when the Order had been hunting those with magic, the hegen had been a part of helping King Porman with his hunt. They had their own type of magic, and though it was tied to their prizes, as they called them, there wasn't anything dangerous about it. They were useful. Until they weren't.

Kanar had seen hegen magic used against the kingdom. The way they would attack using fragments of bone that had been turned into weapons. Explosives, poisons, and other ways of harming entire squadrons. It might not be witchcraft, but that didn't mean it wasn't as dangerous as witchcraft.

Then there were those like Morgan, those who pretended they were much less dangerous than they were. Kanar had been caught up in how she looked and how she had talked, without ever thinking her capable of witchcraft.

He remembered when he'd first seen her. He had been assigned to Vur, to escort the king as one of the Realmsguard, not yet having been brought into the Order. Kanar had been patrolling by blending into the city. It was one of the many skills he had learned as he'd climbed the ranks of the Realmsguard.

He had seen her from across the plaza. He'd been scoping out a market, figuring that was a good place to get gossip. Kanar later learned that taverns were better for gossip, and that making contacts with those who knew the city—and its underworld—was the best way to gather information.

She'd been dressed in a yellow gown. Her flaxen hair had stood out even then, sunlight reflecting off it, and her vibrant green eyes appeared to take in everything with a hint of amusement. Her freckles seemed almost as if the gods themselves had blessed her features, giving her one more way of standing out.

Kanar had woven through the crowd to try to make his way over to her. This had been before the war. Before the southern border had been attacked. The only real threat that the Realmsguard worried about was the ongoing concern about whether the Alainsith would decide to invade.

One of the bells in the city rang, and Kanar glanced up, frowning. The bells sounded different than those of his childhood home of Tolat. They were louder, more vibrant, and seemed to ring for longer, with more of a pause in between each toll. There was also something else about them that seemed as if it settled in his chest. Perhaps these bells found some way of actually summoning the gods.

When he looked down, she was there, standing across from him and smiling at him with a broad expression. He couldn't look away from her freckles, though.

"Were you following me?" Morgan asked. There was a playful tone to it, but there was also a hint of something else. Even then, he had recognized it. It wasn't danger, at least he hadn't thought so at the time. In hindsight, he had probably overlooked the real threat. "I've noticed you for the last several streets. You've been following me. Either you're a cutpurse who intends to rob me, or you have decided to start stalking me."

Kanar smiled but didn't know quite how to respond to a comment like that. "I'm not following you."

"Oh. So you weren't near the Church of Heleth only a few moments ago, and now you're here, in the Amoran Market?"

Kanar wanted to look away, to one of the dozens of stalls that were near him. His mind scrambled to come up with some reason for why he'd come here. He'd heard a candlemaker calling to him when he'd first walked through, and he thought about using that as an excuse for his presence, but he decided to tell her the truth. It was the first mistake he had made when it came to Morgan.

"I'm one of the Realmsguard," he said.

Her smile didn't falter, but the sparkle in her eyes

dimmed. "That means you think I'm a danger to the king."

"I've said nothing of the sort."

"If you're one of the Realmsguard, and obviously not dressed to convey threat, it means he has you searching through the crowd to look for potential dangers. That you have decided to follow me indicates that you think I'm a potential danger. It's a simple matter of following the logic."

Logic.

Morgan had mentioned logic to him and had made a point of telling him how she viewed the world from the very beginning. Had he been paying attention, maybe everything would've turned out differently, but he hadn't known what she meant by *logic*.

"I am tasked with ensuring the safety of the king," Kanar said. "There are always unseen threats within the kingdom."

"See?" The sparkle in her eyes returned, and she tipped her head, watching him. "Handsome and a bit of a thinker. I like that in a man." Her smile had almost melted him. "Protecting a dynasty is dangerous work, I imagine." When he wasn't baited, she'd smiled again. "Care to tell me how I am a threat to the king? Maybe it's my dress. I think the color might be offensive to him, but if that's the case, then the sun must offend him. Or maybe it's my hair. I've seen the king from afar, and I know that he may not share my hair color, but there are some similarities." Her smile slipped then. "Or maybe it's these freckles. My mother liked to tell me that the gods kissed me when I was little and blessed me with them, but some see darkness within freckles. Perhaps you see that darkness and have decided that I must be stopped."

For all his training, and for all the times that Kanar had fought on behalf of Reyand, he had never encountered anything quite like this. It was a different danger.

"It's because I thought you were lovely," Kanar said.

Another truth, and another mistake.

Morgan crossed her arms. "So my appearance is the only value I have?"

"That's not what I meant. And you had said I was—"

"But that's what you implied. Again, logic. Perhaps the king has not trained his men to appreciate logic. That doesn't surprise me. He would expect you to follow orders, not think through such commands. It tells me that you don't have much of a mind of your own."

She smiled as if in victory, and it seemed almost as if Heleth smiled down on her, shining her light through her. As much as he wanted to turn away, Kanar was unable to.

"Are you hungry?" he asked.

"Did you perceive my insults as an invitation to spend more time with me? I must admit that perhaps they were too subtle for a man of your intelligence, and your willingness to follow the king's commands."

"You keep stopping at each of the food vendors," Kanar said. "You stopped at the baker, sniffed two loaves of bread, but didn't purchase either of them. You stopped at the fruit stand, grabbed a couple of apples—along with several other fruits, though I didn't recognize them from a distance—and didn't purchase any of them. You went on to visit the meat stand, where you had your hands behind your back, leaned forward, breathed in, and—" Kanar caught himself. He was revealing too much here, but he was too far in now. "You purchased nothing. Either you don't have the coin, or you simply were inspecting the food vendors. So I ask you, are you hungry?"

Her smile broadened. "A measure of observation. I can work with that." She nodded to him. "I *am* famished, so if you're offering to buy me a meal, I will happily oblige you. I warn you, I won't hold back."

Kanar could already tell that.

"Now. I have a few requirements before we go," Morgan had said.

Somebody nudged him, bringing him back to the present. Kanar opened his eyes and looked over to see the barkeep. The tavern had thinned out somewhat, and he glanced across the table, remembering the first meal he had with Morgan and how ravenously she'd eaten. She didn't always eat like that, but often enough.

"Are your friends coming back, or is it just you?" the barkeep asked.

"They're coming back."

"I need the space."

Kanar swept his gaze around the tavern. He had a hard time thinking that the barkeep needed this space, but he recognized the danger in challenging him. "We'll make sure you're paid well."

"You had better. Tying up a table like this for as long as you have…"

He turned, and Kanar smiled to himself. As he thought of Morgan, he couldn't help but question what she might've said to the barkeep. He had to keep those thoughts out of his mind, though. They were dangerous. Too dangerous.

It was better for him to stay focused, to prepare for what he might say to her when he finally saw her again. Kanar wasn't quite ready, and he had only a few days to get there.

Chapter Fourteen

LILY

Lily was sore from the rapid ride toward Verendal. They had done little more than travel, sleep for a couple hours at a time, and eat, never taking long in one place while swapping out the horses as Malory had directed. She really *was* well connected.

The saddle felt like it was tearing at her backside, though Lily did appreciate that she wasn't the only one who struggled. Each time Honaaz climbed out of the saddle, he winced and limped a little bit more. Jal being Jal, he never struggled. He seemed as if he were born in the saddle, and the horse responded to him as though he had trained it himself. Knowing Jal the way she did, it was possible that he had been training the horse all this time.

Then there was Kanar. Nothing ever seemed to bother him—other than wanting this journey to be over with. Kanar was difficult for her to read, though she tried. She continued to watch him, looking for any subtle signs of what he might be thinking, but found nothing. He had grown increasingly quiet over the last few days. Ever since leaving the small town, they had stopped two more times to swap their horses and ridden fast the following day. She had begun to worry that they were overexerting themselves.

Jal didn't seem at all concerned. He often murmured into his mount's ears, whispering to him, unfazed by the fact that they were pushing their horses so hard.

"We need to talk about what we're going to do," Kanar said to them. "I know Verendal reasonably well. Morgan has been sentenced to die, and I know where they're keeping her."

"You said the prison is going to be difficult to break into," Lily said.

"If she were being held in the women's prison, maybe it wouldn't be so bad. But she's in a prison known as Declan, and it is a fortress. Lily, you will have to find us a way in. Jal and Honaaz, you'll need to ensure that we have a clear path through by removing any guards that might be there. And I'm going to break her out."

"It doesn't sound that difficult," Lily said.

"The prison is a fortress, as I mentioned, and it's old. I've never even tried breaking into a prison, let alone getting out. It's going to be harder than we think."

And so it was that they neared a city.

It was late, several hours after dark. She kept thinking that they would camp for the night—something she was not looking forward to, especially not out in the open. They had to be getting close to Verendal, though she had started to question whether they would reach it in the time frame Kanar wanted. He had been pushing them hard, but there were limits. Not only their own physical limits of how long they could sit in the saddle without pain, but also the limits to how hard they could push the horses.

None of it seemed to bother Kanar.

"Where are we?" Jal asked, breaking the silence that had stretched between them.

"That's Verendal," Kanar said, looking to the city in the distance. His voice had dropped to a whisper. Perhaps he simply didn't want to disrupt the quiet of the night, but there was a certain somberness to him that hadn't been there before.

"Are we staying there tonight?" Honaaz asked.

"You want to stay on the road?" Jal asked, grinning at him. "We got a city right there. A warm bed, a warm meal, maybe even a cold mug of ale. What could be better?"

"Not being back in Reyand," Kanar said.

"You don't have to take this job," Lily reminded him.

"Well, since we're here, we could break into the palace, get the king's jewels, and sell them," Honaaz said. He glanced toward her but then turned away quickly.

He'd been odd around her ever since they had left Sanaron. Kanar must've said something to him. Either that, or he had seen her fight when the caravan had dealt with the highwaymen. She had demonstrated her skill with her knives then, but she had not shown off anything with her other art. She had made a point of not revealing that to anyone.

"The job is the job," Kanar said. "We are going to finish this."

He started forward, riding steadily. She appreciated that he wasn't pushing the horses quickly at this point. She could take some of the pressure off her backside by pressing her heels down into the stirrups, which gave herself a bit of a break. She had shifted during the day, trying to position herself from side to side, and had ultimately decided that it might've been more comfortable if they had hired a wagon.

Maybe it wouldn't have been as fast, though. They wouldn't have been able to navigate through the trees as easily, but surely it would've been better for all of them. They could have lined up their horses, loaded them on a wagon, and made nearly the same time.

Lily found Honaaz watching her again, and she flashed a smile. His brow furrowed, and he turned away. She chuckled to herself. Maybe he really didn't care for her. Or maybe it truly was something Kanar had said to him. She would have to ask Kanar about it later. Whatever he had said seemed to keep her from dealing with Honaaz, though it wasn't as if she really minded him.

From a distance, Verendal was dark, little more than shadows with small glimmers of light shining in hundreds upon hundreds of windows. A massive wall surrounded the entire city. She didn't see anyone standing atop the wall—no sign of soldiers, though she suspected that there would be some. The road led up to another, much wider road, and that one headed straight toward the city. Massive gates were spread open, which surprised her. What was the purpose of the wall if the gates remained open? Anybody could get in.

Colossal towers stretched over the city itself. Some of them looked to have even larger spires twisting above them. In the darkness, they were little more than shadowy outlines, but she knew what they represented. The churches of Verendal.

She had heard that the people here were far more religious than they were in any place she had ever been, though she understood that. They enjoyed a certain comfort in believing that the gods looked down upon you and might influence how you thrived. Too many people believed that the gods somehow controlled what happened to them. Even when she was younger, there had been a belief that the gods, or someone else, had some way of guiding them.

A shape to the right of the road caught her attention, and she looked over at it, trying to make out what it was. Two platforms rose up on either side of a gleaming base made of pale stone, with…

It was the executioner stone.

Gallows.

As they approached, Honaaz stiffened in his saddle. "What is that?"

He pointed, and she saw a small collection of buildings far to the right, tucked almost to the edge of the forest. The homes were lit from within, and there was a familiar sound of music from it. She knew the song, and she would even be able to hum the words to it if she was pressed to do so.

"That's the hegen," Kanar said. "They don't live in the city."

"Witches?" Honaaz asked.

"They aren't witches," Lily said. As soon as she did, she realized that she might've been far too emphatic with that comment. Kanar looked over to her, and her hand went to her pouch, toward her own collection of prizes, when she glanced over to the hegen. "Witchcraft is violent."

"The hegen can be violent," Kanar said.

Honaaz glanced toward her, and Lily shrugged.

Seeing the hegen village outside of the main part of the city brought back too many memories. She could easily remember the look on Ezra's face when she had left. She could remember the sound of the songs that had been sung as she'd departed. She could remember the promises she had made, and the promises she had not kept.

Kanar kept moving, but she found her gaze drifting toward the hegen section.

Then she saw movement.

"There's someone out here," Jal said.

"They must've had an execution recently," Kanar said. "The hegen are collecting their prizes."

Lily saw several people standing along the stone, working their way around what she could only imagine was a body. The executed weren't dangling from a rope, so they must have faced the sword. There were some in this land who believed that falling to the sword was somehow more honorable. If it were to come down to it, Lily had always thought that it might be better just to face the rope, though there was some appeal to the idea that you wouldn't see the blow coming. It might be better that way.

That was how she'd been trained. Ezra had taught her how to use the art, but Tayol had taught her how to truly use it. He had been responsible for the subtle art.

As they passed the execution stone, she found her focus drawn to it.

What kind of prize might be there?

She had collected recently so she wasn't hurting for her own supplies, but something like this might be useful. Surprisingly, those who were condemned to execution often offered great value. There was something to be said about the kind of person who was willing to commit a crime. They often had a certain vibrancy in life. She hated to acknowledge that, but it was a simple truth.

"Look at them," Honaaz said. "Scurrying along there like roaches. It might be better just to smash them."

Kanar urged his horse closer to the gallows, his agitation increasing.

"What is it, Kan?" Jal asked.

"We needed to get here *before* the execution… no. Not her," he said, his voice dropping to a whisper at the end. "Gods."

What is this?

Kanar got closer to the hegen, which Lily didn't care for. He didn't need to interrupt their collection. *I wouldn't want anyone interrupting me.*

"Let them be, Kanar," she said.

He pulled up and returned to the group, saying nothing.

She had been hiding in Sanaron much like it seemed Kanar had been. At least she hadn't been hiding all aspects of herself, but enough. She'd been hiding her skill set, concealing talents that she had been trained to use. But after she'd failed the citadel, there had been no going back for her, so Lily had gone looking for other opportunities. What she'd found in Sanaron probably wasn't the kind of opportunity she should have gone after, but it was something.

Those were the troubling thoughts that stayed with her. Troubling thoughts that left her uncertain about what she might have to do to avoid Kanar Reims coming after her.

They were on the same team, at least for now. What would happen when she could no longer serve on the same team as him? What might he do?

They reached the gates to the city, and she hazarded one more look back. It seemed as if one of the hegen stood upon the executioner stone, watching them. It was easy for her to imagine Ezra there among them, though

Ezra was not from Verendal, and would have no reason to be here. Then again, there would be someone like Ezra. There always was. Someone who helped direct the people, mentored them, and tried to ensure that they were safe.

"What now?" Honaaz asked.

"Now we make our preparations," Kanar pointed at a stable.

When they reached it, they each climbed down from their saddle. Kanar took the reins of their horses, leading them away.

"You think we'll take the same horses back?" Honaaz asked.

"We can take the best horses," Jal said.

Honaaz scoffed. "I don't think there's any such thing as a best horse."

"You'll hurt their feelings if they hear you."

"They hurt my ass, so I'm not so sure that it matters," Honaaz grumbled.

Lily grinned. "And I thought I was having a hard time. You seem like you struggled even more than I did."

He looked over, glowering for a moment, before shrugging. "I'm not used to the saddle."

"Even though you were escorting Heatharn?"

"I was sitting in a wagon, not on top of a horse. I'd much prefer to be standing on a ship, looking out over the sea, and—"

"You're a sailor," Jal said, his smile spreading widely. "I should've seen that before. You have a look."

"What kind of a look is that?"

"The kind that says you might push me over the edge of the ship." Jal shrugged. "I don't know. You just have a look that screams sailor. Now that I see it, I'm not sure I can unsee it."

"I'm not a sailor any longer," Honaaz said.

"What happened?"

"Nothing happened."

Jal frowned. "Something must've happened. You were in Sanaron."

"I lost my ship. I stayed in Sanaron. That's all you need to know."

"A sailor doesn't just lose his ship," Jal said.

"Like a farmer doesn't lose his farm?" Lily asked. Honaaz glanced over to her, and she smiled at him. "I'm sure you've heard him talking about his farm a time or two. That's all he wants to talk about these days."

"That is not all I want to talk about. I have plenty of other things to share with you, including how poorly we have taken care of these creatures…" He trailed off as Kanar returned, moving carefully through the streets, his eyes darting around.

"Let's get moving," Kanar said.

"Why do you look like you're waiting for an attack?" Jal asked.

"Because I'm sure there's going to be one. We're newcomers in this city, and most of the crews in places like this will see us as a threat. As well they should."

Kanar started off, and Lily hurried to keep up with him.

"Were you followed?" she asked.

Kanar nodded to a rooftop, and she looked in the direction of his gaze.

Strangely, it was almost a comfort to be in a city like this. Now that she was here, she felt as if she were back where she needed to be—where she could explore, and where she had an advantage. Perhaps in a place like this, even a place where the hegen had a presence, she could make her way along the rooftops and scout.

Of course, that was what Kanar expected of her.

"I noticed two near the gate," he said. "A couple in an alley near the stable, though both of them turned away when I reached for my sword. I have a feeling that we have a shadow behind us even now. We need to make sure that we don't get separated."

"We aren't going to be able to find what we want to find if we're stuck with staying together."

He frowned. "You see the darkened building near the center of the city?"

She had seen it from the very first moment they'd entered the gate, as it seemed taller than most of the other buildings. "I don't know how I could miss it."

"That's where we're going. The prison."

Her brow furrowed. "There? It looks like a church."

"It was. At least once. I think. Meet me there."

She looked over to Jal, then Honaaz. They would protect Kanar in the unlikely event that he would need it.

She, on the other hand, didn't like the idea of being trapped here on the street level. And Kanar essentially gave her permission to go.

She slipped off into the shadows of the dark street. There were a few streetlamps, though they didn't cast enough light to truly illuminate the area. Shadows still stretched everywhere, and the air had a fragrance to it from the surrounding forest.

The city was still. Almost too still.

Having been in Sanaron as long as she had, she was accustomed to the steady gusts of wind and the fog that rolled in over everything. The haze made it difficult to see much, but it also hid her presence. In a place like this, there would be no real concealment—other than the darkness.

The roofline here was slightly sloped, and she suspected that she would be able to scale along it easily enough. There weren't too many roofs she couldn't traverse.

As she pulled her grappling hook out of her pouch, she saw shadows moving down the alleyway. She turned and reached for a pair of knives.

At least in Sanaron, she knew about the Dogs and some of the other teams that worked in the city, and she knew who not to offend. In Verendal, she knew none of that. She was the outsider.

The shadows faded away, though she knew that whoever was moving along the street was still there.

Lily tossed the grappling hook, making sure that it set solidly. As she scaled the side of the building, she saw someone moving beneath her.

She hurriedly scrambled onto the roof, wrapped the rope around her wrist, and then pocketed the hook. She crouched and waited for the figure to reappear.

They crept along the street.

"Where do you think you're going?" Lily whispered to herself.

She followed, already knowing the answer. They were tracking Kanar, Honaaz, and Jal.

Lily scrambled along the roof, ducking around one of the spies she noticed, before reaching the main street yet again. The shadowy form continued to trail after the other three.

Kanar wouldn't let them sneak up on him. Jal either. She wasn't sure which of them would be more dangerous in the darkness. Probably Jal, as he could pull an arrow from his quiver and fire it before anyone was even aware of what happened.

Honaaz would need to get closer. He struck her as a brawler. She had caught a glimpse of his daggers one night, though he made a point of trying to keep them concealed, as if he needed to hide his weapons from the rest of the team. If it came down to a fight...

Well, if that happened, then they were in trouble anyway. At that point, Lily might have to reveal her other gifts. She wanted to avoid that as long as possible—really, she wanted to avoid it altogether now that Kanar had shared his little secret with them.

A pair of men stepped out of an intersecting street. They had on cloaks, carried crossbows, and wore metal helms. City watch, she suspected. The shadowy form who'd been following the three drifted away.

As did Kanar and the others.

He must've known that he was being shadowed.

Lily smiled to herself as she darted along the rooftop. She encountered only one other man, and she steered clear of him. At one point, she was forced to use her grappling hook to swing across the street to the next building, but that was easy enough.

This city was different than Sanaron. Nearly half of the buildings there were made of stone. They were tall and narrow, and also brightly painted, as if to cast aside the dreariness of the fog. In Verendal, many of the buildings were made out of wood, and some of them were run-down.

From where Lily was up high, the smells of the city began to permeate around her. She looked for the source of that stench but found nothing. Just the foulness.

A river stretched through the midpoint of the city. A few barges moved along it, and other ships were moored. Her gaze followed the direction of the river, out of the city, and then beyond. She didn't know her geography well enough to know where the river connected, though she suspected that it might even eventually reach the sea. If Honaaz was a sailor, maybe that was why Kanar had brought him along.

From what she could see, the city stretched upward, gently rolling up the hillside, though not quite as steep as the hills found in Sanaron. In the far distance, she caught sight of what had to be the palace. A wall surrounded it, and more lights glowed in it than in any other part of the city. It was like its own island in the midst of Verendal. A city within the city. She wondered whether it truly was impossible to reach.

That's not the job.

If she were to get distracted, she could easily end up endangering the mission. She'd done that enough times when she had been working with a different team.

She tore her gaze away and crept her way toward the prison. By the time she reached it, she had refocused her mind.

Down below, she caught a glimpse of Kanar and Honaaz and Jal. Each of them had taken up a different position to scope out the prison.

She checked for some alternative entry point. Perhaps they might be able to scale a wall, enter through a window, and then exit the same way.

The building itself stretched several stories high. It was all made of black stone, something that looked almost somber to her from here. There were windows, though if Kanar was right and this was an old church, they may have been added later. They were small cutouts with crisscrossing bars of metal worked into them. She wouldn't be able to slip through those. They might be able to cut through the windows, or if she were to reveal her art, she might be able to blast through, but there wouldn't be anything subtle about it.

She wasn't sure if going up would even be possible. The top of the building came to a point, and she didn't see any way for her grappling hook to hold.

Lily picked her way carefully around the entire prison. Each angle was the same. It would not be easy to break into, which meant it would be even more difficult to break out of.

Kanar probably had some plan in mind, but what?

She reached for her pouch. She had several different items that might work here. The windows were small, but they were large enough that she could set something into one of them, activate it, and explode an opening. They might be able to find the person and get them out of the prison quickly enough that they wouldn't even have to worry about pursuit.

All of that depended on her ability to work quickly. Not only that, it depended on her willingness to reveal what she could do.

At what point would Kanar grow angry? Lily could claim that she had bought her prizes from the hegen, but he was too smart to believe a lie like that. Which meant that she might be forced to show him what she could do.

Maybe it was time.

A soft whistle carried up to her.

Lily climbed down, then pulled the hook back to her before turning to Kanar.

"Let's go talk about the plan," he said.

"Do you have a way in?" Lily whispered.

He shook his head. "And from your expression, I doubt that you do either."

"Well, there might be one thing we can try," she said, "but I'm not thrilled with it."

"Let me tell you my thoughts first," Kanar said.

She nodded. All that mattered was that they succeed. In the end, it might come down to her revealing her secret.

Regardless of what that cost her.

Chapter Fifteen

KANAR

The room was small, which Kanar appreciated. Better to look poor and unassuming. Weary travelers passing through, looking for a place to sleep, before moving on again.

At least, until he had a handle on how the city felt. It had been too long since he'd been here.

Too long since he had seen Morgan.

He'd tried not to think about her on their journey but had found it increasingly difficult. When he slept, her face appeared in his dreams, unbidden, and her smile a warning to him. As if she knew he was coming, and as if she wanted to taunt him with his betrayal.

Kanar sat on a stool, the dim light of a lantern glowing near them. There were two narrow beds, and extra blankets that he had been forced to pay for, but enough room for all four of them.

"You can't be serious," Honaaz said, looking over to Lily. "I'd rather sleep outside the city."

"You go ahead," Kanar said. "If it bothers you so much to sleep next to a woman, then feel free to lie out there under the stars. You will get your cut."

Honaaz clenched his jaw. "That's not it."

"I'm not going to bite," Lily practically purred. Honaaz stiffened, as if he were afraid that she might actually bite him.

Under different circumstances, Kanar might be amused by this turn of events. He hadn't expected Honaaz to be the kind of person who'd be so bothered by sleeping in the same room as a woman. Lily, though, wasn't just any woman, and he suspected that Honaaz was completely aware of just how dangerous she was.

"Let's talk through this," Kanar said. "We need to get into the prison. Then we need to make sure that we can get out."

"I was thinking about that," Lily said.

Honaaz frowned at her.

"There are hegen outside the city," she continued. "We could go to them, see what they might be able to offer us, and—"

Kanar shook his head. "We are not going to the hegen."

"You're going after her because of her connection to magic, right?" Lily asked. "It seems like you would want to use whatever resources we can. The hegen might have magic that would let us break in. Why be afraid of it?"

"We aren't using the hegen," he said again. "Anything we do incurs a debt to them."

"That's what you're afraid of? Some hegen debt? I can tell you that they aren't going to make you pay any debt you can't afford."

"You have experience with them?" Jal asked. He sat with his legs crossed on one of the small, narrow beds, his bow and quiver resting on the wall behind him. He looked far more at ease than the rest of them did.

"Everybody has some experience with the hegen," Lily said, waving her hand.

"I don't intend to use them," Kanar said harshly. "Especially the ones near Verendal." Kanar had heard stories about those hegen, about their connections to the king. "We have other resources we can try."

He hadn't been in Verendal during the attack, but it had been one of the first places that had come to know the dangers of witchcraft. The city had nearly fallen. Even the hegen would be compelled to avoid some repeat of that.

"We have a little time," he said. "Not much, but enough. I want Jal and Honaaz to work with some of the underground here. There are crews that run through Verendal, much like they do in Sanaron. Find them. Get information without revealing the reason we came, and see what you can come up with."

"Why the two of us?" Honaaz asked.

"Because you look like a criminal," Jal said, grinning at him. "And because I'm able to calm down any crew leader we might meet."

"I don't look like a fucking criminal."

Jal shrugged. "No. You look perfectly safe."

"Safer than the rest of you," Honaaz muttered.

Lily smiled at him, and he tensed again. Kanar had been tempted to send her with them as well, at least to keep an eye on them, but perhaps he needed to keep Lily with him.

"We can start tonight," Kanar said. "Spend a few hours, and if we don't find anything by the morning, I'm going to reach out to see if I have any contacts who might help us."

"I thought you didn't have anybody left at the Realmsguard," Lily said.

"I don't."

It was an option he didn't really want to use, but it might not be something he had much choice in.

"So you want us to go now?" Jal said.

"Unless you're too tired," Kanar said.

"Oh, I'm not too tired for that. Besides, I got plenty of rest on the ride here." He looked over to Honaaz. "What about you, big man? Didn't you get a little rest on the ride?"

"No," Honaaz growled.

Jal snickered and got to his feet. He grabbed his bow and quiver, then headed to the door. "Come along. We have some danger to explore."

Honaaz grumbled again but got up and followed Jal out of the room, closing the door behind them. When he was gone, Lily's grin faded.

"What did you tell him about me?" she asked.

"Why?" Kanar said.

"Because he's been looking at me like I might cut his throat."

"Why do you care?"

"We're supposed to be on the same team, right? I don't need him scared of me. At least, not *yet*." She winked as she said it.

Kanar snickered. "I thought you had your pretty florist back in Sanaron."

"Oh, I do," Lily said, getting to her feet and stretching. She held one hand on her pouch, where he knew she had her grappling hook, along with some of her other supplies that helped her sneak along the rooftops. Probably a dozen knives, as she always seemed to have more knives than he could count. "But Honaaz isn't exactly ugly himself."

Kanar snorted.

She patted him on the arm as she slipped past him. "Don't worry, Kanar. You're pretty enough as well."

"Thanks."

"But a little too dour for me." She reached for the door. "I'm going to make my way through the city. I might keep an eye on the boys."

"You're not to go to the hegen."

She hesitated, pausing with her hand on the doorknob. "It might become necessary."

"It might," he agreed, and hated that he had to. "I'd like to find another way."

Lily held his gaze. Conflicted emotions flickered behind her eyes—probably irritation at his stubbornness, more than anything else. Then she nodded to him and stepped out into the hall. He didn't even hear her walk down the hallway. Not like the thundering of steps he had heard from Honaaz.

Kanar was left alone in the room, though he wasn't going to stay here for very long. They all had a role to play. His role, when it came down to it, would be not only to break in to find Morgan, but also to get her out and then extract information.

It was hard to plan for after.

He had some thoughts about where they might need to go and how they might get there, but he wasn't entirely sure whether those thoughts were reliable. Kanar had to push aside the emotion, along with his own personal issues that played into it, and focus solely on the job in front of him. He had to, otherwise he was going to fail.

More than that, he couldn't deny that he had a certain curiosity and desire to see Morgan again. Regardless of how she had betrayed him.

He checked his sword, made sure that he had a couple of knives on him, and then walked out of the room, down the stairs through the inn, and back out into the street.

At least they had a place to regroup.

As much as he wanted to believe that Jal and Honaaz would find information, he was doubtful. Jal truly could soothe anyone, but who in the city would have any information about breaking into the prison?

Honaaz was there mostly for protection. And to look intimidating.

At least for now.

As Kanar slipped through the streets, his gaze immediately went to familiar buildings. When he had been here as a part of the Realmsguard the first time, he had escorted the king, guiding him along some of these very same streets and ensuring his safety. When he had returned a second time—the only other time he'd been in Verendal—he had escorted someone else.

Kanar wondered why she'd been brought here of all places. Maybe it had something to do with the protections of the city. It was far enough removed from the capital, and from King Porman, that there wouldn't be much danger to him. But if she had been responsible for the Alainsith slaughter… What had she intended to do?

He had to know. The job was already going to be difficult.

And there was also what Kanar might have to reveal about himself in order to succeed in it. People who believed him dead would learn otherwise. Though if he hadn't taken the job, there was a real possibility that Edward would have rendered Kanar's pensioner's mark useless anyway. If somebody learned where he was, they would change the mark and require a new one. So far, Kanar had managed to use his mark to draw his pension, and he hadn't needed to worry about attracting any real attention to himself. It allowed him to live more comfortably, though not without some measure of guilt. Still, he had earned that pension, regardless of what else had happened.

He breathed out a sigh as he reached the river running through the city. A series of small barges carried cargo down to Verendal, where they then turned around and headed back upstream. Very few other ships traveled through here. It was simply too difficult to navigate the narrow waterway.

Kanar had spent time patrolling along the river, checking ships that came in and out, looking for any sign of danger. That had all been before his time serving in the Order, before he had chased magic.

In his mind, he knew what he needed to do, even if he didn't want to.

Why am I waiting?

There wasn't an answer for that. He was waiting because he hoped to find an alternative, but there wasn't going to be one.

It might be late, but that only meant that anything he did would come as a surprise.

He crossed the river and headed into one of the city's nicer sections. The locals knew the names of these districts, but only some of the parts of the city nearest the wall were truly run-down. Everything else sort of blended together.

At one point, Kanar thought that he'd been followed. He started to slow so that he could give whoever might be after him a chance to catch up. *Let them try.* His hand hovered near the hilt of his sword, ready, but nothing ever came of what he'd sensed.

A patrol of Archers—the city watch in places like Verendal—marched in the distance. Kanar moved to the side of the street to avoid detection. Kanar wasn't sure what they would need to do to get into the prison, but he knew he didn't need the guard alerted to his presence.

I'm the one with the reputation.

At least here.

In Sanaron, and in other places, the entire team had a reputation. There wasn't anything wrong with that. A little notoriety could be useful, especially with the kind of jobs they pulled. Malory had encouraged it.

The rumors about Jal had always intrigued Kanar. Most thought him an oddity. With his tall stature, affinity for all animals, and easy smile, too many people were quick to judge him as a little slow. That was to Kanar's benefit, and Jal's. The man *was* odd, but he was also useful, which was all Kanar cared about.

Then there were the rumors about Lily. So many of them were fantastical enough that Kanar had started to think that she'd spread many of them herself. Sorting through the stories, it was easy enough to get to the heart of the matter, that she was quick with her knives and could climb better than any acrobat. But some of the other stories Kanar had heard about her—including one where she'd taken on an entire merchant ship just to get to the chocolate they were moving—were obviously fabrications. One of the Dogs' higher-ups had claimed Lily had made his little toe disappear. Not chopped off – just vanished. Clearly hadn't wanted to admit being beaten by a girl. The rest of the Dogs apparently felt the same, because the man was replaced by someone just as useless named Rayl within a week.

Honaaz was the easiest for Kanar to read at least.

The street near him had become familiar. The homes were spread out, many surrounded by lawns. There were more patrols here. The Realmsguard would never take on a private commission like that, but the Archers made so little that the king couldn't fault them for wanting a chance to earn a little extra coin.

The target was a home at the end of the street. The last time he'd been here, Kanar had spent an anxious evening visiting with his old commander in his retirement home. Now the decision came down to betraying the man who'd forged him into the soldier he'd become.

If it came down to betraying the king, Kanar didn't expect his old commander to share anything with Kanar at all. If their situations were reversed, Kanar wouldn't reveal anything that would potentially pit him against Reyand. But their situations weren't reversed. At this point, he was no longer sure what role he had within the kingdom.

That wasn't true, though. Kanar knew what role he had. He had made his choice long ago. He had left Reyand.

And hadn't completed the mission.

Part of him felt as if he still owed that. Not because he'd felt strongly, though there was a part of him that did feel as if what he had done, and the reasons behind it, had been beneficial—even if the king did not want to eradicate all magic, which was what Kanar had advocated.

Morgan was the one who pained him the most. He had lost his sister to witchcraft, something Morgan had known about. So when she betrayed him, he had taken it harder than he should have. The Blackheart, now the broken hearted.

He had revealed the story of his sister's death during one of their late-night conversations, time spent sharing secrets about themselves over wine or ale. At least, Kanar had been the one to share secrets about himself. He now wondered how much of what he'd learned of Morgan had been real.

Kanar approached the home. When another pair of Archers made their way toward him, he slunk back and scanned for access points. There was a door in the back of the home that led through the kitchen. It wouldn't take much for him to pick the lock or break the door down, though that would just set Belathin, against him. He could try the main entrance, but if he wasn't careful, he would draw the attention of the Archers.

Kanar eyed the home again.

It was a sizable place, the kind that a man of Belathin's stature would not normally be able to afford. He must have retired in considerable comfort, though maybe his pension had provided that. Kanar's own pension had not afforded him such luxury, though he didn't really know what something like this would cost in a place like Verendal. Maybe he overestimated.

Or perhaps Belathin wasn't nearly as ethical as Kanar had long believed. He found that difficult to believe, especially as Belathin had made a point of lecturing Kanar about serving the throne, not himself.

Kanar had been a new recruit to the Realmsguard, already proving his prowess. In order for him to reach the Realmsguard in the first place, he'd needed to demonstrate fighting skill, something that had always come naturally to him. The other aspect of his training had been the more difficult one. His commanders had wanted them to think for themselves, despite what Morgan had accused him of when they had first met. That was why the Realmsguard were so deadly. Not because they blindly followed command, but because they proactively looked for dangers and weaknesses, and were able to strategize. But Belathin had been more traditional. He believed in doing things right the first time.

It was why Belathin had been among his greatest instructors.

Kanar shook his head. He knew what Belathin would say: "Make a choice, stick with it, and see it through to the end."

But that advice was not enough. Sometimes, when you made a choice, you had to reevaluate. If you stuck with a wrong choice, you could overlook the opportunity to make it right.

After another patrol moved past, Kanar crossed the street, and leaped over the fence surrounding the home. Once inside the fenced-in garden, he paused long enough to get his bearings, then darted toward one of the darkened sections at the north end of the home, the break-in already organized in his mind.

Make a choice, stick with it, and see it through to the end.
Kanar had made his choice.
Now he had to see it through.

Chapter Sixteen

KANAR

Kanar clung to the trellis for dear life and tried not to look down. This was really a job for Lily, not for him. She could have scrambled up to the locked window without making a sound, and without running the risk of the trellis breaking, which it was threatening to do with the way it trembled beneath him. Would it crack before he even had a chance to reach the lip of the windowsill?

Here Kanar had thought that he could force his way in, but so far all he'd managed to do was scrape his hands on the vines' thorns. Gloves protected his flesh a little, but not nearly enough.

Another patrol marched up the street. Kanar leaned in, staying motionless, already thinking through his options if he had to fight. He didn't like the idea of cutting down a pair of simple Archers, but for a job like this, perhaps it would be necessary. Sometimes a job was more important than a man. In this case, knowing what he did about the job, there was a greater good at stake. The Archers might not know it, but he did.

Thankfully, they continued. Even so, there were too many Archers around. In any other part of the city, other than the palace itself, there would just be a singular patrol. How much had these men been paid?

Kanar thought about the additional crossbows he'd noticed since entering Verendal, on top of the usual Archer uniform of leather jackets and metal helms.

Perhaps it was more about a show of force.

Kanar hadn't spent much time in the kingdom following the war. He didn't think that a place like this had suffered that much, but perhaps he was wrong. Perhaps this city had struggled more than he had known. Most cities in Reyand had struggled somewhat, especially when it came to dealing with the threat of witchcraft and the dangers that were inherent within it, but he had thought that since Verendal had faced the attack early that they would have already fallen back into old routines. Maybe that was his mistake.

When he was convinced that the Archers had not turned around, Kanar continued scaling the trellis. His foot slipped, and thorns pierced his gloves, drawing blood.

There wasn't anything for him to do but to keep moving.

He reached the lip of the windowsill. He used a knife to pry it until he heard a soft *click*. He tugged on it a few times until the window opened.

Kanar hesitated. The air that drifted out to him had a bit of a sweet fragrance, likely from flowers that had come from the garden outside the home. No sounds came from inside.

Kanar pulled himself in through the window, crouched, and looked around at the bedroom he was in. The bed was made, and there was a collection of neatly arranged stuffed animals on top. A basin rested on a table next to the bed, the metal catching some of the moonlight that streamed in through the window. On another table sat a vase filled with slightly wilted flowers.

He hadn't known that Belathin had children.

I'm not going to use them.

But wouldn't he? That was what the Blackheart would have done.

That's not me any longer.

Kanar carefully pulled the window closed but left it slightly ajar so that he could sneak back out through it if he were to need to. He moved forward to the door, which was slightly cracked, where he paused to listen.

Now he did hear voices. They weren't far from him. A man, who Kanar suspected was Belathin, and a woman. His wife?

When he had visited before, Kanar had never even considered that Belathin might have a family. Commanding officers were seen as stately figures removed from personal desires. Beyond reproach.

Kanar couldn't tell the content of the argument. The words weren't clear, only the tone.

Finally, the disagreement ended, and he heard the sound of footsteps. Kanar kept his eye to the small crack in the doorway, and he watched as a woman dressed in a pale blue evening gown slipped away. He only caught a glimpse of graying hair hanging loose before she disappeared down the stairs.

He waited again, wondering if perhaps Belathin might go after her, but heard no sign of it. Or anything else.

It was time to move.

Kanar crept down the hall, pausing each time he thought he heard a sound. A floorboard creaked beneath his foot, and he hesitated before moving toward the room at the end. It was the only one that had any light in it, at least on this level. From what he had seen outside, the lower-level rooms were illuminated as well, though he didn't know if anyone was still awake now.

When he reached the door, he paused with his hand on it for just a moment.

The door was slightly ajar, and he saw the outline of a desk occupying much of the middle of the room. He caught a hint of movement inside.

"I said I had nothing more to discuss, Mary."

Kanar stepped into the room and closed the door behind him, keeping his back to it. One hand hovered over the hilt of his sword as he half prepared for there to be someone else in the room, but it was only Belathin.

The man looked much like Kanar had remembered from several years before. His graying hair was still cut short, and his eyes had the crispness that Kanar had long come to attribute to a man accustomed to command. But there was a sallowness to his cheeks, as if age had finally started to catch up to him. When Kanar had joined the Order, he had always been strong, and had always been intimidating.

Now he looked withdrawn.

Belathin jumped to his feet, a knife in one hand. "Who are you? What are you doing—?" His eyes widened. "Reims?"

Kanar held his hands up. "I just came here to ask a few questions."

Belathin jerked his head around, his gaze going to the door. "What did you do to her?"

"Nothing. I came in through the window."

Belathin glanced behind him to his own window, a measure of weakness and unpreparedness that was new to Kanar. The old Belathin would never have turned his back on a potential threat.

"I just came to ask you a few questions," Kanar said.

"If they find you here, you know what's going to happen."

"I know. It's more important than me."

Belathin glanced to the door again. Kanar hadn't moved, though his hand remained close to the hilt of his sword, ready to unsheathe it. He hadn't the need. Not yet. This man posed no threat to him. Well, not in his current iteration. If Belathin were to lunge at him, Kanar wouldn't hesitate to defend himself.

"What do you want?" Belathin said. "You've been out of the kingdom for years. There were some who thought you'd died, but I knew better. Kanar Reims would not die so easily."

"I'm still working on behalf of the Order."

"Are you?" Belathin asked. He raised the knife, looking as if inclined to throw it, before thinking better of it and stuffing it into his belt. He shifted and then spun, raising something off the floor that Kanar had not quite anticipated.

A crossbow.

It was already drawn and aimed at him.

Perhaps Kanar had underestimated his old mentor.

His sword would not be of any use against a crossbow bolt, short of trying to cut down the bolt before it struck him—a movement that wasn't guaranteed success. He could reach for one of his knives, but he'd have to either flick one of the knives into Belathin's shoulders or incapacitate his hand before he fired.

Then there was the last possibility.

Kanar twisted, drawing a knife and flicking it in one fluid movement.

Belathin didn't have a chance to react, though he jerked his hand back as soon as the knife stuck into the table. It had cleaved neatly through the crossbow drawstring.

Kanar strode forward, grabbed the knife, and slipped it back into his belt sheath.

Belathin glanced down at his crossbow, shaking his head slightly. "You could've killed me."

"Would you have hesitated to fire on me?"

"No. The bounty on you—"

"The bounty should never have been placed on me. And that's why I had to do what I did."

Faking his death had been easy. Disappearing from the Realmsguard had been harder than he'd expected.

Belathin sank into his chair and looked at the crossbow again. He shrugged, mostly to himself, and lowered the weapon to the floor. A flicker of a question crossed his brow, as if he was not quite certain whether he wanted to grab for his knife again. Instead, he peered up at Kanar. "You're mistaken if you think that I could have any power in helping to remove that. I'm retired, or haven't you noticed?"

"I know," Kanar said.

"Then why did you come here? To taunt me? Or did the great Kanar Reims decide that it was time to get vengeance for some perceived slight?"

"No." Kanar grabbed a chair that was next to the desk and took a seat. One hand stayed in Kanar's pocket, close enough to the knives. "I need to get a prisoner out of Declan prison."

"So you are after her," Belathin said, getting to his feet.

Kanar leaned forward, and Belathin simply nodded to the fading fire in the hearth. When Kanar did nothing, Belathin threw a log on, then prodded at it for a moment before returning to sit, settling his hands on the desk, as if they were simply two friends visiting.

"I told you that I'm still working on behalf of the Order," Kanar said.

"If you were, you wouldn't have come for her."

He wasn't sure how to explain it. "Did you know there was a recent council with the Alainsith? From what I've heard, a dozen were slaughtered."

Belathin frowned and blinked slowly. "Where?"

"I'm not exactly sure, but someone has collected the blood of the Alainsith, and they will use it soon enough."

"You would have me believe that you have access to resources that the king does not?" Belathin said.

"Are you still so connected to the king that you know what he knows?"

It wasn't meant to be a hurtful question, but he knew the answer. Belathin was a pensioner. In that regard, he was not all that dissimilar from Kanar.

Belathin scoffed. "I'm still well connected enough to know when an old recruit is trying to lie to his commander."

"You haven't been my commander for a long time," Kanar said. He took a deep breath. "I need to know how to get into Declan prison, and I need to break the prisoner out so that we can keep the witchcraft practitioners from succeeding. If I don't, it is likely going to be worse than it was before."

"I'm well aware," Belathin said.

"If they did manage to slaughter a dozen Alainsith, the power in that blood…"

Kanar didn't need to finish, and he could see from Belathin's gaze exactly what he thought of the proposition. It would be dangerous. They both knew it would be. Everything that Kanar had heard suggested that the priests were still active, which meant that an attack like this was far more dangerous and insidious than what they had faced before.

Witchcraft had been powerful in the past. The priests who'd practiced it had used their connections and their wealth to abuse the people of the kingdom and draw power out. Yet they had never succeeded in acquiring anything as powerful as access to Alainsith magic.

"Why would I even think that you were telling me the truth?" Belathin said.

"Because I *am* telling you the truth," Kanar insisted. "I have no reason to lie about this. And I would have no reason to return to Verendal, if this was not true."

Belathin leaned back, crossing his arms over his chest. His eyes were clear, and there was a slight twitch in the corners of them. "We both know you had another reason to return."

"I didn't come back for her."

"It seems to me that you did."

Kanar wanted to argue that he'd had no desire to return for Morgan, but was that the truth? He felt conflicted when it came to her. Angry, for the most part, but it was more than that.

He wanted answers, and closure, but he'd had the opportunity to get that already, and nothing came of it. She didn't want to see him, likely no more than he wanted to see her. And even if she were to want to see him, he didn't know what he might do or how he might react if he had that opportunity.

"She's the only person I think can help," Kanar said.

"The only person happens to be the one person who led you to betray your oath?"

Irritation flickered within Kanar, though it often did when he thought about betraying any oath. He had not done that. At least, he never viewed it that way, but that didn't matter. What mattered was how others saw it, and that was not in his control.

Kanar stomped forward. "Are you going to tell me what I need to know or not?"

"There's the famous Reims temper," Belathin said.

"It's not a temper, it's asking a question. I'm looking for information so that I can stop something terrible from happening in the kingdom. I know you may not care about it, but I do."

Belathin stiffened. "How dare you accuse me of not caring about what happens in the kingdom. I have been here and served far longer than you, and I have never betrayed my oath." He gathered himself before forcing a smile. "Besides, it doesn't matter. You won't be able to reach the prison. The Hunter has it locked down too tightly. If you think the king favored the Blackheart, you've never met the Hunter."

Kanar searched his mind for any reference he knew to

someone referred to as the Hunter. A soldier? He didn't think so. Soldiers didn't generally have nicknames. Somebody working in a crew? Kanar didn't think that a crew leader would have any desire to work with the king.

Which meant that it had to be somebody else, but somebody still affiliated with the crown. And there was one person in Verendal that he remembered.

"You mean the executioner," Kanar said.

Belathin shrugged. "You aren't going to get very far. Not with him around."

"Why? Who is he?"

"The only way you can get into Declan. Unfortunately, he's not even expected back in Verendal until late."

That was a problem. Kanar's plan relied upon the executioner.

"I don't need an executioner to get in the way, anyway," Kanar said.

"Then you might be disappointed. I'm sure he'll be back in time for her execution tomorrow." Belathin's tight smile pulled his lips into a sneer. "And if you go after him, you'll never get away. He has a reputation for a reason. He'll chase you until he captures you, and then he'll bring you back to ensure that you face the sentencing you deserve."

A soft thud came from behind the door, and Kanar frowned.

The sound was unexpected, at least to him. From the look on Belathin's face, he had anticipated something.

Kanar got to his feet, leaving his sword sheathed, though he reached for one of his knives, glancing toward the fire. White smoke plumed upward. *A damn signal.* And Kanar had missed it.

"You called for help."

Belathin smirked. "I'm not helpless here."

"No. Maybe you're not. But it seems to me that you intend to betray the king."

"That's rich coming from you."

"I'm the one who's here intending to serve the king."

Kanar looked behind him, grabbed a knife, and flicked it with a quick spin of his wrist. The blade sunk into the door, pinning it to the frame.

He shoved Belathin forward and jerked the window open.

"They will know you're in the city," Belathin said.

"It doesn't matter."

"Why are you doing this?"

"I told you," Kanar said, "I intend to stop another attack. I will do all that I can to ensure that witchcraft doesn't destroy everything I cared about."

"It already did, Reims."

Kanar couldn't even argue with that.

He looked down to the street, saw that he had an opening, and began to climb.

By the time he had worked his way through the city toward the city gate, he had to slip past a few of the Archers, though that wasn't difficult. They weren't skilled soldiers, not like the Realmsguard, and he didn't worry that any would pay any attention to him.

If they did...

Kanar wasn't sure that he was prepared to take out Archers. That felt as if he were going beyond a line he wasn't sure he wanted to cross.

And he'd have to be careful he didn't let the others do the same.

Belathin had given him the idea about how to find the executioner. There was only one way into Verendal, and that was through the massive, gated entrance to the city. Wait, watch, and then act.

A line of shops near the gate was the perfect place to wait. The city had a maze of alleys running through it, so he could just duck into one of them and linger.

How will I recognize him?

Executioners tended to have a look. Kanar didn't know this man but had heard rumors about him. He'd find him.

Once settled into a darkened alley, he leaned against the wall to a general store. The alley stunk of dampness and decay, reminding him of too many nights spent chasing witchcraft throughout the kingdom. Kanar had wanted to forget those days but coming back into the kingdom reminded him of who he'd been. The jobs in Sanaron had used the skills but had let him be someone other than the Blackheart. That wasn't who he was any longer.

Can I ever be someone different?

He'd noticed several people coming through the gate, though none of them looked like they could be the executioner. Kanar could wait. He had practice.

As the time passed, he wondered about the rest of his team, curious what they were doing. Jal would probably have taken Honaaz somewhere to make their plans, likely listening to some hunch of his. And Lily was waiting on him.

A hooded figure stepped through the gate leading a wide-bodied mare. The man was tall and solid, with close cropped brown hair and intense eyes seemed to sweep over and see everything—including the alley. They lingered for a moment but didn't seem to see him. Kanar had been careful about how he positioned himself so that no one *could* see him.

That has *to be the executioner.*

When the man walked past, Kanar made his move.

He stepped out of the alley. The man turned, as if aware that Kanar had been there. His brow furrowed a moment, then his gaze flicked down the street.

Looking for Archers.

Kanar darted toward him, one of his knives unsheathed.

The executioner's expression never changed.

This was a man who didn't fear. Had Kanar not known better, he would have thought him a soldier—and a skilled one. Even surprised, he showed no sign of it.

When the hilt of Kanar's knife slammed into his temple, knocking him unconscious, his expression changed. Not to fear but to curiosity.

Belathin's words came back to him: *He has a reputation for a reason.*

For the first time on this job, Kanar wondered if he'd made a mistake.

Chapter Seventeen

HONAAZ

"This is a waste of our fucking time," Honaaz said as he stood outside the tavern.

Jal wore a wide grin that Honaaz was tempted to smack off of him, but despite this, Honaaz found himself warming up to the kid the longer they'd been spending time together. He thought of Jal as a kid, though Honaaz didn't know if he was that much younger than him. It was difficult to tell his age.

"It's not a waste of time," Jal said. "We're looking for any way that we might be able to get into the prison. That's what Kanar wants from us."

"He doesn't know what the fuck he wants," Honaaz said.

The prison was stout. He'd seen places like that before. They weren't made by a commoner, but rather by somebody who understood the stone in ways that laypeople could not. The place was far too tough for them to breach. And somehow Reims thought that they would just be able to break in and out?

It would be easier to make it inside the palace.

After learning about the palace jewels, Honaaz couldn't help but feel his attention drawn in that direction. He wouldn't be able to pull a job like that on his own, but his mind already started to work through what would be involved. He'd seen the protections in the city. The guards here didn't seem particularly adept, and they were small enough that a good bash against their skull might bring them down pretty quickly. And with someone like Jal with him, somebody who was quick with the bow and skilled with his aim, Honaaz didn't think it would be that difficult. Take down a few targets, slip inside, and let him go to work.

Of course, a job like that would be much easier if Reims was involved. He'd seen the man fight. The rumors were not just rumors. Reims was deadly, and far more dangerous than anybody he'd ever seen before.

And then there was Lily. He tried not to think about her. He didn't want her to even know that he was thinking about her. It would only draw her attention, and it might end up with her jabbing one of those knives into his belly while he was sleeping.

It was definitely best that he not think about her at all.

"I don't know," Jal said. "I'm getting a little frustrated with all these different crew leaders myself. That's five now without answers."

Honaaz found himself smiling. The tall bastard getting frustrated? He didn't know the kid very well, but he had a sense that Jal wasn't the kind of person to get upset easily. Honaaz couldn't deny that he had spent far too much time with hotheaded men. When sailing, there were too many who got upset easily. He saw value in a man who could keep control of his emotions when the situation called for it.

"We can go back," he said.

"I think we're going to have to, but I keep hoping we will... Wait. Is that Lily?" Jal pointed, and Honaaz looked in that direction.

Sure enough, Lily crept along one rooftop. She looked like little more than a darkened smudge, but knowing what to look for made it easier for him to spot her.

"Don't look," Honaaz said. "It's bad luck."

"For her, or for us?"

"Probably both," he muttered. "But we don't want to draw any attention to her. She needs to finish her job."

"I didn't figure you to be all that concerned about her."

"I'm concerned that she might know we've revealed her presence."

If she thought they were responsible for her getting caught, or even being noticed, Honaaz wasn't going to be the one to have to explain what had happened. He wasn't going to be the one to have to tell her why she'd failed.

No. It was far better that he just look the other way, make it seem as if he wasn't aware of her presence, and try to put some distance between them.

"Are you afraid of her?" Jal asked.

Honaaz tensed, flexing his arms and balling up his fists. "No."

Jal smirked. "You *are* afraid of her. You know, she might be skilled, but she's little," he said, holding his hand up waist high.

"You don't have to be big to be terrifying," Honaaz said.

Jal grinned. "I won't tell her she scares you. You'll have to work through it, though. If we're to do this together, you and her are going to have to deal with whatever's going on."

Honaaz grunted. "There's nothing going on."

"Maybe not yet, but I see the way you're looking up at her."

How was he looking up at her? He shouldn't be, that much was true. He should avoid looking in her direction, not just out of safety for himself and for her. But she did intrigue him. He couldn't deny that. How could somebody so small be so powerful and deadly?

"Let's just get on with it," Honaaz said.

They pushed open the door and stepped inside. Taverns in this world were all the same. They served food and drink, and some offered music, but it was the gambling that Honaaz cared about. He loved to sit and play cards, though no one in these lands really understood how to play. They liked games like dominoes, something that involved more chance than skill. Honaaz didn't mind that, but he preferred something to challenge him. He doubted he would find that here. They were far removed from the rest of the world, isolated as they were in this backwater part of Reyand.

The tavern was busy for this time of night. Most tables were occupied, though Honaaz didn't see anybody playing cards or dominoes. Too many people waved their hands animatedly as they spoke, most with mugs of ale in front of them. Part of the crowd had pushed to the far end of the tavern where a musician played. The music was fine, though a little rough. The singer had a nice voice, a sweet melodic sound, but the words were too fast for Honaaz's liking.

Jal took a seat at a table and leaned his back against the wall.

"Is it always like this in here?" Honaaz asked.

Jal tipped his head in a nod and grinned as a server approached. "Do you have any food?" he asked.

"Not at this time of night," the woman said. Her dress was low-cut, revealing ample cleavage. She was lovely and looked to be about ten years older than Lily. She saw him looking and flashed a grin. *Part of the ploy*, Honaaz realized.

As he looked around the tavern, he saw other servers much like her, all of them dressed similarly, drawing the notice of the men and boys. There weren't many women here other than those working.

This was the kind of place where he and Jal could find gossip, Honaaz was sure of it. Of course, this was also the kind of place where he could find men to pull a job.

If things went south with Reims, maybe he could find some men here and go after the jewels in the palace. He could then head back out to Sanaron, buy a ship, and be gone from this land. He'd finally be able to get back to the Isles.

Even if things didn't go south with Reims, that wasn't the worst plan. He needed to be gone from here. It was time for him to return home.

Not until I have my revenge.

Revenge. That's what he called it, but he wasn't sure he'd be able to get it. Answers were the most he could hope for. Only then could he find his way back to the Isles—and home.

And now he wasn't even sure he was going to be able to get that.

Honaaz realized that he'd been staring off in the

distance, and he pulled his attention back to the woman.

"He always look stupid like that?" she was asking Jal.

Honaaz blinked. This one was blunt. "Ale," he said.

"That I have. Plenty of it. A big man like you might benefit from two mugs."

Honaaz shrugged. It might be terrible and taste like piss, like too much ale in this land did. The people here liked to water it down, but that wasn't even the worst offense. Most of the places kept it cold. Who drank their ale cold?

"You have a way with people," Jal said, shifting his bow and touching his quiver. "I figured you might want to sweet-talk folks rather than trying to blast through them."

"We aren't going to be here long," Honaaz said.

"Maybe. Who knows when it comes to Kanar."

"You trust him?" He said it before he realized what he was doing. This was a man who had been working with Reims for a long time. Of course he trusted him.

"More than I've trusted anyone since I left home. I hadn't been in Sanaron for long, but I had gotten into it with the Dogs. You know how they can be."

"I don't."

"Well, they can be ruthless," Jal said. "And I didn't fit in with them. I had to either choose to work with them or against them. And in Sanaron, working against the Dogs means going against the Prophet. Can't do that, either."

Honaaz had heard of this man, but as long as he kept his head down, he didn't care who ran Sanaron. The Prophet apparently had even more control in the city than Malory, and that woman had made her influence well known. Not that Honaaz would ever visit a place like the one she ran, but a man got lonely from time to time.

"What did he do?" Honaaz asked.

"Oh, he did his Kanar thing. Kept me safe. So now I figure I owe him."

"And that's the only reason you have stayed with him?"

Lily and Reims fit, at least somewhat. They were both lethal. Jal, on the other hand, certainly was skilled with his bow, but he didn't strike Honaaz as having the same violent nature.

"Not the only reason. He needs me," Jal said with a shrug.

The server brought over a tray and dropped several mugs of ale onto the table. True to her word, she set two in front of Honaaz and gave one to Jal, who raised it and drank slowly. He grinned and then nodded.

"You can pay me now," she said.

"Oh. Sorry about that," Jal said. He fished into his pocket and drew out several coins.

She held them up. "What are these? They aren't Reyand coin."

"I'm not from Reyand," Jal said.

She laughed. "No kidding. Like I couldn't have guessed with your height and that easy smile. You come from Reyand and you lose a smile like that." Jal grinned at her again, and she shook her head. "I suppose I can take them. There's got to be a bank in Verendal that can change this."

"Silver is silver," Jal said.

The woman flashed her own smile. "I like that. Silver is silver."

She headed away, and Honaaz watched her leave.

"Should've figured that," he muttered. "If Reims doesn't want anybody to know about our presence in the city, we should have gotten local coin."

"I don't think he expected us to be here very long."

"So what happens when we find this woman?" Honaaz asked.

"Then we have to figure out where this ceremony is going to take place. And stop it."

"You think it needs to be stopped too?"

Jal shrugged, then took another sip of his ale.

Honaaz used that as an opportunity for him to take a drink, and he was pleasantly surprised at the quality of the ale. It might be a little colder than he preferred, but it wasn't too bitter and had a nice mouth feel. There was one problem with spending so many of his days on board a ship—you got to sample many of the supplies. A man came to appreciate some of the finer things, such as ale and wine. What did it matter if a cask disappeared?

"It's not so much the magic that I'm troubled by," Jal said. "I know Kanar doesn't really care for it, and I can't speak to his experiences during the war. They weren't my experience. But it's what happened that bothers me."

"So you've bought in."

"Can't say that I've done that either." Jal grinned and took another drink. "It's a job. It pays. And if it all goes well, I'm a little closer to buying my farm."

"You don't intend to stay with Reims?" That surprised Honaaz. The two of them seemed thick as thieves.

"I don't think Kanar intends to stay in Sanaron that long. I'm not sure why he stayed as long as he has. Maybe because the jobs have been good and he feels comfortable with Malory. Well, as comfortable as anyone can be with her. Or maybe he thinks that he can save Lily." Jal frowned. "Or she's trying to save Kanar." He shook his head. "Can't say that I know. It's one of the two."

Honaaz took another drink. He looked around the tavern and spotted something near him. A mark on one of the men.

"Turn slowly," he said, leaning forward and reaching for one of his daggers. He didn't draw it out, but he wanted to be ready in case he needed to. "Do you see anything there?"

"On the man nearest us?" Jal said.

"That's right."

"I… Oh. Dogs," Jal whispered.

"Right."

"We didn't think they had a branch here. It might mean they're after the same thing we are. Or they're following us."

"I thought you dealt with it."

The smile on Jal's face faltered. "I did. As much as I could."

"Then we should deal with it now," Honaaz said.

"If we do anything here, we're going to get caught, and then… Wait. Maybe that's exactly what we need to do."

"Which is what?"

"Get caught." Jal's grin spread across his face. "Isn't that a great idea?"

"You can't be serious."

"We have a chance of getting thrown into the right prison."

Honaaz stared at him. "You *are* insane."

"I'm not insane, I'm just trying to think it through. If we do this the right way, then it will give us a chance to get in, get what we need, and break out. If anyone could break out of prison, it would be Kanar."

"I thought he was on a timeline," Honaaz said. "Only a

few days here, and then we have a short time before we have to stop this ceremony. Wherever it is going to be held."

"Well, there's that." Jal leaned back, frustration evident on his face. "Maybe it's not the best idea, but I have hunch it'll work."

"Not the best?"

"I said maybe. We might need to work through the plan a little bit better. We certainly don't want to end up getting trapped and not getting out in time."

Jal actually thought they could do this? There was confidence, and then there was foolishness.

He'd been around men who were confident in their skills. When it came to Reims and his fighting ability, that confidence was certainly warranted. The same could be said about Lily. Maybe even about Jal, though he wasn't sure how much Jal would brag about himself. But getting out of a prison was something else entirely. Maybe Lily could do it. She certainly was skilled when it came to various techniques, and with her other abilities, it was possible. If there was one thing Honaaz knew, though, it was that no fucking idiot would be able to get into a prison with anything that could be used to break out of it.

"We have to come up with a different plan," Honaaz said.

"You're probably right," Jal said. He leaned back, turning his mug of ale from side to side as he looked down into it. "I just wish I had the answer."

Somebody bumped into him, and Jal looked up, smiling. His smile immediately faded.

"There you are," said a voice with a Sanaron drawl.

Shit.

Jal pushed back, but the man stood close, holding his

hand down on the chair. Jal wasn't going to be able to push away from the table. Another man stood next to him.

"Let him go," Honaaz said.

The lead man looked over. He had flinty eyes and a chiseled jaw, but not much muscle. A tattoo around his neck signified his rank within the Dogs. "It would be best if you just walked away."

"Yeah, probably," Honaaz said. "But I'm a fucking idiot."

He lunged. His dagger was already out, and he jabbed it at the man.

The Dog was quick as he twisted, releasing Jal's chair. The movement freed Jal, who suddenly scooted back from the table and kicked. Honaaz kept his focus on the first Dog and left the other one to Jal.

The man had a pair of knives in hand. The way he held them—one twisted outward, the other held down at his waist—suggested that he knew how to use them. Honaaz had been in plenty of fights with men like this before. The key was not being afraid of getting stabbed. Unfortunately for him, he *was* a little afraid. He wanted answers, not to bleed out before he had a chance to get them.

"Just step away," Honaaz said.

"Not going to do that. Where's Reims?"

Honaaz shrugged. "Probably dead."

"Good."

The Dog launched at him. Honaaz spun off to the side, but he bumped into a table. He kicked, sending the table across the room, and drove his fist up into the man's jaw. The man grunted but kept plowing forward.

He was skilled, then. Most would just drop, making themselves helpless. This man knew better than to stop the attack. The moment you stopped fighting was the moment you died.

He slashed at Honaaz, who barely moved his arm back to keep from getting cut. Another slash, and then another. Each one forced Honaaz to back away.

Jal looked to be having a little more success. He tangled with the other Dog, moving with a certain fluid grace that Honaaz would normally marvel at, but the only thing he wanted to do at this point was to knock down this fucking Dog.

The man surged toward him. Honaaz dropped his shoulder, ignored the knives, and slammed his skull into the back of the other man's head. The Dog fell.

Honaaz rubbed his forehead and smiled to himself, then started toward Jal to give him a hand.

Someone grabbed Honaaz's arms. He tried to thrash, but the grip holding him was too tight. He looked over on either side of him and saw a metal helm in each direction.

The fucking watch.

So much for keeping a low profile. How were they going to get out of this?

Two more men stormed into the room, and they grabbed Jal.

Honaaz tried to fight, but the men holding on to him were strong. He resisted the urge to fight again. As they were marched into the street, he looked over to Jal, who ignored him. Instead, his gaze was up to the sky, toward a nearby building, and he whistled several times in quick succession.

It might have been Honaaz's imagination, but he could've sworn another whistle came in return.

Chapter Eighteen

LILY

Lily sat in the small room, getting more and more annoyed. Kanar had been gone for most of the night, and she had no idea how long she would have to wait before he returned. She had no idea what would happen to Jal and Honaaz now that they been caught.

They'd be put in prison, no doubt. Maybe that was their plan all along, but if so, it would've been nice of them to give her a heads-up. Jal's whistling had helped, but not nearly enough for her to make any sort of preparation.

They had to plan for all of this, and now there was no way they were going to be able to come up with one.

Where was Kanar?

He could be so frustrating, especially with this. He had not shared much with them about his plan, though increasingly, she started to wonder if he really had much of one. Come to Verendal, break the person out of prison, and then what? Lily wasn't even sure if he had a clue after that.

It was getting late. Or early, as the case may be. Soon

the sun would come up, and then they would have to deal with the consequences of Jal and Honaaz's capture.

There would be questions, for Jal in particular. He was obviously not from Reyand. Honaaz didn't look it either, but at least there were large men like him everywhere.

She didn't know how long Honaaz would hold out if he were questioned. Jal wouldn't say anything. At least, she didn't think he would.

If they waited a day, they might have time to regroup, but there might also be time for something worse to happen.

Everything was going to fall apart.

One thousand gold. Lily had been telling herself that ever since leaving Sanaron, but the thousand gold wasn't really worth it.

She wanted to get away, sail across the sea, leave the city behind her, and find a new place for her to explore, maybe settle down. Find some pretty merchant, have a few babies, and forget about everything she'd been through.

But she couldn't leave Jal behind. Or even Honaaz.

Finally, the door opened, and a hooded figure came in. Rather, was pushed in. Kanar came behind, holding a dagger to the man's throat.

Lily jumped to her feet. "What is this?"

Kanar closed the door and shoved the man onto one of the beds. He was taller than her, though most people were, and there was a certain muscularity to him.

Had Kanar grabbed a soldier?

Maybe he had learned about what happened to Jal and Honaaz and this was his way of dealing with it.

"This is the Hunter," Kanar said.

She frowned. "Hunter?"

Kanar nodded, and he flicked his gaze around the room. "Where are the other two?"

"The city watch hauled them off. I followed them to that same prison we were—"

Kanar raised his hand, cutting her off, and she glanced over to the hooded man. This time, she really looked at him.

His clothing was high quality. The pants looked to be almost silken, and his jacket had a layer of embroidery around it, along with a crest for the king on the lapel. Some servant of the crown?

"That might work out for the best," Kanar said.

Lily gestured to the man. "What is this exactly?"

"This here is the city's executioner." Kanar strode over and jerked the hood off the man's face.

He had to be in his late twenties. Maybe a little older. He had short brown hair and hard eyes that blazed with anger as Kanar removed the gag from his mouth.

Lily had been around dangerous men before. Kanar, for example. Even Jal, under the right circumstances. This man struck her in a way she couldn't quite place. It was something she *felt*.

"You have made a grave mistake," the Hunter said.

"Probably," Kanar said. "But you're going to help us get into Declan prison."

The man looked over to him. "That's what this is about? You intend to break some friend of yours out of prison? A poor plan, especially if they were just captured."

"Not them," Kanar said. "But you're going to help us break them out of prison as well."

"Then who?"

"Does the name Morgan Raparal mean anything to you?"

To his credit, the Hunter kept his face as neutral as possible. "The war is over. You will find that the king has little tolerance for those who attempt to see its return."

Kanar snorted. "I have no interest in bringing the kingdom back into war."

"If you free her, that is what will happen."

Kanar leaned forward. "Actually, if I don't free her, I'm afraid something worse is going to happen. Is she still in Declan prison?"

The Hunter frowned. "She is. It's unusual. Normally, most female prisoners are kept in the women's prison, but her crimes were such that we were not confident we could ensure her safety. Nor ours. She is set to be executed tomorrow."

"Why the urgency?" Kanar asked.

"You don't know? I figured that you're here because she had some of the Alainsith blood on her. I suspect you know how that can be used, though we destroyed it."

Kanar fell silent.

Lily recognized the pain on his face. Kanar had come to rescue this person, and she was exactly what he feared her to be.

"He's not telling you something," Lily said.

The Hunter turned his attention fully on Lily. When he did, she realized that those eyes were the real threat. She couldn't take her own off him.

"You won't be able to get her out," the Hunter said.

"Why not?" Kanar asked.

"Because protections have been placed around her. I cannot remove them."

"What kind of protections?"

Lily thought she already understood. She'd seen the potential for that. When she'd prowled the city, she had seen other signs of it but hadn't really paid much attention to them. She should have, though. Even a few people carrying the hegen cards were more than she expected.

"The hegen," she said.

The man said nothing.

The hegen had been outside the city collecting the prizes, but they must also have a presence inside Verendal. That was rare. What reason would they have for welcoming the hegen into the city?

She didn't know, and not knowing meant that she was potentially at a disadvantage.

But the Hunter knew.

"It's a mistake to hold me here," he said.

Kanar snorted. "I've made plenty of mistakes. Especially lately."

"This one may end with you under my watch."

Did Kanar have any idea how dangerous a man this was?

"Do you even know what she did?" the Hunter asked. "She was captured leaving the site of a slaughter, where a dozen of the king's men were killed. I believe you understand the consequences of such an action."

What had Kanar gotten them into?

"I need her to stop something worse," Kanar said.

"You intend to use magic to stop… what?"

Kanar ignored him. It was a mistake, Lily knew, but she also wasn't sure how much they should reveal to this man. And what did they intend to stop? Rescue Morgan, learn how to find the Alainsith blood, but then what?

"Most believe the war over," the Hunter went on. "Very

few have seen the aftereffects. We have. In Verendal, there are still some who think to chase that kind of power. Mistakenly, I might add. They rarely understand the techniques involved. They think they can control it if they learn about it, but too often they simply torture, or worse, because they believe it will lend them something they couldn't have otherwise. Is that what you are after?"

Lily could see the barely contained anger in Kanar's eyes.

"What's your name?" she asked the Hunter.

"I will give you mine if you give me yours."

She drew a knife, quickly brandished it, and rested it on her lap. Kanar watched her, though he said nothing. "I asked a simple question," she said.

The Hunter shook his head. "Your knife doesn't scare me, if that's your intention."

"No? You don't know what I can do with it."

"And you don't know what *I* can do with it."

There was a hardness to him. Lily didn't know *what* he'd done, but she'd been around men like him before. Rough men. He didn't look like a threat—but he most definitely was one.

"His name is Finn Jagger," Kanar said. "Also known as the Hunter. Trained by Henry Meyer, former master executioner within Verendal, and assigned as master executioner following Henry Meyer's retirement."

What she really needed to know was whether he knew the hegen. Did he recognize her connection? If so, she would have to deal with him. She couldn't risk him revealing anything to Kanar before this job was over.

Jagger looked over to Kanar. "If you've heard of me, then you shouldn't have made this mistake. You will face the entire executioner court, along with King Porman himself."

From the way he said it, Lily couldn't tell which of those was the greater threat. Maybe both were. She didn't know much about the executioner court, other than that they were an arm of the king's justice in Reyand.

She looked over to Kanar. This was his plan? Grab some dangerous man, force him to help them break into the prison… and then what? What did he think they would be able to do?

Maybe Kanar didn't know. Maybe all of this was because he didn't have a good plan in place.

"We aren't going to be able to linger here too long," Lily said to Kanar. "If he's the executioner, someone is going to notice that he's gone missing before too long."

"We're going now," Kanar said.

"Great planning."

"We don't have much choice. Besides, we don't really need much from him. We just need *him*. He's our key to getting into the prison."

As much as she hated leaving like this, if there was anyone who could handle this kind of a poorly organized attack, it would be Kanar Reims. And all they were really doing was breaking into a prison, springing a few prisoners free, and then getting back out once more.

That couldn't be that hard, could it?

She knew better than to think like that, though. It absolutely could be much harder.

Kanar affixed the gag back on Jagger's mouth and slipped the hood back over his head.

Lily leaned close to Kanar and dropped her voice to a whisper. "Are you sure about this?"

"We don't have much choice."

"And this was the one you chose?"

"Again. Short timeline," Kanar said. "If we don't do this, the ceremony will finish, and then it's going to be too late."

"I get that, but…" She watched Jagger. He had some hegen connection, she was sure of it. But there was more to it than that. He had threatened to come after them.

The Hunter. Somebody didn't earn a name like that unless they really were one.

What would that mean for her?

"The only choice," Kanar said.

She sighed. "It's almost morning."

"Which is why this has to happen now. We need to get in and out before they try to sentence Jal and Honaaz—and before anyone realizes the Hunter is missing."

Lily suspected there was more to it than that, especially with the expression on Kanar's face, but she wasn't going to push him.

"Let's go." She slipped her pouch over her shoulder, patting it to make sure that all of her supplies were in place. She checked to make sure that she had enough knives. If it came down to it, she would remove Jagger before he had a chance to hunt any of them.

She glanced over to Kanar and saw the look in his eyes, and she knew that he had already come to the same decision.

He was nervous. Not that Kanar would ever admit it, but there was something about this man that unsettled him. Why? Was it only that he was an executioner, or did it have more to do with the fact that Kanar was going against his king?

They slipped through the inn and out a back door that Lily hadn't even known was here. Kanar had discovered it. That, at least, answered how he'd managed to bring the executioner into their room without drawing the innkeeper's attention. Once out on the street, she took the lead. They had chosen this inn based on proximity to the prison, so it was only a short walk before they reached it.

They stayed in the shadows once they neared. She kept an eye out for any sign of the city watch, but she didn't detect anything.

"You've brought me to Declan," the Hunter said.

"How do you know?" Lily asked, getting closer to him. He smelled slightly of mint and an oil she recognized. It had been part of her training. A couple ingested droplets would be lethal. Any more than that… Well, that had other uses.

Why does he smell like that?

"I know my prison."

She looked over to Kanar, who nodded.

"Get him across the street," Kanar said.

"And then what?"

"Then we have him unlock it. We march inside, and we get our people out."

She sighed. It could be easy. And if they did this the right way, they could even lock the executioner up inside one of the cells and slip out without anyone becoming aware.

That was, *if* they did it right.

The Hunter wasn't fighting them. That raised alarm bells in Lily's mind.

What did he know?

What was *he* planning?

She started forward, but she caught sight of a pair of men from the city watch making their way up the street. Kanar covered Jagger's mouth and pulled him back into the shadows, silencing him before he had an opportunity to call out.

Lily slipped away as well, making sure to stay near them both. When the watch had moved past, their boots loud in the quiet of the night, Kanar nodded to her.

She made her way to the door of the prison, where she paused and motioned for Kanar to follow. He pushed the executioner across the street, then positioned him in front of the door.

"Unlock it," Kanar said.

"You have my hands bound," Jagger replied.

"I'm going to untie them. Once you are freed, you'll have a pair of knives at your back."

Jagger scoffed. "I've been stabbed in the back before."

"Then you know it will hurt."

"It depends on where you stab," the Hunter said.

Lily heard the cocky confidence in his tone too.

Who had dared stab a king's executioner in the back? And what reason would there have been?

She stayed to the side of him, holding her knives, ready for him to do something that would put them in danger. To her surprise, he simply reached for the door, pulled out a ring of keys, and unlocked it. As soon as he did, Kanar tied his wrists behind him once again.

Lily breathed out a sigh of relief, then glanced around the street. There was still no sign of other guards.

Kanar shoved Jagger forward into the prison, and Lily followed.

Darkness enveloped them. And a foul odor.

During her training, Lily had come to experience many different torments. Some of them involved learning to discern odors, including simply by scent. That had been a difficult part of her training. The process had required her to get far too close to things that she would rather have run from, but it had proven valuable over the years. She was able to identify different medicines, but usually it was more valuable when she could identify poisons. In her line of work, that was far more likely.

In this case, it wasn't a matter of poisons or medicines, though there was a faint undercurrent of medicinal scent here. If she were to focus on it, Lily thought that she might be able to discern the various compounds used, but that wasn't what caught her attention.

No. It was the overwhelming, cloying smell of piss and shit and rot.

Kanar didn't seem to struggle with it. Neither did Jagger, but then again, this was his prison.

The entrance to Declan was a narrow stone hallway that led in opposite directions. Two lanterns were set into the walls on either side of the door, but the light didn't cast anything more than a dim glow. Shadows swirled, as if they were attempting to squeeze out any sense of life that might be here.

"Where is she held?" Kanar asked Jagger.

"We have a special place for her. I will show you."

Kanar shoved him forward but glanced back at Lily. In the pale light of the prison, she caught him mouthing words to her, and she knew.

She had to find Jal and Honaaz.

When they reached an intersection, Jagger directed Kanar up.

But her nose directed her down.

She took the stairs leading down into darkness. Lily's heart pounded, and she had to force it to slow, using techniques she'd learned long ago.

A man standing guard on the stairs turned toward her, but Lily was quick. She drove the side of her hand into his neck, and he crumpled. She'd been careful with the strike. She didn't necessarily mind killing the prison guards, though they weren't guilty of anything other than doing their job. It was more her concern about the Hunter—and his promise.

She couldn't shake the feeling that he would do exactly what he claimed. She didn't want to give him any more reason to come after them.

Lily crept down the stairs. Another guard stood with his back to her, one foot propped up on the wall, a knife in his hand. He was running the blade along a stone, either sharpening it or using it as a way of intimidating the prisoners.

Someone called out, and the guard started forward. Lily followed and drove her fist into his back, before chopping the edge of her hand down on the side of his neck. He fell to the ground much like the last man.

A shadow moved behind her.

She dropped low. Lily spun, bringing her knife up, and at the last second she flipped it and slammed the hilt into the guard's belly. He grunted. She jumped, swung her fist up, and caught him under the jaw. It was technique, not the size or strength of the attacker, that made the biggest difference.

The man crumpled.

Lily breathed out slowly.

Now to find her team.

She checked the guards, found a ring of keys, and hurried along the cells.

Most of them were occupied. Some of the men were haggard, with long beards and hollow eyes, but others looked as if they had not been here very long.

One of the men tried to reach for her, but she chopped down on his arm and twisted his hand before he could grab her. He jerked back, crying out.

"I don't think so," she whispered.

One of the other men called out to her, but she ignored them all. Some of them begged her to free them, others made lewd comments, and still others were seemingly talking in tongues.

She found Jal first.

He was seated in the center of his cell, legs crossed, hands resting on his thighs. He opened his eyes. "Hey there, Lily. I was wondering when you might make it in here."

"Nice clothes."

"You like them? I'm not a fan of the brown but—"

"Come on," she cut in, trying to find the one that would unlock it. None of them worked. "Damn it," she muttered.

"You can get it," Jal said. He got to his feet and stood across from her. He towered over her, and he'd already started to take on some of the prison stench.

"And here I thought you needed a bath after the last job," Lily muttered.

"Is it that bad?"

She wrinkled her nose. "It's not good."

"It's this place. It sort of gets under your skin."

The door sprang open as she finally found the right key.

Jal joined her outside. "Did you see my bow?" he asked.

"No. And if you go running off—"

Lily didn't have a chance to finish. Despite the warning she'd started to give, Jal did just that.

She shook her head. Some team they were. She slipped along the hall and found Honaaz in a cell several down from Jal's.

"Do you want to get out of here, or do you want to stay?" Lily asked him.

Honaaz frowned. "He sent you after us?"

"Kanar is a little busy. He's going after the woman."

"And then what?"

She shrugged. "Well, then I presume we're going to get out of here."

"There's nowhere."

"What do you mean?"

"Guard's key doesn't unlock the prison door from this side," Honaaz said.

"How do you know?"

"I've asked questions."

She frowned. Here they had been more concerned about getting inside, thinking that it would be a simple matter to break out. Since they'd brought the executioner with them, it should have been. Unless, of course, he had some way of preventing them from escaping.

Clever.

"There has to be another key, then," Lily said.

"There is, but no one here has it. Just the warden."

She worked through the keys in the lock, and it finally made a quick *click*. As soon as the door opened, she stepped aside. She knew that Honaaz didn't want to be close to her, so she wasn't going to force him. He eyed her for a moment before joining her in the hall.

"Are you going to go running after your knives?" Lily asked.

"Daggers. Those fuckers took them."

"Well, maybe Jal will find them. He went after his bow and quiver."

"Fucking idiot," Honaaz said, looking along the hall. "Do we need to help him?"

"We need to get to Kanar."

"I figured Reims could handle himself."

She bit her lip. "Most of the time, I would say yes. In this case, I'm worried he's underestimated the threat."

"What threat?" Honaaz asked.

"The one that got us in."

Lily started down the hall, and Honaaz followed. The guards were starting to come around, so she kicked them and knocked them unconscious again. She dropped the keys in front of them, then thought better of it and grabbed them.

She hurried up the stairs, with Honaaz chasing her. She didn't know where Jal had gone, but as she focused on what she could hear, what she could smell, and the senses of this place around her, she recognized something.

Hegen magic.

It was near. Not only that, but some aspect of it had been disrupted.

It would set off an alert.

And Kanar wouldn't even know.

Chapter Nineteen

JAL

Jal knew that Lily thought him ridiculous for running off, much like he knew he couldn't leave without his bow. He didn't have many memories of his family, and he refused to leave it behind. Especially in a place like this.

The prison *stunk*. Manure piles didn't even reek this way, and those could be foul. At least there was something natural about the stench of manure. With this, there might be something natural about it, but that didn't mean it was right. It filled his nostrils, as if the stink wanted to cling to everything as a punishment.

He tried to ignore the smell as he jogged through the halls of the prison. When they'd been brought here, they'd been placed in a small room for processing. There, he and Honaaz had been forced to strip down to nothing and put on their prison clothing. If Jal could help it, he'd get out of here with his own clothes. If not, at least he could escape with his bow. Well, that and his life.

Jal paused to listen for the sounds of pursuit. He didn't hear anything, but that didn't reassure him. There were still other guards they hadn't come across. Lily would have neutralized the dangers that she'd faced, but he doubted she'd gone floor to floor searching for anything else.

What about Kanar?

Jal didn't know where he'd slunk off to. He had to be somewhere in the prison, but Jal wasn't sure it mattered until he came across his bow. And Honaaz's daggers. The man loved his daggers.

The halls were poorly lit, which made it easier for him to sneak along without fear of someone spotting him, though it was early enough anyway that he didn't really expect anyone to pop out and catch him.

A staircase led up. That was probably where Kanar had gone—and where Jal would need to go once he found his bow.

Did Kanar know the prison locked from the inside and couldn't be reopened without a second key? He had to give credit to Honaaz for discovering that little nugget. For a guy his size, he didn't look like he'd be smart enough to be able to pull information out of someone, especially when he was the captive, but maybe it was *because* of his size that they'd been willing to talk. Jal had been around plenty of people like that. Around people as big as Honaaz, who looked like they were carved out of the stone of a mountain itself, men wanted to prop themselves up by bragging.

Jal pulled on the door to the intake room and found it locked.

Of course it would be. Everything in this prison was locked. Keys needed to unlock more keys. What kind of thing were they worried about? Probably the very thing that they were here to accomplish.

He smiled at the thought, wondering how many times

the prison had been targeted. Kanar had mentioned thieves breaking into the palace for the jewels, and having seen the defenses there, Jal imagined the job would be difficult.

He jiggled the handle and tried to force it open. It was stout, and he could feel some resistance in the lock, but not so much that he didn't think he'd be able to get it open. At this point, they'd already revealed their presence, and breaking the priest out wasn't going to conceal anything anyway.

He squeezed his hand around the lock, then slammed his shoulder into the door once, twice, before it popped open. A shriek of metal and wood screamed all too loud in his ears.

Nothing to do now but keep moving.

Jal stepped inside the room. When he had been here before, he'd been in chains, sitting in the open space. He'd been forced to undress with two guards on either side of him watching. They were only doing their duty, he was certain, but that didn't make it any easier for him. He didn't care to get undressed around other people like that.

Jal wished he had a lantern, though he had a feel for where the cabinets were, and he made his way over to one of them. With a sharp blow to the lock, it sprang open. It was like anything, really. With the right pressure, the right coercion, and the right training, anything was possible.

He glanced behind him for a moment. Then he turned his attention back to the cabinet. Inside he found clothes hanging from hooks.

Not this one, then.

Jal moved on, feeling his way along until he came to the next locked door. With another sharp strike, the door popped open much like the last one had. The security here wasn't nearly as robust as it had been in other parts of the prison. Of course, they probably thought it was unnecessary. Somebody who got into this room either had been escorted here or had a key.

This cabinet had more clothing.

He rifled through them until he found the familiar fabric of his clothes. He let out a soft whoop of excitement and bundled the clothing up, then tucked it under his arm. He could change when he had more time.

There wasn't much else here. He didn't find Honaaz's clothing.

The next cabinet had weapons. Knives, mostly. All sorts of different ones. This was the kind of place that Lily and Kanar would've probably appreciated. Both had their own affinity for knives, though for different reasons. Kanar could hit something from a distance with his. So could Lily, but she was just as deadly slipping up behind you and driving the blade into your back. Jal had never met anyone so quiet.

He grabbed as many as he could and stacked them onto a cloak. He thought he came across Honaaz's daggers, but it was difficult to make them out by feel as well.

No bow, though.

Jal found another locked cabinet. With another precise hit, he popped it open.

This cabinet was tall, and he hoped that it would be large enough to hold his bow, but he didn't feel anything like that in there. A couple of swords and even a crossbow, which he grabbed and stacked on the pile of knives, and that was it.

Not quite, he realized. As he picked his way through it, he felt one more thing. One more familiar item.

His quiver.

He'd almost overlooked it because it was tilted toward the side. Jal grabbed it and strapped it onto his waist. He felt almost whole again.

There were no further cabinets here.

He cursed under his breath. Where was his bow?

His grandfather had made that bow, and the artisanship involved in creating it was something that wasn't easily replicated. Jal might be many things, but he couldn't carve the same way his grandfather had. Not with the same draw weight, and not with the same accuracy. Jal had tried. There'd been plenty of times when he'd been bored in the forest, wanting to pass the time, so he had gone searching for the right branch to carve. None of them had worked as well.

"You have to find the right kind of wood," his grandfather had told him. "And sometimes you'll have to wander a little farther than you would expect. The wood calls to you, you see." His grandfather's hair had been graying even then, his face heavy with wrinkles around his silver eyes. He'd still been strong, and still a better shot than Jal. He cupped a hand to his ear. "If you listen, you can hear it."

Jal had been standing in the forest, resting his hand on a pine tree, though he'd known that the tree wasn't going to make a skilled arrow or bow. He closed his eyes at his grandfather's suggestion, and listened. He heard nothing, until there came a soft whistling sound, then a painful strike on his shoulder.

"Even when you listen, you have to pay attention," his grandfather said.

Jal grinned. "You just wanted an opportunity to hit me."

"Do I need one?"

Jal grabbed the bow. "I suppose I don't need another bow, anyway. I'm just going to keep yours."

His grandfather's face turned serious. "You're welcome to it. Eventually, you will need to find your own call to understand the song, and when you do, let's just say that you will be surprised at the difference."

His grandfather had shared other advice about making his own bow, carving his own arrows, and aiming, but none of it had ever really made that much sense to Jal. Most of the time, his grandfather had spoken about it in ways that seemed almost mystical.

The bow was the only reminder Jal had of his grandfather. They'd lost him before Jal could ever learn to make his own bow the way his grandfather had. He might have succeeded in making arrows, but arrows were easy. With a straight piece of wood, a few feathers for fletching, and dried leaves, you could make a passable arrow.

Jal needed that bow. He was not about to leave it here, not in this strange land, and not in this place.

A shout came from outside the room, someplace else in the prison. Maybe he *would* be leaving without his bow.

It was that, or leave his friends to suffer.

Another shout.

Jal sighed as he grabbed the bundle from the ground, tied the cloth together, and hurried out. Once in the hallway, he cast a glance behind him back into the room, but he couldn't see well enough.

It was lost.

Jal raced forward until he reached the stairs. He paused for a moment, listening, and when he heard the sound of fighting somewhere nearby, he sprinted in that direction.

On the next level, Honaaz was pushing back two of the

guards, shoving them with enormous strength. Some of the light in the hall gleamed off his bald head. Lily stayed low, jamming one man in the ribs, which gave Honaaz an opportunity to push him back. Both were making attempts not to kill. They didn't even try to seriously maim. There had to be at least ten guards in the hall, and all were converging. But within moments, Honaaz and Lily brought them down.

Jal strode toward them.

Honaaz looked over. "Where the fuck have you been?"

"See anything in here you like?" Jal asked, pulling open the bundled-up cloak.

Honaaz frowned at him for a moment, before ducking his head forward and peering into the cloak. "Where did you get this?" His hand shot forward, and he picked through the blades, then withdrew a pair of daggers with a tight smile across his face.

"The intake room," Jal said.

"You went back for that? For your clothes? Wait. Where are my clothes?"

"Will the two of you be quiet?" Lily said. "I'm trying to figure out what to do so we can finish with this."

"And how are you dealing with this?" Jal asked.

He probably should have asked *what* she was dealing with. Lily tossed a few items forward. Every so often there came a loud pop and a faint gust of air, and then a strange, almost pungent aroma would drift toward them. He had no idea what it was.

"Just be ready," Lily snapped.

Jal looked over to Honaaz, who shrugged at him.

"Why did you go after my daggers?" Honaaz said.

"I wasn't sure what I was grabbing. I just took anything

that was long enough to be a knife. Not much use to a sword. At least, not for me." Jal grinned at him. "Are you good with a sword?"

"Not like Reims," Honaaz muttered.

"I don't know that there are many people who are as good as Kanar with a sword." Jal had seen Kanar fight enough times for him to know that the kind of skill he had was significant.

"Be ready," Lily said.

"Ready for what?" Jal said, turning to her. He had his quiver, but without his bow, he felt helpless. He had the knives he'd gathered, but he didn't like using them.

"Can you feel it pushing against us?" Lily asked, her voice tight and her words clipped. "Can you feel it?"

Jal frowned. Without his bow, he felt helpless. "What am I supposed to feel?"

"Sorcery," Honaaz answered. "That's what we call it in the Isles."

Lily glanced back at him, holding Honaaz's gaze before nodding. "They have protections all through here."

"And you are removing them?"

"I'm doing what I can," she mumbled.

"What's going to happen when Reims learns that you did this?" Honaaz asked.

Lily glowered at him, then tossed something into the darkness. There was a flash of white light, followed by another gust of air. Everything went still, even Lily.

After a moment, she took a deep breath and let it out slowly, then turned to them. "We can move. We have to go quickly, though, and we have to be prepared for other protections that might've been placed."

"By who?" Jal asked.

"I'm guessing by the Hunter, but I have no idea why the executioner would be leaving hegen magic behind."

Jal shared a glance with Honaaz, who just shrugged.

They made their way along the hall, and Jal was thankful for Lily's presence. He was always thankful for it, really. Despite Kanar's reputation and what he wanted people to believe of him, he had a good heart. Sometimes men with a good heart let themselves get hurt. Sometimes they needed somebody like Lily to watch their back. Somebody who wouldn't be afraid to throw a knife.

They reached a doorway. She paused for a moment, then reached into her pouch and grabbed another item out of it. She glanced back at them and nodded, almost as if to herself, and then darted forward.

Jal motioned for Honaaz to go first. "I don't have my bow."

"That's the only way you can fight?"

"Well, it's the easiest way."

Honaaz grunted, shaking his head and muttering under his breath. Jal heard only a few words. Mostly *fuck*, *piss poor*, *useless*.

Jal lunged forward after him, expecting to find violence on the other side of the door. He was surprised to see a pale-haired woman strapped to a chair in the center of the room. She was awake, and Kanar stared at her like some long-lost pet—though hadn't gone to talk to her. A ring of strange objects rested on the ground around her. Most of them were made out of gleaming white bone, but there were several that were carved out of stone or wood. Hegen items, he knew.

Jal looked around, and his eyes widened. His bow rested against the wall.

A wave of relief swept through him. He darted over to it, grabbed it, and slung it over his shoulder. Why would it be here, though?

Kanar stood just outside the circle, though there was another man with him, a hood over his head. How had Kanar gotten in without fighting through the magical protections the way that they had?

"I take it that's the Hunter?" Jal asked as he moved closer to Lily, who had crouched down on the ground.

"We aren't going to be able to get through the circle here," Kanar said.

"That's not necessarily true," Lily answered.

Kanar frowned. "What do you mean?"

"There might be another way through here. You just have to give me a moment."

"I doubt that even you will be able to get through it," a hard voice said from the opposite side of the room.

Jal's curiosity got the better of him. He made his way over to the man and pulled off the hood, even though he knew it might be a mistake. The man would know what he looked like, but seeing as how they had no intention of staying in Verendal, there really wasn't a point in worrying about those things. Besides, Jal wanted to know.

The man had an unyielding face. He looked like he'd been in a scrape or two, but he also had intelligence that gleamed behind his eyes, along with quick observation. His gaze paused on both Jal and Honaaz as if to memorize their features. He must have already seen Kanar and Lily.

"Not locals," the executioner said. "None of you. Well, other than the man who dragged me from my home in the middle of the night. A soldier, I suspect. From his skill and the way he bound me, Realmsguard probably." Jal did his best to avoid giving any sort of reaction, but somebody must have reacted. "As I suspected. Realmsguard. And because he's coming here, that would make him… Ah. I should have known. Had I known you were alive, I would've prepared, actually. Kanar Reims. The Blackheart."

Kanar straightened and faced the man. "You don't get to interrogate me. Everything I have ever done has been on behalf of the throne."

The executioner looked past Kanar, his gaze settling on the priest strapped to the chair.

"Even this," Kanar said, his voice soft. "And when it's over, you can run back to the king and tell him that."

"Oh, that won't be necessary. I will have each of you to question, and you can provide the king with all he needs to know about why you came after the Priest of Fell."

"Morgan," Kanar said, turning to the woman. "Her name is Morgan."

As he said it, Jal watched the executioner. Had he not, he might have missed the slight twitch of his eyes, the hint of a smile on his lips.

Even had he not seen that, it might not have mattered.

They were in trouble.

He had heard the way Kanar had spoken Morgan's name. This was more than about the job for him. More than about coming and finding a resource. This was personal in a way that Kanar had cautioned them against.

What had Kanar gotten them into?

Chapter Twenty

KANAR

Kanar tensed at the executioner's mention of his past. He'd already moved beyond his own connections to Reyand, so hearing them from the executioner wasn't what bothered him. Nor was it the undercurrent of threat.

It was seeing Morgan.

When he'd come up the stairs, he'd found Jal's bow hanging on a hook, so he'd grabbed it, eliciting a strange look from the Hunter. When they had reached the next level up, he had been on edge, especially as it wasn't where he expected that he'd need to go. There was a possibility that the Hunter had misled him. He wouldn't put it past this man, but he also didn't think Jagger would. Besides, if he had misled them, all Kanar had to do was head deeper inside.

And then they'd entered this strange room in the middle of the prison.

When they'd scouted Declan yesterday, he didn't recall seeing windows made out of painted glass such as the ones that ringed the upper portion of this room. The air wasn't quite as foul in here, more antiseptic, though he had a feeling that this place had known violence.

The row of metal cabinets near the back of the room were what he noticed immediately. He knew the kinds of things that took place inside of prisons. Men were brought in for questioning, often coerced into answering and forced to make claims that were of dubious validity. How much could you count on what a man said under threat of violence?

But it was the chair, and the woman seated in it, that had caught his attention. Demanded it.

And so Kanar had frozen in a way that he never did in a fight.

It was one thing to think about Morgan, and to dream about her, and to reminisce about days when they had once been friends, and then more, before he had been forced to betray her. It was another thing for him to be face-to-face with it again.

She looked just as he remembered. Even now, despite her time in prison, she was breathtaking. Her face was a little leaner than he last remembered, her eyes more hollowed, but she was still Morgan.

And he couldn't move.

"I am going to work at it, Kanar, but you're going to have to back up," Lily said.

He'd been distracted by Morgan, by the executioner, and even by the sudden appearance of Lily and the rest of the team, but he did as she said and backed away from the circle that surrounded the chair. Kanar recognized the hegen magic. He'd been trained to differentiate between witchcraft and hegen methods, and so he'd immediately identified the different items that encircled the chair, even if he had no idea what they were. The only thing he knew was that they were designed to keep anyone from getting close.

Even the executioner. At least, that was what Jagger claimed.

The man would have to have some way of getting past those protections, but he had not revealed them. Jagger was much like Kanar had once been. He followed the king's orders, and didn't question them.

"What are you doing?" he asked Lily.

"I'm just working through this," she snapped.

Morgan looked up. She locked eyes with him, and only him.

It was almost as if she didn't see the others in the room, each of them trying to help get her free. It was like she didn't even see the executioner, though Kanar was certain that she had interacted with him before. He'd probably come to this very place to question her. Kanar was left wondering how she might have responded to that questioning. Probably with the same steely resistance that he had known from her. Maybe even the torment of her logic.

Lily grunted, and only then did Kanar look down. He couldn't see what she was doing. She was crouched over one of the hegen items, and he could hear a soft scraping sound, as if she was working her knife under it.

"That's not working to work," he said. "I tried something similar when I was deployed, and—"

A soft burst of air exploded out toward him. A sense of pressure that he hadn't been aware of began to ease, and Lily tumbled forward through the barricade of hegen artifacts.

But she almost wasn't fast enough.

Morgan moved. Her arms and legs were strapped, but

as soon as the hegen protections were lifted, she did something with her fingers, wiggling them or contorting them into some strange pattern. The straps around her wrists and her ankles snapped.

Kanar unsheathed his blade. He held it out, its point angled toward her heart. "Don't even think about it."

Morgan's gaze drifted down to his sword. "It's lovely, but not something I would've expected you to carry."

"Do not move," he said again.

"You came here for me?"

Kanar glanced to the side, where Lily gathered the various hegen items off the ground and stuffed them into what looked like a cloak that Jal held. There was a clatter of metal, and he wondered what else might be in there, but he made sure not to turn his focus away from Morgan.

"I came here because I need something from you," Kanar said to Morgan.

"Go on, then. Do what you need to do." She crossed her hands behind her back, but not before he watched to see if she was doing something with her fingers again. She wasn't. She was waiting.

She leaned forward slightly, closer to the point of his sword.

"What did you think I came here to do?" Kanar asked.

Morgan held his gaze. "You're the one with the Order. Do what you must. End me."

There was defiance in her eyes. There was no hurt. No anger. Only a calm resignation, as if this could be the only possible outcome that would ever result from this.

The anger that Kanar had felt for so long toward her—anger that had built up when he'd learned more and more about her betrayal—threatened to spill out. It tried to keep him from reacting the right way. He had to refrain from driving the blade forward.

There was a quiet part in the back of his mind that whispered to him and suggested that might be the best outcome, but if he did, he feared what might happen. He had been sent here for a reason, and though he may not be as concerned about magic in the kingdom any longer, he still cared about preventing it from being released upon the world.

Kanar pulled back his sword. "I'm not driving my blade into you, but you know that I can."

She locked eyes with him again. They were the same shade of deep green that he remembered, the color of a forest canopy, and they regarded him with a measure of curiosity, but also a measure of disdain. He had earned that, he figured.

"Let's go," Kanar said, motioning to the others.

"What about him?" Lily asked, turning to Jagger. "We can't use him to get out of here."

Kanar froze. "What do you mean?"

The executioner looked at him with a flat expression, as if he did not care that they were trapped here with him. Or that he was trapped with them.

"Honaaz learned that two keys are required to leave the prison," Lily explained.

"Could you not say my fucking name?" Honaaz muttered.

"Sorry. Anyway. When he was down in the cell, he got them talking."

Kanar grabbed Morgan. "Is it true?" he asked, trying to ignore the sudden awareness of her being so close to him and the way he felt with that proximity. He shoved her forward, then turned to Jagger. "Are two keys required?"

He shrugged slightly. "They might be. Or perhaps there's a schedule when the door opens."

They were trapped.

"Let's go," Kanar said, forcing Morgan with him toward the door.

"Are we leaving him?" Lily asked, leaning in close.

"For now. We can lock him in here and come back for him if we need another way out."

"He will find you," Morgan said, her voice sounding dispassionate, which only irritated Kanar even more. "If you leave him alive, he's going to—"

"I'm not killing the king's executioner."

Kanar had done things against the kingdom, but that was a step too far for him.

Besides, there was no need to kill the man. At this point, the only thing he really needed to do was to lock him in the room. Once they were out of the city, they wouldn't have to worry about Jagger chasing them down. That was not his obligation, and he'd be confined to Verendal. Kanar knew the function of the king's executioner well enough to know that much, at least.

Once everyone other than the executioner were out in the hall, Jal pulled the door to the room closed, squeezing the handle for a moment before looking up at Kanar.

"Why don't you have her do something to lock it?" Honaaz said, motioning to Lily.

"It's not as easy to lock the door without a key," Kanar said. He turned to Jal. "I don't suppose there's an extra knife in that collection you have there."

Jal grinned at him. "How did you know?"

"Consider it a guess."

Jal held the cloak open, and Kanar looked inside. There had to be a dozen knives. They were all different sizes, and he plucked the slenderest one. He jammed it into the lock, then bent it until it snapped off, leveraging it into the door.

"Is it going to hold?" Jal asked.

Kanar twisted the handle to try to pop the door open, but it stayed closed and locked. "Until someone comes, but we need to block the door as well."

Honaaz grabbed a table in the hall and dragged it in front of the door.

"He's going to come after you," Morgan said.

"If he does, then he's coming after you as well," Kanar said. "Now let's go. Any suggestions?"

Jal pointed down the hall. "Stairs."

"They just lead down into the prison," Lily snapped.

"No, not only down. I saw another staircase that went up."

Kanar motioned for them to go, and he followed, keeping Morgan in front of him. He had his sword unsheathed. The blade might have to find its way into her back, regardless of what he might want. If she made any attempt against the others, he would not hold back.

They reached the stairs that Jal had found, and they gathered there for a moment. Sounds of shouts rang out from below.

"Seems like the guards woke up," Honaaz muttered. "Should've let me deal with them."

"Kill the guards and you have Kanar after you," Lily said.

"That's the only reason you didn't?" Kanar asked.

"Well, I figured the fewer people we kill, the fewer we have to make amends for."

"I thought you liked to kill," Honaaz said.

"Interesting company that you're keeping now, Gray," Morgan said.

Kanar tensed at the use of his nickname. It had been a long time since she'd called him that. "Let's climb. There had better be a way out from up here."

"Don't go getting upset with me if there's not," she said.

"I was talking to Jal," Kanar replied.

"You can get mad at me," Jal said. "Say, maybe we send Lily on up ahead, see what she comes up with."

"We aren't sending anyone up ahead. We stay together. We finish this."

"You don't trust them?" Morgan asked.

"It has nothing to do with trust."

At least, Kanar told himself that it didn't. Jal and Honaaz had gotten themselves locked up, which had not served their purpose whatsoever. They would've had an easier time breaking into the prison with the team intact. Of course, had they been together from the beginning, they might not have learned about the one-way locks.

"Climb," Kanar said.

So they did.

They went up several flights, ignoring different halls that led off the staircase. No one spoke much.

What sounded like an explosion sounded in the direction they'd come from.

Kanar paused, looking behind him.

"The Hunter is free," Morgan said.

"Aren't you afraid of him?" Kanar asked.

"I'm afraid of many things, but he wasn't going to force me to say anything I had not already admitted to."

He'd expected a different response, but she said nothing more.

They hurried up the stairs, which ended with a locked door. Jal tested the handle and shoved his shoulder against it. Kanar was going to tell him that they should let Honaaz try, when the door came open.

It was nothing but a supply room.

"What is this?" Kanar said.

"There's a window," Lily offered, heading to a tiny skylight. She jumped and quickly wriggled through, before poking her head back down. "Opens to the roof. We can get out from here."

"Go with her," Kanar said, motioning to Jal.

Jal was tall enough that he barely had to jump to grab the edge of the window. He started to twist as he pulled himself up.

"He's not going to fit," Honaaz said.

Kanar suspected that was true. Honaaz definitely wouldn't, and Kanar might not even be able to. Jal…

Surprised him.

He seemed to draw his shoulders in and contort himself until he slithered through.

"Well, fuck."

"Yeah," Kanar said.

"What about us?" Honaaz asked.

"We take the long way down." Lily had popped her head back through the opening. "I hope you have your grappling hook."

"Always."

"Will it hold you both?"

"Just us?"

"We won't fit that way. We're going to have to make a run for the main entrance. And that's where I'm going to need your help. You go down and open the door from that side. Take Jal with you. Honaaz and I will bring Morgan through the prison."

Lily looked behind her a moment. "I don't know that it's going to hold Jal."

"Oh, I don't need the rope," Jal said from behind her. "At least, I don't need most of it. I can use the building."

"If you damage my hook…"

"I wouldn't dare. I know how much that matters to you. It's like a little puppy to you."

"It's not a puppy," she said.

"You can scale down sheer stone?" Kanar asked Jal.

"Alainsith stone," Morgan said.

Honaaz's eyes widened. "Alainsith?" He glanced from Lily to Jal and then back. "What do you mean?"

"All of this is Alainsith made, including the stone."

Being this close to freedom was excruciating. The first hint of dawn was breaking over the horizon. Kanar inhaled the damp morning air one last time before turning back to the prison.

"Probably not, then," Jal said. "I'll be careful with your puppy, Lily."

"Let's go," he said. "If you try anything…" He held Morgan's eyes.

She said nothing. He had no idea what she might try. That, as much as anything, worried him.

"Well," Lily said, having disappeared for a moment before poking her head back into the window, "I'm not sure how much time you have. It looks like we have some company down the street. I suggest that I be the one to go down and draw some of them away, while the rest of you make your way down."

"Then I'll wait to ensure you get out," Jal said.

Kanar could imagine him pulling his bow off his shoulder.

"If you kill any of the Archers, the Hunter will definitely come after you," Kanar said.

"I can chase away a few," Jal said.

Kanar grabbed the keys from his pocket and then tossed them to Lily. He had grabbed them from the Hunter, though he hadn't really thought much of it at the time. He'd figured that they would need to use them to get back out, but not that they might need them to get back in.

"Good luck," Kanar said.

"Now you've gone and jinxed it," Lily muttered. She disappeared from the window.

Jal's shadowy frame remained for a moment, then he pulled an arrow from his quiver and disappeared. "You better get moving," he called.

"Don't wait here too long."

"Only long enough to make sure she gets down."

Kanar gave Morgan a shove. She started toward the door.

"The Hunter is down there," she said.

"He's not a fighter," Kanar said. The executioner was a thinker, an interrogator.

Kanar knew the nature of men. The look the Hunter had given him suggested that he knew men as well, but more that he knew their hearts and could read their intentions. That was a gift, there was no doubting that, but Kanar still didn't expect that the Hunter would be able to do much on his own. He'd need the support of the Archers and the prison guards to be effective.

Between Kanar and Honaaz—and Jal, when he finally came along—they should be able to handle it. But without killing? He wanted to avoid killing here. The problem was that he didn't know if it was going to be possible.

He stepped past Morgan and glanced over to Honaaz. "Take the rear. Keep her from doing anything. If you see her using her hands in any strange way, knock her out."

Honaaz frowned as he looked at Morgan. "She doesn't look that fucking dangerous."

"More than you can know," Kanar said.

Then he started down. He descended a dozen steps, making a point of glancing behind to make sure that Morgan and Honaaz were still there.

Three soldiers waited on the stairs. Maybe prison guards. Maybe Archers. He couldn't tell. It was too dark.

His training took over. He couldn't use his sword. Not in the small confines of the staircase, and not without definitely killing someone. They didn't hold back, though. They were armed with swords and crossbows, and one man had a curved knife in hand.

Kanar dropped and slid, ignoring the sting of the step as it scraped his back. He drove his heel into one man's knee, then turned in a roll. With his elbow out, he jabbed it into the side of another, following it with a quick strike upward into his back, which elicited a soft groan as the man collapsed. That left only one. Kanar twisted and got back to his feet, and he drove the heel of his hand up into the third man's chin. The man went stumbling down the stairs. Kanar raced after him, catching him before he fell too far and lowering him to the steps.

Morgan and Honaaz followed.

"You never were afraid of killing before," Morgan said.

"I'm not afraid. There are times when it's necessary. This is not one."

She frowned at him, but Kanar ignored it, continuing down the stairs.

He kept moving until he reached another landing. There was no sign of the Hunter, but he had to be around somewhere.

When they reached the next landing down, Kanar paused a moment at movement.

A dozen men waited. Half of them had crossbows aimed toward them. Others had swords.

Behind them stood the Hunter, who seemed completely at ease. Almost as if there was no other outcome that could have come from this.

Kanar clenched his fists.

"What now, Reims?" Honaaz asked.

"Now you let her go."

Chapter Twenty-One

LILY

A FAINT BREEZE PULLED ON LILY'S HAIR AS SHE CLIMBED down the rope, swaying slightly as she did. The walls of the prison were a dark stone, and they seem to be stained with a bit of soot. Alainsith stone. That meant there had to be some sort of power within it, though she didn't know what kind of power that might be.

She had to get down.

That thought stayed with her as she continued descending the rope. She could have let the others attempt to climb down with her, but she didn't know if the hook would hold any more weight. She kept it light and compact because it did not have to hold anything more than just her. If she put more strain on it, it could snap.

The job wasn't nearly over yet. Even after they got this woman, they still had to pull the other half of the job. The main part, in fact. Of course, it had started to feel as if this was the main part. She could've probably taken the woman with her. She doubted that she would've been too heavy.

But how would Lily have kept an eye on her?

No. Kanar could manage.

An arrow whistled past her. On the street below, a solder crumpled, grasping his leg.

She looked up at Jal, who flashed a smile at her. She had to move quickly. She couldn't linger against the wall. All it was doing was drawing attention to her.

Lily scrambled down.

She'd used quite a few items during the attempt to break through the hegen protections. She wasn't sure how much Kanar knew about the Hunter, but the Hunter obviously was familiar with the hegen and had to have a good enough rapport with them to use their prizes to protect and secure a prisoner. That surprised her. She wouldn't have expected any of the hegen to help with a prison like this. But then, there were many things she wouldn't have expected, including the fact that Honaaz had identified that she had access to the prizes.

The way he looked at her made much more sense now. He knew. The real question was how long he would hold out before revealing that information to Kanar.

All she could hope for was that it was not until the job was over.

Lily reached the street. She hesitated a moment, long enough that she could make sure there wasn't any further movement around her. She didn't see any of the soldiers, though they were likely out patrolling. The air had a memory of the stench she had found within the prison.

The grappling hook dropped. Lily hurriedly grabbed the rope and began to wind it as fast as she could, but she was forced to catch the hook out of the air before it crashed to the stone. She didn't think the impact would've damaged the hook, but it would've certainly made enough noise to draw attention.

When she looked up, Jal was grinning down at her. Then he brought his bow up, aimed, and fired in one smooth motion. There was another grunt, and somewhere in the darkness another man fell.

Now she really had to move quickly.

She raced around the building until she found the prison door. Lily grabbed the keys and scrambled to work one into the lock.

"What are you doing there?"

She spun, knife in hand, and raised it at the old man standing on the far side of the street. He looked grizzled and slightly confused.

"Just keep walking," she said.

"You aren't supposed to be here."

"And you shouldn't be up. A man your age needs his sleep."

He frowned. She had one hand behind her back, continuing to work with the key, but she couldn't get the lock open. She had to keep trying.

They would not be able to open it from the inside. Assuming that Kanar and the others managed to make it back down the stairs and inside, she was the only way they would get out. Otherwise, they'd be trapped.

The old man whistled, two piercing sounds.

She frowned at him. When the whistles came in return, she realized that was exactly what it was. The man had alerted the city guard.

Damn.

Lily didn't like the idea of killing an old man. *Don't kill when you don't have to.* Strange that Kanar was kinder than so many of her mentors had been.

She whipped the knife toward him and caught him with the flat of the blade on his temple. A wrong aim would've killed, but she never aimed wrong.

"I'm really sorry," she muttered.

She fumbled with the lock, twisting the key until it finally worked.

Lily pushed open the door, poking her head inside briefly, careful not to step all the way in. There was the sound of boots nearby, and she knew she didn't have long before the city guard arrived. They'd see the fallen old man and probably help him first, but then they'd come for her.

Where were Kanar and the rest?

A burst of heavy air billowed toward her, carrying the stench of the prison. The smell of filth and rot washed over everything and blasted out into the street, and it was followed by a faint haze that hung in the air and gradually thickened. It reminded her of the fog that rolled in over Sanaron, though this was obviously witchcraft.

A face appeared near her, and Lily brought up a knife. A strong hand grabbed her wrist.

"Easy," Kanar hissed.

"You got out?"

"With a little help," he said, shoving the woman forward. "We needed to use her particular talents."

"You don't sound pleased."

He grunted. Lily felt Honaaz's presence in the thickening fog, but no sign of Jal.

"Where now?" she asked.

"Now we go," Kanar said.

"Not without Jal. He helped me. He brought down two guards."

"I warned him not to."

"I don't know how much choice he had in it," she said. That wasn't true. She knew that Jal had some choice. He could have elected not to fire on them, but then the guards might've sounded the alarm sooner. Knowing him, he had struck them in just the right way so that they wouldn't be able to call to any others.

"Back toward the city gate," Kanar said.

"We need to know where we're going."

"And we will, but not inside the city." Kanar gave her a slight shove. "If we stay here and the Hunter gets out, we won't be able to get out of Verendal. We need to take this window to do so."

Lily nodded toward the woman. "Did she tell you anything?"

"Not here. I told you, we need to get moving."

Lily looked up, but in the dense and growing fog, she couldn't see anything else. She knew better than to wait. Waiting only put them in more danger of being exposed.

Lily backed toward the prison. Leaving might be the smart thing, but she wasn't going to leave Jal behind.

"What are you doing?"

Jal's voice came from nearby, and she spun. Had she gotten distracted in the fog?

"How did you get down?" Lily asked.

"I told you I could climb down the stone, but I can't tell you all my secrets, can I?"

"Jal…"

"Move," Kanar's voice called from a distance.

Lily looked over to Jal. "Did you close the door behind you?"

"It's closed," he said. He held his bow in one hand, an arrow already brought to the string, though with as thick as the fog now was, she doubted that he could see anything more than she could.

"How are we supposed to know which way we go?" Lily asked.

"I thought we were following Kanar."

"We were, but he's not really leading us anywhere. At least, not anywhere I can tell."

"He wants to get out of the city," Jal said.

He nudged her with his hip, practically catching her on the shoulder. The fog thinned out the further she went. She began to make out shapes as they moved quickly.

She caught up to Kanar, who was pushing the priest ahead of him.

"You sure we're going to be able to get out of the city?" Lily asked.

"We can get out of the city," Kanar said. "We just need to move."

"Sometimes I think he has that phrase tattooed someplace," Jal mumbled to her.

They hurried through the growing daylight.

Nobody spoke, though every so often Honaaz would grunt, swear under his breath, and look over to Kanar before glancing in Lily's direction.

Jal stayed close to her, and they followed Kanar and the woman.

At one point, Kanar raised his hand, signaling for them to slow. A streetlight in the distance captured a pair of soldiers marching along the street. He motioned for them to duck into an alleyway, and they did so.

They leaned against the wall for a moment, and she glanced over to Jal. "We might have to lead them astray," she said. "For all of us to get out, we might have to split up."

"We're staying together," Kanar said.

"At this point, I'm not sure that makes a whole lot of sense. With the guard out there and the Hunter guiding them, we might need to move quickly."

"That says nothing about the Dogs," Jal said.

Lily's eyes widened. "What?"

"Fucking Dogs," Honaaz muttered as he leaned against a nearby building and poked his head out, looking around the street. "That's the reason we ended up in prison. A couple got thrown in near us. You didn't see?"

"It wasn't my fault," Jal said.

"Those fuckers recognized you, not me," Honaaz said. "So don't go and claim that you had nothing to do with it."

Jal shrugged. "I thought I dealt with them."

"You didn't tell us about what you dealt with," Lily said.

It wasn't surprising. Jal didn't always like to take credit for things he did.

"I might've had a little encounter with a few of them," Jal admitted. "Like I said, they were dealt with."

"Or not," Honaaz said. "If you had, we wouldn't have found them in the tavern. Or had them find us."

"How many?" Kanar asked.

"There were about ten," Jal replied. "I knew one of them. They were looking for you."

Kanar frowned. "Ten Dogs. That's too many outside of Sanaron."

"How did you get away from ten Dogs?" Honaaz asked. He backed up, and his massive body blocked some of the light from spilling down the alley. There was something almost intimidating about the way he did it, though Jal didn't seemed bothered by it. Jal didn't seem bothered by much, of course.

Honaaz eyed Jal. "Did you kill them?"

"I didn't have to. They had a little run-in with the laws of nature."

"What is that supposed to mean?"

"It means they found a stronger pack."

Lily found Kanar watching Jal too, a question in his eyes.

"Jal, Honaaz, go and scout how many men we have to deal with," Kanar said. "I need to know if there are Dogs or if they're just Archers and the prison guards."

"You're going to send them and not me?" Lily asked. It wasn't that she was hurt, but it surprised her. Kanar knew that she was the best equipped to find them an escape path.

"You need to go and find us a way out."

She looked up. The roofline here was easy enough to scale, so she tossed her grappling hook, locked it on the edge of a building, and started to climb. When she reached the roof, she saw Jal and Honaaz making their way down the street, slipping out of the shadows. Kanar and the woman were left alone.

Probably the way he wanted it to be.

Lily hesitated while wrapping the rope around her arm, not really wanting to eavesdrop but feeling as if she needed to listen.

"Are you going to tell me what this is about now?" Morgan asked.

Her voice was soft, and Lily noticed a slight accent to the way she spoke. Lily couldn't place it, but she knew it was not from Reyand. Kanar was too smart to have missed that, but he hadn't mentioned anything about where the priest had come from before she had ended up here.

"What's there to say?" Kanar said.

"The reason that you came for me."

"I came because you're going to help us."

"And if I don't?" Morgan said.

Lily peeked over the edge to listen better.

"Then you end up back there," Kanar said. "With whatever he planned. I don't know what it was, but I recognized the hegen magic around you."

"I'm not concerned about hegen magic," Morgan said quietly.

"And if they execute you?"

It might've been Lily's imagination, but it seemed almost as if Kanar's voice quavered a little bit at the mention of execution.

"Then my time will have come to its end. I am prepared for that. Are you?"

"I was prepared long ago," he said.

"Until…"

"Until I met you."

"What do you want?" Morgan asked.

"It's what I need," Kanar said. "And it's what you need. A chance to prove yourself. To prove that what you claimed of your magic is real."

"It is real, even if you didn't want to believe it. It was all real."

From above, Lily saw Kanar stiffen. His hand went to the hilt of his sword. She wondered what his face looked like. He was always so stern, but something seemed to change around this woman.

"I need to know everything you can tell me about what happened there," Kanar said. "The Alainsith that were slaughtered. The blood collected. I need to know what they intend."

Lily could see Morgan smirk. "So the king sent you?" She started to laugh, but trailed off. "No. If the king had sent you, you wouldn't have had to break into the prison. You came for another reason. Someone has paid you." She snorted, shaking her head almost sadly. "Oh, Gray. You don't even understand what you got caught up in, do you?"

"I understand well enough."

"I don't think you do."

"What do they intend to use the blood for?" Kanar asked.

"I don't know."

"You do. You were there for a reason. You were there when it happened."

Morgan opened her mouth as if she wanted to argue with him, before clamping it shut. "Have you considered the possibility that someone is using you?"

"Someone is always using me," Kanar said. He held her gaze, and she didn't look away. "How many were sacrificed?"

"Does that even matter?"

"I think it does," Kanar said. "Numbers matter in such things. At least, that's been my experience."

Morgan tipped her head to the side, watching him. "And you have so much experience, don't you, Gray?" She snickered. "Something like that would be for a binding of considerable power. What purpose would they have for that? That's what you need to know."

"You have an idea," Kanar said. "We need to see where this happened."

"Why?" Morgan crossed her arms. "What will that help you accomplish?"

Lily continued to stare, before she noticed Kanar look up at her. He didn't seem surprised. He'd known that she was there the entire time.

Of course he would. What did she think she could accomplish by listening in on him? This was Kanar, after all. He always seemed to know. At least, he had always seemed to know before this had happened. As soon as he'd gotten around this priest, though, some part of Kanar—some part of his confidence—had slipped. He had changed.

Under any other circumstance, Lily might be worried about that, but with the kind of magic she suspected this priest possessed, she thought she understood. Even the great Kanar Reims had limitations.

Lily scurried off, darting along the rooftops, knowing that she didn't need to stay behind to hear what Morgan said. She feared that she knew the answer already.

The problem was in what Kanar would do next.

Chapter Twenty-Two

HONAAZ

Honaaz had grown tired of this fucking city.

A shadow moved near him, and he slashed out with one of his daggers. At least the tall bastard had managed to find his blades. He appreciated skillfully made weapons, though he didn't have the same affection for his blades as it seemed Jal had for his bow. That was something else. It looked to Honaaz like he wanted to wed and bed the damn bow.

Another Dog appeared out of the shadows.

"How many are there?" he muttered.

The Dog was a little larger than the rest, but had the same distinctive mark on his hand, just like every Dog. They just *had* to mark themselves, as if that made them better, rather than simply making it easier for someone like him to know who to cut down.

A pair of knives, too short to be of much danger, came slashing toward him.

Honaaz had faced better-skilled boys out of Hind than this, but it was a reasonable attempt. The people of Hind made knife fighting into something of an art, to the point where they demonstrated it on the streets of every port. When they'd pulled into there the first time, his uncle had told him that the displays were to make sure men didn't get any stupid ideas in their head when it came to the people—and particularly the women—of Hind, but Honaaz had seen something almost poetic in their movements.

Nothing like this simple and rugged fighting style that came at him now.

As Honaaz stepped to the side, he dropped his elbow. The man cried out and let go of his knife. Fucking amateur. *Never lose your blade.* That was a lesson the Hind would have drilled into him.

Honaaz kicked the blade away, drove his fist into the man's belly, and shoved him.

A shadow raced by above him on the rooftop. Not Lily. She'd already moved past as she scoped out a way out of Verendal. This was someone larger. They weren't dressed in the helm and leathers of the guards, which meant it had to be one of the Dogs or another crew working in the city.

Let them try with her.

Honaaz forced himself to turn away. Trying to help Lily was likely a bad idea. He'd get hurt, or get in her way. She already looked at him like she wanted to take his ears and consume them in a stew for her magic.

Honaaz knew his limits. He could watch the stars and guide a ship, he could handle rough seas without falling overboard, and time spent around those kind of men made it so that he was good in a fight. But someone like her was on another level completely.

A whistle caught his attention, and he tore his gaze from the roof.

The neighboring buildings squeezed closer together

here than they did elsewhere. Another street over, near the stink of a butcher, Jal was swinging his bow around as if it were a staff.

There *was* something graceful about the way he moved. The bow dipped, clipping one man's legs, and then Jal spun and drove the other end of the bow up. The weapon caught the next person in the jaw. Two more pressed in, and Honaaz didn't even know if he needed to break Jal's rhythm. It might actually disrupt him.

There were more than two coming at him, though. The light on the street here wasn't enough for Honaaz to see easily, but he made out the convergence of men moving toward Jal. When Jal had claimed that he'd dealt with ten Dogs outside the city, Honaaz had laughed it off. Not a man like Jal. Dogs were stupid, but stupid in numbers could overwhelm.

Seeing him now, Honaaz had to admit that it was possible that Jal had been able to fight his way through at least a few more than Honaaz had assumed.

It was strange to think that he might be the worst fighter on the team. *Why am I even here, then?*

Another man appeared, forcing Jal toward a narrow alley. If he were to get caught there, he wouldn't be able to use that bow like a staff—or even like a bow.

Honaaz growled, and several men bearing crossbows came toward him.

The city watch.

He lowered his shoulder and got to work. Men went tumbling away. Honaaz even picked up one of the smaller men and heaved him at the others. The oncoming attackers were knocked down as if they were nothing more than strawmen, giving him the time to barrel forward again.

Jal took out a few more by thrusting his bow up. He caught another man in the cheek, then the last with a crack on his arm, which was followed by a soft cry. Honaaz gave the last one a kick for good measure.

"Thought you wouldn't find me, so I needed to give a whistle," Jal said. "Hope you didn't mind."

"That's what I'm here for, isn't it?"

"I guess." Jal looked around him at the bodies lying on the street. "How many of them are the watch?"

"I don't know. Don't matter. None are fucking dressed like they'd be out to dance, now are they?"

Jal grinned. "They danced. Just not well."

Honaaz found himself laughing slightly. "We need to check on Lily. Saw a man chasing her on the roof."

"I wouldn't worry about her. She's scouting a way out for us."

"Who said I was worried?"

Jal looked back, watched him a moment, then nodded. "Lily would have noticed someone behind her. She always does." He turned in place. "And we've got Dogs—more than I would have expected out here, to be honest—and the city watch. Is that about it?"

"That sounds about right," Honaaz said.

Jal nudged one of the Dogs. "They were after Kanar. They wanted him for something." The man groaned, and Jal jabbed at him with the end of his bow. That wasn't going to wake him up. "I never knew there were so many Dogs around."

"Not everywhere." Honaaz shrugged when Jal looked over to him. "I'm just saying I've been to quite a few places. The Dogs aren't everywhere. Plenty of them in Sanaron, sure, but there are other gangs there too."

"None run by the Prophet."

Honaaz nodded. "That's true enough, but that fuckwit can't reach all the way here."

Jal nudged another fallen man. "I don't know. It seems like he can."

"Well, maybe he can."

There was a soft shout in the distance.

"I'm checking on her," Honaaz said.

"Of course you are."

"Fuck off."

Honaaz jogged toward the shout. He had a pretty good sense of where he was in the city, though that was easy enough with the wall that surrounded it. The damn thing made it feel claustrophobic, like they were trying to trap him here. Men were meant to be out in the open, on the sea, with nothing but the stars to guide you. At least, that was what he was meant for. Or had been.

He kept his eyes on the roofs. Jal was probably right that he didn't need to go and help Lily, but there *had* been a Dog chasing her. Even a fast—and dangerous—rabbit sometimes got caught.

A man jumped across the street in front of him.

"What the fuck was that?" Honaaz muttered.

"What did you say?"

Honaaz looked behind him. Jal had come with him. He hadn't expected that.

"A man just cleared the street. In the air."

"That's nothing," Jal said. "I've seen Lily swing across a greater distance than that."

"Right. But that's on a rope. This man just *jumped*."

Jal shrugged. "Should we go look?"

"You go look. I can't climb up there."

"Suit yourself." Jal strode off, looking like a mix between a dangerous deer and a skinny wolf. When Jal reached the nearest building, he jumped, grabbed a window ledge, pulled himself up, then swung onto the roof. All without losing his bow.

I'm definitely not the best fighter on the team.

Not the best at anything.

What was Reims up to, bringing me along?

The one hundred gold vans were a reasonable prize, but a job like this was probably paying Reims five times that much. It wasn't all about the money, though it was nice. Maybe he should have pushed for a little more. He knew his worth.

Or had, before taking this job.

It was one thing to feel like he wasn't much help when it came to a man like Reims. It was another when he was around Lily. That little woman was quick, deadly with her knives, and fearless. She'd probably stare into a tidal wave and dare it to drown her. Having seen her fight, she'd probably come out on the right side of it, too.

Then there was Jal. Honaaz had underestimated him, and he had a feeling that was just what Jal wanted. The kid wanted to make it seem like he was little more than a tall oaf, but that wasn't true at all. It was more than the bow, though he was deadly dangerous with it. More than his fighting. Where did someone learn that skill if he hadn't served in the military?

Shadows slithered near him.

He spun, daggers held out, as men converged on him.

"Where is Reims?" one of the men asked. He was a little taller than the rest, and he stayed in the shadows so that Honaaz had to squint to try to make out his features, but didn't dare stare too long. There were too many others now cornering him.

Honaaz frowned and shook his head. "Can't say I know a Reims. I'm just out for a stroll. Got hired on as a knacker to clean out a few strays in the city."

The guard came toward him. Honaaz circled in place. There were too many, and he didn't want to kill them. Reims had been clear about that.

Unless Jal suddenly jumped down to help, these guards would overrun him. At least he could knock down a few, even if it meant cutting some of them down as well.

Honaaz lurched forward.

Then a darkened shape dropped down next to him.

The air exploded, and three of the men were thrown back.

"Thought you could use a little help," Lily said. "Next time, just give a whistle. That's how we know you need a hand."

Her knives went flying from her.

Honaaz had frozen, but seeing her fight loosened something inside him. He lumbered forward, knocking men back. Lily came after him with knives spinning.

She looked over at him and grinned slightly.

He found himself smiling back. He probably looked like Jal, trying to bed everyone around him. That made him even more irritated.

Honaaz ignored that thought and darted forward. When he saw what were obvious Dogs, he cut them down. When he encountered guards, he just punched or kicked or threw them out of the way.

Lily was quick, but it wasn't just her knives that made her deadly. It was whatever was in that pouch. Honaaz couldn't see what she was doing, but every so often, she'd pull something out, and toss it. Explosions followed, and men were thrown back.

An arrow whistled past his head, and he spun, barely in time to see a Dog fall near him. The man had almost snuck up on him, but Jal's arrow had struck him in the chest and knocked him down. Honaaz nodded, and Jal winked.

Turning again, Honaaz swept his gaze all around him for a sign of Reims or the priest. Maybe they were waiting for them to come back.

A whistle rang out.

He looked up. Jal stood with his bow raised, arrow at the ready.

Then he fell.

Honaaz hadn't even seen what happened.

"Something happened to Jal," Honaaz told Lily. "The fucking idiot was just standing there, and then he dropped."

She glanced up with a frown, then grabbed her grappling hook out of a pouch and went racing across the street. She scaled the wall in little more than a few heartbeats.

Lily had done the brunt of the work and removed more Dogs than he'd been able to. But there were still more coming, along with some Archers.

Honaaz had to provide protection. He was going to buy them time.

Two men appeared. Neither of them looked like the Dogs he'd dealt with in Sanaron, but he noticed a tattoo on one man's hand and a dark look in the other's eyes.

Honaaz launched himself forward and kicked the first man in the midsection. Using his daggers, he carved through the next man's arms, then grabbed him before he fell and hurled him into the street. Honaaz chased after him, and when he reached the rest of the Dogs—a collection of what looked like ten more—he threw himself into the middle of them.

He wasn't going to worry about whether they could get to him. These Dogs had no teeth. He jammed his dagger into one man, kicked another, and drove his elbow back into one more.

They had him surrounded.

But he wasn't going to stop fighting.

Anger bubbled up within him, and he continued to punch, kick, and spin as much as he could. Honaaz drove his fists into their stomachs while avoiding their knives and swords, but there was no end to the onslaught.

It was almost as if the Dogs were calling men out of thin air.

But then he wasn't alone.

Another figure fought with him.

Reims.

His blades were a blur. He darted through the remaining Dogs, slicing through the back of one man's leg, jabbing a knife into the belly of a second, cleaving cleanly through another man's arm. He went through one after another, and before Honaaz could do much of anything, the rest of the Dogs were down.

A cloaked figure stood at the end of the street, and it took Honaaz a moment to realize that it was the woman they'd rescued from the prison. She was watching Reims, an unreadable expression in her eyes.

"You whistled?" Reims said.

"Actually, Jal did."

Reims frowned. "Where is he?"

Honaaz jerked a finger.

A face appeared on a nearby rooftop, and Lily looked down. "I'm going to need help! He was hit. Crossbow bolt. It's in his right shoulder so he should be fine, but we're going to need to get him some help."

His right shoulder? Jal wasn't going to take well to that. That was his drawing arm.

Reims looked over to him. "Watch the street," he said.

Rather than arguing, which Honaaz was tempted to do, he just nodded.

The street was empty. He kept waiting for the guards to appear. With what they had gone through inside the prison, he wouldn't put it past the guards to react quickly. This city seemed better organized than Sanaron. The watch should've found them by now.

He waited and glanced back to see Reims scaling the wall of the building, much like Jal had, though not with the same fluid grace, nor the speed. Still, Honaaz didn't know if he'd be able to do it quite so easily.

"He intimidates you."

Honaaz jerked around. He hadn't realized that the woman was still there.

"He's got a reputation," Honaaz muttered.

"It's well earned," she said.

"You know him?"

"Now?" She shook her head.

Honaaz looked over at her. She ran her hands through her golden hair, pulling it back and squeezing. Her green eyes narrowed.

"He was different when I knew him," she said. "Less ruthless. Less determined."

Honaaz grunted and turned away. She hadn't made a run for it, so he doubted that she would. Maybe Reims had said something to her to talk her into staying. Maybe she bought into the mission. Or maybe he'd simply paid her. That was probably more likely.

"How much did he offer you?" Honaaz said. She remained silent, so he glanced back over at her. "He had to have paid you, right?"

"How much is he paying you?" the woman asked.

"I'm starting to think it's not enough. Not nearly fucking enough."

"He's going to use you. That's what he does."

Honaaz stared up at the rooftop, where Reims and the other two were now. "I'm sure he is," he said. "I figured that from the moment he hired me for the job. That's sort of the thing, you know. You take a job, you get used. You deal with it."

"And you don't mind that you're getting used?" she said.

Honaaz shrugged.

"It doesn't sound pleasant."

"Some jobs aren't."

He frowned, staring into the distance. Now he could make out movement, and there was no attempt at trying to conceal it. The men—and there were many of them—marched toward them. Streetlight caught the gleaming metal helms, and he knew the guard was about to bear down on them.

Honaaz whistled, trying to mimic the same whistle Lily had used. She looked down at them, and he pointed. She raced along the rooftop, disappearing for a moment, before darting back. He shook his head. He knew what she had found.

The guard had arrived.

There was nothing to be done about it now. Nothing but to just get moving.

That was, if Jal could even do so.

"We need help," Reims called down. "I'm going to need to lower him down to you."

"Lower him down?" Lily said to him. "What do you think you're going to use for that?"

"Your line."

"If you break it—"

"Then I'll buy you more rope."

Honaaz smiled to himself. It seemed Lily felt the same way about her grappling hook that Jal felt about his bow.

He moved to stand beneath the building they were perched on. "I'm ready," he said.

Reims carefully began lowering Jal. The kid had the rope wrapped around his arms and his bow slung over his shoulder. His face had grown pale, and a crossbow bolt was sticking out of him.

"That's not in his fucking shoulder," he said. "It's damn near in his chest."

As soon as Jal was lowered down to him, Honaaz grabbed him and pulled him closer. He guided him over to the side of the street and then waited.

It didn't take long for Lily and Reims to drop next to him.

Lily checked over her rope before stuffing it into a pouch.

"He's going to need healing." Kanar looked to the woman.

She frowned. "What exactly do you think I can do, Gray? I don't have access to the same resources I once did."

Reims stormed toward her, towering over her. Honaaz

found himself marveling at this woman for meeting Reims' murderous gaze without flinching.

"Just help him."

"I've told you that I can't." She glanced behind her. "And it seems as if you don't have much time. What are you going to do? Leave your man here?"

"I'm not leaving him behind," Reims said.

"Interesting. You must have found some loyalty. That's shocking."

"I never had trouble with loyalty when it was reciprocated."

She looked up at him. "You know that it was."

"Would the two of you stop bickering?" Lily said, moving to stand between them. She gave Reims a push in the chest and peered up at the woman. "You can't help him?"

"Not here."

Lily clenched her jaw and looked as if she were waging some war in her mind, before coming to a decision. "Fine. Then we're going to get him out of the city and over to the hegen compound." She turned to Reims. "Before you object, you know you can't do this job without Jal. He's our friend. Our teammate. We're going to get him help."

Reims looked as if he was going to be sick.

That was almost enough to make Honaaz laugh.

Surprisingly, Lily looked almost as bad as Reims, as if this decision was a painful one.

Chapter Twenty-Three

LILY

LILY HATED THAT IT WAS COMING DOWN TO THIS.

She didn't want anything to happen to Jal, though. Were she better equipped, she might be able to seal off his injury, at least long enough to make sure that he could recuperate. But she wasn't well equipped, even if she had *that* skill with the art. Also, if she were being honest, she also didn't want to expose herself to Kanar. She already had enough questions from him and didn't need him to come at her with even more. The way he looked at her made her uncomfortable.

They managed to reach the edge of the city. There was no sign of them being followed, but eventually, the guard would catch up, and the team had to be ready to either fight or run.

She was ready to run.

They'd accomplished what they needed to do in the city. Getting to Morgan had been the entire purpose of this mission. Anything else was simply extra. Now Lily wanted nothing more than to leave the city, get back on the road, and figure out where they needed to go.

She looked over to Morgan and found the woman watching her with a knowing look, as if she were fully aware of who Lily was and, better still, what she was.

What has she seen?

If Morgan had seen Lily using *any* of her art, then Morgan would know what Lily was. Witchcraft users understood the hegen art.

But it's not just *the art.*

It was *how* Lily had used the art. Morgan might even know where Lily had trained.

The citadel.

It hadn't been that long since she'd trained there. It hadn't been that long since she had left so she could try to make something of herself and have an influence on the war. And ever since leaving, Lily couldn't help but feel as if she was a failure. She had not gotten the vengeance for her people that she deserved.

They reached the gate, where a pair of men stood at either side of the wall.

She motioned to Kanar, who looked up at soldiers and frowned.

"Can you take care of them?" he said.

"From here?" Lily eyed the distance. She could hit one of them with a knife, and maybe both, but it was going to be a tricky thing. Her range wasn't quite that accurate.

They needed Jal.

"I wonder if he'd mind if I used his bow," she said.

"He'd mind," Jal muttered, slumped against Honaaz.

"We don't have much time," Kanar said. "The moment

they start to put out word, we're going to have to get through the gate."

"How are they armed?" Honaaz asked, keeping his head down.

"Crossbows. There are also probably more of them than what we can see. It won't take long for them to stir the rest into action."

Lily sighed. "If we get caught in here, we aren't getting out of the city, and we aren't going to be able to accomplish what we need. How are we going to figure out what they intend to do with that blood?"

The woman looked over to her, and there was a hint of amusement in her eyes.

"One thing at a time," Kanar said.

He was right, but this was one thing that Lily knew she needed to be careful with. She had to move as quickly as she could.

A pair of shrill whistles rang out.

"Too late," Jal said. He still managed to smile, despite the crossbow bolt jutting out of his chest, and his skin looking even paler than it had before. He looked to Kanar, and the smile faltered. "You can just leave me behind. I can find my way out when I'm better."

"We're not leaving you behind," Kanar said.

"Because we can't do the job without you," Lily added.

Honaaz shook his head. "Fuck," he muttered.

Lily laughed.

Honaaz looked over to her and then quickly looked away.

Either he didn't like her or he didn't trust her, but either way, he knew too much about her. It didn't matter, though.

She just needed to keep her secrets from Kanar until they finished the job.

More of the guard began to march through the street. "Time to move," she said. "We don't have enough time to stay here, so why don't we split up?"

"We are not splitting up," Kanar said.

She was surprised that he felt so strongly about that. In Sanaron, he didn't have nearly the same issues with splitting up as he had ever since they'd left. Even when Jal had gone off into the trees to draw the Dogs away, Kanar had been somewhat reluctant. Dividing themselves up then had been the right move, though, and it still was now.

Lily looked over to Kanar. "You can't keep all of us safe by trying to smother us. We're a team for a reason."

Morgan smirked. "Your team understands logic better than you do, Gray."

Kanar clenched his jaw, and he flicked his gaze up, then along the street, before finally seeming to come to a decision. He grabbed a pair of knives from beneath his cloak. With a fluid motion, he tossed both of them.

They struck the men up on the wall at the same time, and they both fell.

"So much for not attacking your king," Morgan said, her voice soft.

Kanar stiffened. He turned away as if he'd been slapped. "Let's get moving," he said.

Lily shot Morgan a look. "Why do you do that to him?"

"Because he deserves it."

"Does he?"

Morgan tipped her head to the side. "Does he know about your background?"

"He knows what he needs to know," Lily said, keeping

her voice quiet. Kanar had moved ahead of them and didn't seem as though he was listening, but she still wanted to be careful. She never knew how much Kanar paid attention. "What were you planning with that blood? What do you intend to destroy?"

"I don't intend to destroy anything," Morgan replied.

They reached the gate. The sound of boots on the cobblestones came loud, and a shout rang out behind them.

Honaaz, who was ahead, turned to them. "Get moving."

"You can't stop all of the guard on your own," Lily said.

"I don't intend to."

He grabbed one of the massive doors of the gate and began to push on it. To her amazement, it started to budge. There was a groan of metal and a soft screech that came with it, but gradually, he forced the door closed behind them.

Lily looked over to Kanar, who wore an expression she had rarely seen before—surprise.

"We have to get past the stone," Lily told them. "Stay close to the wall, and the guards atop it shouldn't be able to see us quite as easily." The hegen section was still lit, despite the early hour. That wasn't altogether unusual, especially as the hegen kept different schedules than most within the city would. They were probably still celebrating the collection of their prizes. "We will be exposed for only a little bit," she said. "But if we're quick enough…"

There came another scream of metal, and when she looked back, Honaaz was pushing on the other gate. How was one man forcing the colossal gates closed?

"I guess it's a good thing we brought him," Jal muttered.

"Is that why you did?" Lily asked Kanar.

"No."

"You're going to have to tell him," Morgan said.

Kanar looked over. "I'm not going to tell anyone anything."

Morgan shook her head. "Still haven't changed, have you, Gray?"

Lily had so many questions, but she didn't dare ask them—not with the little time they had. Instead, she knew to move quickly. If Honaaz managed to close the gates, they wouldn't have to worry about the guards following them, though it seemed too much to expect any man to close the gates completely. It might be better for Lily to use her art to help with the gate, though if she were to do that, then she might not have enough for when they actually needed it.

What a waste that she hadn't had the time to collect from the Dogs. There might have been a few useful prizes among them. Now she wouldn't know.

They hurried along the wall. The wind had picked up, reminding her for a moment of Sanaron, though it didn't carry the same force. The air held the smell of pine from the nearby forest, but it was mixed with something else, a familiar spice that she remembered from the days spent training when she was younger.

They passed the stone. There were no hegen climbing on it. Now was the time for celebrating the collection and then beginning to prepare for the use. She was surprised to find that she missed those festivals. The people all came together, a celebration of death, but also of life. A time to recognize the gifts that they'd been given through the sacrifice of another.

"That's fucking creepy," Honaaz mumbled.

She looked at him, and he tensed.

"Sorry. I blocked off the gate," he said, motioning toward it with his thumb, "but couldn't get it all the way closed. Should buy us some time. Anyway, I wasn't trying to upset you."

Kanar watched Honaaz and frowned at Lily.

Honaaz was only going to draw more attention to her.

She needed to keep him quiet, but with the way he looked at her—the fear in his eyes—she had to say something that might help him as well. She didn't need him fearing her on this job. There was too much they had to get done.

"No. You're right," she said. "It can be creepy. I think that's a good way of describing it."

"There is power in death," Morgan said.

"You need to stop," Kanar growled.

"And you need to stop fearing what you don't understand. Just because your king fears what he can't control doesn't mean that you need to. You're smarter than that, Gray. Or you once were."

Kanar stayed silent.

They moved ahead, making their way past the stone.

A battering sound at the gate drew her attention.

Lily looked back. Honaaz had managed to slip something into the gate to keep it closed, though she couldn't tell what it was from here. Not one of his beloved daggers. Maybe a rock? Or a board?

They had *some* time, but not much to spare. They had to get to the hegen and ask for help. Then they would see what it would take to get out of the city.

It had been a long time since Lily had gone back to her

people. Then again, the hegen were no longer her people. They had not been ever since she'd left to train at the citadel, using her art to get vengeance. That was not something her people would understand.

She looked over to Morgan, but the priest almost seemed to make a point of ignoring her.

That might be for the best. Lily didn't need to have her attention, and certainly didn't need for Kanar to start asking questions that would only cause more strain between the two of them. She didn't want there to be any reason they couldn't keep working together.

At least until this job was over.

When it was, then she might have to plan for an alternative, like leaving Sanaron. That wasn't what she wanted to do, but increasingly, she thought she might need to. Sanaron had been a gift—a place where she could collect her prizes without anyone really paying much attention, and where it wouldn't draw the notice of the watch. Plus she was comfortable, though that comfort had come because of her relationship with Kanar. Once that soured, she doubted she'd be comfortable any longer.

Lily looked behind her. The guards still hadn't gotten past the gates, but that didn't mean it would take long for them to do it. All they had to do was overpower whatever Honaaz had used to block them off, then they could slip out and get to them.

"Keep moving," Kanar said.

They hurried across the open grass separating the wall from the hegen section. A shout came from behind them, and she felt a soft hiss as a crossbow bolt came streaking toward them and sunk into the ground. It was followed by another, but the bolts didn't hit any of them.

They were lucky.

Jal had not been.

He moaned. The pain of being moved this far had to be incredible. She couldn't imagine what he must be feeling or how he must be suffering with the crossbow bolt sticking out of his chest. She hadn't removed it, and when Kanar had started to, she'd caught him and warned him against it. Just as much damage could be done trying to pull out the bolt as there was with it going in. Jal needed someone who could remove it and avoid that damage.

That was, if the hegen were willing to help.

They reached the outskirts of the section, and Lily found herself relaxing more than she would have expected. It was dark, though there was a flicker of light in the distance. The muted and soft strains of a familiar song drifted toward her. Would she know any of the people?

There had been other hegen who had returned when she'd still been with the people, and they'd been welcomed back. But none of them had gone off and done what she had. None of them had betrayed the teachings, taken them, and twisted them the way she had. She had left, abandoned the people.

But with the soft notes of the song, the hint of spice in the air, and even the familiar confusion of the streets, she couldn't help but feel as if all of this were simply *right*. There was something almost peaceful about returning to the hegen, though she knew it should not be the case.

"What is it?" Kanar asked.

"It's nothing," Lily said.

"I can tell that it's something. If there's a problem here, you need to let us know."

"Leave her alone," Morgan said. "She must focus on navigating through here."

Kanar glanced from Lily to Morgan, but he fell silent.

Lily frowned. That wasn't the help she'd expected to receive. Why would Morgan offer her assistance? Something to consider another time.

Now she had to stay focused on finding her way through.

She took the lead, guiding them through the section.

In most places, the hegen lived apart. They didn't care to live in the city, and certainly not in a place like Verendal. Not when there was so much more that they could do in their own places, ways of conveying the art that could not be done by being with those who didn't understand and those who did not appreciate it.

Lily weaved through the street. There was a pattern to it, though it was one that only those who had grown up with the hegen could identify. Most people found the hegen layouts too confusing. Even though she'd never been here, Lily knew her way through and came to a small plaza.

She paused. There was music and dancing and singing.

"What the fuck is this?" Honaaz muttered.

"This is a festival," she said.

He looked over to her. "Why?"

"Because they have reason to celebrate."

"Again, why?"

Jal moaned.

She raised her hand, motioning for them to wait. "I won't be long."

"I can come with you," Kanar said.

Lily shook her head. "Stay there."

Kanar held her gaze, and she knew that she might be

forced to provide answers, but not yet. He might want the answers, but she wasn't sure she was ready to give them.

She moved forward, into the music, the crowd, and the people around her. A few of them looked in her direction, but they didn't mind her presence.

She found herself drawn toward the center of the festival, toward the middle of the plaza.

A dark-haired woman watched her approach. Lily realized that others were moving away, giving her space.

The woman's gaze dipped to Lily's pouch before she looked back up at her. "Have you come to kill me?"

Lily stiffened. "Is that what you saw?"

The woman pulled several cards from her pocket. It was one of the gifts that only hegen with real power were able to access. She flipped one card over, and it showed a knife. Another showed a noose, and another showed a dark-haired woman.

"I'm not here to kill you," Lily said.

She withdrew one of the hegen items she had taken out of the prison, holding it carefully. There was something about this woman's demeanor that reminded Lily of Ezra, though Ezra had a warmth to her, whereas this woman was more distant.

The woman pulled out another set of cards, and she flipped them while looking briefly up at the item Lily held. "I've seen you coming."

"No one sees me coming," Lily said.

The woman glanced up. "Evidence of your coming. You have gained too much skill to be seen easily." She smiled, though it was full of sadness. "If you look around the fringes, you can begin to see some subtle influence.

That's what I saw of you." She turned another card and there was a bow. On another was a dog, and then a ship.

"This was you?" Lily asked. She held out the item she had claimed from the prison, waiting for the woman to take it. "You're the one responsible for keeping the priest there?"

"You rescued her for them?"

"What did the cards tell you?"

"They tell me much," the woman said. "They tell me that you chose not to kill when you could have. They tell me that you have brought someone to me that you care about, and that you are not finished with your journey."

She flipped cards quickly, faster than Lily could keep track of. She could've sworn that she saw a building that looked like the citadel, but then it faded. The ink on the cards was specifically designed, and Lily hadn't remained with her people long enough to learn that part of the art. It was something she would have loved to have learned, but she had twisted the art in a different way.

"And they tell me that you have upset the Hunter."

There was a hint of warmth in the word.

Lily looked up, understanding dawning on her. "You not only made them for him, but you're with him. How do the people feel about that?" She looked around, at the space they'd been given.

The woman watched her. "All of our people get a choice. You made yours, much like I've made mine. And my people understand the choice."

"Of course they do," Lily said. She nodded to the cards. "If you have been paying attention, you would've seen the reason I am doing this. There's danger."

"There is always danger."

"Alainsith were slaughtered. Did the cards show you that?"

The woman's hand froze, and she didn't turn the card this time. Instead, she looked up, holding Lily's gaze. "You would help?"

"I need help for a friend. He's been shot. I know you can do something about it, and I'm not here to bargain for your services." Lily was in no mood to have somebody try to tell her what she would have to do so that Jal could get the healing he needed. "And then we need a way out."

"You have your way."

"Passage," Lily said. "I know that you have passage."

"It won't matter. I can't stop the one pursuing you."

The Hunter.

"Why not?" Lily asked.

"Because he makes his choice, much like I make mine." The woman flipped more of her cards, before finally stopping. She closed her eyes, took a deep breath, and seemed as if she had come to a decision. A troubled expression crossed her brow, and Lily wondered if the woman would show her what she had seen on the card. Even if she did, it was possible that Lily wouldn't understand it. "I will help your friend. The price will be—"

"I'm not paying any price."

The woman pressed on as if Lily had said nothing. "The price will be that you must complete your task." She looked up. "You should understand that they cannot succeed."

"I do."

"You know what would happen if they were to accomplish what they're trying to do."

Lily clenched her jaw. "I understand, but it's not on me to prevent them from succeeding."

"You made it on you when you left the people. Which is why you must do this."

Lily couldn't argue. The woman wasn't entirely wrong. Not given Lily's experience at the citadel.

The woman flipped the card and another, then slid them into her pocket. "Now we must move away from the festival. It might be a time of celebration for our people, but not for you. And if we don't move, then the Hunter will find you."

"How long will you give us?"

"I will give you nothing. You must take it, though from what I understand, you have always taken, haven't you?"

Lily wasn't about to argue. The only thing she'd needed to do was to get help for Jal, and she had done it. No matter what else happened, she had done what she had come to do.

Why was it that she didn't feel quite right?

Chapter Twenty-Four

LILY

Lily looked at the small square. It was so familiar to her, so similar to what she had known. The fires glowed brightly, and there was an energy here. The dancing had a rhythm to it, and it was one she felt as if she could fall into very easily once again. All it would take would be for her to stand, join the hegen, and dance. There were even a few pretty boys here that she thought she could dance with.

Lily pushed those thoughts out of her head. That was not why she was here.

The hegen woman crouched over Jal. She had started working her hands over the wound in his chest. He was only semi-conscious, and he moaned periodically. A wound like that could be fatal for some people, though Jal wasn't just "some people."

Lily cared about that man. He was a valuable member of the team, and regardless of what Kanar might say, he felt the same way.

"Get down here," the hegen woman said.

She crouched down. "You can help him."

The woman looked up, and she nodded slightly. "I can. But I would ask for your hands."

Lily resisted the urge to say she couldn't help because that wasn't true. She recognized the technique, even if it wasn't something she practiced any longer. It was the subtle art that she preferred. She liked to use bone and carve it into forms that worked effectively for her, though it wasn't as if she wasn't familiar with the type of healing that this hegen woman used. She used a different kind of art that reminded Lily of her mother.

"The wound itself isn't so bad, though his skin seems to want to hold the bolt in place. I've seen worse. There will be a cost."

"His life is worth whatever you want to charge me," Lily said.

"I meant for him."

"I will pay it."

The woman scoffed. "And what makes you think that I would permit you to do that on his behalf?"

Lily hesitated. Where was Kanar? She couldn't see him. A crackling fire behind her made it difficult to make out anything beyond the lighted circle.

"You know who I am."

"I don't know if *you* even know who you are," the woman said. "But I do know *what* you are, and I know what you could be. Even if you don't."

Lily frowned. "So does that mean you will help?"

"I never said I would not. A man like him deserves all the help he can get." She paused with her hands on Jal. "I do wonder why he is with you," she said softly.

Lily laughed. "I wonder that all the time."

The hegen woman began to work her hands across Jal's

chest. She ran her fingers in a thin circle, which gradually began to widen. Jal moaned, and the woman cupped her hands over him while steadily working.

It was a different skill with the art than what she had seen her mother use. This seemed much more highly controlled. There were some hegen who were rumored to have far more talent than others. Lily had known it. When she had worked with Ezra, she had seen that her mentor was far more skilled than many of the others they worked with. But Lily had never considered the possibility that somebody would be able to control the art so well that it would heal a wound this quickly.

Finally, the woman sat back. Lily hadn't even seen much of what had happened.

"It's done. At least, I've done as much as I can. He'll need to rest and recover. I suspect he won't be able to use this shoulder for quite some time, and given the weapon he seems to prefer…" Her gaze drifted to Jal's fingers, of all things, and Lily realized that she was likely looking at calloused fingertips. "It may take him more time to be comfortable with it. I would caution you to keep an eye on him, and to keep him safe."

She started to stand, and Lily hurried to catch her. She wanted to stay with Jal, but she also needed answers.

"What have you seen?" Lily asked.

The woman pulled the stack of cards from her pocket and began to flip them. She looked at the cards one at a time, and not up at Lily. "Things are changing. The cards become more difficult to read. Whatever it means is dangerous for our kind."

The woman slowly started turning the cards over again, until she paused once more. "I see you. I wonder if perhaps even you can see what it is, or what this means, but then I see something else. A place, I suspect, but I don't know if that is what it is, or if it's perhaps something different." She flipped another card, which revealed a stream and what looked like a city in the background, but Lily couldn't make any sense of what the woman was trying to show her. "And I see change. Not only for you but for me. My people." Her voice dropped. "For all of us."

It was a strange comment. What might it mean?

"I told you what happened with the attack," Lily said. "That's why we've come."

"I have seen this."

"You knew that's why she was there."

The woman tipped her head slightly. Her dark hair seemed to catch the shadows of the early morning more than it should. "I know what is believed about her, but I'm not one who can make claims contrary to that. I have done my best, but unfortunately, there is only so much that I can say to those who have the authority to change it."

"You knew?" Lily said.

"I knew what I was asked."

Lily snorted. For all the claims of not getting involved and not using magic or the art in particular ways, the people often got involved when they should not. Lily had seen it too often for her liking. And now it was essentially an admission of what the woman had done, how she had been part of this, and how she had been responsible for placing the trap that had held Morgan in place.

It was a potent trap, even for Lily. She had experience in disrupting such things, but even her experience had limits. Had she not trained in the citadel the way she had, she wasn't entirely sure that she would have managed to completely break that pattern.

"The priest claims she wasn't involved," Lily said. She glanced over her shoulder and just now found Kanar wearing a dark expression that he often did when he was upset.

"I don't believe she was," the woman said. "I would challenge him, and you, to question everything you know. Find your own answers, and come to your own understanding. With what I've seen," the hegen woman said, flipping another few cards before looking up and meeting Lily's eyes, "I believe that we may need those who can challenge and question what they assume to be correct."

Lily nodded but wanted to move on to more pressing things. "We need help getting away from the city."

"You keep asking," the woman said.

"You won't help?"

"You truly intend to find what happened?"

Lily nodded. "Alainsith were slaughtered. Their blood was collected. I don't know how much experience you have with witchcraft out here." She didn't really know either, partly because Verendal looked far more intact than many of the other places she had seen during the witchcraft war. They may not have suffered the same way that so many others had. And if that was the case, then perhaps they wouldn't care. "But I can tell you what I've seen. Families broken. Towns destroyed. Lives lost. All for power."

"It was for more than power," the woman said. She took a deep breath and then shook her head. "I suppose that I am obligated to offer whatever I can to one of the people." She smiled tightly. "Even one who has wandered. There is one thing I may be able to offer you, and it will involve some work on your part. I don't get the sense that you mind a little work, though."

Lily frowned. "No."

"You can leave from here, and find it to the west of the city."

"If this is some sort of trap—"

The woman smiled. "Do you always see traps when they don't exist?"

It was an interesting question, and one that struck Lily. Perhaps she *did* always see traps. "I've suffered." She said it quietly and felt a bit ashamed of admitting that.

"All of us have suffered in our own way," the woman said. "Everything should help you grow, even what you don't understand."

Lily wondered what it might've been like to learn from somebody like this, with the same calmness and the same calming demeanor that Ezra had. That was what struck Lily the most. When she had gone to Ezra, it had been partly to learn her type of art, but partly to learn more about others. Lily had never had the talent her mother would've liked, though she had tried.

She had wanted to have an aspect of her art that would allow her to understand elements of the world that were more than just destructive, but that had not been her mother's plan for her.

Instead, Lily had come to master something that her people would never embrace.

"Thank you," Lily said.

"You don't need to thank me," the woman said. "You must do what will make us proud. That is all we ask." With that, she walked away.

Lily crouched down next to Jal. His eyes were closed, but his breathing had become far more regular.

"You can wake up at any time," she said, touching him on the shoulder.

He moved slightly, moaning just a little bit, and gradually opened his eyes. "You didn't have to." His voice came out in a whisper.

"I didn't," she said.

There was a hint of his usual amused expression. "Good. I was worried you would reveal what you didn't want."

She took his hand and squeezed it. She had never really known how much Jal knew, yet despite what he wanted everyone to believe, he was far cleverer than he let on.

"One of the hegen outside Verendal helped you. I think it's the same one who placed the trap around Morgan."

He coughed. "A difficult trap," he murmured.

"She shouldn't have placed the trap," Lily said.

"Who's to say what somebody should or should not do? That isn't for others to decide."

She snorted. "Only you, Jal."

"Is it done?" Kanar asked. He towered over her.

Lily elbowed him in the thigh. "You don't have to stand so close. Jal needs time to heal from this."

"And the cost?"

"She claims there wasn't one."

"There is always a cost," Kanar said.

"She said we had to finish the mission," Lily turned to Honaaz. "Can you help him?"

Honaaz grunted. "I guess I can carry him."

Lily backed away as Honaaz scooped Jal up. It looked easy for him, but Jal was tall and, she suspected, heavy.

How strong was Honaaz? Then again, he had managed to close the city gates by himself.

"Where are we going?" Lily asked.

She turned her attention to Morgan, who was standing behind them. The other hegen shielded them in a circle. The dancing was a steady movement, a swaying energy that flowed around them. The fire encased everything in a crackling, shimmering glow. It was an amazing thing to see, but even more amazing was the fact that no one from the city itself would be able to get past the hegen without raising an alarm. They had simply welcomed Lily and the others and permitted them to enter this place, where they could get the healing they needed and have a measure of privacy.

"I'm not bringing it to you," Morgan told Kanar.

"We need to see where they were going," Kanar said.

"I don't have it. Listen, Gray, I know you think that I'm this terrible witchcraft practitioner, but I'm not."

"You had some of their blood on you."

Morgan shook her head. "You don't understand. It's not as simple as you think. And I didn't have all of the blood."

Lily looked over to Kanar. There was tension in his eyes, along with a lingering sense of pain and anguish. How much had Kanar suffered because of this woman?

Kanar stayed quiet, and he glanced at Morgan, then to the others. "The task was to get to you, and you would lead us to the blood."

Lily felt the same reservations that Kanar did about that.

"Have you even thought about why they wanted you to do the job?" Morgan asked.

"I have fought against this kind of magic for years," Kanar said.

"Oh, I know, Gray. But why now?"

"To prevent something worse," he said. There was real sadness in his voice.

"We should get moving one way or the other, because I don't know how long we have here," Lily said, motioning to the hegen. "It might make sense to head north, to the west side of the city, as the woman claimed. She said there would be something for us."

Kanar frowned. "There is nothing there."

"She said there would be a way."

"How bad can one executioner be?" Honaaz asked.

"He controls the city," a hegen man said from nearby. He was dark-haired, and pretty enough. He motioned to Lily. "I was told to lead you."

"See?" Lily said to the rest of the team. "She even has a guide for us."

"I'm not sure we should go with him," Kanar said.

"Would you relax? She helped us. She saved Jal, and now she's giving us a way out of this place. Isn't that what we need?"

It was more than just a way out of Verendal. They had to go wherever Morgan knew the blood to be. They needed to stop whatever the witchcraft practitioners intended.

Lily turned to Morgan.

"I can show you, but it will be dangerous," Morgan said.

Honaaz grunted. "Of course it will be. We're dealing with fucking sorcery. How can it be anything but dangerous?" He cradled Jal like some tall child.

They headed through the hegen section, following the

pretty dark-haired man. They stayed to the west side, steering clear of the city wall. As they moved toward the forest running alongside Verendal, Lily hazarded a glance back. There were nearly a dozen guards starting to encircle the hegen section. They didn't go in, probably because they were afraid.

"They're going to get us," Honaaz muttered.

"I don't think so," Lily said. "I get the sense that the woman and the Hunter are together, but I also feel like she's not exactly pleased with what he did." She frowned and looked over to Morgan, who stayed close to Kanar, though she was walking a step behind him. It was almost as if she didn't want to walk side by side but also didn't want to get too far.

Lily smirked at that thought. She had seen the hurt in Kanar's eyes, and she recognized how much he seemed to struggle, but she also saw the way Morgan looked at him. There was hope that they might be able to reconnect. And maybe they could—in another life. Kanar would never get past Morgan's use of magic.

They followed the trees, and Lily hurried forward to catch up to the hegen man. "What's your name?"

"Josepan. Esmerelda told me that I should make sure you get to the boat safely."

Lily glanced back at where Honaaz was carrying Jal. A boat? Could Kanar have known? There had to be some reason that he brought Honaaz with them on this journey, certainly more than just as muscle. Honaaz had been valuable with that, but he was an extra body otherwise. Knowing Kanar and how he prized efficiency, she wasn't entirely sure that having an extra body simply for the sake of it fit with Kanar's plans. And he had plans.

"I didn't know the people traveled by boat," Lily said.

"We don't usually," Josepan said. "Esmerelda likes to make sure we can move upriver if we need to. So much trade comes through here, and with her and the Hunter together, we've always been cautious."

Here Lily had assumed that Verendal had been generally untouched by witchcraft.

"Have you been attacked?" she asked.

"Not here," Josepan said. "We had an episode many years ago, but it was before others really struggled in the war. We mainly heard about the experiences through tradesmen." He shrugged. "I think it's because we have such a strong Hunter, as well as Esmerelda. And to be honest, we're so far away from the rest of the kingdom that it doesn't really matter."

Witchcraft had spread quickly throughout the kingdom, sweeping from city to city and beyond. She'd seen it herself. Had been after it herself too. The citadel hunted witchcraft, and it had generally done a skillful job, but there'd been times when the practitioners managed to escape the citadel's reach.

"Is that what you were here for?" Josepan asked. "I thought the war was mostly over."

Lily glanced back at Kanar and took a deep breath. "Not entirely."

Josepan guided them to another section of the forest. He finally slowed and then waved ahead. "The river is not far from here. You're going to have to remove a tarp covering the boat, and then you can go wherever you need to go. It's probably safer if you head upriver. More boats that way."

"Thank you, Josepan. And give Esmerelda my thanks as well."

She bowed, tipping her head slightly and making a point of doing it in the old style—one that she hoped Josepan would recognize.

"Now I know why she wanted to help you." He returned the bow before shooting a look at the others. "Be safe. That big one scares me a little."

Lily chuckled. "He scares me a little too."

Josepan headed back toward the hegen section, and then they were alone.

"There's a boat up here," she said to Kanar. "He said that we should go upriver. More ships to hide among."

"That's not the way we need to go," Morgan said.

"Where, then?" Kanar snapped. He was too harsh with her.

Then again, Lily wasn't sure she could even challenge him. He was that way with Morgan because he hated magic. If Lily spoke up and revealed herself—and who and what she was—how would he feel about her? She'd managed to avoid questions so far, but he would eventually see through that. He was the Blackheart, after all, and she doubted that she could keep her abilities from him for too long.

"You wanted to see what they were after," Morgan said. "This is what they were after. I can show you."

"You can bring me to the blood?" Kanar asked.

"I don't know how much of it is left."

"You had something to do with this."

Morgan shrugged. "I won't be able to convince you otherwise."

"I know what I heard, and I know what I saw."

"That's just it, Gray. Sometimes you don't know what you saw. Sometimes what you think you saw is not what is real."

"Fuck," Honaaz muttered. "The two of you need to just go off into the trees and get this over with."

Lily barked out a laugh. Even Jal started to smile, and then coughed.

She motioned for them to go. "Well, Honaaz, I think once we get into the boat, it's going to be up to you."

"Figures," Honaaz mumbled. "Fucking Kanar Reims brought me to get me onto a boat. Not even a proper one at that."

At least he talked to her this time and didn't look at her with that fear in his eyes. Then again, she didn't necessarily mind that fear. It amused her, much like Honaaz did.

Honaaz jostled Jal so that a branch brushed against Jal's cheek.

"You be kind with Jal," she said. "He's a good man."

Honaaz looked down at him. "Fucking figures."

"What's that?"

"Even the tall bastard isn't a bastard."

Chapter Twenty-Five

KANAR

The Vinlen River rippled in small currents that swirled around hidden rocks, making the otherwise clear water slightly cloudy. Trees towered over where Kanar stood on the bank, fallen leaves littering the surface.

Kanar didn't care for it. At this point, he didn't care for any of it. The only thing he appreciated was that they had gotten away from the city. But now they were going to head back through it?

"It doesn't make any fucking sense," Honaaz grumbled.

They were near the river, though on the wrong side of the city. They had needed to head back through Verendal to move past it and reach the west. Otherwise, they would have needed to portage the small boat, which risked encountering the Hunter and his guards.

"They're looking for us in the hegen section—and over ground," Kanar said. "If we move quickly enough, we should be able to get on our way before they even know we came through here."

"Still don't like it," Honaaz said.

"You're not being paid to like it."

They'd hidden their weapons beneath a tarp, and Lily and Morgan had also concealed themselves there.

"What am I supposed to like, then? Him getting shot?" Honaaz motioned to where Jal lay on the narrow barge. His color was better now than it had been.

They needed Jal. That wasn't the only reason he wanted Jal to recover, but at this point, it was the only reason that mattered. Jal's eyes were closed, and his fist squeezed around the bow, his quiver next to him. He always managed to have enough arrows, but even he might have to resupply before they finished this.

Lily had been quiet ever since they'd visited the hegen. She sat on the barge, resting near Morgan, who had also been silent. Kanar would take her silence, but he didn't like that Lily was being so quiet. She had some connection to the hegen, or experience with them, and going to them had upset her.

He'd have to talk to her about it. He had his own reasons for not wanting to work with the hegen. Maybe sharing those with her would help her understand that she wasn't the only one who had to struggle with whatever she dealt with.

"Let's push it off," Kanar said.

"Still don't like it," Honaaz mumbled. He helped, though.

Neither of them spoke as they shoved the narrow barge away from where it had been moored along the shore and deeper into the water. Kanar had been surprised that the hegen had access to the barge. The raven-haired woman had told them about the boat, and though he'd been skeptical about her claim, thinking that she'd lied so they would leave the hegen and be run down by the Archers, Lily had flashed a strange card with an image of a barge, as if that were all the proof she needed. When they'd found the barge where Lily claimed it would be, he had no choice but to believe she was right.

Once the barge splashed down, he climbed aboard with Honaaz following.

"So we just float through the damn city?"

"We wait for the boat traffic that comes through at daybreak," Kanar said, looking to the sky. It was early morning, and the sun would be up soon enough. "Then we join the rest of the ships and float through the damn city."

It sounded easy.

Which meant it wouldn't be.

When the barge neared the city wall, Kanar realized there were a couple of other boats making their way downstream. Another narrow boat moved toward them. The river gate on this part of the wall was open, so they floated right through. Once they did, Kanar's nerves started to get to him.

He shared Honaaz's concern. If they were exposed, the Hunter would come for them.

Not if he thinks we're out of the city.

That might be the blessing. They could travel through Verendal and then beyond, then move further downstream.

Kanar didn't know where they needed to go, but this way led them toward Yelind, which felt appropriate. He'd dealt with Yelind when he'd been with the Realmsguard, and he wouldn't be surprised to learn that they were the ones responsible for attacking the Alainsith. There had been rumors within the Realmsguard that Yelind had tried to target them before, though they had failed. Why not try again?

But deep down, Kanar didn't think they were responsible.

It all came back to witchcraft. Yelind might still be a part of that, but it was less likely.

Or should be.

The boat floated steadily on the river. Honaaz stood at the bow of the boat and propelled them forward using a long, slender pole. He appraised the other boats.

A waste, Kanar knew.

The real threat would come from shore.

"What do you think, Kan? We going to make it?" Jal said.

"Are you feeling any better?" Kanar asked.

"As well as I can after having an arrow in my chest." Jal shifted and sat up, moving his bow so that it didn't stand quite so upright and reveal them. "That's a neat use of magic. I've never experienced anything like that before. I can't even feel where it went in."

"It's something," Kanar said.

Morgan eyed him, which only made him look away.

He saw no sign of Archers patrolling the shoreline. They passed other boats that moved easily along. When he *did* see Archers, none paid them any attention. His gaze drifted toward the palace, and he remembered his time in the Realmsguard when he'd been tasked with protecting their king.

By the time they reached the far side of Verendal, he was starting to actually think they wouldn't have any difficulty getting out. A surprise from the hegen.

Then they reached the gate across the river.

It was closed.

"Reims," Honaaz called, "what do you want me to do?"

Kanar looked for signs of guards but didn't see anything.

No one was patrolling here. No Archers. No soldiers. Nothing. Just a shut gate.

The river narrowed as it flowed through the city, but the massive iron gate in the surrounding wall was meant to inhibit boat traffic from easily reaching Verendal. The king didn't pass goods beyond his city. The times when he *did* move beyond Reyand, it was to work with the Alainsith, not because he wanted to escape his borders.

That didn't mean leaving was impossible, but with the gate closed, it became more difficult.

"Do you see a lock or anything you can break through?" Kanar asked.

Honaaz looked around. "There's a lock, but I'm not sure I can get to it."

"Let me try," Jal said, grabbing for his bow.

"You shouldn't exert yourself yet," Lily said. She tried to pull Jal back, but he'd already stood up.

He drew back on the bow and took aim at the rope that worked the lock and kept the gate closed. He missed.

Jal frowned deeply as he looked at the bow. "That's never happened before."

"Everybody fucking misses once in a while," Honaaz said.

"Not me."

"Because you still need to rest," Lily said. "Sit down."

"I can do it," Jal insisted.

"In time. But we need you to be well, so stop risking your health."

Jal sat down, sulking as he stared at his bow. "I thought the hegen fixed me. Isn't that what you agreed to with them?"

"Just sit," Lily snapped. She tossed a knife, and it connected with the rope. The gate made a soft grinding sound.

"What did you agree to with the hegen?" Kanar asked.

There was always a cost. That was one of the things that bothered him most about them. They took and took, forcing those who needed their help to make dangerous bargains.

"I agreed to complete the job. That's it," Lily said.

"That's all they wanted from you?"

That didn't seem like enough.

"They knew what we planned, and they wanted us to succeed. That's all they wanted. Do the job, then they'd heal Jal."

Lily took a seat while Honaaz used the pole to push the gate open. They floated through, and when they were past it, Honaaz hurried and tried to close the gate again.

He shrugged when Kanar looked at him. "Just want to make sure they don't know we've come this way. I bet they'll inspect it, but we can buy some time."

"That's a good thought," Kanar said. "Too bad it won't work from this side."

Honaaz grunted. "Fuck."

Kanar moved along the boat, and he stopped in front of Morgan. "Let's talk about your involvement."

Morgan sighed. "I had some of their blood. They were attacked, I tried to intervene, and they believed me responsible."

"Because you were using witchcraft?"

She took a deep breath, as if she were going to explain, but then held back. "Because I nearly escaped."

"How were you even there?" Kanar asked.

"I'd heard some rumblings about what was planned. It took all of my resources to find anything. But when I did, I encountered signs of the citadel with some Alainsith relics."

"The citadel wouldn't be involved in killing Alainsith," Lily said.

"I know what I saw," Morgan said. "I spent time researching in the citadel. I know they were involved."

The day passed slowly. The forest streamed by as Honaaz continued to guide them along the river, though he kept his focus fixed straight ahead of him as if he were uninterested in the rest of the team. Perhaps he was. They hadn't needed Honaaz's particular talent quite yet. Kanar thought they might've while they'd been in Verendal and rescued Morgan from the prison, but it had not been necessary.

If they found themselves in the citadel…

The citadel was a strange place, and one of power. It was situated in a city that was isolated in the heart of the Nevalahd Forest. Those lands had once been Alainsith strongholds, long before their people had retreated and moved north out of this area. Through the strength of the citadel, the Alainsith had positioned themselves as rivals to Reyand, though they had been allies just as often. The leaders of the citadel had their own goals and objectives, though. They had been a part of the witchcraft war but had taken their own side and used their own type of power to intervene. Even now, Kanar didn't know if they'd gotten involved because they opposed witchcraft or because they wanted to be the ones controlling it.

That made the connection even more worrisome. What could the citadel do with Alainsith blood? Maybe they had decided to try a different tack. Perhaps they would no longer ally themselves with Reyand.

There was little talking as they traveled. Kanar didn't force it, though he wondered if perhaps he should have been trying to draw more information out of Morgan. As the day ended, the group fell into a stupor. Eventually, Jal suggested that they get some rest. Lily dug around and found a musty woven throw that she insisted on sharing with Jal in case he experienced some delayed form of shock.

"No anchor," Honaaz peered into a cubbyhole. "But there's a bunch of herbs here."

"Ooh, sage?" Lily asked.

Honaaz flinched and scattered the leaves over the polished wood. "Look, I'm not letting any more weird shit happen today."

"I meant to eat, touchy."

Kanar slunk to the rear of the barge. The moon was a sliver. It turned the overhanging twigs into skeletal fingers. There was still no sign of pursuit, but the collision of water against planks felt too loud for comfort.

"We'll stop by a stream to collect berries and water tomorrow," he said. "But for now we should stay adrift. Honaaz, can you watch first and wake me in a few hours? Can't risk someone finding us on the shore this close to the city."

"Yeah, not to mention Kanar's snores will alert half of Reyand." Lily fluffed up her pouch before settling onto it as a pillow. Honaaz eyed the action in horror, but Kanar had seen men find comfort in stranger things than blades. He'd once fought alongside a guard who'd clung to a toy hedgehog while facing five opponents armed with scimitars. The guard had won, so Kanar figured he couldn't judge.

"I do not snore." Kanar attempted a dignified voice.

"Oh please! Jal thought we were being cursed by the gods the first night of the trip."

"It did sound pretty ominous," Jal said apologetically.

A snicker came from where Morgan was curled beneath the canvas. They'd decided she'd better stay there until tomorrow since she had the most distinct appearance of the group.

Lily strained her head. "You all good under there?"

The others were on edge around Morgan, Kanar had noticed. Not only because of her gifts. She made you feel too crass, too blunt by comparison. Even caked in prison dirt, she glowed. Every move was elegant and deliberate, like she was a diplomat sent from a heavenly realm.

Or a hellish one, Kanar reminded himself.

Morgan was quiet for a moment. "Did you know what I was sentenced to?"

"Death."

"Hanging." Kanar's stomach twisted. "In prison, I sat still for hours. One of the guards began to throw food scraps at me when my eyes became too glazed. He claimed I was trying to put a love spell on him—as if I would waste the breath. I was practicing. Often, the prisoner's neck will not break during the hanging, and they die by suffocation. They manage to hold their breath and stay conscious far longer than usually humanly possible. So far, I've made it to around four minutes. I imagine that would feel like a long time, in the moment."

"So. The boat's comfier then?" Honaaz's question was met with silence.

A strand of Morgan's hair had spilled out over the deck, curving like a silver question mark in the moonlight. Kanar wondered if he should risk sleep at all, but presumed she would have made a run for it already if she was going to. Of course, an escape attempt was hardly the worst thing she could do to them.

"Lily, how is it that I'm double your height yet you're using nine-tenths of the blanket?" Jal grumbled.

"Sorry. I have to create a barrier. Your feet are cold." Lily shuffled closer. "Star game?"

"You've had three guesses already. I'm out of ideas."

"What's the star game?" Honaaz asked. He'd always been out like a candle on the previous days of travel. Maybe his body grew tired under its own mass.

"You have to guess what's in the heavens. Like a city or a series of fires or scattered toffies. Go on, try it," Lily urged.

Honaaz screwed his face up at the night sky. "Once saw a painting of folks who floated up there. Like they were in the sea but didn't need ships. They looked happy. I don't know."

"Hmm, not bad," Lily said. "I think the stars are crannies or stepping rungs, and if you get high enough, you can reach the top and look over the whole universe. Watch someone dumping flour over Malory's head in Sanaron's Mill district. See sprites leap over the cliffs of Xianal. And when you peer further, you can find everyone who's passed on to the After, and they're all waving at you."

"Need a hell of a climbing hook."

"I know, right?" Lily beamed over at Honaaz.

"What about you, Kanar?" Jal called.

"Nothing. Just disappointment. Dots in the abyss."

He turned onto his side and pulled his cloak around his shoulders, but not before he'd caught Lily's "And good night to you too."

Despite the exhaustion of the past few days, sleep didn't come easily. Some godawful toads kept calling from the reeds. And just when Kanar was about to nod off, he was startled by the sound of Honaaz relieving himself over the side of the boat.

Trying to position himself without having to dangle his legs off the back, Kanar spotted a puff of breath come from under the canvas and disperse in the night air.

The hegen restraints had been strong, and Kanar didn't doubt the Hunter's will for a second. If the team hadn't shown up, would Morgan have lived to see another day? It would soon be time to switch with Honaaz, but Kanar found himself focused on those breaths, making sure that they didn't stop.

Over the next few days, the group chattered quietly, though Morgan grew ever more withdrawn until she pointed to a small inlet. They pulled up to the shoreline, only several days outside of Verendal, and Morgan indicated they should stop. This wasn't exactly where Kanar would've expected the attack to have taken place, but Morgan insisted that this was where it was.

"Are you sure?" he asked again, but he had already done so too many times.

And now it was at the point where he could sense that she was growing irritated, and the others were as well. He had to keep his team together, and he had to try to prevent them from raising the kinds of questions he didn't have answers to. How could he have answers when he wasn't sure why Morgan had been all the way out here?

"We're nearly to the border," Lily said.

Kanar glanced over to her. She wasn't wrong. It just surprised him that she would know that.

"Almost to the border," he agreed. "But not quite. We're still in Reyand."

"Not for long," Morgan said. "This is why the meeting took place here."

"It still doesn't make any sense." Kanar let out a frustrated sigh. "Why were the Alainsith meeting here?"

"This is where it is," Morgan said again.

Kanar motioned to Honaaz. "Hide the boat, but make it so that we know where it is. Then we should be ready."

Honaaz looked as if he wanted to say something in retort, but he bit it back.

The man had been good with the boat. Kanar had anticipated a possibility that they might need to use a boat at some point, but he'd figured that might come with getting back into Sanaron, not that they would need to travel along the river. Still, having Honaaz and his obvious familiarity with the water gave them some comfort.

Morgan stood to the side, waiting.

Jal approached Kanar. He was still weak, though he seemed to be growing stronger with each passing day. "We won't have long." He tilted his head at Morgan. "A prize like that, like what they must've been after, won't hold up for long. It's going to be used."

Kanar nodded. Jal wasn't wrong. They had come to break out Morgan, and now that they had, finding the blood was the next part of the job—but Kanar wasn't entirely sure how they were going to accomplish that.

"Any thoughts?" Kanar asked.

"Nothing that you're going to like."

Kanar snorted. "With a job like this, I don't know if it's possible for me to like anything about it."

Jal grinned. He rubbed his chest, his hand lingering for a moment, as if tracing over the wound that had been healed by hegen magic. Kanar wondered how much Jal minded that healing.

"The boat is hidden as well as I can fucking do it," Honaaz said. He glanced over to Lily for a second, then Kanar. "Branches and grass. Should keep it from anyone who comes looking, but can't say we can keep it completely hidden."

"You did good," Kanar said.

Honaaz grunted but didn't say anything more.

Kanar turned to Morgan. "Show us where you were when you were here."

"I was only observing, Gray. Studying. That's all I've ever done. You, of all people, should know that. I wouldn't harm anyone."

Kanar *wanted* to believe that, only he wasn't sure he could. "Just show us."

She frowned and then motioned to them to follow.

They started off through the forest, none of them talking. Jal held his bow, though he didn't reach for an arrow. Given Jal's ability to sniff out danger, Kanar figured that they were probably safe enough.

They walked for the better part of several hours through an overgrown section of the forest, trampling over fragrant pine needs and passing a few small streams that tumbled over buried rocks. Thorns pulled at their clothes, though they couldn't slow. The air around them continued to cool.

Morgan finally signaled to them. "It's just up here," she said.

Kanar slowed, and Lily came over to him. "I don't know what she's after, but I think we need to be careful here, Kanar," Lily said. "If the Alainsith were slaughtered here, there's something more to this than just... Gods, I don't know what it's about or what we're going to find here."

"I know. I've dealt with plenty of witchcraft in my time, Lily."

"It was up ahead," Morgan said. "This is a place that was once sacred to the Alainsith."

They stepped into a forest clearing ringed by moss-covered boulders. Kanar had been part of the Realmsguard designated to protect the king on one of his expeditions to meet with the Alainsith, though Kanar had never interacted with them himself. He wasn't sure what would have brought them all the way out here. Could the king have been meeting with them again? It wouldn't be typical for the king to come this far away from Verendal, or even this far away from the safety of Reyand.

Kanar made a careful circuit, looking for signs of the destruction.

"How many did they kill?" Honaaz asked.

"There were a dozen," Morgan said, her voice soft. "Along with the representatives of the king who had come with them."

"What the fuck happened to the bodies?" Honaaz asked.

It was a good question.

"The Alainsith would've claimed them," Morgan said.

"Unless the witchcraft practitioners kept them for some other purpose," Kanar said.

They were like the hegen in that respect.

Morgan shook her head. "The Alainsith wouldn't have left the bodies behind."

"Well, if whoever came in here was powerful enough to slaughter the Alainsith, then they were powerful enough to take the bodies with them. Right?" Honaaz asked.

"I have to admit," Jal said, "the big man isn't wrong." He grinned at Honaaz, who shot him a hard look.

"The bodies and the blood are gone," Lily said. "And you want us to believe the citadel did this?"

Kanar was tempted to side with her. It seemed a stretch to believe the citadel would be involved in this, especially given how they had fought on Reyand's side during the war.

"Let her look," Morgan said.

Lily walked carefully around the clearing. At one point, she paused next to a log and ran her hands along it, and then she moved further, stopping by a tall oak tree. She inspected a patch of grasses.

"Why?" Lily asked, her voice a whisper.

"What is it?" Kanar said.

"She's not wrong." It was obvious that it pained Lily to say it. "They taught us to mask our presence. All around here are signs of the citadel. If this was where things took place—"

"It was," Morgan said.

"Then it means that the citadel was here."

Lily turned away. Kanar wasn't sure what to say to her. He felt like he needed to say something, but he wasn't sure he could offer her anything. Jal watched, and he didn't get close. The only one who approached was Honaaz. He said something to her, dropping his voice softly.

Kanar sighed. "What will this involve—"

A *crack* came from the trees nearby.

He spun, reaching for a pair of knives and sliding them out. Jal grabbed his bow. Lily slipped her hand into a pouch, and Honaaz had a pair of daggers in hand.

"I see about a dozen, maybe more," Jal said, his voice low.

"Who?" Kanar asked.

"Can't tell. Smells like…"

Kanar took a deep breath, fearing that this might be Alainsith. They were skilled warriors, he knew. His crew wouldn't be able to win in a fight with them. How had anybody managed to do that in the first place?

"Dogs," Jal said.

"We can fucking handle Dogs," Honaaz said.

Jal shot him a look. "We can, but how many would we lose?"

Kanar breathed out. They didn't need a fight. They had come here looking for evidence of what had happened, but it seemed as if Morgan already knew.

"Back to the boat."

"Kanar?" Lily said.

"Let's go. We don't fight unless they attack. We hold them off."

They backed through the clearing, retreating the way they'd come, but no one chased after them.

"Why do you think they left us alone?" Lily asked.

"Because they want to know where we're going," Jal said, shrugging slightly. "They want what we are after."

"Well, do we even know where we're going?"

Kanar shook his head. He didn't, but he had an idea how he was going to find out. "Back to the boat," he said again.

By the time they reached the river, Honaaz had already pulled the boat out from the branches and grasses he'd used to hide it.

They climbed in. Jal stood, seemingly unmindful of the way the boat rocked, arrow nocked and ready. Honaaz gave a hard shove, and they went sliding into the river and quickly picked up speed.

Kanar breathed out as he glanced to the forest that swallowed the river. He made his way along the barge and took a seat near Morgan.

"It's time for you to talk," he said. "What happened?"

"I know you want to blame this all on witchcraft, and perhaps that is part of it, but those responsible for what happened here don't have the blood any longer." She looked over to Lily before turning her attention back to him.

"Then who does?"

"The citadel. I don't know why they were after the Alainsith blood, but between that and the relics involved, it has to be something powerful."

Kanar hated that she was right. This was part of the reason he had been compelled to take the job. Not just the task of rescuing Morgan, though he had done that well enough to earn their pay. He couldn't leave the blood, and the attack, alone.

"I'm not lying about this, Gray," Morgan said.

It had been too long since he had been her Gray, and yet there was a part of him that was still thrilled to hear her say it.

It was all too easy for him to remember the first time she had referred to him like that. They had been sitting atop a restaurant in Vur. The city was spread out around them, and it was not all that different than Verendal. He'd been assigned there to protect the city and ensure the king's safety, though he was never in any real danger in places like that. When they traveled beyond the borders of Reyand, that was when he got nervous, but not in Vur.

"You look worried," Morgan had said. She sat close to him, her hands resting on either side of her, close enough that he could practically touch her.

Kanar had been surprised to see her here. She would come and go—gone more often than not—but she would often pop up in unexpected places. Occasionally, she would send word about where she would be so that he knew to look for her during his travels. This time, though, he hadn't expected to see her. It had been a pleasant surprise. The best kind.

"Not worried," he said. "I'm watching the city."

"Do you always watch it that way?"

"And what way is that?"

"You have this intensity when you study it," Morgan said. "It's as if I can practically follow every threat you see, with your eyes flashing with the dark gray of a thunderstorm. What's it like, Gray?"

He smiled to himself. "I need to ensure the safety of the king, for the sake of the kingdom."

"And what do you see?"

Kanar shrugged. "Three thieves working their way through the plaza. If you watch, you can see a pattern to their movements." He had been observing them for a while, noting how one man would bump somebody in the crowd, another would rush up against their other side, and occasionally the third would pop in. Pickpockets. Minor thieves. Not a real danger to the king. The Archers were fully capable of handling that kind of threat. "I don't worry too much about them."

"The people they're stealing from would be worried."

"Then they should guard their pockets better," Kanar said. He looked up, realizing how ridiculous that sounded. "I'm not trying to say that the people are asking to be robbed."

"It sounds like you are," Morgan said.

He shook his head. "I'm not worried about that kind of crime. I'm looking for other more threatening things."

"Which is…"

"Nothing here," Kanar said. He shifted, and his hand brushed hers. She smiled and didn't draw away.

"How often do you find any real dangers?" she asked.

"When it comes to the king, not often. Not within Reyand."

"And outside the kingdom?"

"We have trouble with Yelind, though it has been quiet lately. Minor skirmishes here and there. The king has soldiers on the border to defend it. Sometimes there is difficulty to the east, but we have a good relationship with the Khophen. The north, across the Bitter Sea, is not really for me to worry about."

That was for the navy. Kanar would rather have his feet on the ground than on a ship. He'd traveled by sea once before, and he didn't care much for it. Too many days rocking side to side, trying to fight back the waves of nausea that roiled through him. Too many days with the ship's crew laughing at him and the other Realmsguard who struggled.

"And then to the west, we have the Alainsith, but I haven't been drawn in for those negotiations."

"You think you will?" Morgan asked.

"I think that eventually I'll get asked to escort the king."

"When is he visiting with them next?"

Kanar thought about it but didn't really know. "Probably soon," he said, shrugging. "He's been more active these days. Moving around, making preparations for a longer time away. Either he's going to Verendal to stay in the palace there, which happens now and again, or he's going to meet with the Alainsith, which is more likely."

"You seem bothered by that," Morgan said.

"It's not my choice."

"Why does it worry you?"

"It's not a worry," Kanar said.

"You know, when you mentioned the Alainsith, your face took on a cloudy expression. A little stormy. You don't like them."

He looked over. "I'm one of the Realmsguard."

"That doesn't mean anything to me," she said. "Well, other than knowing that you've been trained to fight on behalf of the king." She smiled, and the sunlight danced across her freckles. "You're a brave soldier."

"You don't need to make fun."

"There are places for soldiers. I've just known too many who aren't thinkers as well." She made that comment to him too often.

"Now you're accusing me not only of being a soldier, as if that is something I should be ashamed of somehow, but also of being a mindless one."

Morgan watched him, and there was a slight curl to her lips. "I don't know that I could ever call you mindless. At least tell me why you don't care for the Alainsith."

"Because I've learned my history."

"Oh," she said, nodding. "That explains it. You have heard the stories of the terrible Alainsith and how they have destroyed the kingdom time and again. Only through the bravery of King Ophan the Bold did the great nation of Reyand push back the horrible Alainsith threat."

"Now you're mocking me," Kanar said.

"The war was a long time ago. It seems as if your king has recognized the need for conversation."

"He may choose what he decides."

"You don't agree with your king?" Morgan asked.

Kanar frowned. "I didn't say that."

"It sounds like you did. It sounds like you have made it quite clear that you don't agree with him."

He sat up. A patrol moved into the city. Realmsguard, Kanar could tell. And their presence, especially in that number, suggested that the king had come with them.

"Thank you for your conversation. It's been entertaining as usual," he said. He bowed, taking her hand and kissing the top of it. "I hope you will send word of where you're traveling to next."

"Always," she said. She didn't get up, and she didn't move. Instead, she just sat on the side of the rooftop, staring out over the distance.

Kanar climbed down, joined the Realmsguard, and couldn't shake the feeling that Morgan watched him the entire time.

She'd been pressing him for information even then.

He took a deep breath, pulled himself away from the

memory, and let it out. Kanar opened his eyes and looked over to her. It was his turn to press her for information.

"Are you going to tell me about the citadel?" he said.

"I will tell you what you need to know, Gray," Morgan replied.

"You can stop calling me that."

"I remember when you used to like it."

He shot her a look. "It's been a long time."

"Has it?"

She watched him, her green eyes catching the sunlight. When that faded, the green practically blended into the forest, as if the color was meant to.

"The citadel," Kanar said. "We need to have a plan for getting in. You can't want this ceremony to take place."

"You think you know what I want?"

"I don't think you want it to succeed."

"You have no idea what I want," she said softly. "You've never known. You've never cared."

"That's not true."

Kanar found Honaaz looking in his direction. The man turned away, focusing on pulling them forward through the river. They were moving steadily away from the Dogs' pursuit, putting distance between them. At least it was fast enough that they were able to use the current to guide them. It carried them more rapidly than they would've been able to manage on their own, even on horseback.

In that way, it was more pleasant. At least this boat wasn't nearly as unsteady as the ones he had traveled on when he was with the Realmsguard. Honaaz seemed comfortable, despite the uneven footing.

Kanar turned back to Morgan. "If they use the Alainsith blood, they will create dangerous magic. The only reason anybody would want blood like that would be for some sort of ceremony. Why would they have slaughtered the Alainsith otherwise?"

"I think we can both agree that you don't care about the Alainsith."

She was right. He did not really care. The Alainsith were dangerous, and they had been Reyand's traditional enemy for so long that he couldn't see them as anything other than that. He knew that Porman wanted to keep them close to try to bridge a connection between the Alainsith and Reyand, but how could they when the Alainsith were what they were?

"Why won't you tell me about why you had blood on you?" Kanar had a hard time with that aspect of this.

"If I don't, what do you intend to do?" Morgan said. "Do you intend to leave me here? Or have your muscle drive his daggers into my heart? Or maybe your friend here will fire an arrow at me. Even with his injured arm, I'm sure his aim would be accurate enough for that." She held Jal's gaze, and Jal shrugged as if to acknowledge that he would. "Or maybe her," she said, looking over to Lily. "Perhaps you would have her use her own art to destroy me. Of all of you on this boat, she's the only one I fear."

Honaaz was nodding, but Lily had stiffened. The choice of words was not lost on Kanar. *Art.*

He looked at Lily. "What's she saying?"

"It's nothing," Lily said.

Pieces started to fit together. Things he'd heard in Sanaron, along with what he had seen ever since they'd left. He hadn't wanted to believe, but what choice did he have now?

"Lily?" he said slowly.

In all the time he had known Lily, Kanar had never questioned her on what she kept in that pouch. He knew she had the grappling hook, but beyond that, he didn't know what other supplies she kept there. At one point, he had thought it was nothing more than her knives, but how many knives did she need to have on her?

And there was the ease with which she had navigated through the hegen section.

"You're hegen," he said.

She didn't answer.

They continued to drift up the river. Honaaz silently continued to monitor the banks. Kanar increasingly thought that he'd made a *much* better decision bringing him along, though not for the reasons he'd initially intended.

"Not exactly." Lily took a deep breath and looked up, holding his gaze. "Maybe by birth, and partly by training. I learned how to use the art from my mother, was sent to train with a woman who could better teach me about bone, and then returned to find my people." A hard edge had entered her voice. "That was when I left everything I knew. I was brought to a place where I could learn to exact revenge. I was trained to use these." With a flourish, the knives appeared in her hands, and then just as quickly disappeared. "I was trained how to use stealth. Poisons. I was trained to kill."

Honaaz had stopped poling through the water and instead watched Lily.

"I had a different kind of gift with the art," she said, now unable to meet Kanar's gaze. "It was one that my mother couldn't teach, so she found someone who could. The hegen consider themselves all part of one people. One family is the same as another, so she found someone to teach me what my people call the natural art. I was learning how to use it when I got word that something had happened." Lily closed her eyes, as if remembering that all too well. "I went to find out more, but they were gone. All because of witchcraft. So I went to the citadel to find a way to get vengeance."

"So you're a hegen who trained in the citadel," Kanar said.

He found himself more hurt than he expected by this betrayal. Had she known who he was all along? Had she been using him somehow? Or was she simply cautious?

"I can't claim to be part of the people any longer. I gave that up when I began to learn the subtle art." Lily looked up. "I took on assignments that were designed to help protect my people—or what I believed to be my people—and did what was necessary." She shrugged. "I'm not ashamed of what I did."

"How did you end up in Sanaron?" Jal asked.

"The war was over, and I still hadn't done what I wanted. The citadel wanted me back, but mostly because they wanted to use me and the art."

Kanar looked down to Morgan. "Why did you tell me this now? What does this have to do with anything?"

There had to be some reason. He knew Morgan well enough to know that she wouldn't tell him something of this significance without having a purpose behind it. Maybe it was just a matter of her wanting to drive a wedge between him and the rest of the team—and it would work. If Lily had been using hegen magic and their disgusting prizes around him all this time, then how could he trust her to do what he needed? How could he rely on her?

"Don't ask me. Ask her," Morgan said, pointing to Lily.

"I still don't know why they would have been involved," Lily said.

"You said you saw one of the citadel in Sanaron. Could it have been him?" Kanar asked.

Lily looked at him with a sharp-eyed stare. "If it is, we are in real danger. He is one of the most brilliant and ruthless instructors I had there."

And they were going to have to stop him.

Chapter Twenty-Six

LILY

Lily stared into the distance. They were getting close to the citadel. She could feel it.

That wasn't the only thing she could feel. She was all too aware of Kanar's eyes on her back. It wasn't even part of the art. It was more a matter of instinct that she'd honed.

After shifting to the bow of the barge, she had been surprised when Jal joined her. Honaaz remained standing there, using his pole to drive them forward through the water with a steady rhythm.

When Morgan had revealed what she'd seen of the attack, Lily hadn't really known whether to believe her. It didn't fit with the citadel, at least not what she was familiar with. She had tried to tell Morgan and Kanar that the citadel wouldn't do that, but when Morgan had asked if they would use their powers to stop witchcraft, Lily had not had a good counterargument.

She sat stewing over those thoughts. They plagued her because she didn't really know. Back then, she'd thought she understood the purpose of the citadel, but they had started to ask her more and more about her use of the art and wanted her to demonstrate her techniques almost as much as they'd been willing to teach her theirs.

The Dogs had also been following them. They had seen evidence of them, but there had been no skirmishes. Why were they after them? Could it be because of Morgan? It didn't make a whole lot of sense for the Dogs to want to collect Alainsith blood.

They left the forest behind, and the landscape stretched into the plains. After discussing the layout of the citadel as well as Lily remembered it—which was perfectly, as she had spent enough time there—they spent the better part of two days on the water, and in silence. It had become painful.

They had a plan for getting in, but she worried that wasn't going to be enough.

Getting to the citadel was not going to be the challenge. Getting in might be. In that, it would be more like breaking into the prison in Verendal. Getting out would be the hard part. It meant she'd have to sneak past people she'd trained alongside. People that she had effectively abandoned.

Her people.

Or they *had* been.

After a time, she'd begun to see things differently. That had pitted her against her people, but they would have left her alone.

Was facing them worth one thousand gold? She didn't know how much it would take for it to be worth it, but that didn't seem like even close to enough. There was still time for her to get away, but that would mean leaving Jal behind. And even Kanar. The thought bothered her, though she knew it shouldn't. He wouldn't hesitate to leave her behind now.

"You have to stop worrying about Kanar," Jal said, looking over to her.

"I've heard the rumors about him," she said.

"Are you afraid of him?"

She frowned. Was that what it was? Maybe that was the reason she'd been so troubled by all of this. Maybe it was fear. That would be a new emotion for her, if so. She didn't think it was fear. Not exactly.

Something else, though.

"He has a reputation," Honaaz said. "Of course, that fucker has earned it." He stared straight ahead and still did not look at her.

"You don't like him," she said.

"What's there to like? He hired me for a job. That's the only reason I'm here."

There was something between Honaaz and Kanar that she didn't understand, but that didn't matter to her. Or it hadn't before her own secret had gotten out.

It was time all their secrets came out. Kanar had shared his first. Jal was too much of an open book to have any secrets, but they still had to deal with Honaaz. Kanar might have hired him, but that didn't mean he was trustworthy. He'd taken the job and didn't even seem to be concerned about what they had to do.

Lily jumped to her feet. "What brought *you* to Sanaron?" she asked Honaaz.

"A ship," he said.

"You're a sailor. Were you a part of Heatharn's crew?"

Honaaz snorted. "That fucker wouldn't know his way around a ship if he had a Larch to guide him."

"A Larch?" Jal asked. He'd sat up and looked over, a slight smile on his face.

Lily couldn't be certain, but he seemed to have recovered, at least as well as someone could following a near-fatal crossbow injury. The hegen woman had healed him, but it hadn't taken as much out of Jal as Lily would have expected. She'd seen hegen magic—and had used the art herself—so she knew what such things cost. Jal hadn't appeared to struggle the way she would have anticipated.

"Don't know about the Larch?" Honaaz said. "Famous sailors from across the Opain Sea. Probably too small an island for many to hear about."

"Is that where you're from?" Lily asked.

"Fuck no." Honaaz glanced to Kanar. "I'm from the Isles. Spent my days on ships, though. My uncle's ship."

"What happened?"

"Nothing happened," he said, turning away and using the pole to push them down the river. He worked with more aggression than he had before, each movement sending them through the water faster than the last.

Honaaz guided them quickly to where Lily had pointed him to. Everybody seemed to be caught in their own thoughts as they sailed. Minutes stretched into hours, until Honaaz spoke.

"Better be ready. We've got something coming up."

Lily looked past him. When she'd come to the citadel before, she'd traveled by land. Plenty of ships came through, but most arrived from the sea.

The citadel was at the heart of Taluf. The massive city was ancient, supposedly older than even the Alainsith. There was a certain power to it, though Lily suspected that was imagined more than anything else.

Taluf sprawled out from the tower, though there was an organization to the way things were laid out. Those in charge of the citadel ensured that much. Direct access to the citadel came from the dozen roads leading toward it, like spokes on a wheel. The river wouldn't quite reach far enough, though it did bring people into the city.

The city was relatively easy to reach. All they had to do was approach directly. There were plenty of people who went in and out of it, especially as the entire city existed in order to provide for those within the citadel.

Once they got inside, though, they would run into the real problem. Lily had no idea what they might encounter. The only thing she knew with any real certainty was that the Alainsith blood would be protected in the most secure part of the citadel—the heart itself. That meant that they would have to enter the part of the citadel where she had spent time training. She hadn't been there for a while.

Lily moved along the barge to take a seat next to Morgan. "Everybody else has shared, by choice or not, so I think it's your turn. Kanar said you betrayed him, but you're sitting there looking like you're the one who was hurt."

Morgan glanced back at Kanar, who stayed at the stern of the boat. "He did nothing to hurt me. He hurt others. And he hurt himself." There was a hint of anguish in her words.

What Lily didn't know was why those from the citadel would want to collect Alainsith blood. She could understand why operatives would have stopped witchcraft, but they wouldn't have kept the blood. They would've destroyed it. There would be too much power in something like that. But if there was some place in the citadel where they would have brought the blood, it would be one that Lily knew all too well. It was where she had been brought to learn about the art, to focus on it, and to help those within the citadel understand it better.

Lily glanced at Kanar and found him staring out at Taluf. The buildings gradually grew larger the closer they moved toward the city. Most were constructed out of a white stone that was quarried not far from here, though some of them had been hastily erected out of wood, then fortified over time. Those buildings were painted white to look like the rest, but it was obvious to anybody who traveled through here that they were different. Still, the citadel never made anyone tear those down.

"Have you ever known someone who hates the very thing you are?" Morgan asked.

Lily looked over. "Do you think that's all you are?"

"I know that's all I am." Morgan's voice dropped to a whisper. "And I have done all I can to try to open his eyes, to get him to think, but he has followed his king to a fault."

"I have never done that," Kanar said, shifting as he glanced over to Morgan. "I serve my king. There wasn't anything ignorant about it. I did my duty, the same as all must do."

"Not the same," Morgan said. "You made choices that were different. You relished what you did."

"As did you."

There was a real anger between them, almost a hatred, and Lily couldn't help but wonder what had happened. Kanar had suffered. That much she believed, but why? What exactly had taken place between the two of them to cause him to suffer the way he had?

"Why does he hate you?" Lily asked Morgan.

"He hates anything involving magic. Yet, look at you. A prized member of his team." Morgan's gaze flicked towards Jal. "And him. When he was injured, did he hesitate to go to the hegen?" Her lips curled slightly. "Which means that he knows the truth."

"What truth is that?"

"That magic is a part of the world, and that it should not be feared."

"Magic has killed more people than any war ever has," Kanar said.

"And magic has saved an equal number," Morgan spat. "You have believed that witchcraft was defeated, but it has only been slowed. Perhaps the only way to stop it is through magic."

Kanar looked away. "We can stop here." He motioned to a series of docks that jutted into the river. They were long, slender slats of wood, similar to what they had in Sanaron, though not nearly as busy. There were several other ships moored, but very few people around.

They pulled into the dock. Honaaz remained quiet, irritation in his eyes as he quickly tied up the boat, glancing from Kanar to Morgan and finally to Lily. He jerked his gaze away from her as if afraid. She was going to have to deal with that eventually. She didn't know what reason he had for fearing her, other than her art. She hadn't done anything to him.

When they came to a full stop, they all stood. Kanar and Honaaz climbed off the boat, followed by Jal and then Morgan. Lily got down last.

"It's not going to be easy getting in there," she said.

Taluf was much like she remembered. Most of the outer buildings were small and wooden, though the deeper you got into the city, the taller the buildings rose, until you reached the massive wall that surrounded the citadel itself.

Strangely, everything seemed quiet. Empty. As if the city had fallen under some witchcraft spell. There was normally steady activity, with carts and wagons carrying goods up the long roads leading to the citadel. There was some of that here, but not as much as she remembered.

The river ran around the perimeter of Taluf, out toward the sea, connecting this place to other parts of the world.

"Are we just walking up to it?" Honaaz asked.

"We take the direct approach," Kanar said.

"It would be better if we had some way of justifying where we were going," Jal said. "This isn't my place, but it seems that they would be less inclined to question our presence if we look more natural here."

"You don't think we look natural?" Lily asked.

"I don't know. Is this normal?"

"There are plenty of people who go to the citadel," she said.

"Like this?"

"Sometimes like this."

"If the reason we are here is accurate, then don't you think we should be a bit more concerned about that?" Jal asked.

Lily nodded. "A bit more. And we should be ready for different protections than what I remember. Or what she remembers." She nodded to Morgan.

Morgan stiffened slightly but nodded back.

Lily laughed at that. The priest seemed as if she wanted to pretend that she was not more familiar with the city than she was.

Lily knew her way around. She remembered places she had visited, buildings that had been part of her training, including the theater that she'd been instructed to sneak through without detection. She had stolen from some of them, all as part of her training. There was the place where she had made her first kill, a stealthy job where she had used her knives, though later she had learned to use poisons. The hegen were a practical people, and didn't view life and death the same as others, but that had been harder than she'd expected.

"Just push through your resistance. Everything gets easier," Tayol had said.

Easier.

The knife in the man's chest had been easy to aim, but hard to push herself to throw. Even knowing what the man had done—torturing a family before burning them alive—she'd hesitated. The citadel existed to train people to handle such things. Most in the city believed they were immune to the dangers of the citadel, or perhaps were ignorant to those dangers. Not her.

As she looked over and saw Morgan watching the citadel, she realized that the woman was not ignorant either. She knew what was there and the danger of it.

They found their way along the road, and as it neared midday, they slowed enough that Lily could pick out the patrols through the city. She motioned to Kanar, who tensed.

"We have to watch for the patrols," she explained. "As I said, getting through the city is going to be easy enough."

Outsiders weren't necessarily viewed with much suspicion, but the citadel had ways of detecting when newcomers arrived in the city. Lily didn't think they would be able to sneak in.

"Don't worry about that," Kanar said.

"You wanted my input," Lily said. Irritation started to rise within her, and she wondered if she should suppress it. This was Kanar, after all. She'd worked with him, fought beside him, but now he seemed to dismiss her. Ever since learning the truth.

That irritated her far more than she could explain.

"I wanted your input, but I also wanted your honesty," he said.

"You have it. Don't mistake me keeping this secret from you for dishonesty." She took a step toward him, looking up to meet his eyes. "And have you been so honest with us? Kanar Reims, the man who hunted witchcraft. The Blackheart."

"Careful," he growled.

Jal strode up next to her, and he leaned down to whisper in her ear. "I don't know if it makes sense for you to get into an argument with him before we go and try to pull this job. From what I understand, it's going to be dangerous enough for us to get inside, so…"

"It's not going to be dangerous to get inside."

"Look at that place," he said, shaking his head. "I thought the prison looked intimidating. And there are tracks here that I hadn't expected…"

Lily watched him but Jal didn't explain anything more.

Honaaz grunted. "I would've rather broken into the palace."

"What if the king doesn't keep the jewels in the palace like they claim?" Lily said. "What if it's all just some ploy, a tactic to try to draw in those stupid enough to try to break in?"

"I'd like to know," Honaaz said.

Lily nodded to Kanar. "Maybe you ask him, so he can tell you exactly what happens there."

"I'm just saying that it would be a fun challenge."

Jal grinned. "I'm with him. I think it would be fun. I don't know that I'm up for that kind of a challenge, but I'd like to try. Wouldn't you, Lily?"

"I just want this to be over."

Get in, get back out, and then go their separate ways. Only after Kanar paid, though. She would leave him then. She suspected he would want her to anyway.

They passed a series of shops. There was a calm that wasn't present in other places. Certainly not in Sanaron, where the fog settled over everything, forcing shop owners to shout and try to draw attention to their stores. Not even in Verendal, from her brief experience there. The shops had been dingy and run-down, but there'd been a vigor that she didn't see here.

An immense wall separated the citadel from the rest of the surrounding town. The stones had Alainsith marks on them from the harvested stone used in the wall's construction. Those who lived in town understood they were serving something greater, even if they didn't understand all of what the citadel did. As far as most knew, this was a school —and it was, of sorts.

Jal glanced around. "Everything seems so…"

"Boring," Honaaz said.

Jal nodded. "Boring is right. There's something here that's not quite the way I thought it would be." He looked over. "Maybe it's just this entire place."

"It's because of what the citadel deals with," Lily said. "There's a need for a measure of control."

At least, there was when dealing with the subtle art. With the art she'd learned from the hegen, chaos added to it. Sometimes you could have much different outcomes based on the mayhem. It was part of the celebration, the vibrancy, and the energy.

Lily looked up at the towering citadel looming in front of her. The walls were made of onyx too smooth to be carved by a human, making the whole place feel unnatural. She couldn't help but wonder why the Alainsith blood would be here. The people of the citadel were chasing things they shouldn't, even if they claimed it was for the right reasons.

It was easy to remember the very first time she'd come here. Another hegen had found her after her parents' slaughter, or someone she'd believed to be a hegen. She'd been wandering, looking for a safe place, knowing there would be none. Anger had already started to burn in her heart. When Tayol had come across her, he'd seemed different. Skilled. The pouch he carried made Lily think of the art, and he'd accepted that as fact.

They'd traveled a while, until Tayol had helped her by offering her a place to stay and an opportunity to continue her education. When he guided her here to Taluf, she looked for the hegen section within it. There was none, so she kept asking questions until she was brought farther and farther into the city, closer and closer to this massive tower that rose over everything.

He told her then that she could learn, but it would be different than what she'd been taught before. He explained that the subtle art was the key to protecting their people and ensuring that none suffered the same fate. He had made her believe that she could do that.

"We need a wagon," Kanar said, pulling Lily back to the present. "We need robes. And we will need her." He nodded to Morgan. "That's how this is going to work. We're going to walk up to the entrance, get in, and then we're going to finish this."

Lily looked over to him. He held his gaze on her. She had no idea what he was planning, but robes and a wagon?

"I'm not sure that's going to work," she said. "We can't just walk into the citadel. I know you don't really understand what this place is, but I do." She glanced over to Morgan, frowning as she saw the other woman watching her. She had to know, as well.

"I have my own thoughts on what we might need to do," Kanar said.

He saw the world in a different way than Lily did. Much like he looked as if he was studying the city now. Was it anger in his eyes? There was anger in hers, she was sure. From here, though, the rest was going to be straightforward.

"There's one way we can get into the citadel," Lily explained. "If we look like we belong, we won't be stopped."

Kanar looked over to her.

Lily shrugged. "I'm just giving you a suggestion."

"It's not a bad suggestion, Kan," Jal said. "But even when we get inside, I'm still worried about the Dogs."

"There's been no sign of them lately," Lily said.

Honaaz scoffed. "Them fucks wouldn't abandon the hunt." He turned to Kanar. "I can get the wagon if you still need it."

"How do you intend to do that?" Kanar asked.

Honaaz gave a slight shrug. "I'm going to ask nicely. Someone's going to provide it for me."

"I can get the robes," Jal said with a grin. "I wouldn't want one of you to get the wrong size for me. Or for Honaaz. He's pretty big."

"What about you?" Kanar asked Lily.

"I have something else that I need to do," she said. "We don't have too much time remaining today. We'll need to head into the tower before evening. It gets harder after hours. There's more activity in the daytime, and more reason for us to be heading in." She nodded to Morgan. "And you have to keep an eye on her."

Lily didn't know if this would work. The citadel was typically locked down, and even with her experience heading inside, she wasn't exactly sure that they would be able to break through and get further in.

"That's not an answer," Kanar said.

She shook her head. "No, it's not. Because you aren't going to care for my answer. But if you have to know, I have a little searching to do. I need to find supplies."

And it would be much easier if she didn't have anyone with her when she did.

Chapter Twenty-Seven

JAL

"What do you think he wants the robes for?" Jal asked, hurrying to keep up with Lily.

She was quiet, though she'd been that way during the last few days of their journey. For somebody who was as skilled as she obviously was, she certainly didn't want to reveal what she could do or how she could do it. Jal understood that. She had a past. They all had one, though, so that wasn't particularly unique to her. That said, her reaction to it was.

"I don't know," she finally replied. "Kanar has his own ideas."

He did have ideas, and they were often useful. But ever since this job, Kanar had been a little unusual. He'd been on edge, which made Jal nervous. He wasn't sure what was going on in Kanar's head, only that finding that woman had been a problem for him.

"It's your citadel," Jal said. "You have to have some idea."

"I don't. Now can we go on and get these robes?"

"You don't want to climb the roofs?" He smiled at her, but Lily didn't seem to be in the mood for smiling. He needed to take a different approach with her.

"I'm not climbing anything. Not here."

"Why not? Is it too dangerous?"

"This is where I trained," she said, her voice going soft. She'd been that way ever since the truth of her training had come to light.

Jal didn't really understand it. Not all of it, at least. There was some aspect to what she had done that seemed significant, but because he wasn't from these lands, it wasn't clear why it was so significant or why Kanar would be so offended by it.

"Do you want to talk about it?" he asked.

"Not particularly."

"It was hard for me when I left my homeland too," Jal said.

"I think it would've been harder had I stayed."

"Why?"

"When I was young, I learned what my people call the art. It's a way of using life. Of using death. To create something else."

Jal nodded to her pouch. He'd started to pay attention to the way she was protective of it. Now he understood why. She wanted to keep what she had in that pouch from them, but it might be the key to all of this.

"The art was never meant for harming people," she said.

"And that's what's bothering you?"

"I moved past that a while ago. Maybe it's just because of going to Verendal and seeing the hegen there."

"Why would that be hard?" Jal asked.

"Because they're different than what I've become," she said.

"All of us are the result of our unique experiences. That's what makes us special."

Lily looked over to him and shook her head. "Sometimes I think *you're* a little too special, Jal."

He smiled. "You know what I mean. If I hadn't left my home, I don't know what I might have become."

"That's how you look at the world?" she asked.

"Experience is the best teacher, Lily. Your experiences—with your people, your family, and even here—have made you what you are. Much like my experiences made me the way I am."

He turned his attention toward the citadel in the distance. The building loomed over them, and there was a strange undercurrent of energy that seemed to come from it. Perhaps it was just that many of these buildings were ancient Alainsith structures that had been repurposed into something else. "It was an accident. I…" He forced a smile before he said too much. "We should find these robes. Kanar isn't going to be very happy if we don't accomplish that much, at least."

Robes. Where were they going to find robes in a place like this?

Lily would know, but she seemed distracted. She was struggling. He didn't know all of what she had going on, but he suspected that it was tied to returning to this city, to the citadel, along with whatever memories Morgan had dredged up.

His own memories were buried. Jal made sure of that. But her questions had brought up thoughts and reminded him of things he would have rather left hidden.

Lily nodded and then pointed. "There's a general store up here. I think it will have what we need."

"And that being robes?"

"Robes. Dresses. Other things." She shrugged. "The supplies I need."

He looked over. "When you said that you needed to gather supplies, I sort of assumed that you would need to *gather* supplies."

She snorted. "It's not always like that. Sometimes it is. In places like Sanaron, or elsewhere, supplies aren't as easy to gather. But here, near the citadel, what I need is going to be pretty easy to find."

"And that is…"

"Supplies."

She led him to a store near the end of an alley. The buildings here were made of a white stone, though there was a hint of yellow to it. All of it was stacked neatly. Out where they had docked, though, the city looked less organized. The street was more jagged, as if the city's engineers had not thought to convince those all the way out near the edge that they needed to align themselves with the rest of Taluf.

The inside of the store was dingy. Jal had to duck his head to get in, but once inside, there was plenty of room for him to stand. Lily hurried away, giving him a chance to look through the shop. The inside of the store was dingy, and smelled of mold, though there was a hint of dung that reminded him of his time working with rabbits. *Mice?* Not good for a shop like this.

When he'd volunteered to find robes, he had anticipated that he would steal them, not that he would come to a store to buy them. He didn't have any money. Lily didn't either, at least not that he knew.

He found Lily standing near a shelf off to one side. There were no windows here. A couple of lanterns sat on high shelves, leaving everything in a dirty light. The shop owner remained on a stool near the back and hadn't even bothered to look up at their entry.

"Did you find what we need?" Jal leaned close to her.

"There are a few things that could be useful. It depends on what surprises we find."

"If anyone can handle surprises, it would be—"

"Kanar Reims," Lily said softly. "I know."

Jal smiled at her. "Actually, I was about to say that it would be you."

Lily shook her head. "I'm not like him."

"No, you aren't. You are you." He grinned. "And that's exactly what we need."

"Get the robes," she said, motioning to one side of the shop. "You can find some fabric there."

"Fabric isn't robes."

"Fabric can make robes."

He found rolls of fabric in black and blue and purple and deep green. Most of the cloth was soft, far nicer than what people in other cities could afford.

Jal looked over at the shop owner. "How much for the fabric?"

"Depends on how much you need."

"A roll. Maybe two."

That got the older man's attention. He had gray and thinning hair, with a narrow face, high cheekbones, and the kind of bulbous nose that suggested that he'd been deep into his ale for too long. His eyes had a hint of yellow to them as well.

"Well, I don't do bulk discounts, if that's what you're trying to get at," the shopkeeper said.

"I'm not, but why wouldn't you do bulk discounts?"

"I don't have any trouble selling this."

Jal ran his hand along the fabric, and his hand came away with dust. "It looks like it's been sitting here for a while."

"Well, maybe it will sit here a little longer, then. If you don't want it, you don't have to buy it."

"You haven't told me how much," Jal said.

"You haven't told me how much you have to spend."

"I'll tell you how much I have to spend if you tell me how much the fabric is." Jal turned to see Lily standing in front of one of the shelves, looking confused. She had picked up a few different items, then set them back down again. What was she doing?

"I'm not giving any discounts here," the man said. "That's not the kind of shop I run."

"I'm just asking how much."

"And I'm telling you that we can discuss it based on how much you have to spend."

"Just give him the fabric, Gilbert," Lily said.

Gilbert looked over to her. "Why are you taking the fun out of this, girl?"

Lily spun, and Jal realized she had something in hand. She'd been working with various items from the shelves, mixing them together, and now she held what looked to be something made out of bone. There was a string wrapped around it, and perhaps some cork? He had no idea what it was.

Gilbert's eyes widened. "Haven't seen you here in a while."

"I've been away," Lily said.

"Are you back?"

"Not exactly."

Gilbert shook his head. "A damn shame. Used to be fun with you around."

"Fun is relative." Lily strode toward the counter, set the item on it, and nodded to Gilbert. "We want three rolls of fabric. Also, I'm taking these," she said, pointing to her pocket. "I need some food too. What do you have here?"

"Are you sure you can trust anything he has for you to eat?" Jal whispered.

"I've known Gilbert as long as I've been at the citadel. Of course I can trust him." She looked at Gilbert for a moment. "And he can trust me. You see, he knows that if he were to betray me, my dying breath would curse him, and I would come back in specter form to haunt him."

"It doesn't work like that, girl," Gilbert said.

Lily smirked. "As if you know what it's like."

"I know that you can't come back and haunt me."

"If I were to come back and haunt anyone, it would definitely be you, Gilbert."

"I've got food. I'm not going to poison it." He looked over to Jal. "Leave the purple fabric. You won't like it anyway. It's been here too long. Can't guarantee the moths haven't gotten to it." He climbed off his stool and tottered back behind the door, leaving Jal and Lily alone.

"I didn't realize you were so popular," Jal said.

"I know people in the city. I tried to forget about it, though."

"I don't think you should forget about what you experienced here, and I don't think you should forget about what you have been through. That's all part of who you are."

Lily frowned at him. "Anyway, grab whatever rolls of fabric you think we might be able to use. Kanar thinks we need robes, so we're going to have to make them out of those. And then… Well, I'm not exactly sure what else he's going to have us do. Maybe something stupid, knowing Kanar."

Jal smiled. A hint of the Lily he remembered had come back. Maybe it was this shop, or Gilbert, or creating the item she had worked on. Or maybe it was simply that she buried it, much like Jal buried his own demons.

Surprisingly, Gilbert emerged from the back holding a basket of apples and a loaf of bread. He also had a hunk of moldy cheese. He sliced off part of it and offered Jal a mold-free piece.

Jal frowned as he sniffed it.

"I told you it's not poisoned," Gilbert said. "I wouldn't want her to come back and haunt me."

Lily nodded. "And I would. You know that I would."

Gilbert grunted. "What brought you back? You got strange company too."

"Him? He's harmless. He likes dogs."

"Rabbits," Jal said.

She frowned at him. "Rabbits? I thought you liked dogs."

"Well, I like all animals. I've had a little trouble with dogs lately."

"He likes animals. I suppose that's enough." Lily leaned on her elbows. "Things look different from the last time I was here."

"When was that?" Gilbert asked.

Lily seemed to debate how much to tell him.

Gilbert stared, waiting for her to say something.

"It's probably been a few months," she finally said, which Jal knew to be a lie.

"It feels longer than that, but everything feels longer. These days, things are a little strange. There's gossip going around, as there always is."

Lily smiled. "What kind of gossip is it this time?"

"Oh, probably nothing," Gilbert said. "After the war, there were some in the citadel who wanted to finish it fully, and others who thought to wait. The citadel had lost too many operatives. They figured they could let Reyand deal with it. That sort of thing creates tension."

Lily stared off in the distance for a moment. Jal could see her mind churning, as if she was trying to come up with some answer, connecting what they knew. At least one person from the citadel had been in Sanaron, she'd said. They knew that relics had been moved out of the city. And there was the Alainsith blood.

Jal could piece it together, and he suspected that Lily, who was as bright as she was pretty, could do so as well. The blood and the relics would be used to stop the war for good. It would be used to destroy witchcraft.

How would Kanar feel about that?

Would he stop it?

Maybe not. Which meant that they had come to the citadel for no reason.

Finally, Lily turned back to the shop owner and grinned. "It's been good to see you, Gilbert." She paused at a shelf and pulled a lid off a canister resting there. She dipped her hand inside. "I need to borrow a few of these as well."

"You know the price."

"I know the price." She almost started away, but she paused. "Say. I want you to pass around something for me."

"Not sure I can do that these days."

"Just look into something, would you?" She leaned forward, whispering something softly that Jal couldn't make out, all while Gilbert nodded, then headed out of the shop, with Jal trailing after her.

When they were back in the narrow street, he glanced over to her. "He's an interesting man."

"He's mostly harmless." It seemed she wasn't going to share with him what she'd said to Gilbert. "But he does have sources. Not that he'll ever acknowledge it, but he has access to supplies that not everybody does." She frowned, glancing back to the door leading into Gilbert's shop. "Usually he has more traffic in there."

Lily started down the alley, and she paused. "Something he said bothered me. Artifacts. That's what we've been escorting out of Sanaron. Now, with the Alainsith blood, I can't help but feel as if they are tied together."

"There you are," Honaaz said, appearing down the street with a wagon before Lily had a chance to better explain her thinking. "I've been pushing this fucking thing for the last twenty minutes."

Jal shrugged. "You could have just waited."

"Waited where? Reims abandoned me. Basically said that I was supposed to find you all."

"What do you mean by that?"

Honaaz gestured toward the citadel. "He went in. I went for the cart, then went back to see him heading in on his own. I came for the two of you."

Jal looked toward the tower. "What?"

Kanar wouldn't have gone in without them. He was the one who wanted to avoid splitting up. Why would he suddenly change his mind on that?

"I don't know," Honaaz said. "He was sitting there talking to that woman, and then he suddenly turned to me and told me that it was time for me to go get the wagon and meet up with the rest of you. He said not to worry about him." He shrugged.

There was only one thing that would make Kanar suddenly do that.

Jal had underestimated Morgan. Had the great Kanar Reaves been in love?

Chapter Twenty-Eight

KANAR

As soon as they had split up, Kanar knew what he needed to do. It wasn't going to be easy, not with just the two of them, but perhaps it was the best answer anyway.

He didn't want Jal to be hurt even more. Honaaz deserved better as well. And Lily… Kanar wasn't sure how he felt about Lily. He was still working on that. He felt betrayed, though should he?

In hindsight, he understood why she'd kept what she had from him. There was no reason for her to share with him that she was hegen, especially as it didn't really impact her role on his team. There was even less reason when he'd revealed who he was. At that point, there was no way she could have told him anything more about herself. It was almost as if him sharing about his past had essentially closed down any chance he might have of learning about Lily's on her terms.

Which made him even more irritated with Morgan.

He had suspected Morgan's ties to the citadel but had never imagined that anyone from the citadel was as capable as what Morgan—and now Lily—suggested. It would explain how they had survived in the witchcraft war when only those in the Order had. Their operatives had to know some form of magic. Maybe not witchcraft. It might be more akin to what the hegen used, but that was still magic.

But did Kanar have any reason to argue with that?

"I find it interesting that you have assigned the others to their tasks, but what have you taken for yourself?" Morgan said.

Kanar looked over. Honaaz had waited behind, almost as if trying to decide how he would go about getting his cart. He scoped out the street, though most people were walking empty-handed. If Honaaz was going to find a cart, he would probably have to head to one of the outer sections of the city.

The cart wasn't essential for this assignment, but Kanar had wanted an excuse to get the others away from him. He had known that Lily would go off for supplies. Jal had been plenty eager to go looking for robes. That left Kanar to deal with distracting Honaaz.

The man would have a chance to prove his skill soon enough. At least, if things went the way Kanar suspected they would. Morgan had always liked to taunt him about logic, but it wasn't as if Kanar couldn't think through a problem. If there was one thing that his time in the military had taught him, it was how he could analyze, plan, and solve. In this case, the answer became clear the further he went into Taluf.

The puzzle was a relatively simple one for Kanar. He had to get into the citadel, and he had to figure out what they intended to use the blood for. Lily would be useful, especially with her knives, and maybe with the other ability that he didn't fully understand yet. But he wasn't going to bring that inside, not without knowing where her allegiance lay. Both Honaaz and Jal might also be useful, but Kanar didn't want to risk either of them for something he would have to do, and for something where he might have to reveal his own secret.

He had to be the Blackheart.

"My task is that I have to deal with you," he said.

"Deal with me? You make it sound as if I'm going to be some dangerous threat."

"That's exactly what you are."

Morgan frowned and watched him. "I know you don't feel that way."

"You don't know anything about me."

Kanar turned his attention to Honaaz. There were things that the man could do, the least of which would be to gather additional supplies for them. But he wondered if perhaps that wasn't what was needed.

"Go get a cart," Kanar said.

Honaaz furrowed his brow. "What about you?"

"I'm going to keep an eye on her."

Kanar held Honaaz's gaze for a long moment, and the large man finally looked away. He headed down the street, casting a brief glance back at them, before disappearing around a bend.

"You still have a way with your people," Morgan said. "I suppose I shouldn't have expected that to change."

"Come on," he said.

"You aren't going to wait for the rest of them?"

Kanar had originally intended to wait, but he increasingly wondered if that was the right strategy. Knowing what he did—at least, what he thought he understood—he had no interest in getting the others pulled in and possibly harmed. If anyone was going to suffer, it would be him and Morgan.

He had to get inside, find the Alainsith blood, and keep the citadel from using it however they intended. There had to be a reason why the citadel brought the blood here, and for the eerie quiet they had found around the tower. Kanar wasn't sure what the answers were, only that he was going to be here when they were stopped.

Morgan smiled. "You know, when you broke in and came for me, and then were so adamant that you not split up, I started to question whether you were a different person. I thought maybe the great Kanar Reims had finally started to see things differently. To understand that his way of viewing the world wasn't necessarily the only way." She shook her head. "Unfortunately, I was wrong. I hate being wrong, as you probably recall."

"I remember."

"But I guess I was also right. I never thought you would change, Gray."

He motioned for her to get moving.

"I don't think we can just walk into this place," Morgan said.

"Are you sure? You don't even know what we can do."

"Just because you're angry at your team, especially *her* because she was keeping secrets from you, that's no reason for you to throw yourself into something like this."

"Why are you saying that? What do you know?"

Morgan tipped her head. "I told you that I'm a scholar."

"Which means that you came here."

"I've been many places. And the people in this one hate

witchcraft even more than you, Gray." She looked at him. "Which is what worries me. Think of what Alainsith blood can do in the right hands."

"Are there right hands?"

"The world isn't black and white, Gray."

As they approached the citadel, Kanar continued to look up at the building. "Was her layout accurate?" he asked. He thought back to what Lily had said about where the Alainsith blood would be stored. Up. High up.

"I can only tell you what I've researched," Morgan said. "This was one of the few places I was not permitted to visit when I came. They study ancient powers."

"Like the Alainsith?"

"Perhaps," she said. "The citadel has been around for far longer than witchcraft. They have always sought understanding, and they have tried to influence others. Sometimes too often."

Morgan looked over to him with eyes that were bright with a question. Kanar had no idea what that question was, nor about what she intended by looking at him in that way, but he had seen her studying him like this before. He hadn't had an answer then, and he doubted that he would have one now.

"If you think that you're going to be able to fight your way through the citadel, you will be mistaken," she said. "I doubt that even you could survive this."

"You might be surprised what I can survive," he said.

"I know you, Gray. You might want to think that I don't, but I know you."

He turned away. She did know him. Or she had. Now he wasn't sure if he knew himself.

"So we go up," he said. "Here's how it's going to play out. You're going to lead."

She frowned at him. "How, exactly, do you intend for me to do that?"

"That's not how this works. I've seen enough of how all of this plays out inside the kingdom, and I'm not going to let it destroy any other place."

"You have not been paying attention. That's your problem." She stared at him with a hard-eyed expression, and Kanar refused to look away. Finally, she sighed. "I will lead you through the tower. I will even get you to the top of the citadel, where you can stop this ceremony. That is, if you decide it's necessary."

"Why wouldn't it be necessary?" he asked.

"You will see."

They strode down the street. Morgan set the pace in front of him, and Kanar had to move quickly. He shifted his sword beneath his cloak, wanting to keep it as concealed as possible. He doubted that there would be any true risk up until they entered the citadel. Once inside, then he would be in real danger. He had no idea what he might run into, or how he might have to counter the magic that filled the tower.

Surprisingly, Kanar knew almost nothing about the citadel. He had heard rumblings about places where people could train to use power, though this struck him as quite different than what he had ever imagined. Why would there be something like this here? The king had to know about it. Why had he not worked with the citadel?

Unless he had.

Kanar squeezed the hilt of his sword. The king had made a plan to defeat witchcraft, thinking that he had to use some of its elements to be successful against it. Had that come out of a place like this?

He stayed at a reasonable distance from Morgan. She led him to a small tower that stretched up near the back wall of the citadel. Kanar found it quite odd that they had not seen anyone else.

"Not so welcoming, then," Kanar muttered as he looked at the darkened shape of the tower.

She reached the bridge leading to a back entrance, and something seemed to shift within her. Maybe it was her posture, how she shook out her hair, or maybe it was simply that she seemed to embrace her power. There was a funny sort of energy that rippled away from her, a strange but sudden thing.

"What did you do?" he asked.

"You want appearances. You need me to uphold them."

Her prison clothing had shifted, and now it looked as if she were wearing a long black robe. It was much like what he had wanted Jal to acquire, but this seemed as if it had suddenly morphed out of her clothing.

"Is it real?"

"No more real than the cuffs around your wrists," she said, holding out an item of woven grasses with small stones worked into it. A hegen item.

She flicked her wrist, and he felt something stir around both of his.

Kanar looked down. He now had what looked to be metal chains binding his hands. It was an illusion, but he still didn't care for it. "Is this necessary?"

"It is if you want to go up." She glanced back at him. "You will have your answers, Gray. I think that it might be too late for you, though."

"My answers? I don't think I need any answers. I know what I've done and why I've done it. I know what the king has asked of me, and I've done it willingly."

"Which is your problem." Morgan turned away, striding forward, leading him across the bridge. Once they reached the door, she paused and raised her hand. The door shimmered for a moment, before sliding up. He had no idea what she did, or how she triggered the magic she used. He knew it was witchcraft, though.

When he had served in the Order, he had learned the types of witchcraft that the priests of Fell had utilized. Most of them took their dark power and drew on violence and pain, using that to inflict even more violence and pain upon the kingdom, which in turn made them even more powerful. It was why the war had been so difficult. How could you fight something when the mere act of fighting strengthened the enemy?

It had required those like Kanar to go in and counter the danger. Soldiers without families. They could endure physical pain, and though many of Kanar's comrades were tortured, it was nothing compared to the power that could be derived from loss. The priests had often targeted parent-child bonds specifically. They would kill the children first to harness the worst anguish this world could produce.

One night, Kanar's troop had been scouring the plains for a ceremony that they'd been warned of too late. They'd come across the aftermath. Five families that had once lived and breathed were now nothing but limbs and bones and markings on the earth.

When he tried to picture that scene, his mind got stuck. It came in dreams instead. His captain had suggested he try to get it out somehow. Draw. Write a song. Talk to someone.

But he couldn't. Words didn't fit right. Even his thoughts around it were hollow.

So Kanar had plunged into battle willingly. If his time came, he could pass knowing that there was one bit of pain that was so deep within him, the priests could never use it. Because his family had already been taken. And that night on the plains had emptied out the rest.

Morgan looked over to him. "Are you nervous?"

He wanted to tell her no, but the truth of the matter was that he was. Coming into the citadel this way worried him.

"Take me wherever we need to go," he said instead.

"Then we will."

The back entrance to the citadel was made of simple black stone. It was without any real decoration, and there was nothing that made it remarkable in any way. The only thing Kanar noticed was that he could practically feel the magic of this place, as if there was a distinct and steady hum around him.

They headed through the building. Morgan strode forward, and when she reached what looked to be a flat section of wall, she placed her hand on it. She pressed down, and the walls started to tremble, and then this section began to slide apart.

And then it opened completely.

She stepped forward.

Kanar wasn't sure what to expect inside but was surprised that the room looked considerably different than the others. This one was made of a gray stone, all of which seemed to glow softly, as if with its own light.

She glanced over to him. "Are you nervous now?"

"No."

"Good. Because you have barely seen anything."

"Then let's keep moving," he said.

"Let's," she said, smiling at him tightly. "Because I think there is much for you to see here."

"Why do I get the feeling that you're enjoying this?"

She paused. There was a slight flutter, as if whatever hegen items she used to create the illusion of her robes faded for the briefest of moments. Maybe it was the power of the citadel itself that inhibited it, or perhaps it was some fault in her magic.

"You know so little, Gray. Have you even started to think about why I was brought on this mission?"

"Because I was the only one who could get you out."

She snorted. "Because they wanted you to kill me."

"What?"

"Still so easily misled." She shook her head, her golden hair swaying. It looked as if it had been freshly washed, hanging light and loose at her shoulders. She pulled something out of her pocket and held it out—a hegen item.

"Who hired you for the job?" Morgan asked.

"It doesn't matter."

"Perhaps not. How much did they pay?"

Kanar frowned. "Again, that doesn't matter."

"Now I know you're lying. You care. Especially when it comes to money. If this is a job that pulls you back into the kingdom, and back into your past, it would have to pay well, wouldn't it?"

"Perhaps," he agreed.

"Who suggested that I could be of use?" Morgan asked.

He frowned again. "I was told what happened."

"You were told the Alainsith were slaughtered and that I knew something about it. And perhaps I did, but not for that reason. And here we are, a place that should not have collected Alainsith blood, but it appears that it did. Why do you think that is?"

Kanar shook his head. "I don't know."

"And who do you think is responsible?"

Increasingly, he realized that he didn't know.

Perhaps that was a mistake.

"You need somebody to ask the questions you should have been asking, Gray." Her voice had fallen and was softer now. There was something comforting about it. It was almost as if she wanted to try to prod him to ask those questions, as if she meant it when she told him she was trying to help. Kanar didn't know if he could ever believe her again. He certainly couldn't trust her after everything they had been through.

"Why?" he asked.

"Look at you. Your team, and who you were willing to hire. What role do you think you were to have?"

"I'm not exactly sure," he admitted. "I was sent to get you. I chose to stop these people from using the blood."

Morgan gave him a sad smile. "You still think I'm part of this. That hurts." She turned away, found a staircase, and started up quickly. She took the stairs two at a time, her illusion floating with her and her gown barely moving. Kanar had to chase her.

What had he missed?

He tried to think through what had happened. He'd been hired by Edward to break Morgan out of prison. She was part of the job because Edward had wanted him to find her, but the rest of it had been Kanar's idea. At least, he believed it was.

The team was his. Lily. Jal.

Honaaz... Honaaz had come from a job that had gone sideways. Was he trustworthy?

Here Kanar thought that he knew what was going on, and knew his role in all of it, but perhaps that was the biggest mistake. He knew nothing.

As he looked up at Morgan, he started to question if perhaps she had more answers than she was letting on. And if she did, what would he do?

Not let her betray him. That much he knew.

She stopped and waited for him to catch up to her. Once he did, she looked over to him. "Have you come to any decisions?"

"I'm going to keep them from using the blood. Whatever they intend." He looked at her, and she laughed softly.

"Will you believe me if I tell you what I know?" she asked.

"I don't know."

"Have you ever believed me?"

Kanar found himself meeting Morgan's deep-green eyes.

"Yes," he said, and as he looked into her eyes now, he found himself questioning things he had long believed. It was the reason he had left the Order. He had never wanted to betray his king or his people. But those questions had been hard on him—and had been harder still to ignore. Those questions had lingered.

He had seen the effects of the war. There'd been so much fighting, which only led to more and more powerful witchcraft. He had seen what the king was willing to do to stop it. People like him had been sent to take down those who could destroy the kingdom. And Kanar had done it willingly. Gladly, even.

Until her name had come up.

"Why didn't you kill me?" she asked.

"Because I couldn't. I couldn't kill you," he said.

She knew that, and her asking was more manipulation. He wanted to challenge her, to demand to know why she had betrayed him and used witchcraft. Morgan had known about his sister and how she had gotten caught up in it too. But he didn't say anything. Kanar refused to let her get under his skin. He had left Reyand and headed to Sanaron because he felt as if he might finally get away from her.

Standing next to her now left him with a pang of longing that he tried to ignore. There had been a time when the two of them simply sat, looking up at the stars or the moon or out over whatever city they happened to both be in at the same time. He would tell stories of his patrols and the places he'd visited, and she would tell stories of books she'd read and the people she'd met.

It had been easy. It had been comfortable.

It had been a lie.

All of it.

Those books she had read, those people she had interacted with—all of them had been about pursuing power. She'd been chasing witchcraft the entire time.

And he had been sent to stop her.

"Because that's not who you are," Morgan said.

"Do you even know who I am?"

She smiled sadly. "I've always known who you are, Gray." She turned and headed up more stairs. "But had you been paying attention, you would have known what I was."

Morgan's pace slowed, and there was something funereal about the way her head bowed. Kanar was struck by an awful thought: that he had only delayed her execution, and every step since had taken them closer to her fate.

But what fate was that?

They reached the top of the stairs, and Morgan stepped forward.

As soon as she did, she froze. Everything within her went stiff.

Kanar realized they weren't alone.

Things started to click for him, but he wasn't sure he had it completely right. He had been used.

Morgan looked back at him. "I think I've figured out what they're doing. I hadn't realized how they intended to use the Alainsith blood in their ceremony. I do now. The citadel, and maybe the entire city, is the sacrifice."

Chapter Twenty-Nine

LILY

Lily didn't know why she had expected anything else. Kanar had gone into the citadel on his own, taking Morgan with him. Did he really think he could stop what was coming on his own? Lily knew he was capable, but she also knew what the citadel was capable of. Why leave her behind?

Everything had changed when he'd learned about her connection to magic. It shouldn't have mattered. This *was* Kanar Reims, though.

"How long ago did he leave?" she asked.

Honaaz pushed the cart. "I went and got this thing, then went looking for you, so not that long ago. What's the problem?"

Lily wasn't sure how to tell him about the problem. It was more than about Kanar leaving them. There were dangers in the citadel itself. Morgan wouldn't be able to protect him, even if she wanted to do so. Her kind of magic could only offer him so much, and when it came to Kanar and that magic, Lily doubted that he'd be aware of what he'd need to defend himself against.

Or would he?

It occurred to her that she wasn't entirely sure what he was capable of when it came to fighting magic. He had a reputation, which was the reason that Honaaz was so bothered by him, but was that reputation enough to get him in and out of the citadel without dying? He wouldn't even know that there was much more taking place than he believed. He wouldn't know that the artifacts had been brought here.

"We can't leave him alone in there," Lily said.

Honaaz scoffed. "He's not a baby. He's Kanar fucking Reims. You've seen him fight. You know he'll be able to manage anything he gets into. Let him pull the job himself if that's what he thinks he's going to do."

"We need to keep the citadel operatives—or whoever is responsible—from succeeding."

"Why?"

"If we don't, then you won't earn the one—" Lily looked over to Honaaz, realizing that she had no idea how much Kanar had promised him. Maybe not nearly the same as he'd promised them. She suspected that he had truly agreed to split the fee with them, but maybe that was the problem. The number had been enough that it had made him—and them—too eager. "Whatever he's paying you."

"What's he paying *you*?" Honaaz asked.

"A cut," she said, then glanced at Jal. He had the spools of fabric, and she had a collection of items she'd gotten from Gilbert's shop.

Something whizzed past her head.

"What the fuck was that?" Honaaz growled.

"Dogs," Jal said, voice low.

"What?" Lily spun to face him. The Dogs had been following them the entire journey, but the only time they had really been attacked was in Verendal. Otherwise, the Dogs hadn't actually come at them that aggressively. It was almost as if they were only trying to chase them.

What did they know? Why wouldn't they have attacked along the way?

"I think we've forgotten about one aspect of all of this," Lily said softly.

"The Prophet," Jal said.

"Maybe. But there were others working against him in Sanaron. I saw them, Jal. But even if the Dogs or the Prophet or these others get to Kanar, they haven't been able to do anything. Kanar is too skilled." Their entire team was too skilled for the Dogs, at least so far, and she was determined to see that it stayed that way. "How many people is the Prophet going to waste on us?"

"They're still following us," Jal said. He looked behind him, gaze sweeping everywhere around him. His hand went to his chest, and he rubbed the area where the crossbow bolt had struck.

He should have recovered fully, but they hadn't really tested it. If his aim was off, even a little…

"Better get moving," Honaaz said. "Looks like we got quite a few making their way through here."

Let the Dogs come.

But once Lily started fighting, she had to think that others in the city would be drawn to the commotion.

She reached into her pouch, pricking her finger and performing the binding to the bone. A soft pain floated through her, which she felt each time she used that power, but then it passed.

Lily tossed the bone. It rolled through the street, then exploded.

She had expected something more significant. Yes, it *had* exploded, but weakly.

Gilbert.

I thought he wouldn't betray me. I am *going to haunt him.*

The only hope she had was that he might not have known.

"I'm going to need some help," she said, looking over to Honaaz. Jal could provide cover, and between her and Honaaz, they could cut down a few Dogs. "What would you say about helping me collect a few prizes?"

"Just as long as you don't use them on me," Honaaz said.

"Why would I ever—" Lily thought about it for a second.

"I'm just trying to make sure you're not going to come for me. Don't need you taking my fingers or toes."

"I'd only do it after you were dead, not before. Besides, there are probably more interesting parts I could claim."

Honaaz blinked, then he actually flushed. "Fuck."

She grinned.

Another crossbow bolt streaked toward her.

With a quick whip of his bow, Jal shot the bolt out of the air, knocking it to the cobblestones. "The two of you need to stop flirting. Get moving, as Kanar would say."

Honaaz shook his head. "We're not—"

"Kanar isn't here, so we can do what we want," Lily said. "This shouldn't take too long anyway."

She flicked a pair of knives out of her pocket and

started forward. There were other items in her pouch that might be effective, but she'd have to save them. Now was the time to add new things to her collection.

Honaaz kept pace with her. His daggers were clutched in each hand, and he looked like he wanted to plow through the Dogs.

"Let me give you a little coverage," she said.

He nodded.

She found what she was looking for in her pouch. In Sanaron, she didn't have much need for items like this, but in the citadel and in places like Verendal, they didn't have the same fog to hide in. Once she performed the binding, a trail of smoke began to steadily build. She threw the item.

"Give it a few moments," Lily said.

"What's it going to do?" Honaaz asked.

She smiled at how nervous he sounded. She found it somewhat cute, though a man like him wouldn't like to be called cute. "Smoke, mostly. If I made it right…" She laughed softly, which only elicited more of a concerned expression from him.

The smoke fluttered outward from the item she'd made. Thankfully, it was more potent than the last item.

Honaaz darted forward into the smoke. He moved quickly for his size, and she raced to keep up with him. She debated grabbing something else out of her pouch, but she didn't want to risk of exhausting everything she had access to.

A shadow moved near her, too small to be Honaaz.

Lily started toward him, but the man was fast.

She swept her leg into his, dropping him. Reaching for a knife, she thought she'd have time to slow him, but he spit into her eyes, causing Lily to jerk back.

That freed him. With one hand, the man grabbed her by the throat, bringing a knife toward her belly.

Lily kneed him in the groin.

He grunted.

Then she drove her knives upward, striking the person in the stomach. When she pulled out her blades, she wrapped her arms around his neck to yank him down to the ground. Once he was down, she used her shears and clipped off as many fingers as she had time for.

Another shadow appeared. Lily jumped, collecting the three or four fingers in one scoop. She stuffed them into her pouch to be dealt with later, then drove her blades toward the next Dog.

There was a soft shout, and then more Dogs converged on her.

Lily sorted through her pouch. There had to be something still there that she could use. What she needed was something that could explode as a diversion.

She kicked at someone as they came close, slashed at another.

And then men fell away.

A massive shadow appeared before her.

"Is that you, Honaaz?"

"Who the fuck else do you think it is?"

She laughed. They picked their way through the smoke, only to realize that the Dogs had scattered.

Jal strode toward him, seemingly having no difficulty finding them.

"Are they gone?" he asked.

"For now," Lily said. "I don't know how long they will stay that way."

"How many are down?"

"I killed seven," Honaaz replied.

"A couple," she said.

Jal nodded. "I took out three. I feel like I'm letting you down."

"We need to get into the citadel and help Kanar—"

"What if he doesn't want our help?" Honaaz asked. He looked up at the tower. "It was his choice to go in there. Maybe he doesn't need us."

"He doesn't know what he needs," she said. "Cut off enough fabric to wrap around you. Make it loose so that you can still move, but be prepared. We're going in as monks."

"Could she have controlled Reims to force him into the citadel?" Honaaz asked.

"That's not how magic usually works," Lily said.

She didn't know what exactly Morgan was capable of. Traditional witchcraft involved capturing and storing power in different significant items. From what she'd heard of the prison escape, Morgan hadn't used anything like that.

That didn't mean Morgan couldn't have something on her that would permit her to perform that level of magic. Lily simply wasn't familiar enough with witchcraft to know one way or another. Still, it seemed to her that the Hunter *was* familiar with witchcraft, which suggested that he knew how to avoid it. The hegen traps around Morgan had been designed to drain any additional witchcraft—but she'd still managed to use magic to break free of her bindings.

"You two keep moving," Lily said. "I need to take a look. Don't worry about me."

Before they could argue, she slipped along the side of the strangely empty street, then tossed her grappling hook up to snag it on the side of one of the neighboring buildings. She had first scaled stone here in the city. She'd slipped when she neared the roofline and fallen back, landing on her shoulder. It was a wonder that she hadn't broken anything. The citadel refused to offer healing for mistakes—and that had definitely been a mistake.

Once Lily reached the roof, she slowed and looked down. From above, she could make out the layout of the city and the way it was organized, with all the streets leading straight toward the citadel itself. In the distance, she could make out wagons, though they were closer to the river. The rest of the city generally had more activity.

She found herself searching for signs that might suggest that there were other things going on here. The city was far too quiet. She didn't see any evidence of the Dogs anymore. The only thing she was aware of was how everything here felt wrong. She started to wrap the rope for the grappling hook around her arm, when she noticed movement.

Somebody was coming.

Lily carefully slipped the rope back into her satchel, closed it, and then flattened herself down, looking everywhere until she was convinced that there was no further movement.

Where did they go?

She crawled forward and reached for one of her knives, before changing her mind and putting her hand into the satchel.

Lily found one of the fingers she had harvested. A new prize.

With her knife, she sliced the flesh off the bone and then rolled it back and forth along the slate rooftop to dry it. There was a process involved in trying to harness the prize, but she wasn't sure how long she could wait. She needed to use this because she had to be particular in what she created.

She started to carve the bone, peeling layers away until it was smooth and circular like a cylinder. Then she sharpened one end and used that to prick her finger. She drew her own blood and then let it dribble along the length of the cylinder. Taking that, she jammed it into the slate.

Then she started crawling.

If the art worked, it would give her enough time to keep moving, and then it would eventually cause a steady buildup of heat until it exploded altogether. Lily felt a little bad for whatever shop was beneath this roof.

With the quiet around her, she started to question whether something more had happened in the citadel than she realized. She should've been paying attention to it.

Maybe Gilbert had tried to give her a warning, in his own way. He'd told her that the artifacts had been brought to the city.

And I'd warned him.

The rooftop started to sizzle and crackle. As it did, a shadow moved, scurrying away. She smiled to herself and then whipped a knife, sending it streaking across the empty space. She expected a cry of pain, something to tell her that she'd hit her target, but there was nothing. What had happened?

Lily reached for another knife. Jal had grabbed plenty from the prison, but they'd gone through a lot since then. She should have taken the time to use Gilbert's supplies to restock what she needed.

She only had three knives remaining.

She scurried along the rooftop. When she saw another

flicker of movement, she flattened herself and rolled, using the heat and smoke from her art to conceal her passing.

Popping to her feet, she raced toward what she had seen.

A figure was cloaked in gray, blending into the slate. She darted at them, jumping between roofs, rolling, and then springing up. She jabbed out with one knife, expecting to drive the blade into the Dog's back, but they spun and blocked her. She thrust with her other knife, and it was stopped as well.

Lily twisted with one blade, then the next, thrusting each one forward, before spinning back and dodging away. This Dog was far more skilled than any of the ones she had faced.

She kicked. Her boot connected with her attacker's midsection. Another kick, and she heard a grunt.

"You aren't going to follow us, Dog," she growled.

Something came flying toward her. At first she wasn't sure what it was, but then she saw a flicker of shadow. Thinking it was a knife, she ducked and rolled.

The item exploded.

They had used the art against her.

Lily barely reacted in time, tumbling toward the person rather than away. She kicked, driving her heel into this attacker. Then she drove her fist up, smashed them in the shin, and heard a grunt.

She smiled to herself. Another thrust, and she connected with their arm. Lily brought her elbow down and slammed it into the person's chest. She spun behind them, wrapping her arm around their neck, and then jerked backward.

The hood came off, and the cloak slipped away from

their arms. Her gaze drifted as she looked for the Dogs' markings, but she saw nothing other than a satchel much like the one she carried.

Not a Dog at all.

She pushed the person away and crouched, holding knives in either hand, ready to flick them. The person didn't move, though.

Lily didn't think they were from the citadel, but there was one way to find out.

She flung her knife. The person flattened themselves down, but not before she followed with another. That one struck them in their back.

Lily darted over and grabbed her knives as they took a gasping last breath.

Somebody from the citadel wouldn't have been caught by a second knife. They would have been taught to watch for it.

What was this person doing here?

Lily rolled the person over. The compact man was dressed in green and had a short sword that was sheathed. She didn't recognize him.

She found a strange metallic object nearby. Unfamiliar symbols were written on it, though they were similar to the hegen language. But as she looked at it, different questions came to her—ones about the artifacts they had escorted to Sanaron. The same artifacts that Gilbert had mentioned had come back to the citadel. What was going on here? And why now?

Could the city be the target?

Items like that would be destructive.

They could take all of Taluf down.

And that would be…

Witchcraft. That was what that would be.

A whistle sounded, and she stiffened. Jal?

They needed her.

There was another whistle, then another.

They needed her *now*.

She peered down over the edge of the building. The streets were empty—even more so than she would have expected. Maybe Gilbert *had* spread word to his contacts. It was a simple thing for him, but she hadn't known if he would listen.

If he does, this might work.

When she glanced back up, the figure was gone. They scurried along the rooftop, away from the citadel.

Lily had a choice. She could find Jal and Honaaz, or she could go after whoever else was out there.

With the emptiness of the citadel, the answer came to her.

She ran after the figure so that she could get answers. So that they could stop this—whatever *this* might be.

Chapter Thirty
KANAR

A sacrifice. That was what Morgan had said.

"What are you talking about?" Kanar asked.

The room was different than the others they had seen. Light filled it, but Kanar had a sense that it wasn't natural light.

"Ceremonies require a sacrifice, Gray," Morgan said. "I've been trying to figure out what it is. Why the blood, and why were the relics brought here? If they simply wanted to create something powerful, they didn't have to do it here. But it wasn't the citadel. I was wrong." Her voice sounded pained.

"Who, then?" he asked.

"I don't know." She remained completely stiff, only her eyes and mouth moving.

With sword in hand, Kanar focused. The blade would cut through magic. That was the gift. And the curse. By using the sword and cutting down his enemies, he strengthened the blade, rather than strengthening those using witchcraft.

Kanar remembered that day clearly. It had taken the king little time to come up with the solution. The king had approached him, holding a bundle of cloth wrapped around an ancient wooden scabbard engraved with unreadable symbols. Kanar had taken the sword, unsheathing it slightly, noting the painted blade. A black blade for the Blackheart.

Kanar had looked up, and the king had smiled.

"We defeat them with their own weapons," King Porman said.

The war was not going well. They'd thwarted several of the main threats in the war, but not enough for the king's liking. The pressure continued to build on them to find a way past the different attacks. If they could come up with a method to get through the most powerful enemies, they could stop the war.

That was what Kanar told himself.

When he'd felt that growing power of the sword, he knew it was for the cause.

Then he'd started to notice *himself* changing. It was subtle at first. Little more than a boost of strength that shouldn't have been there. Then speed. Then healing.

Kanar wasn't stupid. He recognized the connection to the weapon that he'd started using and understood that it had begun to turn him into something else.

The others of the Order hadn't noticed, but then most of them had died during the fighting. Not Kanar. He'd learned to move stealthily to take down some of the most powerful users of witchcraft—which only served to make the sword even more potent.

It continued to change him.

That was why he so rarely fought with *his* sword. Knives

were easier. With what he'd been through, he found that his aim was far better than he'd ever known before. Kanar had trained to the point where he mostly didn't miss, but with his connection to the sword, he now almost never did. He was also more than happy to use someone else's sword against them, but drawing his own blade… With the gift that he'd been given and the death that came with it—along with the horrible reward—he hadn't been able to keep at it.

Until now.

The blade came free of the sheath.

He hated that, but now that it was in his hand, he could feel that connection. It struck him as similar to what Morgan and Lily had mentioned about this place. A binding. That was what it was.

"You need to go," Morgan said. "You should not be here."

The rippled and shifted, and the light itself started to change. It reminded Kanar of how Morgan's robes had transformed.

What was happening here?

Then the room was filled with people. Dozens of them. One of them was a white-haired man with icy blue eyes who Kanar had seen around Sanaron—and probably the same person Lily had seen in Sanaron. Tayol.

Tayol withdrew a slender rod from his pocket and held it out. The symbols along the silver surface looked familiar. He had spent so much time dealing with people like this, and with witchcraft.

That was what the man wanted?

"All of this is to power some witchcraft spell *here*?" Kanar said.

"You can't understand," Tayol said. "I know what you did on behalf of Reyand during the war, but we suffered our own losses. And now there's movement from the south. The war isn't over, Reims. It'll never be over unless we are willing to do the same as our enemy. I've seen Galdan. Isant. Merkalai. You have not."

Kanar had only heard of Galdan.

"I get it. I've lost to them as well. This isn't the way."

"It's the *only* way. I am not about to stand back and let those witchcraft practitioners gain increased strength."

"This is all to protect the citadel?" Kanar looked over to Morgan.

"If I do this, we will have the power we need to defeat witchcraft for good. The citadel is built in an ancient Alainsith stronghold. That's why this has to be here. This will make us powerful enough to defeat any form of magic. You can either be a part of it—and I know the Blackheart would want that—or you can step aside."

Kanar glanced over to Morgan again. He had no idea what they needed to do. The only thing he could think about was that they might not be fast enough.

Worse, he also couldn't help but feel as if there might be something good here. How could he not? He wanted to destroy witchcraft no differently than anyone else did.

Tayol turned to Morgan. Was he willing to sacrifice her?

"Let her go," Kanar said.

Tayol's determined expression faltered a moment before he took a breath. "I cannot. You're either a part of it, or you're a sacrifice to it. I'm sorry, Blackheart, truly. You've done the world a service. Perhaps this is how you can continue to serve."

"Do you think you can stop me?" Kanar's voice was soft, anger filling it.

He knew that he wouldn't hold back. He knew that he *couldn't* hold back.

Not this time. Not with what they intended to do here.

"You're outnumbered. Even the great Kanar Reims can't stop this." Tayol started toward him, though several others still blocked him from reaching Kanar.

The wand in his hand was the real threat. There was power trapped in that, much like there was power trapped in Kanar's sword. *Lots* of it.

Still, something wasn't sitting right with him.

Tayol was doing this to stop witchcraft, but ceremonies such as the one he intended to perform were destructive by nature. Kanar had seen several of them during the war. He'd stopped many—and failed more times than he cared to count.

"I don't think you understand what you're doing," Kanar said. "If you wanted to eradicate witchcraft, you could have *used* the Alainsith rather than slaughtering them."

"That wasn't us, but it did tell me that the time to act is now. Perhaps they will serve as a necessary sacrifice."

It was almost as if Tayol were trying to convince Kanar. *Not me. Himself.*

This wasn't a man who wanted to destroy.

He'd suffered.

The same as Kanar.

There has to be a way to reach him.

"Do you realize how you sound? You are just like them."

Kanar shifted his stance, turning his sword and preparing

to move. The longer he stood here, the more he might begin to feel a surge of power through the blade, as if it allowed him to summon trapped energy. He had started to wonder if that meant he could use witchcraft. He didn't want to think that was what it might mean, but he had already been changed. He didn't want to become anything worse.

Unless he already had.

"Lay down your blade, Reims. I know you want the same thing we do. You want all witchcraft practitioners to be destroyed. This is how we do it. The citadel will become stronger."

"What if it doesn't?" Kanar said.

"You lack faith."

Faith. Another thing that witchcraft practitioners spoke of.

He looked over to Morgan, and she mouthed, "Go."

They weren't alone in the room. There were nearly a dozen others here now, all dressed in dark gray clothing, several with pouches like Lily's. Operatives of the citadel, Kanar suspected. They would be skilled.

Are they here to help him?

Kanar took a deep breath. "I'm not going anywhere, and I'm not going to let you complete this. You're making a mistake. As much as I want to destroy witchcraft, I don't think this is the right way. We can work together. The citadel, the Order, others who oppose witchcraft…"

Tayol sighed. "Others like you? Others who have abandoned their vows?"

"You don't—"

Tayol surprised him and lunged toward Kanar, using the rod like a sword. Not only that, he seemed comfortable wielding a sword. Lily had said that the man was skilled and dangerous, but Kanar hadn't expected this.

Kanar darted forward, positioning himself in front of Morgan. He would fight for her. He had to.

There had been a time when he never would've questioned doing so. When the two of them had been on the rooftop looking out over Vur, he would have said he would do anything to protect her. He had been the one who had changed. Not her.

Tayol flew toward him again, which Kanar deflected. The man made another jab, but Kanar was ready. A dozen operatives of the citadel then joined Tayol.

It had been a long time since Kanar had lost himself in a fight. Since moving to Sanaron, he had relied on other aspects of his Realmsguard training, avoiding using his sword. But he was the Blackheart. He would lose himself if he had to. He would not be stopped.

He turned, blade thrusting, then spun and drove his heel forward.

One of the men fell after Kanar cleaved his arm off.

Kanar felt the strange tingle of power as the blade pulled the energy of pain and suffering—the energy of witchcraft—into itself. Magic filled it, and since the sword was bound to him, that power flowed to Kanar.

Another jab.

Kanar deflected it.

One of the operatives stepped too close, and though Kanar didn't want to kill, he had no choice. He knew how skilled they were.

One man lost a hand. Kanar felt power surge into his sword.

Another person came at him, and Kanar stabbed his blade into their chest.

Each time he used his sword, he could feel that power shift, flow into him.

Three came toward Kanar.

He kept himself positioned in front of Morgan. She still hadn't moved. He had no idea why, but he kept his focus locked on the three. Two fell before they even had a chance to fight. His blade dropped the next one as well.

Morgan cried out.

Kanar jerked his head around, whipped a knife in that direction, and then spun, driving his sword to the other side.

Tayol was in front of him once more, surrounded by more bodies than Kanar expected. How many had he killed?

"You're harming your own people," Kanar said, realizing what was happening. The operatives were staggering. Some had already collapsed. Most simply seemed immobile. "Your ceremony is killing them."

"No. We are growing stronger. They will recover."

Kanar looked down. He had a hard time thinking these men were going to get back up.

Tayol's gaze went to the black blade. "I heard the stories but never would have known. Such a weapon. Do you know the truth of its making?"

"Witchcraft," Kanar spat.

The man grinned. "You'd think so, wouldn't you? But no."

The survivors hadn't recovered enough, which gave them space now. As Kanar attempted a feint forward, Tayol shifted, sliding from one foot to the next and positioning himself in such a way that he prevented Kanar from moving and easily fighting.

"It's Alainsith," Tayol said. "Impossibly old."

Kanar almost looked down at his blade but resisted the urge.

"Your king collects them." Tayol sneered. "Why should we not have the same opportunity?"

Kanar couldn't wait any longer. He was aware of power building. He had no idea how he could feel it, only that it was there. This ceremony would be complete, and then...

Stone cracked around him. A massive gap in the floor opened.

Increasingly, Kanar suspected that the citadel would crumble.

Tayol started toward him, his hand moving in a pattern of witchcraft. Regardless of what he might deny, that was the magic he used.

Kanar darted toward him, but Morgan cried out. He spun.

Tayol paused, flicking his gaze from Kanar to Morgan. "Her blood is on your blade."

"That should be yours," Kanar said.

"Oh, you say that as if you care about her. Her blood, like that of so many others, taints that blade. But it brings you strength. You fear it, though you should not. Why fear something that can give you so much power? The hegen understand. Of course, they've always understood only a fraction of what's possible. They don't have the capacity to understand more."

"And witchcraft?" Kanar asked.

He had to keep Tayol talking. If the man continued to talk, then he wasn't fighting. Kanar wasn't sure what he was going to have to do to defeat him, only that it would have to be soon.

He had to disrupt this ceremony. Regardless of what else he did, the ceremony had to be stopped.

"Witchcraft is merely knowledge," Tayol said. "It's how that knowledge is used and applied that matters. Do you think the hegen view what they do as witchcraft?"

Kanar faltered for a moment.

"Do you think we should be forbidden from that knowledge? We can stop that use of power."

"You intend to use that same power!" Kanar yelled.

Tayol darted forward.

Kanar blocked it by raising his blade. He caught the wand on the edge of it, and the sound of metal rang out.

Pain shot down Kanar's arms, and he tried to brace himself for the sudden blow, but it was too difficult. His arms shook. As much as he tried, he couldn't fight.

And yet Morgan was behind him, crying out softly.

Morgan.

The girl he had met all those years ago, the woman who had challenged him, tested him on his logic, and proven that he couldn't think things through quite as well as she could, but who had also shown that she wanted him to. She had pushed him to be something more than what he was, had thought he had the potential, and had demanded that he prove it.

Morgan.

If he failed, he knew what would happen to her.

He couldn't fail.

He *wouldn't* fail.

Kanar drove his blade forward. Tayol blocked him,

blow for blow, strike for strike, and doubt crept in. The Blackheart, stopped by this man?

He'd heard himself referred to as *great* so many times that it had gotten to him. He had come to believe it about himself and had come to think of himself in the same way. But he wasn't that great.

At this point, he wasn't even good. If he couldn't save Morgan, if he couldn't protect her, what was he? Who was he?

Kanar focused, squeezing the sword.

When he did, he felt something different. At first it was a subtle shift, almost as if it were imagined more than real. It was as though some part of the sword had changed for him, but he knew that wasn't the case. The sword itself hadn't changed—but the effect of the sword and how it connected to him had.

And it did connect to him. He had always known that. The blade had changed him. Kanar tightened his grip on it, feeling that power, and he braced for what was within.

Witchcraft.

Or perhaps not. Maybe what Tayol told him was true. If so, it wasn't witchcraft at all. It was nothing more than Alainsith magic. That was a natural power, much like hegen magic was.

Could witchcraft itself even be natural?

He would have to ponder that later. Right now…

Right now, he lunged toward Tayol and drove his blade out.

They began a dance. Kanar had never been bested in sword battle. Ever since he'd been gifted his blade, he had never known anyone equal to him. It wasn't arrogance that made him feel that way, it was confidence that he had earned.

But it was also confidence that came from knowing what he did about the blade.

Even the simple act of unsheathing the sword left him feeling invincible.

But he wasn't.

Tayol jabbed with his wand and seemed to move faster. It was starting to glow and took on a faint yellow that emanated from the end of the long, slender rod. The color moved along the surface, glowing with symbols that Kanar realized now were in the Alainsith language, which he'd seen on buildings throughout Reyand. Dark ink stained the symbols. Blood.

Alainsith blood.

Tayol flew forward. The wand slammed into Kanar. He staggered back, pain starting in his abdomen and blooming through him, but he wasn't bleeding. He tripped, his feet tangling as he spun the blade around.

"You see the difference," Tayol said, watching. "You wield an Alainsith relic, while I am using their power. This will stop war for good."

Tayol turned and dipped the wand into a small chalice. It had to be filled with more blood.

Morgan, seemingly fully released from what held her, staggered toward Tayol, who turned and drove the wand into her belly.

His eyes widened as her gaze turned to Kanar.

There was nothing he could do.

Chapter Thirty-One

HONAAZ

"What the fuck is going on?"

A wall of Dogs blocked them from moving up the street, and Honaaz wanted nothing more than to lower his shoulder and make a run at them. He wasn't about to do that on his own, though. The tall bastard might offer a measure of protection when it came to dealing with the Dogs, but Honaaz would much rather have Lily fighting alongside him. That was a thought that should have left him shitting his pants.

"It seems the Dogs have gathered here," Jal said.

He sounded more intrigued than bothered by all of this. How could he not be more annoyed? Honaaz was. In fact, he was starting to think that he had made a serious mistake in following Reims here.

The tavern in Sanaron had been cozy. He could have stayed right where he was, winning a few rounds, losing a few more, but having access to decent ale. Not good, but decent enough.

But there had been too many Dogs there as well.

"You think?" Honaaz grunted. He tried whistling again, but there wasn't any answer. "Why isn't she coming back? Isn't this how your team talks to each other? Whistle one way, then another, and you follow where the person is leading?"

That was what it had seemed like to him, but maybe he had it wrong. When they had fought before, the whistle seemed to be a big part of it.

"She must have gotten distracted," Jal said, looking up, but Honaaz knew he wasn't going to see anything.

Lily was gone.

She'd climbed up to the rooftop to check what they might have to deal with up there and hadn't come down again. Had Honaaz not watched her fight a few times, he might be concerned for her. *Might.*

"She got distracted. Reims got distracted. Seems to me the entire team is just one big fucking mess. And you pulled me into it."

"I believe you let yourself get pulled in," Jal said.

Honaaz shook his head. "Fuck," he muttered.

"That's how I'm feeling too."

Honaaz readied an attack. At this point, he didn't know what good it would do other than get himself killed, but he also didn't want to sit back and wait while the Dogs came at them.

Jal whistled.

Lily didn't respond, but there was an explosion somewhere nearby. A burst of air, a rumble, and debris that shot into the sky.

Below it all was a strange growl. The sound set the hair on his arms on edge.

"What was that?" Honaaz said.

Jal smiled tightly as he swung his bow from side to side in front of him. "That's our signal to get moving."

"Right. Care to tell me where we're to get moving to? Better yet, how? We've got probably two dozen Dogs in front of us." Some of them were hidden behind the buildings, and he couldn't get a clean count. "We've got to get up *there* somehow"—he motioned to the citadel—"and Lily has gone and run off."

"You've got it right," Jal said with a grin.

The tall bastard actually smiled.

Then he whistled again. The sound came out differently than when Honaaz whistled, and there was something to it that seemed a little somber.

"We really should get moving, as Kanar would say," Jal said. "We aren't going to want to be here when the berahn arrives."

"What's a berahn? Some kind of warrior?"

"An animal. Let's just say they are most decidedly deadly. Not to me. I don't know if it would leave you alone. I think I could send word to it to guide it away from you, but I'd rather not take the chance. I've decided you aren't all bad."

"That's what I tell women."

Jal smirked. "Oh, I think Lily knows."

Honaaz shot him an annoyed look, but Jal had already spun away.

"What about the Dogs?" Honaaz asked, looking toward some of the buildings but not sure what they would have to do. "You're not worried that they're going to chase us?"

"We just need to give it some space. Let the berahn have its run. Then we can go into the citadel."

The creature howled again, closer.

What was coming?

Jal worried for his safety. Having seen him around other animals, Honaaz decided the smart thing to do would be to listen to Jal.

So he followed.

"What's going to happen to the Dogs, exactly?" he asked as he caught up to Jal.

They cut around one of the buildings, and Honaaz looked up to the sky, checking the position of the sun. It hadn't moved that far. They still had time before it started to get dark, though increasingly he was thinking that he might want to be done with this job—and this place—before it became completely dark.

"Are you worried about them?" Jal said.

"Not the Dogs."

"You shouldn't be worried about the berahn either. The Dogs won't even see it." Jal looked over to him and the smile that normally clung to his face was gone, replaced by a serious expression that looked out of place. It was the way Reims usually looked. "The berahn are known as silent killers for a reason."

"But it's not silent. I hear it," Honaaz said.

"Because it wants us to."

"You're saying these things are smart?"

Jal nodded. "Deadly."

"So you've trained them before."

"Oh, you can't train a berahn. They work with you, or they don't."

Curiosity overcame Honaaz, despite Jal's warning. He'd never heard of berahn. The howl sounded something like a wolf, and he knew they had unique wolves in this land. He'd seen evidence of them, even though he wasn't much of a tracker or hunter. Out on the sea, a man didn't need those skills. He could fish with the best of them, but following some creature overland was not his skill.

What kind of strange connection to animals did Jal have? It had to be something supernatural, but if that were the case, why would Reims keep him around? He *hated* all things magical.

The berahn howled again. It was getting closer. Now it was near enough that Honaaz noticed a mournful note within it. Almost as if it were a warning.

Jal continued loping along the street, weaving between buildings at a rapid clip. He paused, looking back toward Honaaz, then whistled again. It wasn't the same whistle that he used to call to Lily. This was the one he must use to reach out to the berahn. This was a whistle meant to summon.

The silent killer.

The look on Jal's face was one that Honaaz had never seen on him before. He always seemed so jovial, full of life, amused by everything. The look he wore now was not one of amusement. It was like Jal was trying to force himself into maintaining that cheerfulness. The berahn made that difficult, or at least seemed to.

There was another explosion. Dust flew into the air, and Honaaz coughed.

The citadel was getting destroyed.

It was a fucking trap, and Kanar Reims had brought them into it.

The sound came again. Honaaz shivered.

The Dogs had not chased them. He'd half expected that they would pursue, but there had been no attempt to do so. The Dogs had merely tried to cut them off and keep them from getting too close to the citadel. They'd wanted to divide but not conquer.

Honaaz frowned. He looked up at the massive tower, looking for any signs that might give him a clue as to what was going on, but when the berahn howled again, he knew it was time to hurry.

"Fuck," he muttered, then went racing after Jal until he caught up to him.

Jal had his bow unslung, with three arrows gripped in his other hand. Honaaz glanced at the quiver. Only a single arrow remained. At that point, Jal would only be another fighter, just like him and Lily and Reims.

When Honaaz had first joined the team, he would've said that Jal was the least effective fighter. Having seen the tall bastard with his bow, however—the way he dipped it down to attack, cracking men in the legs, the arms, and the skull as if it were a staff—he had revised that opinion.

Everybody on this team was a good fighter. He was, too, but he still didn't know if he belonged.

Kanar Reims had brought him along for a reason.

Was it so he could be left behind?

A job like this often required a sacrifice. Honaaz had no interest in being that, and certainly not for a man like Reims. He would make damn certain that he got out of here. He would make damn sure that he got paid as well.

"How long before it attacks?" Honaaz asked.

"We might want to climb," Jal said.

Was that a look of worry in the corners of his eyes?

"Why?"

"Well, as I said, the berahn are smart and deadly and have a reputation as silent killers. They make choices about who they will bring down. They might leave one man alive but then slaughter dozens. They typically leave the Alainsith alone, along with anyone who uses magic, witchcraft or otherwise. So they would leave the hegen be." He glanced behind him. Honaaz suspected he was thinking of Lily. "But none of that is what's really bothering me."

"Get on with it. Tell me what's bugging you."

"I think there's more than one."

Honaaz pursed his lips and looked toward the citadel. "How can you tell?"

"They have a certain call. You start to identify it the more you hear it, and I can hear at least two distinct calls."

"At least two," Honaaz repeated.

"There might be a third."

"Gods, Jal. What the fuck is going on here?"

Jal shook his head. "I don't know." His expression suggested that he was telling the truth.

Honaaz motioned with his daggers towards one of the nearby buildings. "Let's get going. We can make like Lily and scale the roof. You can hold out and see if you need to use any of those arrows."

The three arrows took on a different meaning now.

They weren't for the Dogs.

They were for the berahn.

One for each that Jal thought he heard. He would never harm an animal, though, so why would he prepare to now?

"Put those away," Honaaz said. "I don't know what got into you, but those creatures aren't coming for you. They were answering you."

"I don't know if they were or not," Jal said. "I've tried to call to them, but…"

"Is that how you got away from the Dogs before?"

Jal met his gaze, one hand raised so that he could start

to climb. He still clutched the arrows. Honaaz was tempted to pull them away, stuff them into Jal's quiver, and force him to act like he should, but there was that edge to his eyes. That serious expression bothered Honaaz.

"I lured the Dogs away," Jal said. "I thought that was all I was going to have to do. I didn't know they would send more."

"You called the berahn to them?" Honaaz asked.

"It wasn't my intention. I thought it was a pack of wenderwolves that would scare them away."

"Well, it doesn't seem like you are all that broken up about what happened to them."

Jal sighed. "I know what they would've done if they caught us."

"They did catch us."

"Not as many of them as would have."

Jal stared at the arrows in his hand for a few moments, then his expression shifted. Something about his entire demeanor changed, and he shoved the arrows back into his quiver, slung his bow over his shoulder, and hurriedly scaled the side of the building. He worked far faster than Honaaz could even imagine doing. It was fast enough that he questioned whether Lily would be able to keep up with him.

Honaaz looked behind him. There was no sound other than a soft wind and a rumble. That wasn't wind, was it?

It was the sound of breathing.

And the rumble was the berahn growling.

Fear motivated him, and he quickly climbed up the building, then crouched on the roof. He looked out and didn't see the berahn. In the distance, he could make out Dogs but nothing else.

"How long do we have to—"

Honaaz didn't even get the chance to finish before he heard a shriek. The terrible sound was filled with pain and anguish, and it was silenced just as fast as it had cried out.

It was followed by another. And then another. The air was filled with them—tortured and tormented and laden with suffering.

"Not such silent killers, are they?" Honaaz said.

Jal shook his head. "You aren't hearing sounds from the berahn."

There was another explosion. The other buildings that were part of the citadel had started to crumble, but that wasn't the only thing Honaaz felt. The feeling came from some place deep inside him, as if it jarred some part of him loose.

"There was a time when men believed that certain forests were haunted. They thought the dead came back," Jal said with a smirk. "Like Lily promised she would do to a shop owner earlier."

"She promised to haunt him?"

"If he poisoned us."

Honaaz blinked. "Could she?"

"You have to work past your issues with her."

"It's not just hegen magic, is it? It's how she uses it. She can kill with it."

"And she can save with it." Jal nodded in the distance. "Think of the berahn. People think they're deadly and violent, and the Dogs they're slaughtering would say that they are terrible. But the berahn have also been known to protect. It's because of the berahn that my people are safe. Or had been…"

Honaaz found himself watching Jal more than he was looking out into the distance and following the dead and dying. He couldn't really see much from here anyway. Buildings blocked the view, and it was probably for the best. Honaaz wasn't sure that he wanted to see men torn apart by some creature they wouldn't even know was coming.

"What makes you think she would even pay any attention to me?" Honaaz asked.

Jal grinned. "Because I've studied animals."

"Are you calling me an animal?"

"All men are."

"What about women?"

Jal shrugged. "Some are. And some are something more."

Honaaz watched him, and he realized something: Jal was hiding from something else. He was hiding from loss. Honaaz had seen it. Gods, Honaaz had done the same.

"Who was she?" he asked.

Jal glanced over, his eyes flickering for a moment. A hint of an edge returned, but then it retreated, almost as if he was again in complete control over that emotion that flashed in his eyes.

"I don't talk about it," he said.

"If you don't talk about it, it eats away at you," Honaaz said.

"And you talk about what happened to you?"

"Gods no. I don't think anybody wants to hear that sob story. I lost my ship and the people I served with. That's about it. Bad enough, if you ask me, but most people aren't too concerned about that. Not like I was."

"If it's something you cared about, losing it can be painful."

Another shriek rang out and was quickly silenced.

Honaaz realized that Jal must've been right. He kept

hearing the screams from different sides, some in one direction, others coming from another, all of them crying out in a way that filled his ears. They sounded near enough that he did not want to climb down from this building. The berahn were out there hunting, prowling, killing.

Let them finish first.

It was strange to be having this conversation with Jal, though. In the midst of all this death, that was what he was doing, and this was what they were going to talk about?

"It was bad," Honaaz said. "I lost the only thing I ever knew, and I've been trying to get back ever since." Jal glanced over at him before turning his attention back ahead. "I don't talk about it. I've been trying to find my way back on a ship, but how can I find the right one?"

It was more than just the ship. It was dealing with betrayal. The mutiny of his uncle and leaving Honaaz behind. He couldn't go back until he was able to get the vengeance he wanted.

"Maybe the ship you're looking for isn't a ship," Jal said.

"And maybe the woman you're looking for isn't a woman." Honaaz shook his head. "That doesn't make any sense."

"Maybe not."

There was another scream, and then another.

Honaaz had given up trying to count how many men cried out and how many were likely dead. Too many. That much was obvious. Far too many had fallen.

"Can you call to them again?"

Jal glanced over. "Would it change anything?"

"I don't know. Do you think it would help?"

"The berahn are going to do what they do regardless of what I ask of them. And it is an ask, not a tell."

"You almost sound like you think they are more intelligent than humans," Honaaz said.

"It's possible."

Honaaz started to grin but realized that Jal was not returning it.

"How can an animal be smarter than a person?" Honaaz asked.

Jal shrugged. "How can a squirrel be smarter than a butterfly? I don't determine intelligence. Only the gods do that."

"If they're so intelligent, why do they slaughter?"

"Why do we?" Jal said.

Honaaz frowned and turned away.

Everything had fallen silent.

He'd lost track of when it had changed, only that it had suddenly fallen still. There was an emptiness, an eerie quality to the air, as if the berahn had come, killed, and then disappeared again. He heard no howl, no call, nothing other than silence.

He looked over to Jal, who had scooted forward. He still hadn't moved his bow, though perhaps he didn't need to any longer. They were not in danger anymore.

Honaaz reached the edge of the rooftop and started to climb down. Jal grabbed his wrist.

"Not yet."

"Why not?" Honaaz asked.

Jal nodded in the distance, and Honaaz followed the direction of his gaze.

The largest creature he'd ever seen came prowling toward them.

It had to be the size of a horse but as wide as two of them.

Its massive head looked something like a dog's, with a mouth filled with bloody fangs. The thing was thicker around its neck and longer as well. Its entire body was covered with dense fur that seemed brown at one time, then black, then deep green. Yellow eyes tinged with green swept over the buildings.

Honaaz shivered.

"Keep your eyes on him," Jal whispered.

"I'm definitely not taking my eyes off."

The steady breaths and rumbling came again. The berahn exuded vitality.

It was amazing, but it was also terrifying. Honaaz couldn't move. He didn't want to speak. He didn't even want to breathe. The only thing he could think of doing was to sit in place, waiting and watching.

A creature this size, and as powerful as it seemed to be, would probably have no difficulty leaping up to attack them. If it did, his daggers would be of no use. He flicked his gaze over to Jal and wondered if he really would've been able to do anything with those arrows. Not against something like this. It would take a ballista bolt to bring down this creature, and even that might not be enough.

The berahn looked up and met Honaaz's eyes. There was a moment when it snarled and flashed its fangs, revealing a bloody maw. Then it shifted its gaze to Jal and held it on him for another moment before it moved on.

When the berahn had looked at him, Honaaz had seen the intelligence in its eyes. But that wasn't the only thing he'd seen. He was reminded of looking into the eye of a storm. Sailors learned to face it. When the dark clouds moved in, a man could either bow down before it, run from it, or stare into it and try to come out on the other side.

They had to accept the wild vibrancy of the tempest, its thunder and rhythm.

Finally, Jal nudged him. "I bet when you woke up you didn't think you were going to see that today."

"I never thought I would see that ever."

"You may not see it again. Best not forget."

Honaaz grunted. "How the fuck am I supposed to forget that?"

Jal laughed. "We should find Lily. Then we need to get into the citadel. We've got to protect Kanar, even if it's from himself."

Chapter Thirty-Two

LILY

Lily raced as quickly as she could, though she found it more of a struggle than she had anticipated. She skimmed along the rooftops, jumping from one to the next. Her heart hammered. Not out of fear—at least, she didn't think it was fear. This was more a feeling of excitement, a nervous energy, though she wondered if she might be wrong.

Jal and Honaaz needed her help. They had whistled for her, and she had run in the opposite direction.

She needed answers before she went and helped them. She had to do this. Lily had to know what was going on so she could provide answers to her friends. But more than that, so she could know what was happening in the citadel.

She found another person on the roof. Lily whipped three knives in quick succession, cutting the person down. She hurried over and rolled them—another man dressed like the last, in the same green that did not seem as if it was from the citadel. He had a pair of knives strapped to his waist. Lily was tempted to grab them, but she decided against it.

Much like the first person, he was crouching over a strange item. This one was made of stone and had similar symbols etched into it, but there was something else about it.

It was streaked with some dark ink.

Not ink. Blood.

Alainsith blood, Lily realized. *Had the last one been the same?*

These had to be the relics they had been searching for, and scattering them around the city suggested that they were *targeting* the city.

Not if I can help it.

Lily reached into her pouch, pulled out several pieces of bone, and quickly carved them before pricking her finger and smearing blood on them to activate them. This would offer some protection around the relic until she understood what it was.

Another flicker of movement caught her attention, and Lily darted after it.

She scrambled across the rooftops. This was familiar to her. This was what she had done when she'd trained at the citadel, and she knew where to go. When the figure jumped, she knew how to get there first. She soared through the air, flipped two knives toward the figure, catching them in the back and the thigh. They did not get up.

She followed it with a quick flick of a bone fragment that struck the ground and then exploded. It was too much use of the art, but she wasn't going to let them activate the artifact.

That was, if they planned on doing that.

By the time Lily reached the figure, she saw no sign of an artifact.

Which meant they had already placed it.

She crouched and looked at the citadel. This had been her home once. There were so many memories here. This was where she had learned how to turn the art into what the citadel referred to as the subtle art, taking what her people had taught her and changing it into something far different. Something that her people would not have approved of, certainly.

How many other relics had been placed? She could look, but even if she did, she wasn't sure she could find the artifacts in time.

Maybe I've disrupted enough of them.

A whistle pierced the air.

Lily looked up. The whistle sounded more urgent than the last.

She couldn't abandon her people again when they needed her. So she ran.

She rushed back toward the citadel, back toward Jal and Honaaz, back toward the Dogs. Back toward Kanar Reims. Regardless of what he felt about her magic, she was going to help him. She didn't care whether he wanted that help or not.

A strange shriek, then another, came in the distance. Then everything fell quiet. That wasn't Jal or Honaaz, but what was it? It had sounded human, but tortured and tormented in a way she had not heard before.

By the time she found Jal and Honaaz, they were hunkered down on a rooftop, looking down at the ground. Neither of them spoke.

"Am I interrupting a moment between the two of you?"

Jal jerked his head around, and he grinned.

"What happened?" she asked. "I heard… Well, I heard something."

"The Dogs have been taken care of," Jal said.

"Do you care to tell me how?"

"It doesn't matter."

Lily shared with them what she had seen, about how the citadel was falling, but neither of them were surprised. They had probably seen it themselves.

"I don't know how many more Dogs we might have to fight through before we get to the citadel, but I'm ready," she said.

"Probably not that many," Honaaz said. "If it's going to make you feel better, I'm sure we can rustle up a few Dogs. I'm sure there's an arm here or there, maybe a leg, or perhaps something else you can use."

Jal jumped down from the building and moved quickly. Honaaz followed him, and Lily joined them. She noticed a massive paw print on the ground. She'd never seen anything quite like it.

She glanced at Jal, who just smiled at her. "A friend of yours?" she asked.

"Not exactly."

She turned to Honaaz. "Will you talk about it?"

"Gods, no. Let's go get Reims and get out of here. I don't want to be here any longer than we have to be."

They were both acting strange. But then, she probably deserved that. She was the one who ran off, leaving them behind to face whatever horror had come through this place. Had she been here with them, she would have known what they had experienced.

She crept forward, and when she found the first arm,

she stopped long enough to take all the fingers. "At some point, you're going to have to tell me what happened here," she said to Jal.

"At some point," he agreed. "But not today. And not now."

Lily went a little farther and found a leg and another arm. Then she found a torso. She collected from the limbs, but then she stopped. There were more than enough prizes here for her. She was tempted to throw some of them back, to mix it up by adding an ear or a nose, but most of those had been ripped free and weren't easy to find. Some hegen used other body parts in their art, pieces like a person's severed manhood, but she had never found those valuable for what she did.

"Are you done?" Honaaz asked.

She looked over to him. "I'm just getting ready."

"I wasn't trying to make you work any faster," he said hurriedly. "I just wanted to know if you were done. We should get moving to see if Reims needs us."

Lily straightened. "You know, Honaaz, I've enjoyed having you around."

He frowned. "You have?"

"You're a good fighter. I don't always get that."

Honaaz glanced over to Jal. "He's a good fighter. So is Reims."

"But you have a different style." She grinned. "And I enjoy making you uncomfortable."

"Fuck," he muttered.

They hurried forward. She marveled at how many Dogs had been slaughtered. She didn't have the same view of death as some people did, so seeing their remains didn't bother her so much as it left her curious. What had come through here?

Something powerful enough to rip through all these Dogs without them being able to put up a fight. She saw no sign of the animal other than that one paw print, and that had almost seemed intentional.

Lily watched Jal, but he still said nothing about it.

They reached the bridge leading to the citadel. They had seen no signs of any other Dogs, no other attackers, and nothing that slowed them. She started to feel more at ease, as if they might actually make it.

"We should cross—"

Something whizzed past her face.

Lily spun. She was getting tired of having crossbow bolts shot at her, especially from these stupid Dogs.

Jal grabbed her and shoved her across the bridge, then looked over to Honaaz and nodded. The two men started across the bridge behind her. By the time they reached the citadel door, she had pressed herself against it, but it was blocked.

"I'm going to need to use the art on this," she said. "And you aren't going to be able to stand so close to it."

"I'm not sure we have much of a choice," Jal said. "If we stand too far away, we have to deal with them." He pointed, and Lily followed the direction of his finger.

Several operatives watched from nearby rooftops and in the shadows of alleys. They hadn't moved toward them.

They saw what happened.

But why not attack?

"There are relics in the city," Lily explained. "I don't know why, but if the relics are scattered around and if they are using the Alainsith blood with them…" Her mind raced through it to try to understand. "Then there is only one thing something like that will do."

Destruction.

She was far too familiar with that.

"We need to stop them. Let's move."

She reached into her pouch and sorted through the prizes until she found a dry fragment of bone. She didn't need anything particularly powerful here.

Lily carved this one quickly. She tapered it to a point and then jammed that into the lock. Using one of her knives, she pricked her finger and added her own droplet of blood, which flowed along the bone toward the lock. It was called the binding—the last piece of the art.

It wasn't necessary for all aspects of magic, but it was for the kind she performed. Lily would not be able to do anything without the binding. Otherwise, it would just be blood or bone.

"We need to step back," she told them.

Jal shook his head. "We can't."

Lily sniffed. "Then this is going to get interesting in a few moments."

The lock started to steam as her blood flowed down the bone. As it did, she hurriedly reached into her pouch again and grabbed one of her new prizes. It didn't have to be cleaned, processed, or even dry for her to use it. She just needed the power stored within it. A small fragment like this wouldn't contain much power, and she certainly wasn't going to perform a binding to augment that power, but she might be able to use it in a way that would help solidify it and turn it into something useful.

Pressure pushed against her as the binding took hold. The power from her first art flowed into the lock, hissing and steaming and then exploding. The binding contained it, holding it in the lock. Then the door came open.

Lily let out a sigh of relief. "Now we get to see what's inside."

The tower remained untouched despite its disintegrating surroundings. It was usually forbidden for students, but Lily had been invited here to receive recognition for a job near Yelind.

Tayol had organized a hit on a group of supposed priests practicing witchcraft in a village. Bored teenagers, in reality. Lily had locked them in their church, thinking an overnight stay would quell their thirst for magic.

The church was only a makeshift wooden thing, and stone was expensive. Lily's companion had snuck back in the night and burnt it to the ground. When she returned in the morning, there was nothing but ash. A group of citadel elders had pinned silver badges on them for that.

It was the beginning of the end for Lily. Fitting that the ceremony was here.

A twisting staircase led up. The energy of magic built as she climbed.

Another few steps, and she had to fight through pressure. Lily reached into her pouch and came across another piece of pure bone. She grabbed some powdered shavings in her palms and then tossed them into the air.

"What are you doing?" Honaaz asked. "Are we supposed to breathe that in?"

"No. Whatever spell they're placing will absorb this, and the bone will disrupt the spell."

"How?"

She looked over at him, and she realized that he was asking sincerely.

"Everything holds potential within it," Lily explained as she waited for the art to take effect. "Your entire body is filled with it. Yours especially, probably." She smiled at him, and this time he didn't withdraw from her. "You can take that potential and convert it into something real. In this case, I took the potential of the bone, and I'm mixing it with the power of the spell they're trying to use on us."

The pressure on them began to ease. Lily forged ahead, feeling as if she were pushing against a boulder.

"We're not going to be able to get up here," she said. "The power is too significant."

Jal glanced at her and frowned. "Is it witchcraft?"

"The citadel has been trying to understand hegen art for a long time. They've been trying to modify it. When I refused, I was sent away. I had mostly completed my training."

Mostly, but not entirely. She hadn't even finished her testing to be an operative. She had learned the subtle art and still used it, but they had wanted her to use something more.

"Some had started to veer toward something more like witchcraft," Lily said. "That's what I'm starting to fear."

"There might be some Alainsith magic here," Jal said.

Honaaz stepped in front of her and pushed his daggers at the power. Lily let out a laugh, but he gritted his teeth and drove his fist forward, the muscles in his arms trembling until the air popped and he could move ahead.

How had he done that?

Honaaz turned to her. "Try again."

"I can *try*," she said, sorting through her pouch until she came up with another piece of bone that would be adequate. She started to carve through it, but then thought better of it. This time, rather than carving it up first, she used a droplet of blood and created a binding before slicing up the bone. After it was done, she dabbed it in her palms, which streaked them red, and tossed the powder up. As it clung in the air, she could practically feel it battling against the other spell. It slid through the spell until the spell collapsed.

Whatever Honaaz had done had helped. Was he so strong that he overwhelmed magic—or was there something about *him*?

The stairs led them up to a door. White light from the other side drifted out—the diffuse energy of magic. She heard the clang of metal on metal, laughter, and the slow drawl of a voice she recognized.

When she stepped through the doorway, she wasn't sure how to react.

Bodies littered the ground. Operatives. None of the ones nearest her looked wounded. Others had been cut down. Some were missing limbs; some had been stabbed through with blades. She suspected that Kanar was responsible for those.

Tayol stood in the center of the room, a long, slender witchcraft wand engraved with Alainsith writing in his hand. He was holding it near Morgan.

No. The wand wasn't up against her. It was *in* her.

Kanar looked over to Lily, and he had his sword unsheathed. She found her attention drawn to that almost as much as anything else. She couldn't remember when she had ever seen his sword out of its sheath.

"You should go," he whispered.

"No." Lily strode forward and stood behind Morgan.

She grabbed several strips of bone out of her pouch. "You're making a mistake, Tayol. This isn't the way."

"This is the only way," Tayol said. "We can be the most powerful force in this land. We don't have to worry about witchcraft. We don't have to worry about making nice with the Order and Reyand. The citadel can lead."

"That's not our purpose," Lily said.

Morgan moaned. She needed help.

Lily was not a healer. That was not her gift, but having seen the way the hegen woman in Verendal had healed Jal, she wondered if she might be able to do something similar.

Fresh prizes were the key with healing. Lily formed the binding, and Morgan took a deep, gasping breath as she staggered back.

She tried—and failed—to hold onto the wand as she did.

Tayol held it up and pointed it at Lily.

"You're the reason the citadel is falling. You did this," she said.

Tayol shook his head. "The citadel is not falling."

"You haven't seen it. I have. The relics aren't meant to build or strengthen. They will destroy. Look out the damn window, you stubborn idiot!"

"I know what I learned."

"How did you learn? Where?" she asked. With a dawning horror, Lily thought she knew. "It was in Sanaron, wasn't it? I saw you there."

Tayol sneered. "You were the mouse."

"Did you learn about this from the Prophet?" Kanar asked.

Tayol looked at him, then turned his attention back to

Lily. "I know the relics. I know that when they're combined with the Alainsith blood, we will—"

"Be used," Lily said.

It was too late for Tayol. Lily could see that look in his eyes.

It might even be too late for the citadel.

Morgan raised her hands, crossed her fingertips in front of her, and then brought her hands back in a sharp whip crack. A trace of fog built around her, spreading outward.

Honaaz flung one of his daggers, and it caught Tayol in the leg. The man looked down at it, almost intrigued rather than concerned. He plucked the dagger out and dropped it on the ground.

"You can't stop it any longer," Tayol said. "None of you can."

A look of resignation crossed Kanar's face, and then something different. Something Lily had not seen from him in the past. She'd heard stories and rumors, had watched him fight, but had never seen the look of utter darkness in his eyes.

The Blackheart.

"I can," Kanar said.

He attacked Tayol.

Lily had seen Kanar in combat before. She had fought alongside him and knew his technique and skill. She'd witnessed the brutality of every blow he struck.

This was like a different man.

He was a blur of speed and raw power. As soon as he lunged toward Tayol, she understood. It was the sword. She could feel the power emanating from the blade.

It made sense. Kanar Reims, the Blackheart. He had hunted those with witchcraft. But in doing so, and in cutting them down, he had captured strength. That might not have been his intention, but that had been the outcome nonetheless.

Kanar battered Tayol with strikes, but the man deflected the attacks with some unseen magic. Each blow still sent him backing away, though.

Morgan brought her hands up again, and with a circle of her fingers, the air thickened. Tayol staggered backward. He twisted the rod in the air, trying to deflect whatever it was that Morgan used on him. With wand raised, he murmured something and ran his fingers along its surface. Lily felt the power flowing within it before anything happened.

Witchcraft wands were much like Kanar's sword. They were designed to store power, and they allowed the power to be redirected.

That was what Tayol was doing now.

From what Lily could feel, there was considerable power in that wand from whoever he had slaughtered here.

She reached into her pouch for prizes, but she didn't have any.

Lily lunged toward one of the fallen citadel operatives, drove her knife into the body, and cleaved through the bones until she held up a hand. She hurriedly formed the binding to herself, then tossed it to form a barrier around her. Its raw power would drain energy from her, but she had no choice.

As the power exploded, it slammed into her barrier.

But not just hers. Morgan had done something similar, and a rippling wave of energy sent the attack rebounding into Tayol.

He held the wand up and murmured something. He

waved it in a tight, spiraling pattern, then drove it down into the ground.

As soon as he did, the citadel around them started to crack.

"Do you feel that?" Lily asked.

Tayol looked at the wand before turning his attention to her. The other operatives had not gotten up yet.

Are they dead?

A witchcraft ceremony. It depended upon pain and suffering.

"It should have worked," Tayol began. "It should have drawn power into this."

She shook her head. "Not into. Out of. You were used."

He turned to the chalice, which held more blood, Lily suspected.

"You can help me," Tayol said. "You know how to do this. We can still—"

"No," Lily said. "That is not how."

He spun. A surge of power came out of his wand as the Alainsith blood he had plunged it into began to activate it.

Lily reached for her pouch, but she wasn't fast enough. Energy sizzled past her.

Tayol had lost control.

Honaaz jumped in front of her, somehow absorbing the full brunt of the blow. He flipped one of his knives, which went streaking toward Tayol and plunged into his chest.

The rod slammed into the ground again.

Lily darted to the floor, grabbed another fallen operative's arms, quickly carved off a finger, and tossed it. The explosion caused a ripple in the ground, then Tayol dropped.

She sat up, letting out a shaky breath. All around the tower, the citadel crumbled.

Tayol had destroyed it. He had been used in order to do so. One defense against witchcraft was gone. How many operatives had he killed in the attempt?

How many remained?

"We need to go," she said, looking over to Kanar.

"We do."

"I'm sorry."

He shook his head. "I just wish…"

She knew what Kanar wished. He wished that the ceremony would've worked the way Tayol had wanted. But she also knew that wasn't how magic could be used.

If only Kanar could realize that magic *should* be used.

A chunk of the ceiling dropped. Honaaz caught it and managed to hold it up before tossing it onto one of the bodies. He shook his head. "Fuck!"

Chapter Thirty-Three

KANAR

Kanar was exhausted.

They had found no sign of the man. Tayol had disappeared, and so had the remaining Dogs. Most of the Alainsith blood was gone, but not all of it. They didn't know what happened to any surviving citadel operatives—if there were any.

Lily blamed the Prophet for what happened, thinking that Tayol had been used. And Kanar suspected that she was right.

He poured the rest of the blood from the chalice into a vial he found nearby, then stuffed it into his pocket. It might be better to dump it in the river—but this was Alainsith blood. He might hate magic, but for the right person, this could be valuable.

Probably for Lily.

That was something to think on. Later.

They had stopped the ceremony, but most of the Alainsith blood had been used. He couldn't help but feel as if they had failed.

Morgan rested a hand on his arm. A bit of smoke swirled around her.

What kind of magic is she using?

Not witchcraft, but whatever she was doing seemed to staunch the bleeding.

"Do you need a healer?" Kanar asked.

Morgan looked down at herself before looking back at him. It seemed as if something passed behind her eyes, as if she were trying to decide how much to share with him. Finally, she shook her head. "I will be fine, Gray. And you don't need to worry about what he intended. He didn't succeed. Not entirely. He might have destroyed this building, but there are others like it."

"I'm not concerned about the building," Kanar said. He wanted to tell her that he was concerned about her, but he feared admitting that and said nothing.

"There are other operatives still out there. He didn't win. You, her, and your team prevented him from doing the worst of it."

Maybe she was right. Maybe they had only lost those in the citadel and not others.

He still felt that loss, though.

The city had been quiet, though he didn't imagine anyone from the citadel destroying everyone in the city. *Unless that had been the plan.*

More magic had killed the people trying to fight it. But Kanar had done his part. He had also learned something he had not known before. He wasn't sure whether that changed anything for him, or whether it even could, but now he knew they needed to get back to Sanaron. He had to take Morgan there.

"I want to leave the citadel now," Kanar said when they

had reached the base of the tower. "I'm ready to be done with all of this."

"That's it?" Honaaz asked, daggers in hand as he limped slightly. He had been injured, though Kanar wondered when and how. When his eyes met Lily's, he didn't flinch away.

Something had changed between them.

"That's it for now," Kanar said. "We finish the job. Now you get paid."

"You never told me what you wanted me for."

Kanar watched him. He'd heard about Honaaz's kind, about their natural resistance to magic—which was probably a form of magic on its own. And it *had* been useful. Seeing Honaaz now, he could tell the man didn't know.

"You weren't a Dog," Kanar said. "That's why I wanted you."

There was a look that almost seemed like disappointment in Honaaz's eyes.

"Did you think it was something more?" Kanar asked.

"I don't know," he muttered.

Kanar glanced from Honaaz to Lily and Jal before looking to Morgan.

This was the team he had assembled. This was who had fought one of the most dangerous witchcraft users Kanar had ever faced. And he'd survived.

It wasn't over. He knew it wasn't over. Not only had he not finished the job, which he fully intended to do, but he had other questions. He patted his pocket, making sure the blood was secure.

He looked up at Honaaz. "You did well." He looked over the Jal and Lily, offering a hint of a shrug. Jal nodded to him quickly. Lily looked at Honaaz with an unreadable expression before she smiled. "Then it's settled. I think you've earned an equal cut."

"How much is that going to be?"

"If all goes well? More than I told you."

Honaaz grunted. "The only thing I want is the Prophet."

"Why?"

"That fuck is responsible for me getting stranded in Sanaron."

Kanar laughed. "I was going to offer you more money, but I can offer you an opportunity to do that as well."

"I am not saying no to money," Honaaz grumbled.

They stepped outside. Smoke hung over everything, along with a foul odor. Once they made it across the bridge, Kanar saw bodies of what he could only assume were the Dogs. Dozens were littered around, many torn apart and with limbs missing. This could not have been his team's doing. It was too brutal. Not that his team couldn't be brutal if needed.

Buildings all around had crumbled, leaving only the wall that separated the citadel from the rest of the city. That and only part of the tower, but even that solitary tower had started to fall.

He didn't have any answers, but the citadel was gone. Whatever it had represented—and whatever Lily and Morgan had known—was gone. Kanar looked over to them for a moment.

He slipped his sword back into its sheath. "Was he telling the truth about this?" he asked Morgan.

"About it being an Alainsith blade?" She held his eyes, and there was a different question there than what she had asked. Kanar wasn't quite ready to answer that one, though. "It's possible."

"What does it mean for me?"

"It means what you make of it. You can decide."

He doubted that was completely accurate, but he didn't really know. All he knew was that he was connected to it. Bound to it. When he used the blade, he felt it.

Magic, witchcraft, whatever he wanted to call it. That was what it was.

Kanar had been trying to hide from it, trying to fight what he had done, but there were others like Tayol in the world. Even in Sanaron, there was still the Prophet to deal with. They would need every advantage they had.

The citadel continued to crack and crumble as they headed away from it. The only thing that remained solid was the wall that encircled it. How long before the people outside the wall realized the truth? That the citadel had started to fall?

Kanar couldn't help but worry that this place of power was now gone. Allies of the throne, gone.

But they hadn't always been allies.

Kanar frowned. Could King Porman have had something to do with this?

Those were dangerous thoughts. Questions for later.

He heard Lily talking to Honaaz, who mostly responded in grunts. Jal was quiet, though given the slight darkness in his gaze, Kanar wondered what had happened. The slaughter seemed tied to it. Morgan stayed close to him, watching him, not saying anything.

Eventually, he would have to have it out with her as well, but not now. Not around his team.

"How are we getting back?" Honaaz finally asked. "I'm not riding another fucking horse."

"I doubt we'd be able to find horses," Jal said. "I could probably gather something. I'm sure we might be able to find something here."

"Fuck no."

"I was thinking you could guide us back," Kanar said.

"Along the river?"

"Well, the river lets out into the sea, and from here, it's probably only a few days to Sanaron. I figured we'd all want to get back. Warm beds, tasty ale, and the coin we've been promised."

That part was what he was less convinced of.

Honaaz nodded. "It's going to be tricky once we reach open water. I'll keep it close to shore."

"Whatever you think," Kanar said.

Making their way through the city took longer than Kanar would have liked. Everything was quiet, with the residual destruction of the citadel pushing on his senses. Kanar felt that energy, and from the way that Lily swept her gaze around everything in the city, he suspected she felt it too.

"What is it?" he asked as they headed toward the barge.

"It's different than I remember," she said softly. "It's this place. This is where I learned… well, everything. And now the citadel is gone."

"All of it?" he asked.

She shrugged. "There are operatives all over, so probably not."

They were quiet for a few moments as they neared the water. "What will you do?" Kanar asked.

She sighed. "Go back to Sanaron. Then decide."

And that seemed reasonable to Kanar.

It seemed as if something had changed for him—and he wasn't even sure what.

They reached the barge and climbed in. It didn't take long before they made it to the sea, and they spent the next few days slowly making their way toward Sanaron. Though there was some conversation, everyone was generally quiet. Every so often, he heard Lily or Jal or even Honaaz talking about what they might do with their coin. Kanar smiled at that.

What he might do with his reward had changed, though. When he'd taken the job, the idea of that much money had seemed impossible, enough to escape or hide from everything he had done. Everything he had become.

Now he wasn't sure if he wasn't sure if he could, or if he should.

It was early morning, and the sea was calm. An occasional wave pushed them, but Honaaz was skilled and managed to keep them away from rocks and out of dangerous swells. The sky was gray and overcast, and the fog in the distance suggested they were getting closer to Sanaron. The wind had even started to pick up, carrying in the smell of the sea, the salt in the air, and the steady caws of seagulls in the distance.

"I'm not going to take you back to prison," Kanar said to Morgan, who had mostly stayed quiet.

"He's going to come for you," she said.

"The Hunter?"

She nodded. "He won't be confined to Verendal. Are you sure that's what you want to face?"

"I'm not worried about him."

"You should be."

Let the Hunter come. He was another servant of the king, much like Kanar had been. Kanar had done so willingly, without asking all the questions he should have. Maybe that was why he was angry. It was at himself.

He thought about what he had seen in the citadel. There had to be a reason why Morgan was drawn there, a reason why Tayol believed he could destroy the citadel.

And maybe Sanaron.

He'd been there for a reason.

Why Sanaron, exactly?

Maybe he wasn't the one who wanted to.

That meant there might be more to this.

As Kanar looked over to Morgan, he felt the same familiar conflicted emotions. There'd been a time when he would've thought that staying with her would be everything. Maybe it still was. But he also didn't know if that was to be their fate.

Their relationship had changed. *He* had changed.

Perhaps she could understand that, and maybe she could even forgive him, in time, for what he'd done. He wasn't sure if he wanted her to. He wasn't sure if he needed her to.

When Sanaron came into view, Kanar felt a knot loosen in his shoulders. It was a surprising feeling, especially as he didn't particularly feel as if Sanaron was home to him. It was just a place he knew.

Honaaz saw them into shore, and then he slowed as he looked around and picked out a dock to pull them into. "No one is using this berth right now. We might as well take it."

"How much they charge you for dockage?"

Honaaz shrugged. "Never paid it. And we can sell this

barge. Might be worth a little coin."

Lily frowned. "You know that belongs to the hegen."

"What the fuck are they going to do about it? They're all the way back in Verendal. They'd have to come out here and take it from us."

"I don't think we should tempt that," Jal said.

Kanar hopped onto the dock and looked down at them. "The rest of you do what you want to. I have something I need to do."

"I might head back to my room and sleep for the better part of the next year," Jal said.

Lily pinched her nose. "You should bathe first."

"You always think I need to bathe."

"Because you always need to." She laughed.

Honaaz laughed along with them.

Kanar held his hand out to Morgan, and she locked eyes with him for a long moment.

"Are you ready?" she asked.

He nodded. "You were the job. I have to prove that I did it."

"I suppose you do," she said.

She took his hand, and once she climbed out, he released it. Still, they walked side by side. They headed up a hill, making their way toward Edward's home, or what Kanar thought was his home. The air was thick with fog, but it wasn't so dense that he couldn't see.

"You never told me why you went after the blood," Kanar said.

"I did not."

"It has to do with Sanaron, doesn't it? That's what Edward really wanted. He knew you had succeeded and acquired some of it."

"What are you trying to get me to say?" Morgan asked.

"The truth."

"I don't know that there is a truth that will satisfy you."

"What if the Prophet wanted you there as well?" Kanar said. "He runs parts of Sanaron. And given who I think you are, I suspect that he would've loved to see you removed as a possible danger." He watched her for confirmation.

Morgan shrugged. "It's possible."

"Why? You wanted power for Sanaron, but you won't even tell me why? Is it your father, or is it the city?"

It had taken Kanar a while to piece that together, but now he thought he understood. Things that Morgan had said came back to him. He hadn't always been the listener that he needed to be with her and was oftentimes too slow, but he worked on problems until he solved them. This time, he thought he was right. Had he known earlier…

Kanar didn't think it would've changed anything.

I would still have taken the job.

At least he would've known who'd hired him.

"Sanaron has always been an important city, Gray. I pray you don't have to learn why. That's why my father sent you after me."

He shook his head, wishing she could be more honest with him. "You don't want to tell me?"

Morgan regarded him, and then she shook her head. "I don't think you're ready, and I don't think you would understand. You still hate magic in all its forms. Perhaps that will change, Gray."

What was she saying?

She didn't use witchcraft—Kanar believed her now—but what other form of magic?

"Are you going to send your people after me and the

blood?" Kanar said.

"I'm hopeful that you will make the right decision in time. I'm willing to wait."

He wasn't entirely sure. He had seen the look in her eyes when he'd slipped the blood into his pocket. Maybe she wanted it for power, but maybe there was another reason. He didn't know. Until he discovered the truth, he did not intend to provide the blood to her.

"What if I destroy it?" he said.

"You won't. The sacrifices already happened, and you know me well enough to know that I would not use it that way."

"The way Lily knew the citadel?" Kanar said.

"Then perhaps I have to prove it to you." She turned, looking behind her. "But not yet. Be careful with that, Gray. I fear the Prophet isn't done with it."

She was probably right. Worse, there was a magical threat in Sanaron that was far more dangerous than Kanar had realized.

He couldn't shake the worry that his king might have known, or might have permitted the attack on the citadel. It would've been a betrayal of allies, but it would also have removed a threat to Reyand. If Porman believed the witchcraft war to be over, why not remove one more threat?

"I wish it could be different," Kanar said.

"It could be."

"How?" he asked. It surprised him that he actually meant it. His relationship with Morgan had been complicated from the beginning—first by distance, then by who and what she was, and now by this. Could they ever uncomplicate it?

"We just have to make a choice," she said. "I don't want

them to hurt you."

"Then don't let them," Kanar said.

She held her hand out and looked as if she wanted to reach for him, before pulling back and clasping her hands together. He'd seen her use her magic, even if he didn't understand it. He saw nothing like that now.

He had no idea where or how she stored power, or what kind of witchcraft she practiced, but that was her secret and not his.

"You're home safely," he said, "and now I will offer your father one more thing."

"What's that?" Morgan asked.

"I intend to kill the Prophet."

Kanar stepped forward, and before he could think otherwise, he pulled her toward him into a hug. When he started to withdraw, she raised herself up on her toes and kissed him on the cheek. He sighed.

"I still want my money," he said. "He'll know where to send it."

"Is that all you cared about?"

"I care about my team."

He stepped away and left her, feeling as if he were leaving a part of himself, part of his heart. As he headed down the hill, he steeled himself. He had to find Malory and warn her. He had to make preparations.

Kanar patted the Alainsith blood in his pocket. He didn't know what they had intended for it, but it was long past time that he find out. He just hoped that his team understood when he came back empty-handed. For now.

Once he reached the bottom of the hill, he looked up. Through the fog, he thought he saw Morgan still standing outside her home, watching him.

The next book in Blade and Bone: City of Fog and Ruin.

The Prophet seeks a new weapon to rule in Sanaron; few have the power to stop him.

Back in Sanaron, Kanar struggles with the consequences of his last job. In the wrong hands, the Alainsith blood is a weapon. With Kanar's team, it might offer protection, especially as the Prophet remains active in Sanaron and now dabbles in dangerous witchcraft.

When Kanar learns what the Prophet seeks, he must find it before the Prophet, or he'll use the dangerous power to destroy the city itself.

His team succeeded once before, but that was when focused on the same goal.

When each has their own agenda, can they become a team in time to find the artifact, stop the Prophet, and save Sanaron?

Series by D.K. Holmberg

The Executioner's Song Series
The Executioner's Song

Blade and Bone

The Chain Breaker Series
The Chain Breaker

The Dark Sorcerer

First of the Blade

The Dragonwalkers Series
The Dragonwalker

The Dragon Misfits

Elemental Warrior Series:
Elemental Academy

The Elemental Warrior

The Cloud Warrior Saga

The Endless War

The Dark Ability Series
The Shadow Accords

The Collector Chronicles

The Dark Ability

The Sighted Assassin

The Elder Stones Saga

The Lost Prophecy Series

The Teralin Sword

The Lost Prophecy

The Volatar Saga Series

The Volatar Saga

The Book of Maladies Series

The Book of Maladies

The Lost Garden Series

The Lost Garden

Printed in Great Britain
by Amazon